RAVEN

the TORQUED trilogy

SHEY STAHL

Copy Editing: Becky Johnson, Hot Tree Editing
Proofreading: Janet Johnson
BETA Reading: Lauren Zimmerman
Cover Image: Copyright © Sara Eirew
Model: Nick Bennett
Cover Designer: Tracy Steeg
Interior Formatting: A Designs

dedication

For Lauren.

all she ever wanted was
unpredictable kisses and
unforgettable laughter.
~ Brandon Villasenor

Raven
chapter 1
UNFORGETTABLE

I'VE GROWN UP around cars. Though I don't work on them, I can change oil, tell you why your truck's smoking and know the size of the engine just by the rumble. It's a gift I've grown to appreciate.

Another thing I have a knack for is knowing when someone is lying to me. Sometimes I think it would be easier if I didn't have this particular gift. There's something to be said for living without knowledge of knowing someone you thought cared about you was in fact lying to you. This was never more obvious to me than when I showed up at my boyfriend's dorm room with the intention of surprising him. I knew the minute he opened the door, red faced and half dressed, we would never be the same.

"*Jesus Christ*, Holden. How could you?" was my first question as I pushed through the door and glanced around his dorm room. On the floor were scattered sheets and a girl's black heels and panties. "Who the fuck is she?"

He blinked several times trying to come up with a lie and grabbing at my shoulders. "Raven, you need to *calm* down. This isn't what it looks like."

The worst part is he believes he's being serious.

"Really? Oh good, because for a minute it looked like you were fucking a blonde whore in your dorm room! Wow, I'm totally relieved it's not what it looks like!" I pushed him away from me. I needed space and he was sucking the breath right out of me.

Crouching down, I put my hand on my chest trying to calm my heart. I probably looked like a complete mess and I could only imagine what Fuck Me Barbie must have thought but I didn't give a shit. Holden and I have been together since high school and I deserved better than this.

"Four years! Four. Fucking. Years! *Why*? Give me a reason as to *why* you felt dipping your dick in her was worth breaking my heart?" I hated my tears sliding down my cheeks. Showing weakness was the last thing I wanted to do but I couldn't help it. My heart was totally fucking breaking.

He pushed out a labored breath and reached for his jeans. There was movement all around me but I was focused on *him*, the one causing me pain. "Seriously? Damn, Raven. Do you have any idea how controlling you are?" He zipped his pants while the average-looking blonde searched for her bra. Stupid perky fucking tits, tan skin and all. How she looked that good for being in Oregon wasn't lost on me. She was probably from California. All sluts belonged in California as far as I was concerned.

At first, I thought to myself, Holden's assessment of me was ridiculous. Controlling? Yeah, I liked order and yeah I could be a bit of a bitch if things weren't as they should be, but controlling?

Really?

Okay, so maybe what he said was somewhat accurate but it didn't give him a license to have sex with other girls behind my back. He was not the fucking victim.

"If you felt that way why didn't you just break up with me? Why go behind my back and purposely hurt me like this?" I asked because I really wanted to know. Why did we have to end this way?

His eyes meet mine with wide uncertainty. "Look, babe, let's be totally honest here. I'm pledging to one of the elite fraternities on campus. Some of my brothers are future heads of industry with serious family money backing them." He grabbed at the back of his neck, leaning into the wall as he continued, "The connections I'm making will help me to secure my future in business and in order to achieve these connections, I have to live up to a certain persona. Dating my hometown sweetheart isn't going to cut it. Truth be told the only reason I didn't break up with you before this is because of our history. You're lucky I held on this long."

I clenched my teeth together, anger and hatred spilling out of me with each shocked blink I took. *Holy shit.* I couldn't believe what I was hearing. I stared at Holden unable to get my thoughts together. Who the hell was this person? After four years together you would hope you know someone but apparently, I didn't know him at all.

Completely taken by surprise by what he just said, I couldn't even think. All I knew was that I couldn't walk away without hurting him in some way.

"Well, you're an indecisive jerk who can't remember to zip his pants after he takes a piss. Not to mention you're *lousy* in bed, ya dumb dick," I said, the heat in my face reaching record temps. It was like a high fever when even blinking took effort.

Holden smirked, which was the wrong thing to do when I was this mad. "You're overreacting."

"That's the wrong thing to say to me." I look to the average-looking blonde. "Just a little bit of advice, he likes it when I stick my finger up his ass during sex. Careful, I think he might be gay."

Holden's smirk faded and anger replaced it. I knew it was immature but I didn't give a shit. I may not have been able to hurt him the same way he hurt me, but there was no way I was walking away without at least putting a chink in his armor. Asshole.

That night was the start of it. The very beginning. Like in the movies where the main character is sitting there wondering "How did I get here?" and you see a flash of a scene as to why and where it started. That's my why and where. Right then. The unforgettable.

After Holden and I broke up, not only did I have an emotional breakdown but I went into *full-blown* depression. I don't mean slightly depressed and indulging in ice cream and sappy movies because there's that. I'm talking about the type of depression where you just sat and cried for days, barely moving, barely breathing. It was pathetic. But then again, I was with him for four years and he was my only taste of love. Needless to say, it was my first broken heart. And now I wanted to wash my mouth out with soap and never have that horrible fucking taste again.

This went on for weeks before Rawley, my twin brother, finally decided it was time for me to get over my shit and took me out with him and his band one night in March. It should have been a laidback night of watching my brother's band play and having a few drinks. I was only nineteen, but we knew the owner and it was my chance to at least drink and forget the horror of my life. So I went.

My brother's advice before we entered Murphy's Bar? He's a fucking slut so I never listen to him but he said, and I quote: "Raven, one thing always leads to another."

At a bar some Friday night in March

"YOU WANT A drink?" Zack asks me. He went to high school with Red, my oldest brother, and he's always been cool about serving me even though I'm not twenty-one yet.

"*Fuck yeah*, I want a drink." I set my purse on the bar. "Serve that shit up."

Zack smirks. "All right, well hold tight. I'll make you something special. You look like you could use it." While Zack goes about creating whatever surprise he has in store for me, I bob my head to the beginning beats of the song Rawley's doing sound check to. I love that he's playing one of the originals he wrote. He doesn't do it very often because he thinks no one wants to hear it. They'd rather hear him doing covers of Nickelback.

Just as quickly as he's done with that song, he moves onto "Stroke Me" by Mickey Avalon. It cracks me up this one is on his set list because it's unlike him. But I get why. He puts on a good show with it and that's what he's good at. Putting on a show.

Rawley's been in a band since he was I don't even know how old. It's always been him, Linc and Beck. The three of them play good together and someday I honestly believe they'll make it to the big time. That's if my brother can keep his shit together long enough to make it work. He's one of those guys who doesn't like to be told what to do. He wants to play at his own will and if you try to tell him when and where, he just says fuck you and walks away.

The drink Zack makes me is a half piña colada and half strawberry daiquiri and it's the best fucking thing I've had in my life. I suck the damn thing down in less than five minutes risking the brain freeze because I can't believe how damn good it is.

"*Dude.*" My voice is high-pitched and bordering obnoxious already. "You, my friend, are a lifesaver. This drink is amazing!"

Zack laughs as he makes me another and then half turns to help another customer on the other side of the bar. He knocks his fist to the bar lightly. "Hold tight, honey. I'll be right back."

I nod to him, winking. "Take your time. I've got all night. But seriously—" I grab his fist—"make me another one soon because this is *delicious.*"

The crowd starts clapping and whistling, which tells me that Rawley's band is taking the stage. I twist around on my stool so I'm facing the stage and do a quick visual sweep of the bar looking to see what kind of crowd is here tonight. It's then I see a familiar face coming toward the bar.

Tyler Hemming. My older brother's best friend and my childhood crush.

Of all the nights to run into him, it has to be tonight. Awesome. It's only been a few weeks since I last saw him, but still, when you're a mess, the last person you want to see is a hot guy. It's like going to the grocery store with your hair tied up in a bun and last night's pajamas and make-up only to run into someone you know from high school who looks better than you.

A minute later he's standing next to me, our shoulders bumping, Tyler eyes the drink as he sits down next to me at the bar. "Look at you. Drinking someone away, are we?"

I didn't think he'd come in here and not come over. We've been friends for years but his deep voice still sends my heart fluttering. Naturally. Any crush would do that. "Yep."

Zack gives him a nod, waiting for his order. "Whiskey. Bring the bottle."

Looks like I'm not the only one who wants to forget the day.

I give him a look. "Whoa. How about you, what are you doing here?"

His eyes drag over me without revealing anything. Hell, my body is damn near burned by that one look. His gaze narrows before he lifts his chin and nudges his head toward me. "Do I need a reason to get drunk?"

Tyler is a beautiful man. Even when he was younger and I should have been too young to notice, I knew he was pretty. Not like a girly way, just in a rugged man way. His dark hair is shaved close on the sides and long in the front. He sweeps it out of his face, cold blue eyes wandering to mine.

"Well no, but you said it first. And it seems I'm not the only one here to drink someone or *something* away." I eye him carefully. The sharpness of his jaw covered by a slight beard is a roughness I want between my thighs. "Is it a girl? Did she break your heart?"

For a split second, the look he gives me is almost vulnerable and I can't tell why, but our eyes are locked and I know Tyler well enough to know I might have guessed right. He shifts his gaze quickly and laughs a little at the question then turns his attention back to Zack when he returns with his order.

"You gonna join me or am I going to have to finish this bottle by myself tonight?"

"Fuck yeah!" I shout, louder than necessary. "Someone to get drunk with. I hate drinking alone."

He grins, light laughter following and my stomach flips a little because there's the Tyler I have known for twelve years.

The thing about Tyler, he's always been a flirt with me. Really since I turned sixteen and got boobs, he's flirted with me. It didn't matter who we were with at the time, Tyler always had a sexy comment or a wink to send my way. Hell, he even flirted with me during the time he was with Berkley, his ex-girlfriend.

I distinctly remember my teenage years spent dreaming about him going down on me, too. I know, crazy dreams but he was twenty-two when I was sixteen and the coolest guy ever as far as I was concerned. Also the hottest.

You know, those older brother best-friend types, they'll get you every single time. Probably because they're technically supposed to be off-limits. Well you know what, I'm a motherfucking rule breaker tonight, so I shift in my seat to face him.

Tyler seems entertained by my enthusiasm and turns so he's facing me as well, our knees knocking. "Well I'm assuming the person you're here to forget is Holden, so are you gonna tell me *why* or are ya gonna keep me wondering all night?"

Jesus Christ, the way he watches me. I just want to lay myself on the bar right now and beg him to stick his head between my legs.

"Why yes, I will tell you who I'm drinking away, or rather why." I stare at my delicious heaven in a cup that Zack slides my way, my lips scrambling to reach the straw. After a sip, the straw falls away and I remove the pineapple from the edge and take a dramatic bite for no particular reason at all. "The reason for my drinking is that he "whose name shall not be mentioned" is a stupid motherfucker. And for the rest of tonight and all eternity, he shall be referred to by his proper moniker of fucking asshole."

Tyler lifts an eyebrow again, waiting for more of an explanation, one I don't give him. I simply shrug. A hearty laugh leaves his lips, and he raises his drink filled halfway with liquor. He reaches out and grabs the edge of my barstool and in one swift movement, he has me sitting right next to him, our arms touching. "Well, shit…. To me, then."

Giggling at nearly falling off the stool in the process, I watch as he downs the drink in one shot, grimacing at the burn.

"Why you?"

Setting the glass on the bar, he stares at me for a moment, making me slightly uncomfortable. Running his hands through his dark hair, he leans forward slightly, his head turned to me. "Because I'm the lucky son of a bitch who gets to help you forget the asshole."

Sigh. No really, I sigh. Outwardly, like I'm dreaming.

By "forget," I know exactly what Tyler has in mind. As I said, he's never been shy about his attraction to me. He's still technically off-limits but like I also said, all bets are off tonight.

I hold my drink up clanking it against his. "May the force be with you!"

He snorts. "Did you just quote *Star Wars*?"

"Yeah, I think I did." I try to focus on him, and instead I end up squinting.

Tyler's eyes meet mine. "It's still pretty early. You hittin' the town tonight with Rawley?"

I eye him completely straight-faced. "I'm not hitting much of anything these days and all we have in this town are farms and bugs."

He laughs. "You know, I've always said a dirty mind is a terrible thing to waste and girl, you know how to use your dirty mind, don't you?"

The way he watches me makes my knees shake and takes the air from my lungs. It damn near gives me chills. "I'm a Walker. I know how to use my dirty mind for good." I wink at him. "And I think I'm going to stay right here. I want to drink away my sorrows with these delicious drinks and the bottle of whiskey you so kindly bought us." My eyes sneak to his and then the bottle as I raise my empty glass. "Just poor it right in there. I bet it will be delicious!"

Tyler gives me this look, as if he knows where this could potentially go with us getting drunk but with the way his eyes darken maybe he wants that very same thing.

Maybe.

Despite my declaration of wanting to get drunk, my mind is on Tyler suddenly. I shift so I'm facing the stage again, staring out into the crowd hoping to distract myself.

"Can you believe that asshole?"

When I glance over at him, Tyler doesn't look at me but I can see his brow furrow in confusion. "Who? Rawley?"

"No. Holden."

Tyler twists his head in my direction, his brow raised and cheeks flushed in the cutest way. I want to reach out and touch the heat to my fingertips. Running his hand through his thick dark hair, he laughs lightly. "Actually, yes, I can. Holden, sorry, I mean fucking asshole, seemed like a turd to me." His hand raises and flips around. "No offense."

"None taken." I want to slam my head on the bar and knock some sense into me. "Clearly. He couldn't even cheat on me with someone hot. No he had to pick some average-looking blonde with perky tits and a fake tan from California."

"Oh, I'm gonna need more on this. Did he give you a reason? And how do you know she's from California?"

"No, he didn't give me a reason. At least not one I understood and all sluts are from California." I'm sure that's not accurate, but in my head, tonight, it's totally fucking accurate. I reach for the whiskey and pour both Tyler and myself a shot. Zack eyes the two of us and what's happening, like he knows we're having one of those nights where it's best to keep your opinions to yourself. "So... yeah, no real reason but I mean, balls deep in another girl pretty much explains it, doesn't it?"

"Yeah." He rubs his left thumb over his bottom lip. "I *suppose* it does."

I can't help but shift my gaze to his beautiful full lips. Tyler has one of those mouths you just want to suck on. His lips are like your favorite candy that you just want to lick all day.

When I finally force my eyes back to up to Tyler's face, he's staring at me.

My chest tightens as I swallow. There is no missing the way his eyes linger on me, watching my every move.

He's curious, I know he is.

"So you catch him balls deep in some chick and he doesn't even give you a reason why he cheated?"

"Apparently I have expectations no man can ever meet," I tell him. "I mean, seriously, are there any good men left? And I'm talking the honest ones. Ones who aren't dating someone else or are married. Ones who have some fucking chivalry in them."

Tyler flips his hand around, his rosy cheeks indicating he's feeling pretty good with that third drink. "What you're asking for is bullshit," he says bluntly. "Chivalry is overrated. You're puttin' too much pressure on it. A relationship should be simple."

"Simple as what?"

He looks me straight in the eye. "Simple as I want to fuck you."

Is he saying that to me?

"Of course you would say that." I sigh, knowing he is right in some sense. "Guys just want a girl who lets them put their D in their V and it's over, right?"

"Wait." His brow raises. "Did you just say put their D in their V? Do you think you're talking to Nova? Why can't you say vagina and dick?"

"Oh, I can say it, and I'm pretty sure you've heard me say worse."

"True, but I think it's fucking hilarious that you're *not* saying it now. Also I kinda want to hear you say it."

"Dick and vagina."

His eyes meet mine, amusement flickers in them. "Or cock and pussy."

The way he says cock and pussy makes my stomach clench. Straight up fucking clench. It's damn near fucking erotic sounding. My heart pounds, fluttering in my chest. Clearing my throat, I say, "Or… muff and wang."

He shakes his head and lifts his drink to his lips casually but grins. "That's the name of a porno I watched once."

"Really?"

He holds up his hand, a smile lingering in his eyes. "No... not really, but it totally should be."

Why are you so fucking adorable?

"Enough about me. I told you why I'm here so now it's your turn. Spill. What's with you and Berkley?" Of course I asked that. For the last six years Tyler has dated one girl. Berkley Logan. And it ended suddenly about a month ago. In the first few years it was clear they had an open relationship, but then they settled down for the last two years and seemed happy. Not so much anymore.

"Next question." Smirking, he tries to get away with that answer.

Not happening.

"Nope. Answer me."

Tyler leans back slightly and runs a hand over his face before staring up at the television screen playing highlights of the baseball game. "I don't fucking know. Never gave me a direct answer."

"Relationships suck."

He holds up his drink. "I'll fuckin' drink to that."

And we do. Three shots to be exact. Each.

And then comes a little truth. "I came home one day and she had moved out," he finally tells me after his fourth shot. "Said she needed to find herself."

"Bullshit!" I yell, entirely too loud.

"Right?" He nods and then his gaze drops to the shot glass he's flipping over in his hand now. "Four fucking years."

I laugh. "I thought it was six."

"I don't fucking know." He snorts and drops his head in his hands. "Maybe that's where I went wrong."

"Maybe."

I lay my arm on his shoulder. "We're a mess."

"Hot mess."

He winks and then drags his eyes south. "*Hot* is an understatement."

I wish he'd drag his mouth over mine!

Good think I'm sitting or I'd drop to my knees at that look.

THE NEXT THREE hours are a blur. A fucking blur. I keep switching between the whiskey and those delicious mixes Zack should be arrested for serving me to the point that I dance on the bar with Tyler. Considering my vision's blurred, I have no balance and poor motor skills but I'm still standing and doing pretty good.

When I'm drunk I can't feel my lips. It's also a general assessment that they won't work either. Clearly.

I yell, "Drinks on me!" as we stand up there. Thankfully, Tyler saves my lying ass, steals my credit card telling everyone I'm not serious and I have no money.

Partially true. I have fifty-seven dollars in my checking account.

You would think at some point during all of this drinking I would have begun to feel sick. I drank a lot of alcohol, but maybe it was the heartache soaking it up.

Shaking myself from those thoughts, I look over to Tyler who I notice, not for the first time tonight, is staring at my chest. His gaze only lingers there for a minute and when he looks back up to meet my eyes, he winks, and we find ourselves once again smiling at each other.

A switch in the songs draws our attention toward the stage and Rawley's playing a slower song, SafetySuit's "Never Stop," his attention on Sophie in the corner of the bar drinking with her friends. My brother is still in love with his ex-girlfriend, Sophie, but refuses to admit it. He'd rather fuck with her head than tell her how he feels.

I drag my eyes back to Tyler and notice that again he's not looking at me, but instead at my chest.

It makes me sigh. Again. Actually sigh because the way he's looking at me sears my skin with his heat and sends my heart sputtering like a misfired engine. It's there in his eyes that he's enjoying my reaction, along with the slow lick of his lips and the darkness in his eyes.

I think it's worth mentioning again that I'm incredibly drunk. Having said that, I want to be clear, I'm not throwing myself at Tyler. I'm launching myself.

Sipping the drinks a little more slowly, I keep having to wipe the condensation from the glass. It drives me mad, seeing it pool around the glass. I also hate the drips when I would go to drink, and water spills all down the front of me.

Tyler's amused and even keeps taking my napkins to see what I will do if the water pools and I have nothing to wipe it up with.

Teasing bastard. He's done this to me since I was a kid and he realized I had obsessive compulsive disorder.

"Want another one?" Zack asks, gesturing to my empty drink with a nod.

"I'm here to make bad decisions and regret them in the morning. Serve it up."

Tyler laughs beside me when Zack turns around to make the drink.

"What if you *don't* regret them in the morning?" Tyler asks.

"Even better." I point my finger in his face. He tries to bite it, his cheeks flushed from his buzz.

"What the hell is in those drinks?" Tyler asks when I take a drink and moan and then looks at Zack. "Dude, cut her off already."

Zack whispers something I don't hear but they both laugh.

I push the menu at him and then protectively cup my glass. "It's not on the menu. It's a secret concoction." The word cock rolls off my tongue nicely and doesn't go unnoticed by Tyler.

In fact, I think it makes him uncomfortable because he shakes his head but shifts on his stool, his left arm dropping to his lap.

Resting my arm over his shoulder, I hug him to my side. I'm a happy, loving drunk and will love on anyone if they let me get close enough to them. "Man, I've always had a huge crush on you. I remember when I was like fifteen, and you were twenty-one, you snuck a beer from a party for me and took me out in your truck around town. Do you remember that night? It was snowing like crazy and you were doing donuts in the parking lot of the shop. You asked how old I was that night and when I said fifteen—"

"Yeah," he interrupts, nodding. "I remember that night."

"You said damn when I told you my age, but you knew how old I was so I couldn't figure out why you asked." Removing my arm, I stare curiously at him, his smile higher on one side. "Were you mad?"

"Kinda." He shrugs, flipping a bottle cap around in his hand. "I only asked because I needed the reminder. You were pretty hot that night but way off-limits. I shouldn't have even entertained the idea, but I did."

I love the way he says, "But I did," because he's honest with me and I love honesty right now. "Well." I shrug myself. "I'm not fifteen anymore, so there's that."

"No, you're *definitely* not fifteen."

chapter 2
GIVE ME ANOTHER

I'VE ONLY EVER slept with Holden. A shocking reality, huh?

Looking at Tyler, I wonder what he's like and if he's a hair puller. He's a man and all hard lines and bulging tattooed muscles and I *hope* he's a hair puller. I *hope* he yanks the shit out of my hair.

Remember when I said when I'm drunk my mouth gets me in trouble? It's about to happen. I can feel it coming.

"Okay, here's some drunken truth." His eyes on the television slowly drift to mine. "As you know from our previous conversation, I've had the biggest crush on you since I was old enough to crush and one thing always crossed my mind…. Are you *rough* in bed?" I ask with my straw in my mouth.

Tyler smiles widely and with a tip to his head, he runs his hand down his jaw. He glances at my chest and then back at my eyes. "Well, I'm not one to kiss and tell so I guess you'll have to find out on your own." A smile curves his lips as he gives me a narrowed look, scrutinizing my reactions. "If I were to take you home, how far would you let me go?"

Holy shit. Did he just ask me that? It means it's crossed his mind then, right?

Against my better judgment, our eyes meet and his captivate me. "I'm… not sure."

Yes, you are. You're totally sure you'll let him do whatever the fuck he wants. Admit it.

He raises his eyebrows in a playful manner but I can see the hunger in there.

I smirk, knowing how true that statement really is, but never giving him an answer. I hold the cards and I like my hand right now. Slouching slightly, but careful not to fall back off the stool, I look at him again. "You're too sober for this conversation. You should drink more."

"Too sober? Why's that?"

"Because, Tyler, I've decided that my mission tonight is to get you to go home with me and the way I look at it, my best chance of making that happen is to get you drunk. How the hell am I supposed to get you drunk if you're not drinking?" I take a sip from my drink. "Although, I wouldn't actually be taking you home. For what I have in mind, we should definitely go to your place." I sigh, lightheaded, my own intoxicated wave hovering over me. This should probably be my last one for the night or else I might throw up.

Tyler's quiet, so naturally I become a little self-conscious. What the hell is he thinking?

Tyler motions me forward. I do as he asks and find myself hanging on the bar and giving him a clear view down my shirt. He smiles, giving a small nod. "I'm gonna let you in on a little secret, Raven. If you want me to take you home, all you have to do is *ask*."

My voice is lost in my throat.

When I find it, I ask, "Take me home?"

"See, now was that so hard?" He draws his voice out like a whisper. Damn him.

"Kinda." I roll my eyes. "I've had a huge crush on you since I was like fourteen or sixteen. *Whatever.* So I mean, yeah… do you want to?"

"As long as you're sure, I'd be an idiot if I said no." His gaze falls to my lips. "Wouldn't I? Something tells me you're a good time."

I bet you're a good time.

I can't have him thinking he's in control of this. It'd be out of my nature. "Oh, I'm sure. As far as me being a good time, well I guess you'll have to find out." I push the last of my drink away and reach for my purse. "I think I'm done for the night."

He gives me *that* look again, the one where I should be concerned about what he really has planned. "Well that's too bad because I think I'm just getting started."

Fuck yes.

"I BET YOU'VE done this a lot, huh?" I ask when we're outside in the parking lot.

He doesn't answer, shrugging, gravel crunching beneath his feet. The air is cold, whipping around in a gentle spring breeze that's refreshing on my burning face.

It occurs to me then that drunk Raven just needs to shut up but of course, that proves to be impossible because he's Tyler Hemming and pretty much my dream guy.

"I don't know whether to take that question as a compliment or an insult. What makes you think there's been a lot of girls?"

I give him a look, intentionally letting my eyes drink in his strong physique. Olive skin, and sky blue eyes shadowed by jet black lashes search mine. "First of all, it was a compliment. Definitely a compliment. Second, look at you." I wave my hand around in the air and unintentionally smack him in the chin. He chuckles. "There's definitely been *girls*. I saw you in high school before Berkley.

Different girl every night. I remember a party you and Red had when my parents were out of town. There were *definitely* girls."

He gives me a look, so much hidden in those eyes. He knows exactly what party I'm referring to. The one where I caught him having sex in the backyard with Tina Gordon. I can't forget her because her hair reminded me of cooked top ramen.

His eyes meet mine and I stop walking. His face twists and he blows out a quick breath. "Does it matter? I'm only with one girl right now."

I laugh, which to my embarrassment comes out sounding more like a snort a baby elephant might make. "I bet you've used that line a time or two, haven't you?"

Tyler regards me for a moment, his eyes sweeping down my body in an audacious way. Every inch. There's the burn again. He's staring at me, a look I can't decipher. "Maybe."

Stop thinking, Raven! This is the moment you've always dreamed about.

"*One thing always leads to another.*"

Fucking Rawley and his rightness.

I nod this time. I don't want things getting awkward by not talking and him potentially deciding *not* to take me back to his place. I'm not going to lie, my curiosity nags at me. So badly. I want to know. I want to know how many he's treated this same way, but at the same time, I don't want to know. In some ways, I want to remain oblivious to this and enjoy it for what it is. A one-night stand.

As we make our way through the parking lot, my mind is racing with all my internal thinking and unfortunately, I'm not watching where I'm going. Which in my defense is easy to do when you can't see a goddamn thing other than the moon and the lights of the bar. Forget about seeing your own feet. Zack really needs to put better lighting out here.

Tyler notices my lack of balance and says, "Hey, there, watch where you're walking." Before I can do that, I run right into a trailer hitch on the back of Rawley's truck, only to be caught by two strong arms.

"Motherfucker! That's going to leave a mark." I turn in Tyler's arms and push my finger into his incredibly sculpted chest. "I blame you for my inability to walk in a straight line. You let me get drunk," I say, placing the blame on anyone but myself.

"You were already *well* on your way to drunk when I got there." Cupping my cheek, his thumb grazes my mouth, toying with my bottom lip. There's a darkness sparking in his eyes. "I just joined you."

All I have to literally do is turn my head and I'd be kissing Tyler. And just when I think I'm going to do it, he pulls away slightly. It's the sensation, all tingles and sparks when the roughness of his fingers meeting my skin that sends my heart racing.

He keeps his tone playful but his look sears my skin and kick starts my heart. "Don't get shy on me now."

His fingers find the bare skin of my collarbone... hot, damp skin begging to be touched.

I don't reply. I can barely breathe let alone actually reply.

"How long have you wanted to kiss me?" he asks, knowing damn well I've wanted to more than once tonight.

Unable to force my eyes from his, I breathe out slowly, stiffness to my posture, unsure maybe because there's desire here but there's also the need to leave this alone. "I can't remember a time when I didn't want to kiss you."

As soon as I've said the words, without any more hesitation, his mouth is on mine. Pulling his bottom lip with my teeth, I bite down softly drawing him into me with my hands welded around his neck. He willingly comes forward, his kiss eager. It's not one of those kisses that happens suddenly. He eases me into it, brushing his lips lightly before his tongue slips into my mouth.

He tastes so fucking good. A sweet mixture of the drinks and a taste I know is all him.

Steadily, his hand slides around my neck, and then the other, holding me there for him to kiss. He groans into my mouth, deepening the kiss. The sound causes me to shake. No lie.

That kiss. It sets fire to what was sparked by his flirting tonight.

I go a little crazy. My hands fisting in his hair, yanking his face to mine with more force than necessary. For years I've been wanting to touch him, have the weight of his body on mine and now that it's a real possibility, it's a little hard to take and has me desperate not to lose the connection.

Amused by my sudden eagerness, he chuckles against my lips and then kisses me deeper, angling my head to thrust his tongue inside my mouth.

If he can set my mouth on fire with a kiss like this, imagine what he can do with that tongue to other parts of my body.

Oh, the possibilities. My V will be so happy.

Needing air, he draws back and takes a deep breath, his hands moving over my body everywhere, from my neck to my breast to my ass. There's no stopping him. He wants it, and I know a part of him would be willing to do it now in this parking lot.

Not happening. I've waited too long for this.

Our lips slide apart, our movements too frantic for a parking lot. "Let's take this back to your place," I whisper, my lips at his ear as he hungrily scrapes his teeth and tongue along my neck, teasing me. Pulling at the straps of my tank top, he's already working on getting it off.

My hands seek his, pushing them away as I stand before him, rubbing my sore shin from the trailer hitch.

I reach for his hand. "You coming?"

He grins, grabbing my outstretched hand. "I'm hoping to."

"So dirty." I laugh, backing up one step, and he finally follows me.

SINCE I RODE to the bar with Rawley, I didn't have to worry about leaving my car there. The drive back to his apartment only takes minutes, but it gives my drunk mind enough time to worry that he's going to change his mind about wanting to be with me.

Fortunately, those worries are dispelled quickly by Tyler placing his hand on my thigh and slowly working his way up my thighs before we even get to the first stop light.

As soon as we manage to make it to his apartment above the shop, he has my back pressed against the door and his hands are under my shirt, palming my breasts and already pawing at my clothes.

Oh yeah, he wants it all right.

Just as quickly as his hands make their way to my breasts, they are gone and before I can voice my protest, he grabs my waist and twists me around so that my chest is up against his front door. Part of me thinks we need to take this inside but the truth is I really can't focus on anything but how good he feels against me.

Damn, why couldn't this door open on its own?

Drawing in a deep breath, I arch my ass against his hips. He answers me by slamming his hips into me and pushing me against the door, pressing firmly into the cool metal. One hand twists into my hair, tangling my locks around his fingers as he sweeps the hair aside. Hot wet lips take over, and his other hand grips my hip as he rubs his erection against my ass.

I made Tyler Hemming hard!

It's the first time I've ever felt him like that and I know tonight will be anything but disappointing.

"I knew you were a hair puller," I tell him, smiling.

He doesn't say anything, only tugs harder.

Shuddering in anticipation, I remember he still hasn't opened the damn door. Just as I attempt to back up so he can, he offers no room and instead pushes himself deeper, my face now pressed to the door.

I glance back at him and he smiles, heavily hooded eyes prying open. "We'd better get that fucking door open, *or* I'm fucking you against it. Your choice."

I arch my brow at him, maybe challenging, maybe not. A wave of pleasure shudders through me when he shifts his stance, like he's going to do it.

Letting go of me he reaches for his belt, unbuckling it, a wicked grin in place.

"You have the keys, Tyler. It's your apartment."

"Oh, right."

There is a moment where neither one of us say anything. We stare at one another, waiting, because once that door opens, we both know where this leads. Reaching around me with his keys in his hand, he crushes me between the closed door and his body as he unlocks it, his lips on my shoulder. "Goddamn...."

Something in his urgency tells me maybe it's been awhile for him. I know for certain it has for me, which may explain the butterflies in my stomach just anticipating what we're about to do.

Bringing his hand up, his thumb traces over my bottom lip, his eyes dark and needy. His body shifts into mine as the door clicks open, his hips and chest touching me now.

Once inside his apartment, he picks me up, wrapping my legs around his waist, slamming us against the wall. We explode into a frenzy of kisses, neither one of us able to break apart for air, let alone stop kissing. His body shifts as if he can't keep still. With a noise of impatience, he growls into my mouth, deepening the kiss again.

When he finally puts me down, we attempt to move toward the bedroom, but things get sidetracked when I start slowly stripping at the door.

Tyler obviously thinking I'm taking too long as he immediately goes to take off my shirt and actually rips it down the side, just trying to get it out of the way. He attempts to slow down, obviously trying to restrain himself, but fails miserably when he comes back with even more intensity.

I look at the shirt, laughing, even as his lips attack me with a desperation I understand.

With my hands on his shoulders, I try to catch his eyes. "Dude, you ripped my shirt…."

"Who fuckin' cares?" he mumbles, going in for another kiss.

He's right. I actually don't care at all. I manage to push him back again, wiggling out of my jeans and tossing them aside. It's getting hot in here and my clothes need to go.

His large hands are at my waist, guiding me inside the bedroom. From the look in his eyes and the way he touches me, I get the impression he understands how badly I need this.

As we stumble around, the back of my knees find the bed, and we fall back against the mattress. Every line of his body tenses, as if he's trying to slow down but can't.

We don't speak for a moment as he slides his hands over me and I'm swimming in how good this is just being with him here like this, as long fingers and broad palms explore my willing body.

With my heart hammering in my chest, beating so erratically I'm sure I'm about to have a heart attack, he kisses me once more and then reaches for the buckle of his jeans, unbuckling his belt and drawing his zipper down.

I grab his hand to stop him and he raises his eyebrow in question. "I do believe that's my job." I'm not sure where this boldness is coming from, but I'm liking it. "Don't worry, I'll go easy on you," I say, trying to be naughty and hooking my fingers into the waist band of his boxers to pull both them and his jeans down all at once.

He laughs, stepping out of his jeans while removing his shirt. Once he throws his shirt on the floor, he looks at my lips and then my eyes before clearing his throat softly. "Is that so?"

"Well maybe not too easy, I am here to find out just how rough you like it after all." I slowly lay back, eyes roaming over his body as he falls into me, catching himself on his hands.

Sky blue eyes give way to darkness as he rolls to the side, his hand moving south, stroking himself a few times, as if he just couldn't take it any longer.

In the name of all things good and holy, fuck me, that's intensely hot!

Prying my legs apart, he moves to settle between my hips, waiting for me to make the decision.

I quickly shift my gaze from his face and get a brief glimpse, knowing I wouldn't be disappointed by his cock, thick and heavy between his legs demanding my attention.

Placing his elbows on either side of my head, he watches me until his voice drops and his words hit my stomach. "You sure?"

I nod, maybe a little too eagerly. "Definitely sure."

Leaning over the side of the bed to find his jeans, he pulls a condom out of his wallet. I stare as he opens the package with his teeth and then proceeds to put it on before settling back between my legs.

Drawing in a deep breath, I prepare myself. He smells so good. Like man and a rich running engine. It was one of those moments where I literally tingle as he enters me.

Once he's inside me, it's clear that Holden is still only a member of the boys' club, because Tyler, he's a fucking man. Maybe because it's been awhile but still, nothing can compare to him entering me. My breathing stops and brain cells are quickly dying awaiting the oxygen.

Tyler entering me is the only time he takes it slowly or gently. And that's where the softer side of him ends. As soon as he's inside me, his body is heavy, his grip too strong and his hands too rough. It's all hard to comprehend but I'm in no coherent position to stop him. I need this. This is what I'd asked for and what I so desperately wanted.

"Holy shit, I knew you'd be rough," I say when he's slamming inside of me, whole body movements that slide me up the bed. I'm a thicker girl, probably a size ten—it's mostly in my ass—and he makes me feel tiny with the way he's manhandling me.

Tyler hesitates midthrust and then I panic because he's stopping. This is something I've wanted since I was sixteen, long before I should have wanted my brother's best friend and the thought of stopping now is *not* an option. "Should we be doing this?" He swallows hard, his gaze on mine. "I mean, you're Red's little sister...."

Seriously?

It's a slap in my face, it really is, even in this moment I'm only ever someone's sister, but it's not enough to stop me. "What's that got to do with anything? Are you scared of Red?"

He looks offended. At least we're both on the same page. "*Fuck* no."

"Then stop thinking and fuck me."

My nails dig into his shoulders as he pushes inside me, this time more warily, and I think again, maybe it's been a while by the way his body trembles when he moves again. His breathing is rapid as he gives me a look I don't quite understand, or have the mental ability to comprehend with the amount of alcohol in my body.

His hands move over my hips, carefully but with a bit of impatience, his touch almost sweet, as though he's attempting to slow it down. I close my eyes, wanting to enjoy every sensation he's causing throughout my body but they soon snap open when he raises my left leg and reaches between to adjust the angle. Roaming fingers slide slowly over me, taking time to learn my contours. "Jesus, you're fucking beautiful, Raven."

I'm so ready to come just based on those words and squirm against him, needing the friction, needing him to move faster, but he's slowing down.

With my leg hooked around his arm, he has the correct angle, and he pushes inside me again, drawing back, and then giving me a little more.

"I want you to make me scream." I move his hand from beside me to my neck, making him squeeze. "Take me any way you want me. *Any way.*"

For someone who's in a constant struggle to maintain control all the time, it's maybe a personal fantasy to have someone else control me in the bedroom. Having a man like Tyler Hemming take what he wants from my body, yep, I'm down with that. Fucking all over that.

I wonder briefly if he understands how willing I am and how I want it. My eyes search his face but never meet his eyes. I'm so needy for him, if he asked, I'd probably let him stick it in my ass.

Tyler stops midthrust, and looks down at me, giving me a glimpse. "Are you sure that's what you want?"

"Yes. I want you to fuck me. Like, *really* fuck me." My voice lowers. "I want to be able to feel you every time I move tomorrow."

With a growl, one that emerges from deep within, shaking me to my core, he goes for it.

I should have known when Tyler took me home he'd be the best fucking lay of my life, but then again, I've only ever been with Holden and just Tyler's kisses blew that out of the exhaust pipe. With heavy kisses, ones that leave me shivering and shaking, he whispers my name across my neck, how beautiful I am and how badly he's wanted this.

Yep, all he has to do is ask and I'm totally letting him stick it in my ass.

His hands curl around my shoulders and he draws me into his thrusts, which seem harder each time, my breath expelling on contact.

"That's it," he growls into the curve of my neck, biting down on my skin. "Is this what you wanted? You needed to be fucked, didn't you?"

I nod against his shoulder, biting down as the pleasure begins to peak. "God, yes, Tyler! I needed this so bad!"

He groans again, the sound pushing me further over the edge as his mouth moves over my jaw and to my neck, a searing path that sends shivers down the backs of my legs. One hand stays curled around my shoulders, but his right hand moves and angles my hips as he drives into me, harder this time. The angle takes my breath away. "I knew the moment I walked into the bar and saw you sitting there you'd be on my dick tonight."

Yeah, he's pretty sure of himself. Judging by the way he's fucking me right now, he has *every* right to be. The truth is he's always been this way. Overly confident. So sure of himself.

"Why's that?" My lips are at his ear, kissing along his neck. "Taking advantage of the drunk girl, are we?"

"No, I knew it because the minute I saw you tonight, I knew you needed this as much as I did," he says, his face flushed and determined.

Flipping me over, he has me on my knees and entering me from behind, just like our position outside the room. One hand presses into the small of my back, burying my face in the pillow, the other gripping my thigh to the point where it burns.

He doesn't last long like that, and with every move he makes, his body leans forward until eventually he's slumped forward completely, wrapping his arms around my waist. He brings me closer to his chest that way, and it's nice, the thump of his steady heartbeat and breathing against my damp skin. Moving from his grip on my waist, his left hand grabs the front of my neck and squeezes. "Fuck, I'm so close."

It's then I know I'm going to come like this. It's the force, the movements, and knowing if I didn't like his hold, I'd say something, but his body isn't giving me the opportunity to deny him. And there's something incredibly sexy about that.

Flipping me over again, and with just a simple movement of his wrist, I'm on my back with him between my legs once more.

Only this time his arms are hooked just behind my knees, his hips undulated, giving me exactly what I need. It rises like a roller-coaster ride, warmth spreading from my thighs to my toes. I roll my hips, giving in, letting go, sensations gripping every part of me.

I cry out with the switch of positions but it's not from pain. "If you want me to stop, just tell me." Amusement touches his lips when I squirm.

"Don't you dare fucking stop," is my only reply, my fingers gripping his hands, which are placed securely on my hips.

Tyler throws his head back. My eyes lock to his heaving chest, straining as he moves, and on the way the sweat beads on his skin.

Everything is heightened when I see his face contort in pleasure. It's clear, until now, I've never been fucked by a man. I've only ever had nervous touches and sweaty palms. Now I have this, the confidence, the fierceness I've always associated with Tyler.

Warmth jumps in my tummy, forcing a string of needy pleas passing my parted lips. The tingling and then the sudden pleasure ripping through me. Succumbing to sensations, my orgasm is there, all at once, igniting my body in flames.

He knows when I come, clenching and shaking beneath him as my back arches and his grip on my hips slip. His hands move from my hips completely and fist in the pillow beside my head.

"Christ, you're beautiful when you come." Throwing himself into his own movements, his pace hard and desperate, Tyler chases his need, his hips slamming into me, his body tensing at the onset of the pleasure. I bite down on his shoulder muffling my moans of pleasure in his skin.

He lasts three more pumps and thrusts his head forward, his forehead resting against my breasts. Then collapsing as he lets go completely, he gives me all his weight. His hands move from beside my head to my ass, giving me one more long thrust. "Jesus Christ…." He breathes out, long and low into the curve of my neck as he pulses inside of me.

Fearing this will be over before I know it, I don't want to let go—hell, I don't want it to end. Ever. I want to stay here with him buried inside me until the sun peeks through his dark curtains.

Holding onto his neck, I move with him until he lets out a heavy sigh, riding out the last of his orgasm.

Barely able to draw a breath because of his weight on me, I have no words. All I have are shortened gasps, trying everything I can do to keep myself from hyperventilating. I just had sex with Tyler Hemming. My childhood crush.

And it was the best sex of my life. I'm not lying. I want to cry with how good it felt and how badly I needed that. Holden who?

Tyler rolls off me and onto his side, shifting to bring my back flush against his chest, his lips lingering at my shoulder. He is still trying to catch his breath.

"That was amazing," I say with heavy breaths, swallowing and then letting out another forced gasp.

He turns my head to kiss me again, grinning against my lips.

"Turn over," he says, letting go so I can do so.

When I do, he smiles, his knuckles brushing over my cheek gently, his eyes fluttering closed. "You're amazing, Raven." It's his tone and me believing the truth behind his words that draw me in.

I continue to stare at him, his eyes remain closed. Maybe he's still awake, but his features seem relaxed, as if he is already asleep or just getting there.

Staring at him, my eyes follow the line of his jaw, the curve of his cheeks, his lips. Just him. My heart flutters in my chest. Holy hell, no way this can be a one-night thing.

Raven
chapter 3
TONGUE TIED

THE NEXT MORNING

I'M NOT REALLY sure how to wrap my head around the fact that I'm lying here, in the soft bluish lit room, resting my head on the chest of the last person I ever dreamed I would be. Tyler Hemming.

As his lips kiss my bare shoulder, I ask, "Should we talk about what happened last night?"

"We don't have to." I find myself watching his lips when he speaks, remembering how they ghosted across my skin last night. It's morning and the sun's peeking in through his slate-gray curtains as we lay in his bed.

It's weird being in Tyler's room and it's not lost on me the implications this could cause. He's one, my brother's best friend, and two, we're above the shop that my brother now owns. I hope to hell he doesn't come up here.

Given the pounding in my head, I'm not sure I want to remember every vivid detail of last night. And then again, I'm certain I do because there's a spark of emotion in his eyes when I watch him that most would miss. I can't tell you what it is but I know I put it there.

His gaze drops from mine when he rolls out of bed and pulls on a pair of shorts and a T-shirt, motioning to the kitchen. "You hungry?"

Reaching for one of his shirts he has folded on the chair beside his bed, I nod and follow him after putting the shirt on. We sit in silence mostly, the occasional few words uttered as he makes me pancakes.

"Are you regretting it?" he finally asks, setting the pancakes in front of me. Tyler's known me a long time so it makes sense that he can tell my mood is off.

"No, definitely *not*." I try to take even breaths. "I just... well, thanks for being there for me last night."

Leaning back on the couch he's sitting at now, he pulls up his shirt, revealing his chest. "I think you thanked me pretty well," he teases, gesturing at the scratch marks from my nails on his chest. My mouth gapes open as I stare at him. "You could thank me again though. I'm all for that."

My insides do an excited dip, like I'm thrilled with the possibility. "I don't know...."

"I bet I could convince you," he goads, his eyes twinkling with a boyish mischief.

He stands up from the couch and walks over to where I'm sitting at the table and takes the chair next to me.

"How so?"

He leans forward and pulls my face to his, smothering my words. This kiss is nothing like the ones I experienced last night. This one is full of intent, passion, and promise. I'm burning, dying, and wanting to spread my legs for him again. Damn, he's good.

And then, just as I want more, he draws back, smiling. "Convinced?" Keeping his eyes on mine, he draws his bottom lip in slowly, letting it drag through his teeth.

"Maybe." Maybe, my ass, but I have to recover some of my dignity after that soul scorching kiss!

He makes quick movements and has me back in the bedroom immediately. Within a minute, he's filling me, his kisses and touches eagerly worshiping me in all the ways I need him to.

"Promise me you won't regret asking me back here last night." My fingernails digging into the skin of his back as he buries his face against my neck. I have to know. Normally I'm not much for small talk during sex.

His mouth is fierce and needy, kissing my neck, my shoulders, anywhere he finds bare skin. "Raven, I can guarantee you I have no regrets about bringing you home with me last night. Believe me when I say if I didn't want you here last night, you wouldn't have been here. Now shut up. I'm busy."

My head snaps back against the headboard, his hips bucking forward. His lips mix with his hot breath fanning over me, killing me slowly, sweetly, before he fills me again and again. The force of his powerful hips drive me harder into the headboard.

His left hand clamps down on the headboard, his knuckles turning white with his grip. Seconds later, his head falls forward, resting against my forehead. "Jesus, Raven, you feel amazing." His sweaty chest slides across my own, and the moan that leaves my lips shakes the both of us.

Both of us make frantic movements, moaning and grunting, and I fist the sheets between my fingers.

Riding out my high, adrenaline flows through my veins. I can already tell just being with him once, or even twice won't be enough.

His legs tense, his stomach muscles flexing as he pulses into me. Steady, panting breaths capture my own broken breaths. Just as I'm

staring at him, a grunt forces its way from his lips, and then a groan. "So good."

When his body finally collapses on mine, I hear wood splinter from the headboard, and laugh. "Um... I think we broke your headboard."

Rolling off me, he lays sideways so that he can drape his arm across my body, his eyes hesitantly meet mine, and then he shakes his head. "Fuck the headboard," he says, panting against my neck, his heavy arm over my stomach. "I think you fucking broke me."

Less than ten minutes later, I smile when he kisses my neck again and moves me so I'm on top of him. His eyes are hooded, and I know he wants more already. Raising his hands to cup my cheeks, he breathes in deep. "Round two?"

"You mean round three?"

He drops his face so his lips are at my ear. "That too."

This is how Tyler and I began. Secretive, undecided, and unbearable for me to end.

6 Months Later

September

TYLER AND I began just before school let out for me during my freshman year of college. Something that was easily dismissed as two people having fun. We continued to hook up on occasions but summer was where it really took off for us. I was in his bed nearly every night and damn it, I broke the rules.

Now here I am, leaving for college tomorrow and it's killing me not knowing what's going to happen when I'm not here with him. Will he find someone else to fill the void?

That can't happen. It won't happen. It's not that I'm going back to school and need clarification on our relationship, it's that I want it. I was with him for months, in his bed, his D in my V and I deserved some kind of definition, right?

The morning before I leave, I'm waking up in Tyler's bed and it isn't something I experience often. Usually I'm gone by morning. Today though, I lie here and watch him sleep, knowing things are changing. He's asleep on his back, one arm slung over his face, the other on his stomach.

My gaze drifts to his hands. I'm addicted to them in every way. I love hands in general. They can provide so much for you, strength, security, and affection... safety. Looking at Tyler's hands, you can tell a lot about him. Hard working, rough, grease under his nails that will never come out, cuts and scrapes from knocking his knuckles against engine parts. They're the hands of a mechanic, a real man.

Staring at them, running my fingers gently over the scar on his left hand where he cut it open on an engine two weeks ago, I think about how many times over the last six months these hands have pulled me in, cupped my cheek, ran his thumb over my lip and caressed my curves.

I definitely don't want this to end.

We made rules. We did. Did we follow them? I can honestly say looking at him, Tyler did.

We had a few of them. Most friends with benefits did.

One. Red couldn't find out. The last thing either of us wanted was for him to know his best friend was pile driving his sister at 3:00 a.m. most mornings.

Two. And this had a lot to do with number one. No flirting in public.

Three. Don't get attached. Tyler specifically said, no falling in love with me. I laughed in his face at that one but it's proven to be the hardest one yet.

And there you have it. Simple right?

Nope. Not even close. I'm a fucking girl. Telling us not to fall in love is like provoking us to fall in love.

"If I ask you something, will you be honest with me?" I ask when he's awake an hour later.

His body tenses and he nods, probably wondering where the fuck I'm going with this.

"Do you think we should stop?" My voice is plagued with fear as I await his words, his potential rejection.

His eyes cut to mine, a sideways glance. He's silent, but I can feel his resistance like a prick on my chest. My question throws him for a loop. He just sits there blinking, considering me for several silent moments. Does he think I want to go away this fall and not know where we stand?

He sighs heavily and sits up against the headboard.

Am I an idiot to think it'll work out?

Probably.

And then I am left with where I am now. Staring at Tyler wondering how the hell I let myself get caught up in something a big part of me knew could only lead to heartache.

I mean, as much as I never want to admit this next part, you can never truly start out as fuck buddies. I've seen enough romantic comedies to know it never works out in the end for the girl. It's because our girly hormones get involved from the start and we think we can make them feel something more than sex.

"How does this end, Tyler?"

His brow raises, as if he doesn't understand what I'm asking, or maybe why. "What do you mean?" There's emptiness in his voice, the hesitation so obviously written on his face, answers the question for me.

"How did you see this ending? Because it's pretty obvious I'm going to get hurt."

"Don't say that." He scrubs his hands down his face, blowing out a long breath. "We both knew what this was."

It's not like what he is saying isn't true. I mean, it wasn't like we didn't discuss what we were getting into. Hell, he even told me not to fall in love with him, but still. "Yeah, I did." I sit with my legs folded under me to look at him. "But I'm also a girl and our emotions and feelings sometimes take on a life of their own. In the end, every girl hopes for more."

"Well, fuck." He throws his arms up in frustration, moving to stand beside the bed. "How the hell am I supposed to know that? I'm not a damn mind reader. Just tell me what you want from me!"

I draw in a breath, one that comes from deep within and offers no relief. "You know, for six months I've been playing by the rules, putting on a show in front of my brother, your friends, work, all that, but I'm tired of pretending. Tell me where we stand."

I feel bad pushing him. I don't want what we have to end and I don't think Ty does either, but I still need an answer. Hurting me is the last thing he wants but the reality is when sex gets involved, someone always gets hurt.

Honestly, I really don't know what's holding him back. Maybe it's the six-year age difference.

Maybe Holden is right and I'm too controlling and I'm coming across as needy. Or maybe it's Tyler just being too stubborn to see the possibilities.

Why? Why isn't it as obvious to him as it is to me that we have something that could be more, so much more. All I want is for him to be open to the possibility that this has become more than what we intended when we made our agreement. That maybe, just maybe, this could be love. One sided? Most likely. But love just the same.

And now I sound like a cheesy version of a *Dirty Dancing* song.

Staring at Tyler, it's clear he has no idea how much anxiety beats in my chest and how every word we haven't said these last six months took pieces of me.

In a huffed breath, he lets out a sarcastic laugh, shaking his head, unable to say anything more.

My legs start shaking. Breathing too fast, the action too much, my heart threatening to give out. "Seriously, Tyler, *what* does all of this mean to you?"

There's a deep inhale, his chest expanding. He's studying me and gauging my words and reaction to this. I do my best not to give away anything, but I'm sure I fail miserably. "Why does it have to mean anything? We didn't go into this looking for it to mean something. We went into it looking to have fun. We both agreed. Now you're looking for a definition I can't give you and it's not fair. I didn't do anything wrong. I didn't change the game. You did. I didn't go into this looking to fall in love. Had I, sure, maybe it could have turned into something more. But I didn't and you knew that, Raven. I just don't understand why you're trying to find a bigger meaning in something so simple."

I can't meet his eyes when I say, "There's nothing wrong with wanting a bit of clarity."

His teeth grind, his swallow rolling over this throat. "Is that what this is? You're gonna be gone during the week so you're feeling insecure? Don't be. We started with you being gone during the week. Nothing needs to change and this isn't a matter of me not falling in love with you." His body remains rigid, his face impassive. He's putting up a shield, guarding himself from giving away too much. "It's about me not falling in love, period. End of story. I don't want love. I'm not looking for it. It's something I told you from the very beginning I didn't want in my life."

"Okay, fine." There is a tightness in my chest I don't understand as the words spill from my lips. Biting the inside of my cheek, blood pools in my mouth. I force myself to stay calm and not let him see how his words are chipping away at my already fractured heart.

Standing from the bed, I reach for my clothes on the floor.

"I'm not trying to be a dick, Raven." He moves in front of me, refusing to let me get out of his room. "I like my life the way it is. This isn't about you and me. Please understand that."

His voice is pleading. I have to believe him. There's so much vulnerability in his voice. "So, while I'm away... you're planning on having sex with whoever you feel like?" I'm searching for meaning.

"I haven't thought about it." I can see it written all over his face. It's in the pull of his brow. He honestly hasn't yet. Part of me is thankful for that.

"I just—" I don't even know what I'm trying to say now.

"Come on, let's not fight about this. We don't fight. We have fun." He cups my cheek, his thumb dragging over my lip when he pulls me in. It's relaxing in a sense because the last thing I want to do is fight with him. "Why can't we just enjoy the moment that we have now? Stop worrying about what will happen once you're not here every day." He watches my face close, the desperation to change the situation clear. "Come here."

I do as he says, our chests touching, my emotions all over the place. Once our bodies are coming together, he turns me around so my back is to his chest. His breathing changes, his heart thumping between my shoulder blades and I know then this, us being together, is having some sort of effect on him. Maybe that's why he's doing it, making me stand this way. He knows if I could see his face, I would be able to see the truth. Whether it's because he's trying to protect me or hide from me is what I don't quite know.

Breathing in deeply, his chest expands into me.

His hand glides across my stomach until he reaches my thighs.

He moves us to the bed with me lying on top of him, my back still pressed to his chest. With heavy breaths in my ear, his hand moving lower until his thumb drags over my clit. "Just relax. Enjoy the moment. Let me take care of you," he breathes out as two fingers slide into me. His left hand moves from my hip to my neck, squeezing and angling my head back so he can kiss my neck.

Arching my back into him, his hips raise at the contact my ass makes with his erection. Every time he touches me my heart races erratically, uncontrollably and I find it hard to catch my breath.

Reaching up to grab a fistful of his hair behind me, I cry out when his teeth sink into my shoulder. I need more. Never before has this ache been so intense. When he moves, thrusting his hips up and dragging my ass against his erection, I search for friction as his fingers continue to move inside me.

There's a heat between us, stronger than the sultry haze in the room as I squirm on top of him. My reactions, my moans of pleasure spark a response in him, his left hand slowly moving back down to squeeze my hip.

With him hard between the cheeks of my ass, his mouth on the back of my neck goes wild with heavy kisses as his groans of pleasure pass over my skin.

And all I can do is remember to breathe and say his name, and when I'm so, so close, I tell him and his mouth bites down on my shoulder again, muffling his groan. He's rubbing and stroking with his talented fingers, and then I'm panting and crying out with my release at his touch. He covers the sounds with his hand that was on my hip, his fingers inside my mouth. I suck on them, my tongue swirling around his fingers, sucking them like I would his dick. His hands are all man, calloused edges of a roughened mechanic, the faintest hints of grease and oil on my tongue. It's a harsh comfort being held captive at the hands of this man, rugged and raw.

His hips jerk, thrilling movements that push me over the edge again with every sensation-soaked arch of my back.

When we part, I sit up, straddling his lap and look over my shoulder at him. The look on his face is one of hunger. While my need has been met, his is still very much there.

I twist around and face him, my hands resting on his chest. His breath speeds as he watches my hand glide down his forearms. Taking a shuddering breath, his eyes close when my I palm his erection.

"Fuck, I have to be inside you. Now." His mouth finds mine, unable to part from me.

My kisses ask unspoken questions. I can't help it.

He offers nothing but hunger and passion, two things he's always shown me.

He moves us back, lying me down on the bed, his hands cradling my head. Deepening the kiss, he groans and presses me into the mattress. My body tenses, my arms stiff, wrapping around him. It's then he remembers the condom and draws back once more.

I'm in the middle of his bed when he's crawling back on after putting a condom on. Grabbing me by the ankles, he slides me underneath him. Lifting my right leg, he enters me in one swift, brazen move.

Just when I think it will be like every other time and I'm waiting for the more dominate side of Tyler, I'm shown something else entirely.

His hand that's on my hip moves to cradle my head, his grip never tightening as he threads his fingers in my hair. Tenderly, his lips cover mine, breathing the words, "Don't think," against them.

Our gaze locks and then falls away as he deepens the kiss again. Thrusting inside me, I can understand what he's trying to do. Make me see that despite me not getting what I wanted, he's giving me what he can. He cares. It's just the place in his life where it's not right. I get that.

Threading my fingers through his hair, I try to give him what I can. My understanding.

His tongue slides across my collarbone, my legs lifting to wrap around his waist.

He shudders, his hands in my hair. Kissing down my neck, he rocks into me with slow languid movements that set my nerves a blaze.

Drawing back, he swallows, his chest heaving with a breath, the muscles in his throat working. "God, *Raven*."

He doesn't last long and I'm not surprised. All I can do is lie there and feel him because it's the best fucking thing I ever felt, being with him like this.

"Raven," he whispers again, his lips close to my ear. It's two more thrusts inside me before his body shakes, his mouth returning against my lips as we share breaths. His hands, his lips, the ones that have touched me so intensely over the last few months, hold me in place.

Breathing heavily against my ear, he holds himself still, gripping my hips so hard they begin to hurt.

I let my hand drift up to the side of his face, running my fingertips along the edge of his cheek. For a spilt second, his eyes open to me. I want to see warmth and connection reach his eyes, and when I don't see it, a hint of fear pricks at my skin because all that's there is sadness. His lids fall shut again as he kisses me harder.

He slows it down and he kisses me softly, pouring emotions he says he doesn't have into them. Under the sadness, there's vulnerability he doesn't want.

Rolling off me, he lies on the bed, breathing heavily.

I sit up, curling into myself and then he's sitting up too, his hands resting on his bare legs. That intense stare lingers on me, as does the confusion. Running his hand over the back of his neck, there's hesitation in his movements. "Raven," he whispers, the lowness hitting my stomach with the fragile way I'm holding onto his expression. "I know when you leave this room you're going to pick apart everything that's been said and in doing that, you're going to focus on me telling you I didn't want anything but sex." He leans in enough for his lips to meet my forehead, his grip around my waist tightening. "But what I want you to understand, no, I need you to understand, it's not that I can't fall in love, it's that I don't want to. Yeah, another time, another place, maybe things could've been different and believe me, hands down, Raven, it would have been you, but it's just not who I am. What we have right now, this is all I can give. I'm sorry if that's not enough."

Reality crashes down on me like a wrench straight to my temple. A wave of heat hits me, this one humiliation because like it or not, I'm emotionally invested.

Stupid girl.

I turn away, my eyes on the wall because I'm about to cry. I know he cares about me but what we're doing doesn't matter to him in the same way it does to me.

To him it's sex. Always will be.

He kisses the spot between my shoulders and then the back of my neck.

Goose bumps shiver over my skin. "I have to go. I'm heading to Eugene in the morning. My classes start tomorrow." My voice breaks apart, much like my heart. "I'll be back on Friday though."

Blinking at my words, he turns me around, his eyes on mine. I don't recognize the expression on his face. It's one I've never seen before. Regret? Doubtful.

"I'm looking forward to it." A smile plays at his lips, and though it's a familiar sight, one I've seen often these last few months, something seems different about it. He leans toward me, kissing the shell of my ear. With his hands on my shoulders, he pulls away.

Removing my hand from around his neck, he kisses the knuckles of my right hand and touches my face with the other.

My stomach twists the moment I'm out the door because I know what's happening, I'm falling for him and the gutting reality is he isn't, nor will he let himself.

chapter 4
STUPID GIRL

"So...." Lenny begins. Her eyes widen when I glance over at her. "Red knows about you and Tyler." Lenny is Red's girlfriend and she's quickly become my best friend. I tell every single shitty thing about my life to her. Naturally, she was the only one outside of me and Tyler who knew we'd been hooking up.

"Red knows?" I gasp, my hand over my heart. It's pounding so hard, so fast, I think it's going to pop out of my chest. "Is Tyler still alive?"

When I left the apartment this morning I went back home to get the rest of my clothes I'll need for the week and then over to Red's house to talk to Lenny. It's been something like five hours since I saw Tyler; he could very well be dead by now if Red knows.

"As far as I know, for now," Lenny tells me, digging through the cupboards at Red's house for the tequila. Nova's at her feet asking if she can have some. "They're apparently at the bar. He heard you arguing this morning and I did my best to distract him but he's not stupid."

She's right. Red is far from stupid. Red's my older brother by eight years and me thinking I could hide anything from him was a dumb thought.

"How did he hear us arguing?"

"He was helping me grab the last of my clothes and you two were in the bedroom."

"Shit." I throw my hands up in the air. "He's going to poison Tyler and make it look like a suicide."

She doesn't say anything for what feels like minutes, like she's seriously thinking about it. "Nah, he wouldn't do that." When she finally pulls the bottle down from the cupboard, she holds it above her head and looks at Nova as if she's crazy when she reaches for it. "No, you can't have any. It's alcohol, Nova."

Her hands are immediately on her hips. "So? What's that mean?" Nova is Red's daughter from his marriage to Nevaeh, his wife who died three years ago. Nova, who's almost six now, acts like she's about thirty most days.

"It means you have to be twenty-one to drink it."

Nova scowls. "That's ridiculous."

"So how did this morning go? What did you guys decide?" Lenny asks the moment Nova takes off to her room. Lenny knew my intention this morning was to tell Tyler how I felt.

"I'm pretty sure his dick made love to me this morning, but the rest of him, yeah... not so much."

Lenny frowns and hands me a shot glass and then the tequila. "Here. This will help."

We're just getting started with drinking when Nova reappears, her hands on her hips. "Can we talk about kindergarten?"

Lenny pushes her shot glass away and faces Nova. "Why?"

"I don't want to go anymore."

"You kinda have to."

"No, I don't. You're technically in charge of me. Just call them up and tell them I'm not going anymore."

"It doesn't work like that."

"It does if you're Rawley. I heard Daddy talking about him not calling when he doesn't show up. And kindergarten is like prison." Nova dramatically puts her hands on her hips. "I have to ask to go to the bathroom."

I place my hand over hers on the table. "They're teaching you manners."

"Screw that," she mutters, walking away.

Lenny's eyes widen watching Nova flip her brown curls around. She probably can't believe she just said that. Nova has a bad mouth and Red's been fighting it since she learned to talk. None of us should be surprised by it. Much like me, she grew up with a bunch of mechanics as her role models. Her language should be the least of his worries.

"What's all this?" I motion to the piles of clothes and two boxes sitting in the dining room.

"Red asked me to move in."

"I'm so happy for you," I lie, trying to smile at Lenny. I think I did a pretty good job, because the excited look on her face tells me she's close to buying it.

"Really?" Lenny beams with my words and I almost refrain from my next comment.

"No." I roll my eyes, throwing back my head to down the last of my drink. "I hate you. Don't talk to me about your perfect life."

"I do *not* have a perfect life," Lenny reminds me, and I know that. She doesn't. No one does. "I know Holden is an asshole and cheated on you Valentine's Day and you agreed to this fuck-your-friend arrangement, but let's be real, you *knew* going into it there was a good chance things would go bad, right?"

"First of all, thank you very much for reminding me it was Valentine's Day. I wish that day would burn in hell. I don't ever want to see another Valentine's Day ever again! And second, I think it's obvious I didn't think this whole thing through or I wouldn't have done it. No. Never mind, I *totally* would have done it. The sex is amazing." I look down at my hands on the table. "The truth is I took a risk and I lost."

My chest burns at the memory. It's like any break when you're reminded of why it's there. Like a glass that breaks on your kitchen floor, and for weeks afterward you keep finding little shards of it that cut the shit out of your feet. Not just any cut either, the kind of cut that burns. Like a sharp clean line.

Being cheated on is the same deal. My mind drifts back to Holden and why it hurts. The gut ache and confusion that somehow it was my fault. That I drove him away with my social awkwardness and overbearing demeanor. I mean, is it wrong to be so obsessive all the time? I didn't think so but then again, it's not like I have much of a choice. It's who I am, who I've always been.

I'm a planner. I just feel safer when I know what's going to happen and when it's going to happen. For example, when I was three, I told my mother I would be married when I turned twenty-five and I've stuck to that plan until now. I'm not exactly on the right path to that particular goal, now, am I?

The correct answer is no.

And if I think about Tyler and how wrong it went.

Why couldn't it have been just sex for the both of us?

Because I'm a stupid girl with emotions and the ability to try and see something where there's nothing.

Stupid fucking girl.

If you think my having to have a plan at all times is bad, then the question of whether I'm too controlling is a disaster. If I'm being honest, in some ways I can be. Did I see the signs early on? Yep.

When I was in kindergarten, I used to get pissed when the teacher would be even a minute late or if we wouldn't go outside at the exact moment we were supposed to for recess. I like people to be precise and detail oriented. What's wrong with that?

When I'm at a doctor's appointment, if the doctor is late coming into the room, I'm not pleased and insist he tells me why I wasn't worth being on time for.

If my desk at work is a mess, I freak out. Obsessive-compulsive disorder?

That's an understatement.

By some standards, I should be on medication. Okay, maybe most standards but hey. I'm not as bad as I used to be. Sadly, I haven't improved enough to, let's say, keep a relaxed attitude and let a relationship run its course. *Clearly.*

Sometimes I think I'm having a midlife crisis at twenty.

I've taken about four shots, maybe more when Lenny looks over at me, waiting for me to say more. "It doesn't matter anyway. As far as he's concerned, nothing has changed. I just need to figure out what I want."

"And that is?"

I groan.

"Raven, do you think you could continue with the fuck-your-friend agreement without falling deeper?"

"That's the million dollar question now, isn't it?"

Truth is, I don't know if I can. My heart is already invested and I don't know if I can just turn it off.

I DECIDE TO stay here tonight, get up early and leave for my morning class. Lenny and I are on the couch watching a movie around midnight and I hear a rumble. My stomach drops when I realize it's Red's car pulling into the carport. "Shit!"

When his car door shuts, Lenny and I scramble to hide the bottle of tequila. I'm not sure why because it's not like it matters we're drinking on a Sunday night.

Lenny flips the blanket over her face. "Shhh. I want to hear this." And then she darts behind the couch out of sight.

I'm not sure why she's hiding because it's not like Red wouldn't talk to me in front of her. I can only assume she's hiding because she's drunk.

Red comes through the door a moment later, his keys dropping to the floor as he kicks the door shut with his foot and turns the alarm off.

I count the footsteps until he's standing before me in the living room. His hands are on his hips and he's watching me with the protective hardened brother look he's had a time or two. He's certainly perfected it over the years and it's kinda scary. "He was fucking you behind my back. *Friends* don't do that."

"Lighten up." I groan, resting my head against the back of the couch. And then I remember Red and Tyler have been best friends since they were kids. Surely Tyler might confide in him, right? I sit up and stare at him. "Were you with him? Did he say anything?"

"Yes, I was with him. He said plenty." Red dramatically tosses himself on the couch Lenny is hiding behind. He's definitely been drinking and grabs the pillow beside him holding it over his face. After a moment, he removes it and stares at the ceiling. "You're not a brother. You'll never understand."

"You're right, I won't. I don't have a dick. Which is good because dicks just seem inconvenient to me. *But* you've never been a little sister and you'll also never understand. I care about him."

He takes my words in. They settle over him and he stares back at me, his eyes softening. "I get it, I do, but I'm going to stay mad for

58

a little while." And then he stands tossing a pillow at my face. It hits me and then falls to my lap. "The fucker deserves whatever shit I throw at him so don't even try to make me be nice."

He walks away after throwing another pillow at my head, into his room where he probably assumes Lenny is.

When he's out of sight, Lenny pulls the blanket from her face. "I think Tyler is about to get all the shit jobs now." She seems pleased by this, the corners of her mouth raising up. She's probably just glad she won't be getting them anymore.

Sliding out from behind the couch, she crawls down the hallway on her hands and knees. "Why are you crawling?" I call out after her.

She grins over her shoulder. "Just saving some time. Red likes me on my knees anyway."

I take the blanket she was under and throw it over my face. "Gross!"

I don't fall asleep right away. Instead, I go over the conversation with Tyler in my head and him telling me if he had been in the position to fall in love, it would have been me. There's a good part of me that's hopeful that might still happen someday.

Tyler
Chapter 5
LITTLE SISTER

LITTLE SISTERS ARE off-limits. It's a bro-code that any good friend would follow.

Too bad I've never been good at following the rules. While my head got the message, my dick didn't. The sex overruled any other thought I could possibly have as to it being wrong. Truth be told, while Red is my best friend and I would do just about anything for him, when it came to this, I just didn't give a fuck.

Raven fell into my life at a time when everything I thought was true in my life, wasn't. Everything I thought I knew about relationships and commitment, fucking life in general was a lie. The people I thought I could trust, I couldn't. With Raven, I had all that. We had it, until we didn't anymore and I wasn't sure what it had become besides a mess.

I've learned, a lot like diagnosing a car with an oil leak, things are never what they seem at first glance. Girlfriends you thought would always be faithful aren't. Parents you thought always had your best interest at heart and would always protect you don't, and your friend with benefits you thought was on the same page, isn't.

I'm not sure what exactly happened this morning but I think it's obvious Raven and I are of very different opinions where we should take our relationship from here.

Relationship? Is that what we have?

I guess some would call it that, but not me. No. A committed relationship is the last thing I want and I thought Raven and I both agreed we weren't headed that way when this whole thing started. It was one of the few rules we agreed on for Christ's sake.

The thing is, I do love Raven, just not in the way she wants me to. Being Red's younger sister, she's been a constant in my life for as long as he has. I care about her and if I was being completely truthful with myself, part of me does love her, but I can say with certainty that I'm not *in love* with her. The extent of my romantic feelings are expressed in the satisfaction of making her scream my name when she comes. At the same time, I care about her enough to never want to hurt her.

I'm not sure I was successful in making her understand my unwillingness to let this arrangement take on a greater meaning has nothing to do with her and everything to do with me. After Berkley, I decided I was better off staying away from love and relationships all together. Like I told Raven, it's not a matter of *can't*, it's a matter of *won't*. Nothing and no one is going to change that, even if she is the first person to make me feel the good and forget the bad all at once.

Staring at the door, the one she just walked out of, I knew I couldn't stay here. Not with the memories of this place—and her— and how it's all changing.

Grabbing my keys off the counter, I head to the bar, the one place I know I can at least try to forget what's happening.

You know when you've had someone in your life for a long time and you just sense when they're around, well that's how it is with Red and me. I know the moment he steps into the bar, and turning to see him take a seat on the stool next to where I'm standing, it's obvious he knows. It's written all over his face.

He shakes his head and licks his lower lip in agitation, turning so his eyes are trained on mine as I stand next to him. There's a split second when he stands up when I think of running. "You're fucking my little sister?"

What do I say? No? I can't lie to him now.

I almost smile at his petulant tone and how dumb I've been, but while I may be dumb, I'm not stupid enough to do that. Utter silence expands between us. Until I clear my throat. "Look, Red—"

Scowling and muttering under his breath, Red draws back and punches me. Right in the fucking jaw and it stings like a motherfucker.

Running my hand over my throbbing jaw, I wonder briefly if he's done some damage and then realize he hasn't, but my pride is certainly wounded.

I glare at him. Though I know I deserved that, it still stings a little more to be hit by my friend.

Shaking my head, I step back. "Message received, I suppose."

I stand there staring at him, gauging when his anger begins to dissipate and he nods to the bar. "Sit. Down."

I do as he says, mostly because I don't want him to hit me again.

"Why didn't you tell me?"

"Man, I'm sorry. But we're adults and I didn't really see the need to ask for your permission. And dude, you're scary." I rub my jaw, a reminder.

"That's bullshit and you know it," he grumbles, raising an eyebrow. "Why did you guys have to go behind my back?"

I think about my answer for a second and then ask, "What was I going to say? Your sister and I decided to be friends who fuck? That's not really a conversation either of us was willing to have with you."

Zack comes by, eyes the two of us and then slides two beers our way.

"Well, did you think for even a minute that by not telling me you made it worse?" Red asks when Zack disappears to the other side of the bar.

"Look," I twist slightly in the stool to face him. "I get that you're upset that we didn't tell you but you know me. I'd never hurt her or use her. So yeah, you can be pissed that we didn't tell you what we were doing, but honestly, I don't think you have any right to be mad at either of us for being two consenting adults who enjoy each other's company."

Taking a slow drink of his beer, he slams the glass down pointing out the obvious. "I'm pissed because you're six years older than her."

"Yeah, but she's not a little girl anymore and you can't be stupid enough to think this is her first rodeo. She was with Holden for four fucking years."

"I don't get it. How did this even happen? Did this happen in the shop?"

"No, the shops all yours, man." I chuckle, bringing my beer to my lips. "It just happened."

He glances away, then nods. Once. Sharp. Like he's really wanting me to consider his next question. "Just for a minute put yourself in my shoes. What would you do if it was you?"

Heavy question.

I'm not sure how to answer it. So I don't, for an entire minute.

"Honestly, dude, I don't know. I didn't grow up with siblings. I'd never be in that position."

"I just don't get it. She was eight when you met her. She was like your fucking sister."

"I know, but she's not eight anymore and I'm not fourteen. I get it, but I would never hurt her intentionally."

Look at Red. He's a perfect example of how things can change even when you don't want them to. He told himself his love was buried with Nevaeh. And then Lenny came along and surfaced every emotion he thought was six feet under.

With Raven, as the weeks went by I realized why this girl had taken a hold of me when she was younger. I thought of her as a little sister myself, but it still didn't mean I wasn't attracted to her.

She just turned twenty in August and I'm twenty-six. I'll be twenty-seven in December. That's a huge age difference.

Given her recent background, and mine, it surprised the hell out of me she even wanted more.

I'll admit I'm a bit hostile when it comes to relationships. Mostly because I've been burned in the worst way.

Last February my now ex-girlfriend, Berkley, found out she was pregnant and we couldn't have been happier. So I thought.

Two weeks later, she miscarried and a week after that she moved out claiming she needed to find herself.

After six years of being together, I think it's pretty obvious if that was her way of dealing with it, she was never truly in love in the first place.

"I'm sorry I didn't tell you," I tell Red, hoping he listens to me. I never went into it with Raven thinking I would deceive my best friend. I told myself I'd tell him eventually and then that turned into six months and how do you start that conversation?

With his elbows resting on the bar, Red laughs low and without humor as he toys with the paper label on the longneck in front of him. "I know you are."

Does he?

Red looks over at me and I think I know what he's going to say next, because I've certainly felt it. "You made her dirty by hiding it."

Guilt hits me in the chest. I should have told him and the fact that he found out this way only makes it worse. The fact that I made Raven look dirty, well that's enough to destroy me.

I moved to Lebanon when I was fourteen and Red has been my friend from that day on. He deserved better from me. I definitely should have told him.

"It's never gonna be the same, man," Red says, bringing the beer to his lips.

Weariness has me rubbing my face before I answer. "I know."

"Do you have feelings for her or what?" There's a curiousness in his tone, one where he's genuinely asking and not looking for me to just say it to appease him.

"I don't fucking know. I really don't." I leave my answer at that.

BY FRIDAY, I'M missing Raven. I told myself not to. Actually demanded that I not, but it didn't work. I miss her like fucking crazy. Mostly her friendship but the sex too.

Friday marks the start of our fall softball league as well and arguably my favorite night of the week in the fall. Mostly because these guys are part of my family and I love spending time with them. Red and his family have become like my second one over the years. They say friends are closer than blood at times and I honestly believe that. I hardly ever see my family but on any given week, I'm at Red's house two nights a week.

Except for this week. He wasn't exactly that nice to me. I can't say I blame him.

I've played softball with Walker Automotive for years and it's always been fun. It's different now because I'm not sure how to act around Raven since last weekend. So I act as I always do and flirt with her and send dirty text messages all week. The last thing I want her to think is that our friendship has changed. To me it hasn't.

I get there just as Red does with Lenny and Nova.

"Uncle Ty!" Nova yells, running toward me as she's scrambling out of the car and pushing up the sleeves of her shirt. She's wearing a black shirt like our team with the Walker Automotive logo on the front only her number is ½ pint.

Kneeling down, she runs to me and then jumps in my arms. A pain hits my chest as she does it, mostly because I'll never have this. I've always had a special connection with Nova though, and she's called me Uncle Ty from the beginning.

"Hey, girly!" I pick her up to carry her toward the field as Red carries his bat bag on his shoulder.

"Raven coming tonight?" I ask Lenny, not Red. Though we're not totally cool like we were, he's getting over it.

I'm not even sure why I ask Lenny but as I do, Red grumbles and steps ahead. I know he can't stay mad at me forever but shit, I wish he could just let it go.

"She's on her way." Lenny smiles, knowing why I did. Because I care and I can't deny it.

I wink.

As we're walking toward the field, I see who we're playing and cringe. It's Berkley's parents' team which means she's here too. Fucking sucks for me. I hate running into her, mostly because she always finds a way to make it awkward.

Despite breaking up, she acts like I should want to be friends with her.

Walking into the dugout, I see Colt lying on the bench.

"Dude, why do you come out here if you're just going to get drunk and pass out on the bench?"

Colt lifts his eyes to mine, a drunken smile plastered across his face as he spits chew at my feet. "Because Mia *asked* me to play. Probably because she needed extra players."

"You got third tonight, right?" Red asks me as they're sorting out the batting order.

"Yep."

I watch closely to see where he puts everyone. He sticks Raven at second and I like that because she's good there. He then puts himself on short stop. I'm concerned how he'll play. A few months back Lenny's ex-husband showed up in town. He caught Red, Lenny and Nova off-guard in the shop only to shoot Red in the chest. It was touch and go for days but he pulled through. Given this information, to me it seems a little early for him to be playing softball but I'd never say that to him.

Quirking an eyebrow when he turns around, he stares at me. Though I haven't said anything, he knows exactly what I'm thinking. "What? It's just softball."

"Okay." Yeah, it's just softball but I know Red and he never goes easy. I don't think he knows how actually. Before you know it, he'll be sliding into bases and diving for line drives.

Raven's rushed when she arrives, having gotten stuck in traffic. Tossing a hoodie on her bat bag and reaching for a water in the cooler, she notices me sitting next to Nova on the bench.

She gives me a nod. "Hey," and then smiles at Nova. "Hey, kiddo."

"Hey, Auntie."

"Auntie looks pretty, doesn't she?" I whisper in Nova's ear, knowing what she's about to do.

"Auntie, Ty says you're pretty."

Yep. Knew it. And yeah, I did that on purpose because just looking at Raven in her tight black pants makes me push Nova off my lap and scoot away from her.

I thought, no, I fucking hoped maybe I could distance myself from Raven since I'm clearly not what she needs, but I can't do it. I'm a weak son of a bitch.

Nova frowns. "Why'd you do that? The bench is cold on my butt cheeks."

"It's for the best," I mumble, making my way out of the dugout on the other side to stand near the fence.

Over my shoulder, I sneak glances of Raven as she puts her cleats on, her cleavage on display. Good thing I'm standing now.

"What's up your ass tonight?" Raven asks Rawley, who throws his phone on the ground and storms out of the dugout when he sees Sophia talking with another guy. If I ever thought shit was messed up in my life, all I have to do is look at Rawley and know it isn't so bad.

Berkley walks by the dugout right then wearing a pair of tight black pants, her white T-shirt with the number 5 on the back even tighter. For being with her for so many years, I feel nothing inside when I see her. Maybe hatred, but certainly no attraction.

Her eyes scan the bench and drift to Raven. I know she has an idea there's something going on between Raven and me, mostly because she asks me constantly which tells me she's concerned.

She gives a nod to Red dragging Nova back from the snack bar with nachos in her hand. "How are you doing, Red?"

I'm not sure why, maybe because we dated for so long but Berkley has it in her head she's still friends with everyone, like Red and my parents. I guarantee even though Red is pissed at me, he still doesn't like Berkley.

Red steps inside the dugout, his arm draped over Lenny's shoulder. "Pretty good."

When Red takes a seat at the end of the bench near the fence, I scoot next to Raven. "Did you miss me?"

She moves away from me and ties her hair up, her mitt on her lap. "Not really."

I scoot next to her and she slides herself further down until there's nowhere left to go without falling off the bench.

This time she glares. "Are you five?"

"Stop acting like you don't enjoy it." And when she doesn't reply to that, I ask, "Did you get my text?"

She shrugs and stands up. "Stop talking to me. You're up to bat soon."

I'd forgotten the game is starting.

WE GO THROUGH the top five in the batting order and I'm standing outside the dugout waiting for my turn to bat, the sky's painted with hues of red, orange and pink, which fade to a matte black as the clouds move in. Lenny's up to bat, with Red coaching first base. He's got one eye on Lenny and one on Nova, who refuses to sit still tonight and keeps running onto the field.

Wanting Raven's attention, I tap the bat to the fence. It rattles with the weight of the bat and when her eyes are on mine, I dip my head a little and wink as I stroke the handle of the bat to get a rise out of her.

She scowls, her uneasy stare sweeping over me.

Nova bounces up from her place on the concrete inside the dugout. "What's wrong with you? You look like you're going to puke," Nova says to Raven as she grabs the sunflower seeds out of her hand.

Raven grumbles something to her I can't hear but I'm distracted now by Daniel, our lube tech at the shop, making his way toward me.

He's batting behind Raven and leans into my shoulder and gives a nod to Raven. "I can't believe you've been hitting that."

Daniel is one of those kids you shouldn't trust. You know he probably has good intentions inside of him somewhere; I've just never seen them. The only reason I tolerate the shit is because of Lyric, Red's dad who passed away last May. He asked me to help the kid out and I've been trying to show him the right way. Only, he's pretty fucking dumb.

I glare over my shoulder. "What are you talking about?"

He steps beside me. "I've been spanking it to images of that ass for years. Please tell me you're done with it."

My body rushes with anger and it nearly blinds me for a moment.

I blink, twice.

Did he seriously just say that?

Taking the bat in my hand, I lift it and smack his balls with the end.

"What the fuck!" he curses, dropping to his knees on the ground.

Kneeling, I get down to his level. "If I ever hear you say something like that again, about Raven, you're going to be pulling this bat out of your ass instead of cupping your fucking dick." Standing up, I point to the dugout. "Can someone bat for Daniel? He needs a pinch hitter."

I'm a good softball player. Baseball was my sport growing up so it's no surprise to anyone I hit a home run.

After I cross home plate, I'm walking back and I stop in front of Raven near the dugout, since she's up next and hand her my bat she likes to use. "Your turn."

She takes it but doesn't meet my eyes. I watch her the entire time as she swings and drives one deep into left field. Their left fielder manages to get to it before she makes it to second.

Daniel's up after her and I have to run for him, seeing how I smacked his ball sac and that leaves me watching Raven run to third. I want to make a run for second but I don't have time.

Once I'm on first, I notice Berkley standing next to me.

Raven, Lenny... they can play softball. Berkley can't. Not even a little. She's too girly. She's mainly out here to look pretty.

Flipping her black hair around, she pushes out her chest. "Nice hit."

I used to think Berkley had good tits. Not anymore. Nothing compares to Raven's. So I look away and I don't acknowledge her at first.

She sighs. "Not talking to me now?"

I don't even look at her and focus on brushing the dirt of my black shorts. "I'm trying to but you're making it difficult."

"Well, I'm just trying to be nice."

"Being nice would have been paying the fucking credit card bill instead of maxing it out," I snap back. There's a lot of things I'm bitter about regarding our breakup and her maxing out my credit card is on top of that list. Did she not realize how hard it'd take a guy like me to pay off twelve thousand on a fucking credit card?

She says nothing.

When I'm back in the dugout, I sit right next to Raven, mostly to annoy her and mostly because I fucking want to.

She's not looking at me still; she's watching Nova with a bat in her hand, who's stroking it like I was just minutes earlier.

"Nova, what are you doing with the bat?"

Nova shrugs. "What do you mean?"

"Why are you running your hands over it like that?"

Well fuck. It does look rather inappropriate now that I see a child doing it. I give Raven a smile and she puts her hand on my cheek to turn my head the other way.

"Uncle Ty said he was warming up so I'm warming up." The innocence on her face makes me feel bad.

Crap.

Raven shoots me a look of disappointment. "You're an idiot."

I laugh and flash her another smile. "Yeah, well I never said I *wasn't.*"

"True."

We sit in silence watching the game when I notice Raven's head down and she's rubbing at her eye, grimacing.

"What's wrong?"

Using her index finger, she's still rubbing at her eyeball, which I find a little gross. I hate it when people touch their eyeballs. But now she's wincing almost like she's in pain.

"I've got some damn dirt in my eye and I can't get it out."

I gently grab her chin to turn her head to face me. "Here let me see."

She lets me help her without argument, which I'm going to count as a win with how today's been going so far.

As tenderly as I can, I use two fingers to open her eye and move closer to softly blow to try and remove the dirt. It must work because when I let go Raven just sits there staring at me. The looks she's giving me is almost curious, like she doesn't know what to make of my helping her.

Staring back at her all I can think is that she's so fucking cute and the next thing I know I'm tucking a lock of her hair behind her ear, running my thumb over her jaw and smiling like a fool before I ever realize what I'm doing. Her breath hitches. Wide chocolate eyes melt me. "Stop being nice to me, Tyler."

I draw in a deep breath of cold fall air. "Sorry. No can do. When it comes to you, I can't help myself."

Our knees touch and I bump hers a couple times trying to annoy her.

Raven eyes Daniel, who's holding an ice pack to his nuts. "What's wrong with him?"

"How should I know? The guy's a goddamn idiot."

She leans in, whispering, "I saw what you did."

I shrug. "Well then, you know what's wrong with him."

She squints at me to try and convince me that she means business, I guess. "I know what's wrong with him, but what I don't know is why you did what you did."

There's no way I'm going to tell her what Daniel said so I shrug. Again.

Thankfully, she lets it go.

Raven leans over and grabs my bat, gripping the handle as she pushes around the dirt. Looking over, I can't help but stare at her hands.

Raven has really pretty hands. I know that sounds stupid but she does. Her hands are perfect. Her fingers are slim and her nails are just the right length for scratching my back and when I'm lucky, my chest.

Watching her now, holding that bat, all I can think about is how much I would love to have those nails clawing at me as she moans beneath me.

I lean into her again until our shoulders are touching. "I like the way you *grip* that handle," I whisper in her ear.

She shivers, then quickly stands up sidestepping and reaching up to rub the ear I just whispered in. I can see it; her entire neck is covered in goose bumps. I'm glad I still have that kind of effect on her.

Rolling her eyes, she drops the bat on the ground in the process and then bends over to pick it up. "While you're down there."

Standing suddenly, she slaps at my chest. "Knock it off."

My hand grips her waist as I lean forward toward her ear from behind. "Want me to adjust your stance?"

"No," she snaps, trying to push me away. "Don't touch me." When I don't move, and instead push my body into hers, she fights me off but it's not serious. She's slapping at my arms playfully. "Stop it, Tyler. You're making me mad."

"What's up your ass tonight?"

"*Not* you."

I grab her ass with my left hand. "Well, now I'm thinking about that."

"Don't." She slaps my hand away. "You're not getting any."

"I bet I could convince you."

"Nope." And then she walks away and the reality is, she's right; she controls whether we're together or not later. And that fucking sucks for me.

Tyler
Chapter 6
COMING BACK FOR MORE

AFTER THE GAME, which we won 13-7, we decide to all go out for pizza, which is both a good thing and bad because one, Berkley follows us there, and two, I sit across from Raven. That part's okay, but the fact that she's not giving me any indication of where we stand now, that's frustrating.

Nothing's said between us until after orders are made and there's a few pitchers of beer on the table.

"So, how do you feel?" Lenny asks Red, rubbing his back as he reaches for two pills in his pocket, more than likely pain medication.

With clay covering his chest where he dove for a line drive, he plays it off but I know Red and he's in pain. "I'm good."

Lenny shakes her head. "Bullshit."

He had his chest cracked open in July and I know bones don't heal that fast that he wouldn't be in a little bit of pain come September.

He eyes me as if to say, go along with it. I do. The last thing I'd do is call him out on it.

"Where's the old man with the pizza?" Rawley asks, growing impatient when our waiter hasn't returned. He probably forgot we were even here.

"Should that guy even still be working?" Lenny watches him as he pours water in glasses, his hands shaking as he does so.

Nova looks up for a split second and then takes her crayons one by one out of the cup. "He's so old his armpits stink."

We all look at Nova and she shrugs, like that made perfect sense to her.

As we're waiting for the old man to get to the table, Berkley walks by. "Good game, guys."

Rawley talks to her, as does Mia and Eldon. I don't say a word to her, neither does Raven, but I don't miss the way she glances over at her.

Berkley leans over and ruffles Nova's hair. "How you liking kindergarten, kiddo?"

Nova scowls at Berkley and turns away from her to face the back of the booth we're in. "Don't talk to me. I hate when you do that. You broke Ty's heart."

I have to admit while I wish she hadn't said anything there's a part of me that's grateful for Nova because after her comment Berkley finally gets the hint and leaves.

Red nudges his daughter in the ribs. "Nova, knock it off and be nice to her."

Nova used to be nice to Berkley, but I made the biggest mistake and confided in a five-year-old one Saturday night when I was drunk. Leaning in, I pull Nova to my side in the booth. She slides across the leather and stares at me.

"What?" The word is seethed out as she glares at her dad, and then darts her gaze at me.

"I told you that in private. You weren't supposed to say anything."

Nova eyes me carefully trying to understand what that means and then pushes a green crayon my direction. "My brain is too big to remember that. Now color the grass green."

I do as she says because I never want to piss a kid off.

ALL THROUGH DINNER, I do my best to flirt with Raven unbeknownst to everyone else around us.

She's standing under a street lamp talking to Lenny and Red, the foggy night creating a spotlight on her. A steady gust of wind shakes her hair loose and it falls in her face, tousled and tangled in the night. The hairs on my arms rise with a bite of wind chilling my bones.

With the hood of my sweatshirt pulled up, I take a step in the direction of her car, a vast white blanket of fog rolling through the parking lot. And then I stop, because I can't go over there right now with Red and Lenny.

Turning on my heel, I make my way to my truck and head home. Alone. Once I'm at home, I regret it.

Why didn't I invite her over? *Stupid.*

Call her.

Picking up my cell phone off the coffee table, I call her just about the time someone knocks on my door.

Imagine my surprise when I open to the door to find her standing outside of it, digging through her purse for my call.

"Miss me?" she asks, holding up her phone.

"I could say the same for you," I mumble with a smile. "You're standing at my door."

"My car drove itself here," she says.

My hope was just because she's gone during the week at college wouldn't mean it's over for her, and now I know for sure it's not with her standing before me. She may have been avoiding me, but it's certainly not *over*.

Thank fuck.

Memories rush to the surface. Her skin, her smile, her scent that used to overwhelm me. Resting my cheek against the door frame, I grin. "Raven Walker... is this a booty call? I'm not *that* easy."

Rolling her eyes, she shifts her stance seeming frustrated. "How about you put your D in my V and stop talking," is her soft reply.

I swing the door open. "Ah, the classics. They never get old."

Stepping inside, she closes the door behind her, locking it and greeting me with a soft smile.

Her voice is gentle, like she's suddenly nervous being here. "Hey."

I pass her and sit down on the couch. "Hey."

Coming forward with hesitant steps, her hands slip over my shoulders, familiar, yet different.

My hands roam where I hope no other man has been this week, knowing I should never give another man the chance. I *should* just tell her I want more and get it over with, but I can't because I can't give her what she's expecting. A relationship.

There's a moment when our eyes meet and the fragile way hers hold mine, she's hoping she sees something different tonight. She's hoping my feelings may have changed since our last conversation.

I blink and drop my gaze to her chest. With a deep breath, I stand, picking her up and carrying her with me to the bedroom.

Taking my time with her, we move to my room where I lay her on the bed, yanking away my clothing and desperately searching for the familiar closeness. Is it wrong to fall into this again? Is it wrong to want any part of her, whatever she will give me?

Yes. And no.

Legs spread, bodies tangle and our clothes are carelessly discarded. My knees spread hers further, a depraved sense of belonging consuming the both of us.

My hands grasp hers above her head, needing, moving and dragging her body against mine.

"Tyler," she moans the word into my mouth.

My body screams in approval when I enter her. My hips move on their own, pounding into her, giving her the roughness she craves from me. I duck my head and capture her nipple in my mouth, sucking it in deep to flick the hard nub with my tongue.

She loves it. Grasping my shoulders, Raven moans again. "Faster, Ty, please!" She's panting now, her arms tightening as we rock into one another.

I can't deny her, though my body has other ideas and I want to slow this down and enjoy the way her body curves to mine.

I know the exact moment when she comes, her pussy milking my dick, her thighs clamping around my waist.

My orgasm is nearly there, heat washing down my thighs. I fight hard not wanting my time to end with her.

"I fucking missed you so much." I grunt against her bare shoulder. My movements speed on their own volition, needing the release.

She tightens her embrace, wrapping her legs around my waist, and I lose all sense of existing in anything besides her. Grinding into her, her cries echo through my room and then I'm the one crying out, desperate and loud.

"Don't stop, please don't stop," she begs, desperate for more.

Moving a little slower, I smile against her cheek. "I won't," I moan, pushing deeper yet again, shaking my head lightly.

What the fuck is wrong with me? Do you ever know what you're saying to her?

Though I know she's searching for meaning in everything I do and say, I can give her this, my body, even when I can't give my heart.

chapter 7
CAN'T LET GO

I ENDED UP spending the weekend with Tyler, which should really be no surprise to me. Monday morning, I'm rushing around his apartment trying to find my clothes when I see him at the kitchen table working on his carburetor he has torn apart.

He watches me pulling my jeans on. His eyes regard me with a steady intensity, my face his focus.

Once I have my jeans on, I make my way over to him. There's a cup of coffee next to the carburetor, almost gone. He gives a nod to the counter. "I made some for you."

"That's nice of you."

His eyelids are low and dark, slow smiles and burning blue. "Thought you could use some. We were *up* pretty late." He gives me a once over and twists in the chair, turning to face me with his hands on my hips as I stand in front of him.

Moving my hands to his broad shoulders, I laugh, feeling bare to the world, and especially him when he looks at me like this, but also incredibly alive.

He forces me to straddle his lap on the chair, which isn't forcing because I'll gladly straddle him. Licking his lips, he gazes up at me

UNBEARABLE the TORQUED trilogy

like he's about to speak. I blink and swallow, afraid of what he might say. Pushing his thumb over my collarbone and over my chest to my heart, my eyes hold his. "Are you leaving right now?"

He leans in so our noses and foreheads are touching before kissing me softly.

"I'll be back on Friday."

"Hmmm," he hums, dropping his mouth against my shoulder. "Tell me something dirty."

"I want you to touch me." We've probably had more sex in the last two days than we have in an entire week, but I can't help it when it comes to Tyler. I want him all the time.

His kisses falter, a smile pressing against heated skin. "Is that what you want me to do to you?"

I nod. "Touch me."

"Where?" His voice is rough, enough that I shiver as it hits the side of my neck.

"Down there." I'm not good at dirty talk. I've never really mastered it and I'm afraid I sound like a child asking for candy when they know they're gonna be denied.

He does touch me though, despite the lack of commitment in my voice. His fingers dip inside my jeans to my center when he sticks one finger inside me. "How'd you get yourself so wet?"

My head falls forward against his shoulder. "From thinking about you."

"Thinking about what?" He's forcing me to be vocal and tell him all the naughty things I want him to do to me. I can sometimes do it in the bedroom, but here, in the morning with the sunlight filtering in, I'm somewhat bare and nervous.

My voice shakes around the words, "Fucking me."

Tyler's head is down, staring at the carburetor on the table when he pushes it aside and lifts me up so I'm sitting on the table.

Leaning back, he reaches for the hem of his dark shirt, yanking it over his shoulders. My stomach jumps knowing where this is going on his *kitchen table*.

Holy hell. YES!

His shirt drops at his feet, steady and sure palms hold my cheeks and he leans in, a kiss so heavy I'm drowning in him and I never want to surface from this. I never want to surface from *him*.

My heart kicks against my chest, my breath growing heavy as heat rushes up my thighs. "You've ruined me, Tyler."

His lopsided grin is there, boyish and adorable but so dirty. He knows what he's done to me. "I hope so." Taking my body in his hands, he scoots me to the very edge so my bottom is so close to his face I'm left shaking with anticipation. I watch the muscles in his stomach and arms, flexing with each movement.

Rough and wild, his hands are on me, memorizing the curves before him. His fingers move lower, sliding across my exposed skin to meet in the middle of the button. His touch burns, igniting my nerve endings and making my heart race. My eyes drift closed. But not for long. I can't be denied his stare for long. Moving my hands up above my head, I grip the edge of the table, craving his touch.

He's not looking at me; he's watching my body.

Standing, his body comes in contact with mine. His jeans are still on—as mine are—when he grinds his hips into mine, his arousal straining against his jeans.

Leaning over me, his mouth finds mine. It's eager but controlled. He gives his heart when he kisses me like this. Everything he says and does shows that.

With one hand against my stomach, he unbuttons my jeans and then draws back, watching me closely but saying nothing. I don't say anything either because words aren't necessary. I don't need to hear how much he wants me. He's showing me.

And he doesn't ask if it's okay, because he knows it is.

He moves both hands from my waist and lower to the backs of my knees hooking his hands around them. Bringing both my legs to rest on his left shoulder, his head moves to the side pressing my calf against his ear.

There's a slight grin on his face, but it's more the intensity in his eyes that makes me nervous. It's like the night at the bar.

His fingers dance over the waistband of my jeans. He gives me a wink and I lift my hips for him. Slowly he pulls them down over my thighs as his knuckles graze my skin. When they're at my ankles, he tosses them near his shirt on the floor.

I'm not sure what he's going to do next, but his mouth is lingering on my calf.

"What time do you have to leave?" he asks.

"I'm already late." I bend my knees, sliding my feet down his bare chest.

He stops, grabbing my ankles and spreading my legs for him.

"You're about to be *really* late," he adds when my legs are spread and my lower half is now completely bare for him.

Tyler's mouth twists, a half grin that fades quickly as his eyes drop, his fingertips moving and squeezing my upper thighs as he groans, a low, throaty sound I want more of. When his right hand falls away, he leans in, supporting his weight with his arm beside my head.

Picking up the wrench, he presses it against my center, the cool metal causing me to jump.

He pauses, his eyes searching mine, waiting to see my reaction. My hands move to his chest and then his hair, wanting to fist that beautiful brown hair between my fingers. He lets me pull at his hair, trying to make him come forward, but then he stops, taking my wrists in his left hand and pins them down on the table.

Again, the wrench in his hand rubs over my center but never inside.

I wouldn't think a wrench could do this. But it's Tyler Hemming we're talking about. He knows his way around a woman's body. Just when I think this can't get any better, his lips are on mine, his elbows holding him up while my wrists are still trapped in his hold.

"You like that?" he asks against my lips, his sweet breath blowing over me.

I can't even respond because while he asks this, he doesn't stop moving the wrench in his hand against my clit.

I'm not sure what it is about Tyler and *this*, but everything is exactly right and the friction of the cool metal grinding against me is exactly what I want. Writhing under his hands, I begin to move my hips on my own will without his direction. When Tyler comes forward, his chest is heaving with heavy breaths giving me another angle. I kiss his rough and tensed cheek, his jaw, and then his lips, anywhere I can access.

"Fuck." A shudder rolls through his body. "That's it... *come* for me, baby," he says, just before plunging his tongue into my mouth.

The warmth starts low and it's sudden, first a slow burn and then stronger, like the pop of a firecracker.

Tyler's eyes are dipped, watching the wrench carefully, rubbing where it wouldn't normally be touching me, moving me against him. When I start to shake against him, my heels dig into his ass, begging him to come closer, harder, anything to make this last longer.

He does, *oh God*, does he.

My head is right by the carburetor and the smell of gasoline ties me to him in every way. It's everything I associate Tyler with, cars and engines.

His breath comes out in short gasps, much like mine, when he sees me falling apart on him. "You're so fucking sexy... fuck." He moans it this time.

"Oh God!" I scream, my eyes squeezing shut as I throw my arms around his shoulders hanging onto him and clawing at his skin.

"That's it, baby." His rough voice is low and tense as he whispers to me. "There you go… fall apart for me." One hand moves from beside me, wrapping around the back of my neck and bringing his eager kiss to mine. He's excited and his kiss shows me, wild tongue and frantic gasps telling me how beautiful the sight before him is.

But then he pulls away, dropping the wrench on the ground.

"Have you done that before?" I'm still trying to catch my breath.

"No, never."

His fingers trace my cheek bone. He gives me a long stare, searching for any regret. When he doesn't see it, a grin appears and he steps back.

"I'm going to be late for work."

I look at him like he's crazy. "We can't just leave you hanging. That's not fair."

"Watching you come apart in my hands was enough." He helps me up from the table and hands me my jeans. "Come back tonight and we'll take care of it."

Oh, I'll be back. For sure.

I know it's a forty-five minute drive but whatever. I smile when he picks the wrench up and places it in his back pocket. "At least you'll be thinking of me today."

He winks. "Not just today. I'll think of you every time I pick up a wrench from now on."

Why am I excited about that?

IT'S CLEAR I'M not making it to my nine o'clock class so I take my time once I leave the shop.

I'm dragging ass and in desperate need of caffeine, mostly because I was up all night with Tyler. I stop off to get coffee before getting on the freeway. Inside the small café, I see Sophie waiting for her order. It's been a while since I've seen her. She and I were friend's way back in middle school but when she and Rawley used to date in high school, we became even closer. I'm not sure why we drifted apart after their breakup.

She spots me immediately. "Hey, Raven. I can't believe how long it's been since I've seen you."

"I know. It's been a while. Probably since the Fourth of July party, right?"

She frowns, probably remembering the night where her and my brother got in a huge fight in the driveway. She also doesn't realize I know all about the fight since I was there watching them.

They call her name for her coffee, and then mine and she nods to a nearby table. "Are you in a hurry? How much time do you have?"

"I've got time. Do you want to sit down and catch up?" I don't have time but something in her eyes tells me she needs someone to talk to.

"Actually yeah, if you don't mind I've been wanting to talk to you."

I have a feeling I know what the answer is going to be, but I ask it anyways. "How are things going?"

Tying her hair back in a ponytail, she lets out a heavy sigh. "Shitty. Completely fucking shitty."

"Rawley being a dick?"

She rolls her eyes. "When is he not?"

"I can't think of anytime actually."

We both laugh and then she shakes her head. "I just don't get him. I try to help. I mean, after your dad died, I reached out to him to tell him how sorry I was about everything. Your dad was an amazing man and was always so kind to everyone. It's hard to believe someone that alive is gone. "

"Thanks for saying that. He was pretty great." Naturally, I thought my dad was the greatest but that was the thing with Lyric, everyone thought he was a good man. "We were all concerned with Mom after we lost him and I think we forgot how hard Rawley took it. He and Dad got in a huge fight the night he died and I think he holds it against himself."

Sophie lets out a sigh, as if she's gone over this a thousand times inside her head. "I can only imagine. I called him and asked him if he wanted to grab some coffee or maybe dinner and talk or something, and he suggested I meet him at the bar one night."

"Makes sense. I swear that place has become a second home to him."

"It has." Sophie nods. "The only way he can stand to be in the same room with me is if he's either high or drunk. That night we met at the bar, we got drunk and ended up in bed together. The next morning Rawley was such an ass. I thought…." She sighs, as though she honestly thought hooking up with him would have changed anything between them. In some ways, I can relate. "I spent the next day in bed. The breakup with us was hard enough that I don't know what I was thinking that night. I guess I thought if I was there for him he'd see I made a mistake and didn't mean to hurt him senior year."

"What did he say?"

Her eyes well up with tears. "Just that it didn't change anything and thanks for letting him get his dick wet. Typical Rawley behavior lately."

I'm actually surprised he said thanks.

"He's not the same guy he used to be. He's drinking and smoking more than ever. Beck's a horrible influence on him and I just… he's going to end up doing something he shouldn't."

Everything she's saying is just a reminder to me that I don't even know Rawley anymore. Sure, we still act normal around one another and he still uses every chance he can to annoy the shit out of me but she's right, he's not the same.

When I was younger, I took it upon myself to watch over him. He's always been a little different, more the brooding type but I was always the one to keep him from going too far.

I'm the normal half of the two. I swear, but he's the fun-loving joking half where if there's fun to be had, I'm going to weigh my risks first. Rawley will just react and think later.

I know when the change happened, but I don't want to tell Sophie because it happened when they broke up. It was slow at first, but then when Dad died, there was no coming back from it. He distanced himself from everyone but music. Gone was the automatic smile every time he walked into a room. You could always count on him to ease the tension when things between Dad and Red would get heated, which believe it or not, happened more than you'd think.

I've been so wrapped up in Tyler lately I haven't stopped to look at Rawley and what I could do to help him. I know if it were me, and I was going through this, he'd help me.

When Holden and I broke up, he came to my college and spent the entire weekend with me making me laugh.

"Why don't you just distance yourself from him?" I know it's probably way harder than I realize. Probably for the same reason I know there's nothing ever going to change Tyler's mind about wanting a relationship, but I still stick around.

"I still love him," Sophie tells me and then takes a sip of her coffee. "I know I made a huge mistake spring break. I don't even know how it happened and I tried explaining it to him. One minute I was fine and the next I'm waking up next to some random guy. The last thing I ever wanted to do was hurt Rawley. Ever. Nothing compares to the way we were when it was good. I just hoped maybe with time he could forgive me, but he just keeps acting like he's going to and then when we start spending time together, he sleeps around, as if it's payback or something."

"You don't deserve to be treated like crap though, Sophie. Yeah, you made a mistake but you were eighteen and in Mexico. A lot of people make mistakes in Mexico. I bet you if the tables were turned and it happened to him, he'd be a lot different."

Her eyes dart around the coffee shop and then back to mine, tears falling now. "I just don't know what to do."

"I think you need to consider letting him go. If you're meant to be, he'll figure his shit out. I know he loves you."

She laughs through her tears. "He has a shitty way of proving it."

I laugh and look down at my phone to check the time. "Yeah, well, he's Rawley. As Nova would say lately, we shouldn't expect so much from him."

My words have me thinking though. If it's meant to be, it'll happen. I guess I could say the same for Tyler and me. Why am I trying to push something he doesn't feel? Probably because I don't want to lose him, so I settle for what I can have. Much like Sophie. If she can't have my brother in the ways she wants, she settles for what she can have. The jerk.

Drawing in a deep breath, Sophie lets it out slowly. "How's college life? I heard you're with Tyler now?" You can't miss the gleam in her eyes. She definitely wants me to be happy but if only she knew. "College is okay. Lonely sometimes, but good. It's nice being able to come home on the weekends."

"And Tyler?" I know she's curious because like I said, Sophie and I were friends in middle school, long before her and Rawley got together or Holden and me. She knew I secretly had a crush on him.

"So take your situation with Rawley, take away the cheating and add a guy who refuses to commit."

Sophie laughs. "What's with the men in this town?"

"I'm not sure." I look at my phone again. "I'm sorry but I have to get going. I have an eleven o'clock class I need to make it to."

Sophie waves her hand around and then stands. "I'm so sorry. I didn't mean to keep you."

"You didn't keep me." Standing, I hug her close. "I'm here for you if you need me."

"Thank you. I appreciate that."

As I'm leaving the coffee shop, my mind races over our conversation and my situation. In many ways—much like Sophie—I felt like Tyler's toy, shelved up high, out of reach of everyone else, and brought down easily when he wanted to play, as sad as that was to admit.

My thoughts are a reminder that I can't change how I feel about him. I'm trying but I'm consumed with one thought, one mindset. Tyler.

He's in my head, wrapped around every thought and decision I'm making.

Why is it that I can't forget him?

Probably because he's Tyler Hemming and the bastard won't let me. Or, it's because I keep going back for more.

As if I needed a reminder of this morning, he sends me a text after my 11:00 a.m. class.

Tyler: My wang is lonely without his muff. I should have taken you up on the offer.

I hate how that one text sends my heart into a rapid beat and my cheeks flush remembering the wrench this morning.

Me: Last class is at 1. Be there tonight. Think you'll be done on time tonight?

Tyler: We're slow today. Makes it worse because suddenly I'm staring at my tools....

I laugh out loud at that one and then put my phone away. Right after my classes are done, I head back to Lebanon, pick up take out and show up at Tyler's apartment to make it up to Wang.

We ignore the food completely.

"Today was torture," he tells me, his palms cradling my face, his mouth crashing against mine as soon as I'm through the door.

A sense of familiarity seeps into my pores.

This is why I keep coming back.

This is why I can't let go.

Maybe that's why Sophie can't either. Familiarity with someone intimately can be everything.

Picking me up, he sets me back on the same table he had me laid on this morning. He unbuckles his belt and then his jeans, pushing them down just enough to free himself, gliding his hand from base to tip twice.

So fucking sexy!

"Did you think of me in class today?" With his question, I begin ripping my shirt over my head and working on my jeans. I'm just a little eager.

I nod. "Yes. I couldn't even pick up my pen today without being reminded of a wrench."

He seems satisfied with my answer and helps me out of my jeans. "Good. At least I wasn't the only one losing focus."

Caught up in him, I watch the movements in his chest, his stomach, the look on his face, always searching.

Holding me captive with his kiss, he enters me. He kisses me deeply, sliding in and out of me as he attempts to keep himself steady holding me against the table with his movements.

He only lasts a minute, maybe two. "You have no fucking idea how sexy you are." He breathes, slumping against me. His hands and arms shake as he tries to control his breathing.

When he does, he gently picks me up and carries me over to his room where he lies down and pulls me against him. "I don't think you're getting any sleep tonight."

And I don't. I definitely don't.

MAYBE IT'S ME trying to fit in, I'm not really sure, but on Thursday, I have the bright idea going to a frat party would be a great way for me to experience college life. I think it's more my obsessively going over the conversation I had with Sophie the other day that has me wondering if I'm hanging onto something that's never going to be. Like Tyler actually having feelings for me outside of sex.

With that thinking, I attempt to socialize and go to a party. I hate frat parties. That much is clear when I'm at one and the guy wearing sunglasses next to me can't stop talking. Why he's wearing sunglasses is both surprising, and not. He's a tool so it makes sense.

Surrounded by a thick cloud of smoke, I ask myself what the fuck I'm doing here. It's mostly because I don't have friends in college. I mean, I know people and talk to them but I don't go out of my way to be friendly. Maybe it's the small town girl in me or maybe it's just me.

I should have known better to think I could come to a party like this surrounded by idiots and not run into the biggest douche of all.

"Thirsty?" Holden asks, staring down at me and the guy in sunglasses.

I hate that he's looking at me as if he knows me. He doesn't know me at all anymore.

I raise the beer in my hand. "Clearly… I'm drinking, aren't I?"

With a chuckle, he shrugs, one hand in his pocket, the other holding a drink. He gives a nod to the kitchen. "Come with me. I'll get you something stronger."

I do, only because he's probably better company.

Holden gives me a rum and Coke. Or so I thought, but apparently more rum than Coke. The drink is the extent of our interactions that night because mostly, I don't want anything to do with Holden and if he thought his plan was to get me drunk and hope for something to happen, it's a shitty plan.

After four drinks and three hours, I sit by myself on the wet grass and stare at my phone in silence. Not complete silence. I'm crying too. I'm not even sure why I'm crying, maybe because I'm alone outside the party and missing Tyler.

And thinking of that conversation the day before I left for college.

"It's not that I can't fall in love, it's that I don't want to. Yeah, another time, another place, maybe things could've been different and believe me, hands down, Raven, it would have been you, but it's just not who I am. What we have right now, this is all I can give. I'm sorry if that's not enough"

I'm such a fucking idiot.

Though I don't want to, the longer I stare at my cell phone and the last text message of him sending me a picture of a wrench, I cave. It might be a mistake, but I make the call anyway.

He answers on the first ring, probably thinking it's me looking for a booty call. "Hello?"

"I deserve better," I tell him immediately.

"What?"

"I deserve better!" I yell. "Damn it. Why won't you love me?" I fully admit to sounding like a whining brat but I blame the liquid in my cup and me wanting an answer.

"Raven?" He sounds confused, his breathing speeding up. "Are you okay?"

"I just *want* to know. Why won't you love me?"

He sighs, heavily. The last thing he *wants* to do is admit to me why he won't love me. It's like he's keeping his heart on lock down. "Are you drunk?"

"Yeah." I laugh. "I wouldn't say *this* sober."

"*Where* are you?" He sounds upset now, his tone demanding like if I don't answer, he might scold me like a child.

Or spank me.

Don't answer him. See if he spanks you later.

I do answer him though, because I want some answers. Drunk me is persistent and demanding. "What do you care?"

He sighs heavily. "Raven…. You know I care."

"No." I shake my head adamantly, though he can't see it. "No, I don't. You told me you *didn't* love me."

"I never said I didn't care," he says immediately.

"Whatever." I throw my hand up in the air. "It doesn't matter. Just answer my question. Why won't you love me?"

"I won't until you tell me where you are. I mean it, Raven. Where the fuck are you?"

"I don't know." I flip my hand around and lay back in the wet grass that's seeping through my jeans. "I came to a frat party and Holden was there and I got drunk… and I don't know now. I wandered."

"What frat house?"

"I'm not in a house. I'm on the grass. It's wet."

"Talk to me." I hear doors slamming around and what sounds like his truck starting. "I'm coming to get you."

I shake my head back and forth, the smell of dirt all around me. "If you don't love me, why are you coming to get me?"

"No matter what, I'm your friend and I care about you. I want you to be safe. Tell me where you are? What fraternity?"

"I don't even know. It's a brown house though. Does that help?"

"Don't move, don't talk to anyone and don't drink anything."

"Why would you come get me, Tyler?" I don't wait for him to answer before I say, "I don't need to be rescued."

And then I hang up on him and rest my phone on my stomach, staring up at the spinning sky and ignore the ringing when he immediately calls back.

Why do I keep falling for the wrong guy? Maybe it's not even that I'm falling for the wrong guy. Maybe I'm the wrong girl. I clearly wasn't meant for Holden and now Tyler, he's adamant I'm not the right girl for him to love.

IT'S NOT HARD to know when Tyler arrives. I hear his truck roaring from a mile away and then squealing to a stop in the street. I'm actually impressed he found me.

He slams the door to his truck and stalks toward me. "Where's Holden?"

I shrug and roll over onto my stomach and tuck my arms under my head. "I don't know." Bringing my knees up, I try to stand but it's a moot effort and he has to help me up. "Let's go."

Either from standing up so quickly, or the fact that I've drank my body weight in alcohol, I puke. On Tyler.

He groans, tossing his head back and helping me to the car. "I'm gonna fucking kill Holden."

Stripping off his shirt, he tosses it in the bed and then opens the door, nodding for me to get in. But I'm covered in puke so I strip. Right then and there, pants and shirt gone completely.

Seems fine to me but there's people rolling by on the street, whistling at me.

"Jesus, get in the truck." Tyler's eyes are frantic, and knowing he drove an hour for me, makes me feel way too good, despite the fact I just threw up on him.

When I'm standing there, staring at him, he waits several seconds, like he's waiting for me to tell him what happened, but I don't. I wait to see what he's going to do with me now standing before him in my bra and underwear and not doing what he told me to do, which was to get in the truck.

His jaw flexes, the muscles in his face twitching. But his touch, it's tender as his thumb brushes lightly over my cheek. "Raven, you're in your bra and underwear. Get in the truck."

My stomach burns, the acid in my throat causing my words to come out rough. "Okay."

I THINK I PASS out after that. I'm not positive, but I wake up on my bed in my dorm room with Tyler between my legs. I can't tell if he's taking clothes off, or putting them on.

"What are you doing?" I ask, trying to pry one eye open. It's hard, an effort I don't have. I really do want to sleep but I also want him to love me.

"You're naked. I'm trying to get your panties on." He taps my knee. "Help me out. Lift up."

UNBEARABLE the TORQUED trilogy

I do and smile when he struggles. My head falls back against the bed, my legs dangling over the edge. I have no idea how my panties came off in the first place, but it's then I notice I'm not wearing a bra either, just an old tank top of mine.

Tyler laughs when it's not working getting my panties up my wet thighs. "I'm usually taking panties off, *not* putting them back on." His brow scrunches; he's trying to figure out how to get them on since they're sticking to my thighs. "This is surprisingly difficult."

"Why are my legs all wet?"

"I had to clean you off. There was puke all over us."

I bring my elbows underneath me and sit up slightly. "How did you clean me off?"

Tyler stands from his crouched position and scratches the side of his head, as if he's trying to come up with a plan to get me dressed and in bed. His expression darkens with an unreadable emotion. "I took you to the car wash. You puked in my truck and I had to clean it off. So I hosed you down too."

I want to laugh because I wish I would have been coherent enough to remember that. With a lot of effort, I stand up and help him out by pulling my panties on. "What are you doing here though? I thought you'd drop me off and leave. Remember? You don't want me."

I'm an obnoxious drunk tonight. So much so that I want to punch myself.

His brows draw together in a frown. "I'm not leaving you alone so Holden can come back and have his way with your naked body."

Is that possessiveness I hear?

"Better *you* than him?"

I'm teasing, I think, but he doesn't see it that way. His lips purse when I sway on my feet. "Not quite."

His arm wraps around my waist, the other under my thighs as he picks me up.

"Are you sure?" I ask as he sets me gently on the bed.

Tyler's arm slips around my shoulder as he lies down next to me, his dreamy blues landing on mine. He studies me for a moment but I don't give him much time before I straddle his lap. I want him, right now.

Instantly his body stiffens and his hold on me falls away. "Raven… don't do that."

"Why?"

"Because you're drunk and if I do this now with you, I'm not any different than these fucking frat boys. I came here to help you get to bed, not fuck you." His lips brush the top of my head. "Please just sleep."

I'm so grateful he's here with me that I say what I'm thinking. "I love you, Tyler."

It slips out and I know what I've done, but I play it off like a drunk girl would because I am and I can get away with it.

He chuckles but says nothing.

Closing my eyes, I let my hand wander lower, attempting to seduce him. "Make love to me. I want to know what it's like to have a man love me."

He catches my hand when it reaches the waistband of his jeans and puts it back on his chest. "Why do you want me to make love to you? It's not like we haven't had sex before, Raven."

"No, not *sex*. Make *love* to me."

I think I know what he's going to say next. Something along the lines of he can't love me, he's too broken, blah *fucking* blah. I don't want to hear that. I want love, damn it.

His lips brush my temple. "What was that the morning you left?"

"I'm not sure what that was. I think it was the day you broke my heart."

He draws back and the look on his face makes me want to sigh. "It wasn't my intention."

"I know."

Despite the regret I think he feels for saying no, he offers a smile. "Go to sleep."

I can't sleep. Not with him here and a little bit of courage. I want to know why I'm not good enough for him to love. Berkley was. Why can't I be? "Why can't you love me back? I'm not good enough, that's it, isn't it? What's wrong with me? Was Berkley better than me?"

He ducks his chin to look down at me, his brow raising. "There's nothing wrong with you. You don't know what you're talking about, Raven. You're drunk."

I'm refusing to let this go and sit up and twist to face him. "Yes I do. You don't love me. Holden didn't love me enough. What the hell is wrong with me?"

"It's not you. You're perfect." He sits up too. "There's absolutely *nothing* wrong with you and I told you, if I was going to fall in love with anyone, it would be you."

I take a moment to think about what he says, or I try at least but I turn and realize I'm wearing a tank top and one of my boobs falls out.

"Oh, look. One of the Double Mint twins is looking for a solo career."

He glances down and his eyes crinkle at the corners but I can tell he's desperately trying to not look. "Raven, fix your shirt." Slowly, his hand eases along the dip in my side, squeezing my hip. "Please."

I fix my boobs but then I sigh into his chest when his hands don't leave my side. "You're touching me and it's making me want you, so stop touching me unless you're going to make love to me."

His hand relaxes, as does my breathing when he presses his lips to my forehead and then sits up. "Sleep."

"I can't." A sigh escapes me. "Hold me until I fall asleep."

Tyler doesn't say anything but he lies back on my bed and lets me rest my head on his chest.

I lift mine again. "Are you sure? I mean, I can't believe you don't want any sex."

His lips curl up into a barely-there smile, though his expression doesn't change. "It's not without effort." Staring at the ceiling, he asks, "Why did you go to a frat party anyway?"

"I'm trying to fit in."

He nods. "And that worked out, didn't it?"

I think I should be offended by it, but I'm not. "I don't fit in anywhere."

"That's not true. You fit in with me."

"But you *won't* love me, *or* make love to me right now."

"Okay, stop it." Tyler lets out a heavy sigh and turns to face me. "You're drunk and feeling bad about yourself but you're better than this. Knock it off." He's right. I'm being insecure and it's probably pretty annoying. "It's like two in the morning. Go to sleep."

I didn't think I could, but the moment I close my eyes and listen to his soft breathing, it's a lot easier than I thought it would be.

Tyler

Chapter 8
WHAT SHE WANTS

IT'S AROUND FOUR in the morning when I'm driving back from her dorm and I know I'm not getting any sleep tonight. All I can think about is her and her telling me that she loves me. The more I think about it the more I believe it because I know despite her being drunk, she knew what she was saying, and Raven rarely says anything she doesn't mean.

What do I do now?

I'm completely aware that the right thing to do is to pull back knowing her feelings are getting too deep, but I'm a selfish bastard at heart and the thought of letting her go isn't something I'm willing to entertain. As it is, I'm having a hard time wrapping my head around everything this woman makes me feel. I know why, deep down, this is a struggle for me, but I'm not ready to put my feelings out there just yet.

Sitting at my kitchen table, my thoughts on the night are still buzzing loudly in my brain.

I finally decide to shower and head downstairs to get a head start on the day. Maybe keeping my hands busy will help drown out the battle going on in my head.

Grabbing my keys and phone from the table on the way out, I notice that Raven must have texted me while I was in the shower.

Raven: Sorry about last night. Thanks for saving me.

Staring at her message, I realize I can't text her back. Don't get me wrong, it's not because I don't want to, but because I'm afraid if I do, I'll say something I'm going to regret and lead her on even more.

I'M NOT SURE what my problem is but weeks have gone by and I still haven't talked to Raven. We're approaching Thanksgiving and maybe it's because I didn't reply to her message or she feels guilty about that night but she doesn't text me either and she hasn't come home on the weekends.

I know she's coming for Thanksgiving and the fact that I'm going to see her soon has me sort of amped and on edge at work.

I'm counting down the hours in the day so I can get the hell out of here when Berkley shows up at the shop wearing skin-tight jeans and black leather boots up to her knees.

Typical of her. Always trying to gain attention.

"What are you doing here?" I don't look at her when she leans against my toolbox. I have a car I'm working on and the last thing I need is to get distracted. Besides, I know *why* she's here wearing that outfit. She's looking to hook up. "If you're looking for Rawley, check the parts room."

"Can't I come by and check on *you*?"

I shrug, quirking an eyebrow at her to see that Red's watching us. "Well, you *could* but you made it clear you've moved on. Why keep stopping by?"

"Tyler." There's a long sigh that escapes her, one I've come to know is her being frustrated with me. It's like the wind, you know it's coming, you hear the howling, you're just waiting for the gust to hit your face. "You don't have to be an asshole."

I laugh. "I can be anything I want to be."

Despite my laugh, it's like a knife to my chest that she can pretend like we're friends.

I swallow, the action forced because I just want to scream at her for all the pain she's caused me. She's one of the reasons why I can't give Raven everything she needs. "I think it's best for both of us if you walk away before I say something I'm going to regret."

She doesn't listen, nothing new, and steps forward to stand near the car I'm bent over replacing a fuel filter on. "I know the break up was hard on both of us but you have to understand where I was coming from."

With both hands on the fender, I shake my head slowly. "Go, Berkley. Just get the fuck out of here." My voice is sharp and she knows I'm not fucking around. She needs to leave.

When she does, her heals clicking against the concrete floor, a memory flashes in my head, the night I found out who she really was. It's also the night I hooked up with Raven but it started with the news where my reality crashed down on me by my mother of all people.

"Why did you break up?"

"She decided she wanted something else, I guess. I'm not sure. She lost the baby and then I came home to her moving out."

"Berkley was pregnant?"

"Yeah, like a few weeks or something."

My mother frowns. "Is there any chance that Berkley may have been lying to you about being pregnant?"

"What? No, why would you ask that?"

"Because there's something you should know." She shifts her gaze to the kitchen floor which tells me whatever she's going to tell me is important. "When you were ten and the doctors were finally able to stabilize your epilepsy with the Tegretol, we were so grateful; we really didn't think about anything but you being able to live a normal life. As you got older and it became obvious that you were going to need to continue taking the medication long-term, the doctors informed us that prolonged exposure to Tegretol had been shown to cause some patients to become sterile. They said it wasn't a definite but that when you were older, you should get tested."

She raises her gaze to meet mine and there is a mixture of pain and fear in her eyes. "You may want to go and get tested because there is a good chance that if Berkley was pregnant, the baby was never yours."

"What? Are you fucking kidding me? Don't you think that's something you should have told me before now?" Pissed off, I don't even think before I grab a glass on the counter and throw it against the wall in the kitchen. Mom jumps at the sound but now she's staring at me like she doesn't even know who I am, which seems hilarious since I feel like I don't know who she is either. "How the hell could you have kept this from me? I get that I didn't need to know at ten but how come you didn't tell me when I was older or better yet at some point during my six-year relationship with Berkley. I'm twenty-six now. Fuck. This changes everything about me and relationships I have with women."

Mom rolls her eyes, not seeing the significance behind my words. "It doesn't have to change anything, Tyler. I get that you're upset but please calm down."

I laugh. Calm? Is she serious?

My dad walks in, having heard the glass breaking and stares at me, his stone-cold blue eyes narrowing. "What's going on?"

"Did you know about this?"

Mom gives him a look. "I told Tyler...."

So he knew. He fucking knew too. My own father, a man himself wouldn't think to tell me something like this?

"You fucking knew and didn't think to tell me?" I wave my hand around in front of them. "I'm your only son and no time in the last sixteen years did you think it would be a good idea to tell me that I've been taking seizure medication that probably made me sterile? You didn't think it would be a good idea to tell me I could never have children?"

Mom chokes back emotions and stands, reaching out to me but I back up near the door holding my hands up. She's the last person I want comfort from. "Tyler, honey, you don't know what it's like to watch your child suffer day after day. To be so afraid for their safety that you insist they are never alone in a room because what if he has a seizure and falls and hits his head or chokes."

I can imagine how scary it must have been for her, I can, but it changes nothing. My mom's voice filters my thoughts, distancing me from the past and back to the present. "The fear is so consuming that you begin to feel hopeless because what if the doctors never find a cure, or what if we aren't doing enough to help you? God, Tyler, you have to understand that when we finally found a medication that worked. It felt like we'd been given a miracle. At the time, we didn't care about anything but making sure you had as normal a life as possible. We weren't focused on ten years from now. We were focused on ten days from now. As time went on and you stabilized to the point you could live like a normal child again, we rejoiced in the victory and put the risks in the back of our mind. The last thing we wanted to do was take your future away from you but I'll never regret putting you on it. It saved you."

Normal. Fucking normal. Words I desperately wanted to be but now knew I never would. It's not even all about the medicine; it's about them not telling me and basically finding out Berkley cheated on me and had no intention of even telling me.

"Damn it, Mom. It's not about the fucking medicine!" I shout, only to have my dad glare, his silent way of letting me know I've crossed the line yelling at my mother, but they crossed the line and that's all I see. "It's about you keeping this from me for sixteen goddamn years. I can't have a family! Do you have any idea what that feels like?"

"Tyler."

My throat threatens to close, my pulse soaring. "No. You don't get to say anything else." I storm toward the front door but turn one more time to see both my parents standing in the living room looking at me with apprehension.

"I can't be here right now. Honestly, I don't know if I'll ever be able to be here again."

I'd walked out of my parents' house after those words, slammed the door and headed to Murphy's where I'd began my quest to give myself liver damage and sleep with Raven. Honestly, deciding to take Raven home with me that night was a decision I will never regret. Those six months with her before feelings started fucking everything up, made pushing the shit my parents had dumped on me that day into the back of my mind possible.

AFTER WORK, I head straight to Murphy's bar. I know I'm going to potentially run into Berkley, which would not be a good thing considering I would like to punch her for being a lying, cheating bitch but she's a waitress here sometimes, and I need a fucking drink in a bad way.

I find a stool at the bar and drop into it exhausted. I'm the kind of exhausted where I wish I could go home and sleep but know there's no way it's going to happen with all that's going on in my head right now.

Zack approaches me bracing himself with his hands on the bar. "You look like you need either a good drink or a blow job."

I stare at him as if he's crazy. "Women complicate shit that doesn't need complicating."

"Okay, drink it is." He laughs. "What can I get you?"

"Whiskey."

He takes a minute to look at me and reaches for the whiskey and a glass but doesn't pour it. "You really do look like shit, man."

I drag my hands over my face. "You have no idea."

"Girl problems?"

I'm not in the mood for talking. With anyone. "Can you just get me the whiskey?"

Zack nods. He knows I'm not going to talk about it. I set my phone down on the bar and immediately my mind moves to Raven and the fact that I want to call her, even if it's just to hear her voice. A message pops up from Lenny.

Lenny: Hey, you were looking kind of rough today. Just checking on you. You doing ok?

If she only knew.

Me: I'm fine.

The truth is, I'm so far past fine I don't even know how to find fine again. All this shit with Raven and Berkley and my parents are weighing on me. For the first six months with Raven, I didn't think much about what happened with my parents and the whole Berkley thing. I focused on having fun and enjoying being with someone in the simplest of terms. But now she wants more and the fact that I can't give her more pisses me off and throws everything back up in my face.

I've grown up knowing there's certain things in my life and my body I would never have control over. I'll be taking seizure medication for the rest of my life. Even without forgetting my meds, I still have them on occasion.

My point is, for years I've struggled with not wanting anyone to know. Mostly because I'm out of control when they happen, vulnerable to everything and everyone around me. For the longest time I had a hard time just thinking I was normal, because truthfully I wasn't. I had to rely on pills for my brain to function properly and not drop to the ground in front of anyone.

And then after my breakup with Berkley, my mom tells me the medication I thought made me as close to normal as I could be took away any chance I had at having a family.

Just as I'm going over this in my head, fucking Berkley shows up.

I reach for the glass Zack must have put in front of me while I was having my pity party and down the amber liquid. I can't remember how many I've had but the burn of the whiskey making its way down my throat is a relief.

An hour later, I'm still sitting at the bar when Zack asks, "Another one?"

I stare at the glass long enough to know I don't need another, because I can't tell whether the glass is full or empty.

"Nah, I'm done." I throw down enough cash to cover my drinks and get up to leave. Just then, Berkley comes to stand in front of me, way too close for my comfort.

"What's with you and Raven?" Berkley asks suddenly, her hand over mine like she's ready to be there for me should I want to open my heart to her. That's long gone. It left when I found out she cheated on me.

"It's none of your business."

"Can't you just talk to me and look at me? I just want to talk. We were together for six years it's the least you could do."

The least I could do? What a fucking bitch.

"So I'll ask again... you and Raven? I mean, I'm happy for you."

"What the fuck are you talking about?"

"I heard you and her were dating. I mean, she's a little young for you but whatever."

"I don't see how that's any of your business."

"I'm just trying to have a conversation with you, Ty." She lifts her hand and rests it on mine on the bar. "I just want us to be friends."

I rip my hand away from hers. "Friends? We were never fucking *friends*. Maybe that's part of our problem. We went from fucking to living together and never became friends."

"You can't say that," she snaps, scowling at me, her words so sharp she probably wishes they could cut me. "You were happy when we were together."

"Maybe so but friends don't go behind friend's backs and fuck around after six years."

She's shocked by my words because all this time she thinks her reasoning for our breakup was justified. She miscarried and needed to find herself. It wasn't the truth.

Standing, I brush my body along hers. "Fuck your friendship. You wanna be friends, go suck Rawley's dick. I'm sure he's up for it."

My gaze hardens, letting her know I'm serious and then I walk away, toward the door to where Rawley's grinning, two chicks on his arms.

"What the fuck are you smiling at?"

He holds up his hands after slipping his cell phone in his pocket. "Nothin', man."

Nothing my ass.

I think about texting Raven when I leave because in the reality of all this, she's the only one who hasn't fucked me over. She's honest and pure and loves me simply because she does. There's nothing wrong with that either and in a way, it helps that she does.

I want that night with Raven for the first time back, that overwhelming sensation of her underneath me. I want that feeling I had of being completely at ease with her. Undoubtedly, I'm regretting not talking to her these last few weeks.

Fuck. I need her.

chapter 9
THIS IS ALL NOW

MY LIFE SUCKS.

No, really, I know that's dramatic but those are my thoughts after the incident with Tyler. I mean, fuck, he drove an hour to get me at two in the morning, I puked on him and then told him I loved him and begged him to make love to me.

I can't make this shit up.

And then I texted him the next day and haven't heard anything from him. So naturally, I'm a nervous wreck the week before Thanksgiving and fuck up my marketing management final.

I'm walking back to my dorm room after class, a coffee in one hand and my phone in the other. Last year when I had a bad day, I texted Tyler and he'd come to my dorm or I'd sneak into his apartment late at night and everything would be better the next day.

Now that's changed.

Staring at my phone, I want to text him when a message pops up from Rawley with a picture. Sliding my thumb over the screen, I open the message to see it's one of Tyler at the bar and he's sitting on a stool at the bar with Berkley, her hand over his. It's like a fucking punch to my throat.

Rawley: Thought you should know....

He thought I should know?

I don't reply at first because I'm honestly too shocked to even consider replying. At both Rawley and Tyler.

Me: Dude, why would you even send that to me? Are you trying to break my heart?

Rawley: No. Tyler does that on his own. Wanted you to know he's still seeing her.

Me: You don't know off one interaction that they're seeing each other.

Rawley: True. I don't. But I'd bet money he is.

Me: Shut up. Don't ruin my night.

He doesn't reply after that. I even text Lenny and ask her what's going on.

Me: Lenny... is Tyler seeing Berkley?

It takes her an hour and I'm halfway through my marketing term paper but she replies.

Lenny: No. He can't stand her.

I send the picture to her. Me: What does this look like then?

Lenny: Looks to me he's leaving and whoever took the picture caught it out of context.

I guess I know *why* he didn't reply to my message three weeks ago. Maybe he's moved on and there's nothing I can do about it. Maybe the reason he can't love me is because he's still in love with her? Unlikely. Tyler holds grudges. I know that much. When he was fifteen, the neighbor kid hit him in the face with a baseball. Knocked out two teeth.

To this day, Tyler won't even acknowledge poor Johnny when he walks into Walker Automotive to get his oil changed. Maybe because it wasn't an accident and Johnny meant to hit him, but still, years later, he apologized and Tyler wouldn't accept it.

The likelihood of him forgiving Berkley is low, but there's a girly part of me, the same part that got drunk and begged him to love me, thinks maybe he might because they have history together.

"WHAT DO YOU mean Tyler's coming over for dinner?" I ask Lenny in horror as we stand in my mother's kitchen peeling potatoes on Thanksgiving.

Lenny takes the potato peeler in her hand and points it at my face. "Don't blame me. Mia invited him. And besides that, Tyler's actually my family."

She's right. Tyler is the closest thing Lenny has to family. It's easy to forget Lenny's background because looking at her now, she's completely comfortable in the life she and Red have. You'd never know what she's been through in the last year from her abusive ex-husband to him coming after her and shooting Red in the chest. It's amazing to me how well they've both adjusted to everything.

"I know that, but still…." I start sweating and my heart pounds in my chest, pretty much an indication that once I see him this will be a lot worse and it might possibly lead to me having a heart attack. I don't know why but I assumed I wouldn't see him this weekend and could silently avoid him. I mean, he hasn't messaged me in weeks so it was possible but now highly unlikely unless I left. Which I wouldn't do because Thanksgiving is my favorite holiday.

"What do I do?"

Lenny shrugs. "Maybe play hard to get?"

I sigh, my shoulders slumping forward. "I can't. I'm incredibly *easy* to get."

Trying not to think about him coming over, I turn my attention to cooking. By the way, I'm not good at it. In fact, I usually don't cook at all but it certainly never stops my mom from trying to make me her little Betty Crocker.

I'm good at math and organization. Organization and my mother have never been friends. I'm too methodical for my mother's style of cooking because she doesn't use measuring cups. I can't handle not being precise.

As I measure out the right amount of salt for the mashed potatoes, mom frowns in disappointment. "What are you doing, Raven? I just use a pinch."

A pinch?

I look at Lenny. "A pinch is a teaspoon, right?"

She shrugs, hiding a grin and mixing the gravy on the stove, entertained by my weirdness. Most people are.

Just as I hear the front door open and voices in the family room indicating the arrival of someone I probably don't want to see, mom pushes me toward the dining room. "Okay, let me handle the potatoes. How about you show Nova how to set the table?"

She's not asking me, she's telling me.

Nova's staring at the china cabinet when I walk into the dining room, her hands on her hip. "Why are they kept in a cabinet?"

Reaching on the top of the cabinet, I bring down the key and unlock it. "They're fancy dishes that Grandma wants to keep pretty so she puts them in a cabinet."

Nova shrugs and reaches for one as soon as I open the cabinet. I help her so she doesn't break them and within a minute we have the table set. Tears sting my eyes when I set the plate down where my dad would have been sitting. It's the first Thanksgiving without him and it hurts. Bad. I can't imagine what mom is going through today but the sensation stinging my chest is awful as I stare at the head of the table.

"What's wrong?" Nova asks, curiously watching me. "Do you miss Papa?"

Looking down at Nova I see an understanding no five-year-old should have. I brush the falling tears aside and hand her the forks. "I'm okay. Here, put a fork next to each plate but make sure it's straight."

She doesn't. I mean, she puts the forks by the plates next to the knives I place on the neatly folded napkins, but they're at odd angles and it's just not acceptable.

Each time I adjust one, I find them slightly twisted in another direction when I come back around the table. I know who's doing it and lift the table cloth up to find Rawley underneath of the table.

"You're a dick. Get up."

He falls back on the floor laughing. "Took you long enough. Nova had all those knives straight the first time."

Nova crawls on her knees and high-fives Rawley under the table. "Told you she'd fall for it."

I have a distinct impression I was set up from the beginning. "Jerk."

He grabs my ankle when I try to get away from them and I end up falling face first on the floor. Kicking at his head but missing, the two of us wrestle until he tickles my side and has Nova sit on my head. "Don't let her up, Nova."

"Tap out!" I scream, trying to move a forty-pound kid off my head.

"What does tap out mean?" Standing up, she stares down at Rawley and me.

"It means stop."

"Tap that means—"

I slam my fist into Rawley's side. "Don't you dare tell her that."

He laughs, or attempts to. I knocked the wind out of him with my punch.

Footsteps draw my attention over my shoulder as I frown at my twin brother. "You're such a child."

After shoving me into the table, Rawley walks away. "You started it."

Turning my head, I wish I wouldn't have. I'm not sure what to expect seeing Tyler today but he's here, his back to me as he stands in the kitchen next to my mom.

Heat pricks my chest seeing him and being in the same room. "Thanks for inviting me," he says to my mom, wrapping his arm around her shoulder.

"You're always welcome, Ty. You know that." Setting down the spoon in her hand, she gives him a hug. "How're your parents doing today?"

Tyler's body tenses, his posture tight. "I'm sure they're doing good."

I'm sure they're good? What does I'm sure mean?

He doesn't notice me yet. He's wearing loose fitting dark jeans with a navy blue sweater I know will bring out his eyes and my panties will come off.

Just don't look him in the eyes.

Easier said than done. His eyes are so beautiful I automatically search them out. It's like a habit I can't stop. A nervous twitch or something.

"Is Raven here?" he asks, his hands in the pockets of his jeans now.

Is that excitement I hear in his voice?

Crap. Double crap. He's looking for me. I'm trying to hide behind a dining room chair that probably couldn't even hide Nova, let alone me.

He's not talking to me but his voice invades me, makes me want the roughness against my skin and my name on his lips.

"Yeah, she's in the dining room," Mom says, ratting me out.

When I think I might be able to sneak away without him noticing me, he fucking turns and looks right at me like he knows I was standing here all along.

"Hey," he says, so simple, like it shouldn't mean anything but it does. It means everything to me because they're the simplest of words spoken under the most awkward of situations.

"Why are you here?" I ask curiously, watching him as he walks toward me with a slow gait, his hands remaining in his pockets.

Why do you look so fucking good all the time?

I want to reach up and grab a fistful of his hair as it falls in his face. And then drop to my knees and give Wang a kiss.

Pathetic.

"Is it a problem I'm here?" His brow raises and I'm not sure what to say. He glances at me, and then back down.

Nope. Not a problem.

Liar.

Screw that. Yes! It's a fucking problem!

"It's a free country but aren't you usually at your parents' for Thanksgiving?"

He shrugs, his gaze darting from mine when Nova spots him. His jaw is tight and he doesn't look relaxed any longer. "Things change."

"Uncle Ty!"

Tyler then drops to his knees at Nova's level, the two of them wrestling on the floor of the dining room.

Stepping over them, I walk into the kitchen where Lenny's making whip cream and Red's licking some from her finger, sucking it slowly in his mouth and grabbing her ass at the same time.

"You two are disgusting," I grumble, bumping Lenny's shoulder. When Red smiles and walks away, I give Lenny a serious stare. "What's with Tyler? Why isn't he at his parents'?"

She shrugs and leans into the counter. "I'm not sure. He won't say but for the last three weeks he's been all sorts of weird."

"I told him I loved him when I was drunk," I admit, my gaze dropping to the floor in what I can only describe as a moment of pure let down. I can't believe I put myself out there like that.

Actually, yes. Yes I can. Alcohol makes me an idiot and emotionally unstable.

"Holy shit, really? You told him you loved him? Do you?"

"Yes, really. I did. And I think I do, but I was drunk and he drove to my school and picked my drunk ass up and took me back to my dorm. And I puked on him."

It takes Lenny a moment to process what I'm telling her and then she shakes her head. "I don't think that has anything to do with what's going on with him. He's been acting really weird at work lately. It's something else."

I hope it is but sadly, I don't think she's right. I mean, he's clearly afraid of commitment and I basically told him that's what I wanted. I don't blame him for freaking out.

Within an hour after Tyler arrives, we're all seated at the dinner table, an awkwardness settling over us when Red gives an expansive sigh, his gaze on his child not eating and building a mashed potato volcano. "Nova, stop playing with your food and eat it."

"I don't like food. And I ate dinner last night. Why do I have to eat today?"

Lenny leans over and brushes Nova's curls out of her face. "Because Grandma spent a lot of time on the meal. You want to make her happy, right?"

Nova's eyes dart to Mom who gives her a silly look, one eyebrow quirked and then she sticks her bottom lip out. "Won't you eat, honey?"

"Fine." Nova gives Red a scowl. "But only because Grammy asked."

I don't know why but Nova's been giving Red a hard time lately, mostly in the last month since school started but she's also one of those kids who hates change and disruption in her routine. Kindergarten fucked that all up.

Clearing my throat, I reach for my glass of spiked egg nog and end up dumping it on my plate. Classic move on my part.

Glancing up, I wonder if anyone notices.

Tyler cuts his eyes to mine and smiles, then glances at Red.

I don't get up. I leave the egg nog on my plate and act like it didn't happen because the last thing I want is the attention moving to me.

Jude, my cousin, let's out a laugh at something Rawley says and quickly everyone is paying attention to the two hoodlums at the end of the table making jokes.

Watchful of Tyler's every action across the table from me, I thought, hoped, my feelings would have changed in the last three weeks. But they haven't, and in that moment I realize they probably never will. Drunk or not, they remain.

He's watching me but I can't look at him directly. I won't. If I do, I'll smile and everyone will see right through me. Sure, they know, but it's not that I want everyone here to see what Tyler does to me.

It's then, when no one is looking, he attempts to make me squirm. Something Tyler can do with a wink.

Which he does by slowly sinking his teeth into his bottom lip, but then he takes it a step further, slouching to one side and picking up his knife to cut his turkey. Only he lets it slide slowly out of his hand much like he did with the wrench in his kitchen. I'm immediately reminded of being laid out on his kitchen table while he uses a wrench to get me off.

That son of a bitch and his talented hands!

My cheeks flush to the point where the heat is making me sweat and there's a sudden urge to squeeze my thighs together.

"Raven, are you feeling okay?" Mom asks, and then laughs when she notices Tyler sit up straighter in his chair and clear his throat.

"I'm fine." I shoot Tyler a glare only to have him watch with me that same intensity he did when I fell apart in his hands. "I think the whiskey's getting to me."

AFTER DINNER, I help Mom and Lenny clean up along with my aunts but I spill cranberry sauce all over myself with my shaky hands.

"Fuck," I curse, staring at Mom and then my white sweater. Not sure why I chose to wear a white sweater today but it's obviously a stupid idea. "Do you have stain remover?"

"Yeah," she shakes her head at me smiling at Lenny. They both know why I'm so jittery. But my mom also knows if there's a stain on my shirt, I have to change it. "It's in the laundry room above the washing machine in the cabinet."

With the heaviest of sighs, I walk down the hall passing by the family room where the guys are gathered watching the football game.

Searching through the cupboard, I find the stain remover and spray it directly on my sweater, never bothering to take it off.

His presence is known before my breath can catch up with the rapid beating of my heart. It makes me gasp, the way his body makes mine react instantaneously. "Did you miss me?"

His voice sends a jump through me, physically and mentally. He's right behind me as I close my eyes and inhale, not wanting him to see the reaction he has on my heart.

"I did," I breathe out, his body pressing into mine as his hands rest on the washing machine trapping me in his embrace.

He steps around me so he's standing beside me, his arm brushing mine, fingers dancing over mine. "And that means?"

He's acting like this should be casual and I'll tell you right now, Tyler and I have *never* ever been casual. We're undefined and undecided.

When I don't say anything, he leans in and whispers in my ear repeating his question, "What does it mean?"

His words are no longer a question, they're a statement, maybe even an observation he's found a weakness, because I can't tell him what it means. "I'm not sleeping with you."

He blows out a long breath and tips his head back, looking up at the ceiling. "I might not ask."

Might. It's a big might and potentially a lie. I think.

The wetness of the stain remover soaks through my shirt. "I have to change my shirt." Stepping around him, I separate myself from his heat and retrieve a shirt from my room.

Taking the shirt to the bathroom, I change and I'm stepping out of the bathroom when Tyler's leans outside of it, waiting.

"What are you doing?" I ask when he turns and blocks me from coming out.

"Honestly, I don't know." He takes a step and I back up into the bathroom where he closes the door behind him.

Shit. I'm trapped.

"Tyler…." I sigh. I know where this is heading.

Our gaze catches. "What?"

I reach out to him. I just can't help myself, my hands on his jaw and the roughness of the sharp line.

"I miss you."

I don't say anything.

"Things have really gone to shit lately," he mumbles, dejected and steps forward, a position much like moments ago in the laundry room as he cages me in.

"I wouldn't know," I tell him. "You haven't texted me or called in three weeks. I thought you wouldn't want to talk to me anymore."

He won't look at me; instead, his gaze is on our touching bodies as he traps me against the counter. His body shifts into mine, contact I can't ignore, a sensation of jitters buzzing through me. "I'm sorry I made you feel that way."

I want to cry, I do, but I'm not going to. Instead, I'm left wondering where he's going with this and why after three weeks, he's telling me this. My brain can't wrap around the fact that he does miss me. He probably misses my vagina. That's all. It has nothing to do with me.

This time he touches my chin and lifts my eyes to his. "Do you believe me?"

His fingers on me weaken the hold I've had on myself, the fear that I'll give in and melt for him takes over and I swallow, hard. "I believe you missed my V."

He presses his palm against the bathroom counter and leans into me until our chests are touching and he takes my breath from my lungs with the motion. "I don't know what it is about you, Raven, but it's not going away," he confesses, his eyes cutting to mine and I hardly recognize them. Something inside of him has changed over the last three weeks.

"You act like it's something bad."

He sighs heavily, his chest expanding into mine. "For me it is." His eyes drop to the floor creating a foot of space between us, his warmth dissipating and I want to shiver at the coolness surrounding me. I want his heat to return.

The look on his face sends a pang of guilt through me. I certainly don't have anything to feel guilty about, but then again, maybe I do.

I shake my head. "I'm sorry I'm making this hard for you." I don't even know what I mean by that, but I say it anyway.

His eyes narrow, his breaths hard and fast and he swiftly grabs my face between his palms forcing me to look at him. The heat returns, scorching and uncontrollable as every other moment I have around him.

"Don't ever be sorry," he breathes out in a pained whisper, the smell of whiskey washing over me. He closes his eyes and exhales. He's hurting. I can see that.

Sliding his hand past my hip, he wraps it around the backs of my legs, lifting me, pressing himself against me and the counter. His face moves to my neck, and one of his hands to my waist, squeezing. His grip on me reminds me of *why* I shouldn't be in this room with him. My eyes dart to the door. He locked it. Shit. He came in here with an intention of not wanting to be interrupted. Now what do I do? I didn't even notice he locked it.

"Damn it, Raven. What do I do?" he asks in a pained whisper.

I shake my head, squeezing my eyes shut. "I don't know." When I open them, he's staring at me. Fuck if I knew what to do. If I did, I'd be doing it.

Leaning in, he pauses his mouth on my collarbone. I respond by pulling him closer, our bodies in line again and we're frantic, pulling at one another as our mouths make contact.

"*Jesus Christ*, I can't shake you." His voice is pleading and warm against my skin.

A twinge, a clenching deep within my belly causes me to jump as his words whisper over my skin like a breeze on a summer's day. I melt, never wanting to move, and open my legs to have him fill the space between them.

Tilting my chin, his lips brush the satiny curve where my neck meets my shoulders, his hands working on his belt buckle to free himself.

Well, fuck. This isn't going where I thought it would. I'm about to have sex in the bathroom in my parents' home. Well, that's certainly not a first but still….

"I don't want the sex we had before," he says, continuing his path up my neck. "I want this, right now." With his hands on my hips, he slides me to the edge of the counter and pulls a condom out of his back pocket.

My heart thuds against my breast bone as his chest expands on a breath. "Okay…."

His mouth finds mine again, our lips and breath colliding as one. I don't know how my pants come off or my shirt, but they both do and our eyes remain focused on one another as he moves inside of me, in and out.

"I missed you," he repeats, the words washing over my mouth, bathing me in his scent. His hand lowers between our legs, placing pressure against me in the way I need. "I missed you so goddamn much."

I have to believe his words. I do because they're spoken with truth. I can see it in his eyes.

His mouth sliding over mine is pure bliss and I never want his lips to part from mine. They can't. They just can't.

There's no denying what's going on here because with every moan I give, he takes it, always louder, always rougher, always more in every way. Reaching to the wall, he flips the switch to the obnoxiously loud fan and I know why he does it. Though the bathroom is upstairs and not one most use, if someone was to walk by the door they could totally hear what's happening in here.

His left hand moves from my hip to between my legs, my gaze follows. It's when his thumb drags over the sensitive bundle of nerves that I sigh, my breath expelling from my chest. "Oh God, Tyler...."

"That's it, honey." He breathes into the curve of my neck, his teeth nipping at the sensitive skin. "Show me how much you missed me, too."

Wrapping my arms around his shoulders, I cling to him, my body speaking to him as he pushes his thumb down harder, a quick and focused movement only he seems to know. I've never had someone make me come like he does. He knows exactly what to do and when and how much.

"Jesus... you're so fuckin' beautiful when you come." His tone is guttural as he tries to halt our movements for a second, his dick pulsing inside of me and I know he's close but he wants me to get off first. As soon as those words leave his beautiful lips, I'm falling— falling hard as my orgasm ravages me, my hips rocking back and forth as I attempt to not fall off the counter in the process. His hands dig into my hips, bruising my skin, keeping me in place.

When he knows my need is met, his thrusts become thoroughly focused and I know he's about to come by the way his chest shakes, his feet shifting, his belt buckle clanking, bracing himself for the onset of the pleasure coursing through him. I can tell he's moments away from his release by the tense expression and lust-hooded eyes. That alone distracts me enough to focus my attention on him because, Christ Almighty, his O face is breathtaking.

"Holy shit," he says, and then moans my name. Not wanting anyone to hear us, I take my panties from my ankle and shove them in his mouth.

It doesn't even register with him as he thrusts deeper, his head falling back, the muscles in his neck straining, his hips jerking quickly and then stilling as he empties himself.

Yep, fucking breathtakingly beautiful. I lean forward and press my lips to the protruding veins in his neck, capturing the sensation of its sturdy thump with my breath.

When my mouth leaves his skin, he takes my panties from his mouth with a grin, and then he kisses me with burning urgency. I burn with the same urgency. It's been weeks since we've been together *this* way, and I'm utterly incapable of stopping myself from kissing him.

Our mouths crash against one another in desperation, searching for meaning in the kiss. I know we are. Or at least I am.

Eventually we part, our eyes locked, now searching for meaning in what we just did. Where does this leave us now?

I'm not even sure why, but my eyes water and he notices.

Tyler looks nervous as he tosses the condom in the garbage can and pulls up his jeans. I have my jeans and shirt back on and it's a couple minutes later and he braces his forearms on the counter. "You didn't want it?"

"I didn't say that."

Tyler dips his head to catch my eyes and regards me, a pleased smile softening his features. "Is that so?"

"Yes."

Truth's out now. Can't deny it.

His voice lowers, taking my air with his proximity as he leans in and kisses my forehead tenderly. "Then come back to my place tonight."

An uncomfortable knot forms in my chest, my hand shaking as I reach out to touch his shoulder. "Do you think that's a good idea?"

Stepping back, he's still close but distanced. The soft heat of his breath tickles my nose, his lips near enough to brush my own, but they don't. It's like he's teasing me. For a moment, our stare locked in unspoken questions.

"I think it's a good idea," he murmurs, still watching me.

He closes the distance between us, my body pressed against the wall. It's then the hard length of his cock is against my hip. "Once wasn't enough?"

Tyler makes a sound deep in his throat. It's one I want to record because of what it does to my insides. "It's never enough *with you.*"

It's never enough with you.

"WHERE DID YOU go?" Red asks me, his gaze darting from me to Tyler, whose cheeks are flushed. I can't even imagine what mine look like. It's clear as fucking day what we were doing.

"I stained my shirt with cranberries. Had to change it." My words are snotty, because I know why Red is asking. He's only asking because he's being a dick and wants to be mad.

"Bullshit," he mutters, sitting back on the couch and glaring at Tyler.

Tyler shakes his head and sits down on the couch, away from Red and near me, our fingers touching in the process.

I blow out a controlled breath, not caring if he knows those words affected me like they did. Repeating the words in my head, they make my head buzz. I can't concentrate with him this close and my family in the room. Our eyes lock and his breathing falters, as though he can't either and he might turn his head and brush his lips to mine regardless of who's watching.

A languid smile stretches across his mouth when he knows he has an effect on me even now.

Nova choses then to jump on Tyler's lap. "Uncle Ty, can I spend the night with you tonight?"

He looks at her curiously and it's obvious he doesn't want that but he's not going to tell her no. "Why would you want to stay with me? I don't have any toys or anything for you."

"My dad won't let me sleep in his bed anymore." She eyes Red from across the room. "Can I sleep in yours?"

"No," Tyler says immediately. "Girls don't sleep in my bed." His comment is suggestive because really, I certainly haven't done a lot of sleeping in his bed either.

I snort. "How about you stay with Grammy," I suggest and Mom beams from her place beside Uncle Hendrix where they're drinking wine and talking about my dad and their memories.

"I'd love for you to stay, Nova."

Nova seems happy with that and slides off Tyler's lap, bypassing Red who's trying to tickle her, and jumps up like the little lap whore she is and sits on Mom's lap. "Okay. I'll sleep with you, in your bed."

Mom hugs her tightly. "I love sleepovers with my little lady."

I'm not entirely sure but Red seems bothered by Nova's distance to him the last month. She was so happy for him to come home from the hospital and to have Lenny move in. I don't think she realized what it would mean with her daddy having a live-in girlfriend. She adores Lenny; it's Red who she's taking her anger out on.

We all knew it was coming with her eventually. You can't experience what Nova's been through at such a young age and not be affected by it in some way.

Tyler gets up a few minutes later and grabs two beers from the kitchen during the fourth quarter of the game.

Lenny takes the opportunity to sneak over to me and sits where Tyler was. "Were you in the bathroom with him?" she whispers.

I nod, making sure Red doesn't see. He's not paying any attention to us; instead, he's now arguing with Rawley, who's telling him he won't be at work tomorrow because he's playing in Portland tomorrow night again.

"I don't even know why you fucking work there, Rawley. It's not like you show up for five days in a row." The sour tone to Red's voice draws Mom's attention.

"Red, don't," she warns, scowling at him but keeping Nova cuddled between her and Hendrix. "Not today."

Red shakes his head but doesn't push the issue. The last thing he wants to do is make today an argument, but I can see where the tension comes from. Rawley's a shit these days and cares about music and nothing else. We all thought he'd change when Red nearly died, but he hasn't.

Lenny elbows me. "So what now?"

I shrug. "I told you I was easy. He touched me and I spread my legs." I let my head fall back against the couch. "I'm so disappointed in my vagina and her lack of control."

"Oh, don't be so hard on yourself." Lenny laughs, standing up to sit next to Red on the other couch, attempting to calm him down.

Tyler returns a moment later, hands Red another beer and then sits next to me. Red takes the beer, never missing the gesture. Their friendship was cemented years ago and just because there's something going on between Tyler and me, doesn't mean their friendship isn't still there.

I'm thankful for Tyler's return and relax a little, my stare on the remaining minutes of the football game. I can't tell you who's playing because though my gaze is locked on the television, my mind wanders to Tyler's words in the bathroom and him telling me he missed me.

If he missed me, why is he so fucking distant? Why was he with Berkley just days after he rescued me from a frat party? I'm dying to ask him those questions too but I know the timing isn't right.

"Hey, Tyler," Rawley says at the door after kissing the top of my head. He's standing there with Jude, the two of them getting ready to head out.

Tyler looks up at him, his eyes leaving the game for the first time in the last five minutes. "What?"

"Where's Berkley tonight?"

Rawley is a motherfucker. He really is and I want to punch him in the throat.

Tyler tenses but doesn't give his frustration away, his eyes snapping back to the television. "How the fuck should I know?"

Shrugging, Rawley leaves and no one pays any attention to his laughter. Little shit is so intent on causing a scene all the time I have no idea what's going through his head.

When the game ends, Tyler finds me in the laundry room checking on my sweater, my mind scrambling with jumbled thoughts.

"We have to stop meeting like this," he teases, leaning into the door.

"No, you have to stop following me." I turn around, holding my sweater in my hand ready to go up to my old room and wallow in my self-pity of being in love with a man who will never love me.

Slowly he eases away from the doorway and it takes both of us a minute before our eyes find one another again. Tyler studies me, his blue eyes unnerving in thought. The air between us seems dense, like oil, so thick you can't see through it.

The familiar heat spreads over me when his burning stare captivates me. He smiles, and I smile. That always present electricity and draw linger, charging the air and suffocating me to the point where I think I'm going to burst into flames.

I want to know what he's thinking.

The blood in my face rises to the surface, my ears throbbing. "Why are you staring at me?"

"Come to my place tonight," he replies without hesitation. "Please."

Sometimes I think Tyler is using me for his own benefit, a comforting face when he doesn't know what else he wants. I'm not sure I always believe that, especially now, but it's easy to fall prey to it when I think about the message Rawley sent me a few weeks ago.

I didn't want to believe Tyler would use me.

I raise my eyes to his and he grins, because he knows I can't deny him. Fuck, he's asking nicely and I can't deny a man with manners, right?

I give him a smile. "Okay."

I'm a fucking idiot.

"WHAT IS THIS?" I sigh, knowing what fucking idiots we're both being in all this. We're willingly hurting each other. I know it.

"What?" He's staring up at the ceiling of his room, his arms draped over his head as if he knows how dumb this is himself.

"Us..." I motion around the bed of tangled sheets and scattered pillows making myself look him in the eye. "What are *we* doing, Tyler?"

"Whatever you want it to be." His tone is casual, but his eyes are anxious. He moves and twists to hover over me again. His left hand moving under the sheets, raising my right thigh up his hip.

"No, seriously, what are we doing?" My eyes close when he enters me for the third time tonight, just before the sun's rising. "If this was what I wanted, you'd be with me, *only me*."

He can't miss the way I say only me. And he doesn't.

His stare moves to mine. He's trying to keep the conversation light, but it can't be, and he knows damn well it won't. There's hurt and resentment for what we're doing, though we both avoid it.

I can see something in his life is changing him in ways I hate, something he's not telling me. When I look into his eyes, I see stress where I once saw a bright-eyed guy living life to its fullest every day. Maybe it's the stress of the job or the changes with him and Red, but maybe it's more, maybe it's me or Berkley. There's just so many questions in my head I can't handle it. Could it be that our situation is just as stressful on him as it is on me?

I hide my face in his neck. My breath catches as he rocks against me, harsh breathing and slow moans controlling me for a moment.

"It's not like I'm sleeping with anyone else, Raven." He props himself up with his elbows, his brow furrowing, but he keeps his movements slow.

My gaze drops from his, losing the battle, wilting under the burn of his eyes, and I know the discussion is over, as it always is. He gave me an answer, but I know I'm still not getting what I want. He might be sleeping with just me, but it doesn't mean he wants anything more than he's giving me now.

My body is tense, his words controlling my mood. He senses the change and shakes his head, pulling out of me and rolling to the side, never finishing, the moment ruined by words.

His jaw tightens and he brings the sheet up around his waist after discarding the condom in the trash next to his bed.

"Why can't this ever be easy for us?" He's staring at the wall now. "Why does it have to turn into this every time?"

You have no idea, Tyler. No fucking idea.

"I'm sorry. I just don't want to be this girl." Rolling to my side, I face him, needing to look in his eyes, only his found refuge in the ceiling.

"For fuck's sake, Raven, you act like you're just some girl I call every once in a while. You're not." The biting edge to his words make my entire body shudder with the emptiness of his words.

"Don't you see? I am *that girl* because that's the way it's always been," I tell him, desperate to keep him from pushing me away completely and seeing what this is doing to me by constantly falling back into this.

Tyler snorts out a laugh, his head shaking back and forth as he flops his arm over his face.

"We have absolutely no communication other than you calling when you need me or texting me that your wang misses his muff. What does that tell you about our relationship? Why won't you tell me what's going on? Maybe I can understand where you're coming from. It's not like we just met, I can tell there is something going on with you, aside from us. Let me in." My eyes burn, and I keep blinking, hoping he won't see the tears coming. The thought of him knowing how he truly feels is frightening.

Hearing the nervousness in my tone, he removes his arm, staring at me, his eyes consumed with emotion. There's a scorching pain and anger just below the depths of his pupils but he gives me nothing verbally.

"I have to go," I say, twisting to find my clothes on the floor. Tyler reaches for my hand and when I go to move, he stops me.

His hand closes on my upper arm, his gaze intent on mine. "Why does it have to be like this? You knew I couldn't give you anything more than my friendship and sex. Why does it have to change now?"

"Tyler, I just don't get it. Why can't we have more?" My voice shakes with each word. Flinging my arm up, it breaks his hold on me. I want to punch something, maybe him at how selfish he's being.

His jaw snaps closed and his eyes go wide with surprise question. Then he looks at the wall, the muscles in his jaw clenching. He doesn't say anything, but it's the answer I need.

"This is why I need to go." I reach for my jeans on the floor, but he grabs my arm again.

"Damn it, why do you always do this?" His voice is louder than I'm expecting.

Digging out my cell phone in my bag near my jeans, I move to show Tyler the picture Rawley sent me of him and Berkley, a reminder of *why* I'm not good enough and should leave before this hurts my heart even more. I'll admit, I'm a little self-conscious. What girl isn't? Even if they tell you they're not, I believe they are in some aspect of their life. Like it or not, because Tyler says he's not in a position to love me, I'm constantly comparing myself to Berkley. Maybe I'm not the type he wants, Lord knows she and I are completely different.

"This is why...." And then I show him the picture.

Tyler
Chapter 10
TRAPPED

"ARE YOU WITH Berkley?"

A thickness forms in the air, one that has me wanting to take a deep breath for relief. "No," I say under my breath, but I don't know why. I don't need to lie to her. There's nothing and never will be anything between Berkley and me again. "Where did you get that?"

She stands, her bag on her shoulder now like she's going to leave with those words. No fucking way. "Does it matter?"

Is she serious?

She is.

"Yes, it fucking matters." Ripping the sheet away, I stand, her eyes roaming over my naked body. Bending over, I pull my shorts from the floor on. "Who took that?"

"Rawley." Her voice is timid, as if she didn't want to tell me, but did.

Anger rushes through my veins. My hands shake as I run them through my hair just before yanking my shirt over my head. "What is he, in high school again? What the fuck?"

"He's only looking out for me," Raven mumbles, turning to walk into the living room.

"Yeah, and he's fucking my ex. He's looking out for himself is what he's doing," I yell, following her.

She stops at the door, but doesn't face me. I hate that she's thinking of walking out after accusing me of this shit. "What were you doing talking to her then?"

"She keeps trying to talk to me says she wants to be friends and I told her I didn't want to be her goddamn friend," my words are rushed and damn near pleading despite my anger for the situation and fucking Rawley, "she showed up at the bar to ask again."

She turns now, her eyes on the floor, refusing to meet mine. "What did you say?"

"I told her to fuck off. I don't need any more friends." I snort once the reality of this argument sinks in, simmering below the surface. "And you know, it kind of pisses me off that I'm having to explain this shit to you." I fling my hand up in the air. "Do you honestly think I'd go back to her after everything she did to me?"

Her back meets the door, still no eye contact. "I don't know. I barely know why you guys broke up. And you can't give me more than sex. What am I supposed to think other than she still has your heart?"

"All you need to know is that we broke up. It doesn't fucking matter anyway. It's not like I'm getting back together with her. I'm done with her." I take another step back hoping with the movement, she might look at me. "I've never given you a reason to think I would and just because Holden's a cheating bastard doesn't mean everyone is." I hate mentioning Holden, I do, but I do it so she sees I'm nothing like him.

She doesn't say anything. We both know I've avoided her real question, if only she knew. But I can't open up to her. I can't be who she needs me to be.

"This is what I was afraid of, Raven." I take a step toward her, hoping she might let me touch her. "You're overthinking it. Yeah, we're not in a relationship by the definition *you* want, but when I'm with someone, I don't fuck around."

Raven sighs, shaking her head when my hand cups her cheek. She leans into it; she wants it there. "Tyler." I can hear the dejection in her voice. "I don't want to fight with you." She smiles softly, but the action doesn't touch her eyes. It's more of a reflex, forced. "We used to have so much fun and I don't know why that ended."

"I'm sorry I overreacted." Bringing her into my chest, I wrap my arms around her, my chin resting on her head. "I have a lot on my mind and when I'm with you, I'm able to relax. I just get mad when you question my intentions here and don't give yourself enough credit. Whether you realize it or not, you're one of the most important people in my life."

She nods, her posture weakening.

I draw back, my hand under her chin. "Are you hungry?"

She nods again.

"Come on, I'll make you something to eat."

I FIX HER some eggs and toast that morning but there's a nagging sensation clawing at my chest, I ask, "Are you mad I didn't call? Is that what all this is about?"

She can't look at me, her eyes are focused on her plate as she pushes the eggs around with her fork. Part of me doesn't want her to look at me because I don't want her seeing my guilt for not calling.

She shrugs.

Stepping around the counter, I turn her to face me on the stool. My left hand reaches to tuck a loose strand of her hair behind her ear.

Leaning in, her scent clouds my judgment. "I don't know why I didn't, Raven. It's not that I didn't want to, it's just I've got some messed-up shit in my head. It's not you though. It's never anything you've done." My answer is real and just as raw as the pain hitting my chest because she won't look at me. I can sense she's distancing herself, protecting her heart from me and I get it, I do, doesn't mean I like it.

Raven doesn't say anything and I know what's happening. She's shutting herself down emotionally because she thinks I'm going to break her heart.

In some ways, I'm glad she is. In others, it hurts to know I'm willingly doing it. It's the last thing I ever intended to do.

chapter 11
WHO YOU ARE

I'M TRYING MY hardest not to react. I know I need to just be friends with him and not hope for more. I know I should tell him what's going on between us is bullshit. I should tell him I deserve better than what I'm getting from him but the truth is, he's giving me exactly what he always has. It's me who decided it's not good enough all of a sudden. If someone is going to have to change, it's me and I know deep down that's just not going to happen.

I guess in some ways it's easier to play ostrich and bury my head in the sand to avoid the inevitable because the alternative is not having him at all. I can't take that.

Finishing my eggs, I ask, "How's work been going?" I'm trying to change the subject and I think he appreciates it.

Tyler laughs, taking the pan of eggs and placing a spoonful onto his own plate. He then sits next to me at the kitchen island. "Well, since Red found out about us, I've pretty much been handed every shit job imaginable but I can't say I wasn't expecting it. I changed oil for an entire week."

Setting my fork down, I wipe my mouth with the napkin beside my plate and then fix my fork because it's a bit lopsided. "Sorry, he's a bit possessive."

"Oh, I know." He nods, his eyes on my fork, finding entertainment in my obsession for order. "I saw him when Holden broke your heart."

My brow furrows. "You did?"

"Yeah, we paid him a little visit over the summer." Tyler grins, as though he had fun doing it.

"What? I never knew about that!" And then I feel bad because that's how strong their relationship was. Tyler and Red did everything together before he found out about us. Had I destroyed that? "I'm sorry, I put a strain on your relationship with your best friend."

He holds up his hand to shut me up. "Raven, I was there too, with you, in that bed when it started. If I thought it'd destroy my relationship with him, I would have stopped. But give him more credit than that. He may not *like* it, but it's really not up to him, is it?"

"It's not."

But it's not up to me either.

I don't say that and I know I'm a fucking idiot because despite everything he's said, I know I should leave but instead, it makes me want to wrap my arms around him and give him whatever it is he's willing to take from me.

Incredibly stupid on my part given my history.

"Well." I stand. "I should get going."

He sets his fork down and does the same. "You coming home this coming weekend?"

"I think so."

He pulls me in for a hug, his arms wrapping around my waist and drawing me tight against his hard chest. "See you then?"

I try to control the rapid beat of my heart by pulling in a deep breath. "Okay."

RIGHT BEFORE I'M heading back to Eugene, I stop off at Red and Lenny's house to say good-bye since it's on the way to the interstate and I miss my friend.

"How'd it go?" Lenny asks the moment I'm inside the house and she's sorting through a box on the floor.

I pull my hood up over my head dramatically and sit on the couch behind her. "Where's Nova and Red?"

"I made them go pick out a tree together." Lenny sighs, toying with an ornament in her hand. "I think Nova needs some alone time with him. She cried when we picked her up today."

Leaning forward so my elbows are on my knees, I pull my hood off. "She's just going through a rough patch, L. Give her some time. She loves you."

"I know, I just feel like maybe Red and I moved too fast for her."

"It's not that. She did this when her mom died too. Gave him a run for his money but it's not you, it's just her. Red's the same way. Hates change and then when he comes to terms with it, he's fine."

Lenny moves her legs out from under her, tossing the ornament aside. "Okay... I just don't want them to think I've invaded their relationship, you know?"

I nod, because I totally get where she's coming from on this one. I just don't think that's what's happening. "You're not. I'm telling you, it'll blow over."

"So…." She waggles her eyes suggestively. "What happened last night?"

"Well, we went back to his place, had sex two more times, he came on my face and then I think I pissed him off by bringing up Berkley."

Lenny lets out a whistled breath. "Yeah, that's a sure way to piss him off." And then she frowns. "He came on your face?"

I nod, my cheeks burning with my admittance.

"He came on my face."

"And you liked it?"

"Yes. Is there something wrong with me? I mean, I get into all that dirty shit with him and it confuses the hell out of me because he's so damn nice and polite anywhere other than bed. It's like here, I'll hold the door and then later I'll jizz on your face. And fuck, I'll let him stick it in my ass too. If that's not love"—I flop my arms up dramatically—"I don't know what is."

Lenny clears her throat. "I never saw him that way. Didn't really want to either."

Standing, I grab her arm before she can get away from me because she's trying to leave the room now. "You know what I mean, he's like that saying 'Lady on the street but a freak between the sheets.' Except he's a gentleman on the street but a nasty hair-pulling ass-spanking handcuff-me-to-his-steering-wheel in the sheets."

"You know." She faces me, laughing now. "I don't understand why that's not a saying cause it's not a mouthful at all."

"Right? But I'll tell you what *is* a mouthful—"

"Nope!" Lenny cuts me off. "That's enough."

"But I need someone to talk to," I whine, falling back on the couch again. To add to the dramatics again, I pull my hood over my head once more.

"Fine." She sits down next to me, her posture stiff, as though this is painful. "I get to tell you what your brother did to me in bed first so you can see how this feels."

"Fine." I wave my hand in her face. "Try me."

"Well." She seems way too pleased with this and sits back in the chair, grinning. "I told him I wanted him to—"

I stand up, my stomach turning at the idea of hearing anything sexual about my brother. "Nope. Let's not."

I caught Red and Nevaeh having sex once and it was way more than I ever wanted to see of my brother naked. Way too much. The sight still burns my eyes and I'm immediately reminded of it when she begins to talk.

Lenny looks relieved. "See? I told you it wasn't cool."

"You're right. But seriously, why is he confusing me?"

"I think there's something going on with him and his parents," Lenny admits. "Red told me they called him asking if Tyler was okay, but they didn't go into detail as to why they hadn't heard from him. Apparently he hasn't talked to them since March."

Since March? Wow. Okay…. So maybe he does have something else going on. Still doesn't excuse the fact that he's stringing me along, but I do have a little more sympathy for him than I did an hour ago.

AROUND FOUR, I'M getting ready to head home when Red shows up with Nova and a tree. She's happy, pointing to the tree with a big grin.

147

"We got a tree, Auntie!" she yells as she's running past me into the house to tell Lenny.

I smile, happy that she's in a better mood.

Red sees me and gives me a nod. "Can you untie the other side for me?"

"Sure, if you start being nice to Tyler again."

He groans, a slow shake to his head. "I'm already nice to him. I took the beer from him last night, didn't I?"

"True, but stop giving him all the shit jobs. We didn't do this to piss you off."

"I know that." His voice is off and I feel bad right then because I know he's going through something too. Everyone is. Seems like life these days.

"How's Nova?"

Red sighs, anxiety flooding his face. "She's better. I asked her if it'd be okay if I took Lenny away for a weekend alone and she asked if you could watch her."

"Sure, I can. I have no life. Where are you going?"

"Thought I could take Lenny to the beach. She's never been, believe it or not."

"Why do you have to be such a good guy?"

"I'm not, clearly by your standards." I glare at him and he laughs, leaning into the car with his arms crossed over his chest. "Tyler's a good guy too."

I almost laugh that he's able to say something nice about him. "He is, but he doesn't know what he wants."

Red nods. "He'll come around, I'm sure." Reaching up, he takes the string around the tree we untied and unravels it. "So you can watch her here next weekend, right? I don't think dorm life is for a five-year-old."

"Yeah, here." I turn to head to my car and then look back at him. "Does Lenny know?"

He shakes his head quickly. "No. *Don't* tell her. It's a surprise."

We both look to the door where Lenny's laughing on the porch, Nova at her feet. "I get to stay with you next weekend, Auntie!"

"Too late," I yell out to Red and then air-five Nova. "Can't wait, sweet cheeks!"

"Nova," Red groans, smiling at her as he brings the tree down. "Darlin', that was supposed to be a secret."

Nova shrugs. "Stop telling me secrets. You know I can't keep them."

Once I'm in my car, I watch the three of them for a moment. Red's proudly holding the tree and Lenny has the biggest grin on her face. This will be the first Christmas she's actually had a real family around.

I'm also a bit sad too, because this will be our first Christmas without my dad. Thanksgiving was hard enough, I can't imagine how Christmas will be for us all.

THE WEEK BACK at school seems to fly by, mostly because I have to basically study my ass off if I'm going to pass any class and get my mind off Tyler. And it doesn't work. Why I thought it would is beyond me.

What else doesn't help is when I'm rushing to my marketing management class—the one I'm failing—Holden finds me. "Hey, you okay?"

I give him a confused look. "Yeah, why?"

"Oh, well someone said you had a rough night at the party a few weeks back."

I don't know how I forgot about that. "Oh, that, right." Adjusting my bag on my shoulder, I squint into the sun. "Yeah."

He stares at me. "I would have drove you back to your dorm."

"Tyler did."

Holden's jaw tightens and I have no idea why so I start walking and he follows.

"Tyler... he's Red's friend?"

"Yeah, you've met him, haven't you?"

"I have."

I want to laugh imagining what Holden must have thought when he encountered Red and Tyler together. I can imagine. He probably pissed himself. Though Holden's a football player, there's no chance in hell at standing up against my brother or Tyler.

He bites down on his lower lip and tiny frown lines appear on his forehead. "So is he like... your boyfriend?"

In my dreams.

"No, I just fuck him on occasion."

And he comes on my face every once in a while.

I don't think Holden's prepared for my blunt answer because he blinks several times, and then several more. Then I think it hits him I've moved on and have absolutely no feelings for him.

"Oh."

"I need to go." I point over my shoulder with my thumb. "I'm late. Good luck on Friday."

He doesn't move from his place in front of me. "I'm not playing this year."

"You're not?"

"No. I don't know if you heard about that party we had at Shasta over the summer...." His voice trails off and I can hear the disappointment in it.

"I heard. Most of Oregon did." Holden's fraternity trashed Lake Shasta over the summer and were currently under investigation.

Every year for Memorial Day weekend, the University of Oregon's fraternities invade Lake Shasta in northern California on party boats. Last year it apparently got out of hand.

"That sucks. Didn't know they'd suspend you over it."

"They didn't. I lost my scholarship over it."

Remember when I said everyone has issues? Apparently Holden does too.

"Sorry." Is all I offer him. I can't say I didn't see it coming with Holden. The moment he left for college my senior year he changed. I didn't know him as that sweet boy I fell in love with at sixteen any longer and I honestly should have seen it coming when he cheated on me.

"So Tyler...." He's been dancing around the topic the last two times we've had conversations so I'm not surprised when he finally asks, "You like him then?"

Jesus. Trying to walk away is proving difficult.

I release a pent-up breath. "You could say that and I wouldn't disagree." Liking him is certainly underestimating these feelings but hey, let's just go with that for now.

"How long?" I know what he's asking. He knows as long as I was with him in high school, Tyler was around. What he's asking can potentially hurt him and after everything, I want to be a little vindictive. I'm entitled to be, right?

"Honestly?"

Holden raises an eyebrow, vulnerability dancing in his eyes. "Yes."

"Since I was sixteen."

It's the roll of his throat as he swallows and his hardening that confirms this bothers him more than he's going to lead on, more than he'll ever say. He nods, his lips press together in a slight frown. The look in his eyes, the set anger in his jaw, naturally he'd have this reaction. For so long Holden thought he was the only one. I made him believe he was, so was I any different then him?

"I'm not trying to get back together with you, I swear," he mutters, hurt and anger simmering beneath the surface. "I get it, I cheated on you, but I guess I just wanted you to know I'm sorry, about everything. I shouldn't have said those things to you that day and I'll never forgive myself for that."

I'm not sure how to react, mostly because he apologized and fully admitted to be a dumb dick. Something I never expected from him.

The words get stuck in my throat, but I manage to get out, "Okay," I say, nodding. "I really do have to go, Holden."

He backs up giving me space. "Okay."

And we part, just like that, much different from Valentine's Day last year. I can't help but wonder why he felt now was the time to corner me like that, but then again, maybe he needed closure?

AFTER PACKING SOME clothes, I make the drive to Lebanon and pick up a pizza on the way over to Red and Lenny's. I'm actually excited for a girl's weekend with Nova when Tyler texts me.

Tyler: Free tonight?

I do get a little giddy that he's texting me, despite knowing it's just for sex.

Me: I'm watching Nova. Red and Lenny went to the beach.

Tyler: Want help?

I know where this is going. He'll come over and pretend to help only because he wants some and then when he gets it, he'll leave. Red probably won't appreciate that much.

Me: I have to ACTUALLY watch her. Not just bumping uglies.

Tyler: My dick is NOT ugly.

Me: meh.

Tyler: what the fuck does that mean?

I don't reply. Mostly because I think it's funny and I know what he's going to do with that. He's gonna show up.

Sure enough, thirty minutes into watching Nova, Tyler's knocking at the door.

"Uncle Ty, what are you doing here?" Nova opens the door, motioning him inside.

He looks at me, then Nova, smiling. "I heard there's a party here."

I snort from my place in the kitchen where I'm cutting another slice of pizza for Nova. I don't say anything until he's in the kitchen and Nova's asking him to stay the night with us in the fort she's planning on building in the living room.

He glances around, wearing jeans and a T-shirt that clings to his massive biceps I want to run over and touch. "I've always wanted to sleep in a fort." He waggles his eyebrows at me. "Can't wait."

See, this is the problem with Tyler and me. He won't give me what I want but I enjoy his friendship so much I constantly set myself up to be hurt by him.

Standing next to me in the kitchen now, so close his warmth surrounds me, he whispers in my ear. "Is this okay? Or should I go?"

"I'm not having sex with you," I tell him, rolling the pizza cutter through the slice of cheese pizza.

He chuckles and it's low, the sound flowing through me because the soft chuckle gives my stomach a flip every damn time. "Who said I was asking?"

Sure he's not. I remember the bathroom and by the look in his eyes when our gaze meets, he remembers too. It's why he's here, I think.

"I came to see about a text message," he whispers, his voice so dangerously low goose bumps form.

I roll my eyes. "Jesus, I was kidding."

"Damn right you were." Tyler grins and it looks good on him. I miss his smiles. "How's school, Nova?" His stare sweeps to hers. She's in the fridge digging out the root beer I brought over for her.

"Not awesome." She sets the soda on the table next to our plates and then grabs another paper plate for Tyler. "I want to talk about just getting a job or maybe being a stay at home kid but Red says no."

Tyler chuckles, the corners of his eyes crinkling with humor. "Why don't you like it?"

"School just isn't for me." She leaves it at that and smacks the table with her hand. "Sit next to me, Ty. We can eat pizza together."

It's amazing how much I miss Nova and her quirky behavior when I'm away at school and don't see her during the week. I swear she gets bigger every time I see her and her attitude is more like Red every day. She's got his dry sense of humor.

We're at the table, eating pizza and Nova's telling us everything she doesn't particularly like about school. Tyler's attention is fully on her, listening to her every word.

Lost in my head, the night flies by with the three of us playing Monopoly for what seems like hours. Naturally, I win. No one can manage money down to the very last cent like me. Hell, Nova bought everything she came across and Tyler was more into being ahead of everyone on the board than actually playing the game. His car always had to be in front of my thimble.

Nova decides after Monopoly that she wants to have ice-cream sundaes so Tyler takes her, hand in hand, to the kitchen. She stands on a chair, watching his every move and asks, "Uncle Ty, are you afraid of anything?"

He shrugs and takes the lid off the ice cream. "Spiders. I don't like them."

"Daddy hates snakes."

"I know. It's the only time I've seen him scream like a little girl." Scooping a large chunk of ice cream into her bowl, he waits for her to say if she wants more. She nods so he gives her one more scoop. "Are you afraid of anything?"

She shrugs. "Not really. My daddy is a super hero so I don't have to be afraid of anything."

Tyler grins and taps her nose with his finger leaving a dot of chocolate ice cream on her nose. "I wouldn't be afraid of anything if my dad was a super hero either." Taking two more bowls from the cupboard, he scoops ice cream into them while Nova watches intently. "So he's like Batman?"

"No." Nova grabs for the whip cream on the counter beside the ice cream I set out, considering her super heroes carefully. "He's like Ironman because he has a hole in his chest. But Mommy healed it with her heaven powers when he was hurt and gave us Lenny."

"Lenny's pretty special, isn't she?"

Nova's face lights up. "She is."

When he's finished with the ice cream, Nova and him pour on the toppings and bring the bowls to the table where I'm sitting

watching the two of them. Tyler takes a bit of his ice cream and then looks at Nova. "So why are you giving your dad a hard time lately if he's a super hero."

Nova rolls her eyes, midbite of her chocolate sundae. "Because he's making me go to school. I don't want to go. I want to be a stay at home kid like Uncle Rawley."

"You don't want to be like him, Nova," I add, hoping she never turns out like him. Rawley knows he's a horrible example, but he claims if you can't be a good one, be a horrible example of what not to do. His logic, not mine.

GETTING NOVA IN her pajamas before we are set to watch *Frozen* for the second time tonight is something else. We're in her room, digging through her dresser when she strips down to just her panties and I notice the kid has a wrench in her underwear.

"Ollie gave me a wrench," she says, pulling it out to set on her nightstand.

"Why did you put it in your underwear?"

"Does it look like I had any pockets?" She raises an eyebrow. "I had to put it somewhere."

She is Red's kid so I'm not all that surprised by this.

Once dressed in her jammies, her and I go back out into the living room where Tyler is in the fort waiting for us, still fully clothed. I'm glad he's stayed because he's made the night so much better. Not that we wouldn't have had fun without him, but Tyler has a way about him that makes everything more fun.

For nearly two hours, we lay in the fort watching *Frozen* and eating popcorn, most of which Tyler throws at me because deep down, he's still a boy and when you want a girl's attention, you throw things at her.

"We gotta get her to sleep at some point," I tell Tyler once *Frozen* is over and Nova restarts it again, knowing this kid is never going to go to bed if we're playing with her. Fuck us for being the cool aunt and uncle who don't force her to bed at nine. It's midnight and I can't understand why she hasn't passed out. Could have been from all the sugar we gave her.

"This movie's not very good. What's with all the singing?" Tyler's lying against the pillows in the fort, Nova across his lap, his hands combing through her hair trying like hell to make her sleepy. "I have an idea," he says, nodding to her room and sitting up. "Go grab her bear and blanket she always sleeps with," he whispers.

I forgot she had a special bear and blanket she refuses to sleep without. When I'm in her room, I hear Tyler turn on some music.

I walk into probably the sweetest thing I've ever seen in my life. Tyler slow dancing with Nova as he holds her against his chest and sways in the kitchen. They're dancing to Chris Stapleton's "Tennessee Whiskey" and I nearly cry.

Her head is on his shoulder, her eyes blinking slowly like she's close to sleep and he's singing softly to her. They continue this for the entire song and when it's over, Nova's asleep, just like that.

"How'd you do that?" I whisper, setting her bear on the pillows.

Tyler twists his head to the side after brushing his lips over her forehead. "Do you remember the week Nevaeh died and Red locked himself in his room?"

I nod. I was only sixteen when Nevaeh died but I remember my brother's pain during those first few weeks like it was yesterday, knowing nothing would ever be the same for him. He was so broken and out of it, I didn't even recognize him anymore.

His head tilts sideways and his brows knit together as though he's in pain. "I helped your mom with Nova that week, and the only way I could get her to sleep at night was dancing with her in my arms. And then she'd sleep right on my chest for hours."

"You'll make a good dad someday," I tell him, my hand on his shoulder, rubbing it softly. I wrap Nova's blanket around her before Tyler lays her on the sea of pillows on the floor.

Tyler nods, setting Nova down but there's a sadness in his expression that says he's bothered by something I said. He stares at Nova for a moment and the sadness remains.

Standing, he steps back, his hands buried in the pockets of his jeans. "I should go home."

"No, you told her you were staying. Don't bail on a five-year-old."

It gets him and he sits back down but doesn't say anything.

Fuck, did I say something to upset him?

When we're both lying down, I finally ask him, "Why'd you come here tonight?"

"Because you called Wang ugly," he teases and then breathes in deeply, he takes a moment to think about the question and then says, "I like spending time with you."

Be still my heart.

The look on his face captivates me as it always does. Instantly, he has my full attention, my heart pounding oddly fast.

He sinks his teeth into his bottom lip and then lets it go. With a grin, his fingers brush the edge of my bra strap, teasingly, lightly tickling over my collarbone.

He brushes my hair behind my ear as his eyes roam over my face lit by the My Little Pony nightlight with splashes of pink and purple. "I've told you, I do have feelings for you."

I touch his purple-lit cheek. "Just not girlfriend feelings."

"Well—" His head twists and he kisses my palm. Something in the way he looks at me unnerves me, makes my skin tingle and my breath hitch. "—I don't have girlfriend feelings for anyone else either."

I tip my head. "There's that."

He didn't try to have sex with me either.

There's that, too.

Maybe he's wanting a change of subject, I'm not sure but he smiles and motions around the pink and purple sheets hanging up by a baseball bat stuck between couch cushions. "You know, the last time I was in a fort was when I was eight years old."

I laugh lightly, covering my mouth so we don't wake Nova. "Were you with a girl?"

He nods a bit arrogantly. "Two actually."

"Not surprised."

"It was the neighbor girl's. They were twins and we were playing doctor."

"Oh my God, you were a flirt even back then, weren't you?"

Tyler chuckles softly, rolling on his back, his arms resting on his stomach. "Probably. Got my first kiss that day."

"I bet you did."

Turning his head, he looks at me with curiosity. "Who gave you your first kiss?"

"Devin West."

He groans, his arm flopping over his face. "That little fucker? He slashed my tires senior year."

"Yeah, because you and Red gave him shit every time you saw him."

"We weren't that bad."

"Bullshit." And then as my mind shifts through the memories, I realize Tyler is in every one of them, always in the background, or right beside me. "You know, every memory I have of my childhood you're in it." I have so many of him, mostly protecting me. Aside from the time he gave me my first beer when I was fifteen and then proceeded to hold my hair while I puked for the next hour.

"I have a lot with you in them too."

"Remember that time we went camping at Sun Lakes and you carried me for two miles on your back because Rawley pushed me down a hill and I broke my ankle?"

"Yeah." He gives a slow shake of his head. "Man, I was *pissed* at him. He could have really hurt you."

"Something tells me that was the intention. I mean, it was a pretty steep hill."

This is why I enjoy being around Tyler so much. We can talk about anything. As I remember that day, and the hot sun on my back as Tyler carried me, I can still recall the way his muscles felt, tensing and straining, and the smell of the sunscreen he wore.

"This might sound weird, but did you ever think you'd be fucking me someday?"

He laughs, the corners of his eyes crinkling with the motion. "No."

"Never?"

"Well, once you had tits, it certainly crossed my mind, but I don't know, never really thought too much about it."

Guys don't like to talk about things like this, I can tell. Our whispered conversation fades away and we realize Nova is out cold, snoring away.

Turning off the TV, the room lights up with purple and pink, brighter now and I lay back next to Tyler, Nova at our feet where she originally fell asleep.

Side-by-side we lie, his soft breaths stirring my hair. My heartbeat is a drum in my ears, and I struggle to keep still and not turn over and cuddle with him.

Everything's quiet for about a half an hour when Tyler jumps. "There's a spider beside me. I felt it touch my arm. Hold me."

"You baby, kill it."

"I can't. It's dark and I can't see it."

Instead of killing it, he practically lays on top of me. I'm not much for cuddling and sigh about every ten seconds.

His hot breath stirs my hair, the muscles along his arm twitching as he moves his arm over my stomach. "What's wrong with you?" His fingertips graze the underside of my breast and I stop breathing all together. "You let me put my D in your V but you won't cuddle?"

"What's your V, Auntie?"

And now my heart just stopped.

"*Holy crap!*" I sit up and stare at Nova, who's curiously watching Tyler and me. "What are you doing awake?"

She shrugs. "Can't sleep. Can I have a slice of pizza? I'm hungry."

"Sure." I'd do just about anything for her not to ask what V and D are again. But she does.

"Do I have a V?"

Tyler's sitting up in the fort now, watching me with humor in his eyes, waiting for me to come up with something. I think he can tell I'm moments away from a panic attack when he stands and follows us into the kitchen.

"Uh, well…." Taking a slice of pizza for her out of the fridge, I place it on a plate and stick it in the microwave for a few seconds. "He fixed my car." Okay, bad example and poorly executed and I want to take it back as soon as I say it, but this is Nova and there's no takebacks with her.

Tyler's sitting at the table now and drops his head forward, laughter rolling through his shoulders.

"So like his D is his tool and he can fix your V with it? Is your V your car?"

I'm so screwed.

"Yeah." I smack at Tyler's shoulders when he can't help himself and breaks out into full-on laughter. "Something like that."

Nova shrugs, but something tells me that isn't the last of this. It never is with her.

"You were absolutely no help," I say to Tyler, smacking the back of his head.

His eyes brighten when he looks at me, and I know he's about to say something dirty so my glare intensifies, warning him. "I think… I'm a lot of help. Your V always seemed *very* satisfied with me."

He's got me there.

As we eventually make it back to the fort for the night, I watch Tyler sleep for about an hour with Nova right between us. It's then I realize even though I don't have the relationship I crave. Having him as my friend is something I need and want. It's where we started and essentially what ties me to him in every way. I can't lose that over what I think my heart needs.

Raven
chapter 12
YOU

IT'S OFFICIAL. I'M an idiot and I'm trying to force him to be my friend just so I don't have to let go of him. And it's okay, right? Because I'm not trying to force him into loving me. I'm just a friend and you know, that's okay.

He wants to be my friend, too. At least I think he does because he never said he couldn't be my friend. He just said he couldn't love me.

My attempts to spend time with him become so bad that when I'm studying, I'm constantly thinking of him and checking my messages to see if he's sent anything. Consumed is an understatement.

It's this obsession that leads me to asking him to a football game. No way did he want to go to a college football game where my ex would be. Guaranteed. But I didn't want to go to the game alone and I knew Tyler enjoyed football.

Me: Come see me. We can go to a game.

He replies within a minute. Tyler: I'm not into football.

Me: Bullshit. You are too.

Nothing. He doesn't reply for five minutes.

Me: So you'll come?

Tyler: Sure. Why not.

Me: Ok, see you Saturday morning.

Tyler: K... but hey, wait...

Me: What?

Tyler: What are you wearing?

Me: Pervert.

Tyler: D misses V.

Me: Muff is going to study.

Tyler: Wang could help you relax.

Me: I'm sure... Night, Tyler.

Tyler: Fine. Study HARD.

He knows exactly what he's doing with that last text because now my mind is on his wang... and my muff is sad.

I DON'T DO much all week, between studying and a Skype session with Tyler, it fills my week pretty well.

Saturday morning I have him meet me at my dorm room. He's dressed in a black hooded sweatshirt and jeans that make me what to squeeze him. When I do, he smells like fall, crisp leaves, and foggy mornings.

"How's that bed of yours? Sturdy?" he asks with an unintentional sexy smirk he has. Or maybe it is intentional. Knowing him, it probably is.

I look back over my shoulder when he steps inside and then back at him. He's ripping the comfy sweatshirt off his shoulders as we speak and stalking toward me. "It's *sturdy* enough."

It's the same scenario we find ourselves in every other time we're together. A battle of dominance to get clothes off, grunting with each forceful move. His hips frantic, my body arching into his, begging he fulfill my every need and knowing he will.

His mouth, soft and tender, quickly gives into the urges, his arms of steel grasping me closer. "Fuck, I missed you," he rasps just before his mouth finds mine again and he enters me.

High five! He missed me.

I can't speak to respond verbally. I can barely breathe. A week apart and we are right back to where we know, a place and a moment we are comfortable with one another.

"Oh God, Tyler!" I moan when he finds all the same spots he knows so well, like the back of my neck and the spot above my left collarbone. "Don't stop."

With school and missing him, I've been so wound up and this is exactly what I need. Screw the game, I don't want to leave this room.

"Never," he grunts, flipping me over. His large hands cover my own as I dig them into the sheets. His stomach presses to my back, pushing me harder into my mattress. "I'll never stop."

His hands withdraw about the time I'm finding meaning in his words, slowly moving their way over to my hips. His thrusts are dominating, moving me up the bed with each movement.

"Jesus, Raven... fuck...." His grasp tightens. "Tell me I'm the only one, *please*." His voice breaks a little at the end as he nods a couple times. "Tell me you haven't been with anyone else."

What? Why would he ask that?

"I haven't." I moan before finding his lips. "Only you, Tyler."

He pants, nodding against my shoulder, the scruff of his jaw scratching against my back. "Thank fuck," he grunts, pushing harder into me, his hips erratic and just as forceful. His hands wrap under and over the tops of my shoulders, pulling me into him.

Now do I dare ask the same of him? It would kill me if he tells me he went back to her.

"Have you?" I blurt out against the sheets, hoping maybe the fabric muffled my words enough.

His thrusts never let up, his breath pelting my neck as he whispers, "No, *only* you." His mouth is hard against my skin, kissing and biting, so desperate, so possessive I'm light headed.

When he comes, he doesn't stop and I look at him, a smile playing at my lips. "Not done yet?"

"One more...." And he goes for another. One is never enough for him. Last weekend after I watched Nova, we had sex four times on the Sunday before I left. Four! In a matter of two hours. Needless to say, walking was a little difficult Monday morning.

He turns me around so his weight is pressing between my hips. I want it too. I always want more so I wrap my legs around him drawing him in deeper. He groans at the position as his lips finally find mine. Giving me intoxicating kisses, I'm searching for an answer in his, one he won't give. I'm asking what this is with passion-infused kisses. And every time I'm left with the same answer: I'm afraid to let go. If there was anything I was holding onto, just within reach, it's Tyler Hemming.

A moment later the rumble that leaves his heaving chest, the way he throws his head back and the way his arm pins me to the bed, it's worth the whole world to see.

Body trembling, he looks down at me as he shakes, eyes dark as he gazes at me, his brow scrunched in concentration. His breath expels in heavy gasps when he draws his bottom lip in and I know I'm staring at him but I can't stop. He's absolutely beautiful when he fucks me like this.

He hasn't come a second time, yet, so I push him back, my hand on his chest, and kneel in front of him for a moment. Removing the condom, I toss it on the floor next to my bed. Taking him inside my mouth, I taste the latex from the condom but I don't care. I have to have Tyler like this, all of him, in the most intimate way.

Tyler leans forward, his hands on my ass, body slumping against mine as he thrusts his hips into my movements. Moaning, one hand moves from my ass to fist my hair in his hand, and I grab onto his hips, driving him into my mouth as hard as he wants to go. He comes again, just as strong as the first one, hunched over and clinging to me. My mouth fills with the warmth of him a second later, his dick pulsing inside of me. "Fuck... Raven." His words fall away just as quickly as they're spoken. Quickly I peek up at him and his head is thrown back, his muscles flexing and contracting with each heavy breath.

Sadly, there's a twinge of pain in my chest that this might be all I give Tyler. A release. He doesn't give me the forever I so desperately want, but I give what I can and what he needs.

What does he give me?

"I DON'T KNOW about this," Tyler says as we're walking out of my dorm room, swarms of Oregon Duck fans doing the same. He doesn't like crowds. Never has.

"It'll be fun." I loop my arm in his, walking with him to my car.

Tyler laughs before ducking his head a bit to get in my car. "Oh yeah, sure." His blue eyes flash with humor. "I can't believe you convinced me to go to a college football game."

Something swells between us, warm and unfamiliar. The very thought of knowing he's going to the game for me makes me emotional.

Tyler clears his throat, noticing the change. "So do I get to take you back to my place after this?"

"You want to?" I raise an eyebrow in surprise.

"I'm pretty sure you know I do," he says, kissing me briefly again.

I don't know what to say so I go with, "Let's just get through the game."

I can't wait for after the game now!

TYLER AND I make it to the game and by the second quarter I'm convinced I need to take him to every game with me from now on. Between his constant dirty words whispered in my ear to the heckling he gives the refs on the sidelines, it's extremely entertaining.

I also don't miss the way every girl in the student section, bundled up in their Ducks hoodies, stare openly at Tyler and his arm around me.

Be jealous girls. Be extremely fucking jealous because he's mine. Kinda. Sorta. Maybe not really but still, he's here with me.

Tyler gets up to go to the bathroom and I move to stand near the rail. The games getting good, the score tied up at this point and Oregon has the ball on the twenty-yard line.

When Tyler returns, he's smiling and holds up a piece of paper. "That chick gave me her number." He gives a nod to one of the girls in the student section who had been watching him. She's blonde and reminds me of the girl Holden had been with.

"Really?" Who the hell has the balls to give a guy a number when he's clearly with someone?

He nods. "Yeah. When I walked by she stuck it in my pocket."

That's bold. Taking the paper out of his hand, I wad it up and then throw it at the girl hitting her in the back of the head. It's paper. It's not like it makes an impact but she must notice it hit her hair and turns around to glare.

I wave and then grab Tyler by the front of his shirt and draw his lips to mine. I give this kiss intention, meaning, and Tyler does too. I know he does when his arms wrap around my waist and he draws me into his warmth. There's hundreds of people all around us in that moment but I only know what he's giving me. The thrill that shoots through me when his tongue meets mine causes my knees to weaken as I sink into the taste of him.

I know then I'll never tire of kissing Tyler. He's unlike anyone I've ever met so naturally kissing him would be an entirely different experience, right? He has this way about his kisses that shake you, take away every other thought you have except for his lips and tongue on yours. I feel it in my spine, between my legs and I know he feels it too when he makes almost a growling sound in his throat and deepens the kiss despite the world around us.

Cheering around us, a touchdown scored, brings me back and I pull away from him. Tyler's body shifts as he makes a sound I know means he's smiling.

My cheeks heat. I'm almost embarrassed I just did that. "What?"

His long fingers trace idle patterns along my back, his eyes on mine. "I'm not complaining, but what was that about?"

"I have no idea. I guess I have a jealous side when it comes to average looking blondes."

Tyler utters a short laugh. Slowly, his hand eases from my back along the dip in my side and he squeezes, once. "Well, you won't hear me complaining."

I guess not.

What the hell is wrong with me?

TYLER AND I are intently watching the game, the final five minutes of the third quarter approaching when I notice Holden walking toward us. Last year I remember cheering for him from this very spot. Now I just want to hurl his body over the rail. "Wow, did hell freeze over? What brought you to a game?" he asks, smiling at me as if I should be happy to see him.

"Thought I'd get in the team spirit," I tell him, huddling into my coat. It's fucking cold today and I wish like hell Tyler would wrap his arm around me again, but he doesn't. We're standing near the rail, the team just below us along with about a hundred other college students chanting "Go Ducks!" at the tops of their lungs.

It's hard to hear much else but I do hear when Holden talks to Tyler.

"You don't have anything better to do today?" Holden asks him. I can already tell he's had way too much to drink. Holden isn't exactly the best drunk, but neither is Tyler, who's holding a beer in his hand too.

Tyler's brow lifts a little and it seems he's struggling not to punch Holden. He then moves his eyes back to the game, leaning into the rail, closes his eyes, giving his head a sharp shake. "Yeah, well, someone's gotta watch out for Raven since you can't," he says to Holden; the lines around his mouth are tight. His eyes shift to mine and stay there.

Crap.

Holden becomes defensive, scowling at me, and then Tyler. "Who the fuck do you think you are accusing me of not looking out for her?" he asks, stepping toward Tyler with a new confidence. I'm in between them, and then suddenly I'm not. I'm pushed aside by the two of them, maybe intentionally.

Tyler laughs softly setting his beer down on the ground. Standing, he runs his hand through his hair, and I know where this is heading. His jaw twitches, and he doesn't back down to Holden. I've never seen him back down to anyone, not even Red. "If you were looking out for her, why did I get a call to pick her up at one in the morning because you fucking got her drunk and left her?" There's an arrogant edge to his voice, relatively civil despite the murderous expression he's holding onto.

Oh God, I know where this is going. Shit.

Holden lets out a disbelieving laugh, looking at me with his next comment. "Dude, I get it. It's cool. I know what it's like to have her moan your name while your dick's in her mouth."

How is that possible if your mouth is full of dick?

I give Holden a what the fuck look but then I watch Tyler.

Tyler freezes when the words hit him. His jaw twitches, unstable breaths attempt to calm himself down, but there's no use. Not now. His stare sweeps to Holden.

Tyler lunges for him at the comment and it becomes a frenzy of fists and elbows and I'm not even sure who's hitting who at one point.

"Tyler!" I shout, pushing him back away from Holden though I know it's stupid to wedge myself between two men throwing punches. "Knock it off. Stop!" I scream at the two of them when a security guard gets in between them.

Tyler and my stares meet for a split second, a fiery angry look I've never seen before flashing in his. Stepping around me, his glare returns to Holden. "Don't you ever fucking talk about her like that again!" And then he's right back in Holden's face.

Holden shoves back, hard. "Fuck you! She was my girlfriend for four fucking years!"

People begin to stare, their eyes wide in disbelief when Tyler hits Holden again, this time landing a right hook on his jaw that makes me cringe with the sound it makes.

Given we're in the middle of the stadium, they're pushed apart by security guards and we're told to leave, along with Holden, but pushed different directions.

Wiping blood from his lip with the back of his hand, Tyler's eyes meet mine but there's no emotion, at least none I can make out.

I still haven't caught my breath once we're in the parking lot and Tyler's stalking through, no mind to anyone around him. He's bumping into people, his intent on getting away from the stadium, maybe even me.

He doesn't speak to me the entire way back to my dorm.

When we're in the car just outside my dorm, he finally talks to me and I kinda wish he wouldn't have.

He's looking at me with a hardened face and vacant eyes. "I didn't want this. This is exactly the fucking drama I didn't want. I got enough shit in my life."

My pulse races, pounding in my ears with each word. "I didn't know Holden was going to be there."

"It doesn't matter," he says immediately. "I've got no place in my life for this shit. I'm twenty-six. I don't need this."

I'm never more aware of my age than I am right now. My eyes squeeze shut and I know he sees the pain those words give me before I deny him the sight. "Why are you always reminding me of your age? I don't want this shit either but welcome to my life." I flip my hand up and then flop it down on the steering wheel. Still sitting in the parking lot, there's drops of water hitting the windshield now. "I'm so sorry being in my life is so unbearable for you."

He swallows heavily, his eyes full of hurt. "Have you been with him? Since we started… have you been with Holden?"

I'm surprised he's asked and I'm not sure how to answer it. Moments pass, and he presses again. "*Have* you?"

"I can't believe you'd even ask me that. I told you earlier this morning I haven't been with anyone."

His eyes pierce through the car, steady on mine. The heavy thudding in my ears drowns out the rain hitting the top of my car, each pop more distinct than the last and fogging up my windows. "Just answer the question. Are you fucking him?"

"I'm *not* and I just… I can't believe you'd ask that, *Tyler.*"

"Kinda like *you* doubting me with Berkley?"

My mind scrambles to provide some sort of justification to the words, but it won't do anything. It won't mean anything. He's made it pretty clear to me.

He blows out a breath, as if the next part is painful for him to say. "I don't want to be this guy," he tells me, suddenly seeming angry, or at least angrier. He brings his hand up and covers his mouth, air rushing through his fingers when he releases the breath.

I flinch at his words, having never been on the receiving end of his anger before. At least not like this.

His posture stiffens. "I thought you knew how I felt, regardless of what was said. I don't want to be this guy sitting around all week wondering if the girl he's having sex with is fucking someone else."

I'm shocked by his words. I didn't think he cared for one.

Tears begin to stream down my cheeks. "Then don't be him."

Tyler's hand cups my cheek but he doesn't say anything. The guarded side takes over, and I know my next set of words have the possibility to end this, or see where it goes with us.

"Tyler, what is this about? This isn't like you. I don't understand what's happening between us. One minute we're cool and the next we're arguing. I'm tired of it. Just be honest with me, what do you want from me? Because if it's just sex, you have no right to be acting like this." With every word, my legs shake in the seat and it's a good damn thing I'm sitting down because if I had been standing, I would have fallen.

He's quiet for a long time, longer than I would expect. Sighing, he rests his right arm against the window sill in the car, running his hand through his hair. "Nothing. I'm just overreacting." His voice is low but I know I heard him right. I just don't understand why he's acting like this.

He turns to look at me, pain evident in his features by the tightening of his jaw and the pull of his brow. "I should go."

"Tyler." I reach for him, my hand on his arm as he's getting out of the car. "Don't you fucking dare get out of this car after acting like this," I warn, my glare so focused on him I could have burned a hole in him. "Get back here and explain. You *will not* treat me like I'm your fucking doormat. Talk to me. Tell me what's bothering you and let me help you through it."

He doesn't listen to me, the slamming of the door just as harsh as his words.

Scrambling to get out, I run after him as he stalks to his truck, my feet splashing in puddles as I do so.

"*Don't*, Raven."

He's warning me but I'm not listening.

"Tyler, please don't leave like this." I'm pleading and I know I sound desperate, but it doesn't matter. I don't want him leaving like this.

He stops, turning to face me. I stop, too, because the anger in his eyes makes me. Icy-blue eyes pin me in the moment. "You don't get it. You're *twenty* years old and you shouldn't have to deal with this." His voice breaks and I'm left wondering what the hell he's talking about.

"Understand what?"

He doesn't say anything. Nothing. And then he begins to walk away and I watch him, rain pelting my face, blurring my vision of him walking away from me.

As though he knows he's made a mistake, he pauses, hesitation in his step and turns to face me wearing the same expression he wore in the car... sadness... confliction... I can't place it.

He jogs back to me, rain blurring our vision but his eyes are alive with regret. Crying, I wrap my arms around his neck tightly. He pulls me snug against his chest. His strong arms wind around me, pressing his face against my neck.

His lips brush across my skin as he speaks softly, "I'm sorry. I shouldn't have yelled at you." The low resonance of his voice sends shivers down my spine.

"Tyler, just tell me what's going on with you." Raising my hand up, I touch the side of his wet face, my other hand wrapping around his neck.

He takes my hand in his and kisses my palm after pulling it away from his face. "I don't even know what's going on with me anymore."

Taking in his words, I'm not sure what to say to him when he pulls away further but stares at me.

My heart is beating so loud I fear he can hear it. Slowly, I reach out and wipe a drop of water from his nose. His eyes close tight, a sigh leaving him, and he bites the corner of his lower lip. "It's not you though."

My hand drops away and I take a step back. "Okay."

For a moment, we simply stare at each other. I'm not sure what to say either. I want to know what's going on with him but if he's not ready to tell me, or can't, what am I supposed to do? Maybe it's something Holden said, or maybe it's my college drama he can't handle.

"I'm gonna go," he says, nodding to his truck, rain drops dripping from his hair.

I nod, unable to say anything else.

I know Tyler well enough to know he's not going to tell me. Not now.

Tyler
chapter 13
OUTSIDE

FUCK, I'M THE biggest piece of shit around. I can't believe I said those things to her. I had no right to treat her the way I did.

I hated this. Being an asshole wasn't working out for me.

For a while, pretending as though I didn't care and acting like I'm a cold-hearted prick worked, but I never wanted to hurt Raven.

Watching from my truck as she walks through puddles back to her dorm room, my mind scrambles with apologies I should have said to her, or need to say. Mostly because of fucking Holden and one of the many reasons why I hate him so much is because he can give her a life I can't. That's exactly what it comes to. Plain and simple.

I send her a message when I make it home.

Me: I hope you believed me when I said it but I'm sorry I reacted like that.

I hope she'll reply but I know she won't. I keep overreacting, which is the norm for me. I react and then have to clean up my messes. It's not a good trait to have, but I'm stuck with it.

I'm not really sure what to do with myself when I get back to Lebanon, mostly because it's a Saturday night and I wanted to be spending it with Raven, not here, alone in my apartment.

Just when I'm thinking of breaking out the whiskey, I get a text from Red.

Red: Wanna go to Murphy's with Lenny and me?

That sounds way better than drinking by myself. Mostly because I do really stupid shit when I drink alone. Like shopping at Bath and Body Works.

Me: Sure. Meet you there.

I'm actually surprised he asked, and that's part of the reason I get up off the couch and go to the bar. Maybe it'll get me out of my funk.

SOMETIMES WHEN I walk into Murphy's, I have flashbacks from the night Raven and I were here. They're good flashbacks but it makes me wish my situation was different.

I'll never forget that night and what she did for me by just being Raven.

Walking through the doors, I see Lenny and Red at a table to the left of the bar. Red nods to me holding up a glass of beer and I walk over to them. There's a pitcher of beer on the table and an extra glass.

178

"Hey!" Lenny yells over the music, smiling at me. She knows I went to the game today and I mentally count down the seconds before she's going to ask me how it went. "Did you have fun today?" And then she sees my lip and cheek. "Oh."

I chuckle, peeling off my jacket to sit across from them, slouching. I'm actually a little sore. Fucker got me in the ribs with his knee somehow. "I met Holden again," I tell them with a smile, one that cracks my lip a little more. Immediately I taste blood.

Red laughs, shifting his weight to lean into Lenny. "Told you."

Lenny rolls her eyes, pushing him back a few inches with her hands gently on his chest. She's still mindful of his injury. I think she always will after what we saw that night.

"Told you what?" I raise an eyebrow.

"I figured Holden would be there and you two would get into it." Red pushes a glass my way. "I'm right once again."

Taking the glass, I pour myself a beer. "Yeah, well, he's a fuckin' pussy."

We relax into steady conversation about the shop and cars we've been working on for the last couple of weeks. I've got a Ford in my stall with a blown head gasket. I've been waiting on parts and Red tells me they're finally in.

Three beers in, we're laughing and joking as we always do. It's nice to know what happened with Raven and me didn't ruin my friendship with Red.

Rawley's on stage and they're just starting their set when Berkley walks in and takes a seat at a table with three guys. Rolling my eyes when she smiles at me, I try not to pay any attention to her, but I'm a little curious what's going to happen with her here, and Rawley on stage.

Berkley no sooner takes a seat when Rawley stops the song he's singing and breaks into Buckcherry's "Crazy Bitch" and moves to stand near her table.

Shaking my head, I watch Berkley's reaction to it. I don't think she's paying any attention, her hand raising to tuck her black hair behind her ear.

It's when the music fades, he drops to his knees in front of her and repeats "crazy bitch" three or four times that she's finally looking right at him.

She flips him off, glaring and then turns her gaze to me briefly, after tossing her friend's flannel shirt at him.

I smile. I've already had something like four beers and I'm sorry, but it's entertaining that she's sucking his dick yet he's calling her crazy. They're both crazy if you ask me.

Just like I expected him to do, Rawley takes the shirt she threw at him, puts it down his pants and then throws it at her face.

Chuckling, I turn to Red and Lenny, his arm around her as they both sip their beer. "Where's Nova tonight?"

"Ma has her," Red says, giving a nod to the stage. "What the fuck is he doing?"

I don't want to look but I do to see Rawley now shirtless, his half naked body being whistled at by the twenty-some girls, acting as if he's a god up there. He's good, I'll give him that but he's turned into an ass since he turned eighteen. Probably around the same time his girl fucked him over too. I'm telling you, women, they have a way of destroying everything sometimes.

Rawley used to be a good kid. He was an *amazing* quarterback, could have gone to any college he wanted but he threw it all away his senior year and it's been a downhill slide since then. Music has always been his passion. I can't ever remember a time when he didn't have a guitar nearby but still, he's throwing away a lot these days.

"He's just having fun," Lenny tells Red, smiling. "He puts on a good show."

Red raises an eyebrow at her and then flicks his hand at the stage. "You gonna go throw your panties on the stage too?"

She scowls at him, her hand on his thigh raising higher and causing him to squirm in the seat. "No, but I'm going to shove my panties in your mouth if you keep being an ass tonight."

Red buries his head in Lenny's neck, whispering to her and I turn away. It makes me miss Raven and that's the last thing I need to see. Mostly because I'm thinking about Thanksgiving when Raven shoved her panties in my mouth.

I miss her. I'd be stupid if I said I didn't. Every time I see her, she lifts the weight the world is putting upon me.

Whether I like it or not, the shell I put around myself cracks every time I see her, breaking away piece by piece. I know I'm being a fucking dick to her half the time but I just can't get over that I can't give her what she needs. Maybe that's why I keep torturing myself with her. I can't give it up either.

I'M DRAGGING ASS Monday morning. It's all I can do to actually make it downstairs by eight.

Red hands me a repair order for a Dodge Durango in my stall as I'm stirring my cup of coffee. "What's wrong with you?"

Drawing in a deep breath, I set the repair order on my toolbox. "Rough night." I hate being hungover. I welcome the numbness, but the hangovers, I can go without. So it surprises me that I've been drinking so much lately.

Truth is, after I left the bar with them, I finished off a bottle of whiskey on Sunday. In my head, it was better to be drunk than deal with my own shit.

He shrugs and makes his way toward Lenny, hip checking her and handing her a repair order of her own. She laughs and takes it from him.

The morning starts off slow. I spend most of my time doing an alignment on the Durango and then timing chain on a van.

Nova stops by with Mia at lunch time. I guess she had a field trip this morning and worked her way out of not going back to school for the rest of the day. Red's definitely going to have his hands full with her. She's only in kindergarten and already looking for ways to get out of going every day.

"Uncle Ty!" She runs up to me immediately hugging my legs.

I look down and smile as I lift her up and set her on my tool box. "Hey princess. How was your—"

"I'm not here to talk about stupid school." She points to the van in my stall. "What are you working on?"

"Timing chain."

She leans to the side to peek around me at the van, her brow scrunched in concentration and then hands me a torque wrench next to her. "Here. This should fix it."

Her face is beaming and I can see that she believes she's solved my problem. So proud of herself for helping.

I laugh and when she joins me, it's the sound of her laughter that sends a punch to my chest, so potent I almost hear the shards of it clatter against my ribs. I stop and look at her and I see so much of both Red and Nevaeh in this little girl.

This is what I struggle with. This right here is why I push Raven away. I will *never* have this moment. Standing at work, laughing with my son or daughter while I look at their laughing face and see my eyes and Raven's smile.

How can I ask her for forever when I can't even give her something as simple as having our own child visit me at work?

BY LUNCH TIME, I'm eating a burger on a crate and staring at my cell phone. The bay doors are open to the crisp afternoon and it's actually nice out. The sun's shining, it's beautiful but the wind is cool. I want to kick the leaves blowing inside the shop away because it makes me think of Raven and her brown eyes.

Scrolling through Facebook, I check her page to see if she's posted anything this weekend. I stalk her on social media when I don't have the balls to send her a message. She hasn't posted anything since last week and even then, it was just her complaining about needing caffeine before her class. I even scroll through the comments from her friends at school to see if any are guys. None seem to be but you can never tell these days. I eye the one from Taylor Hunt. He seems harmless but I don't like his comment of: *Help me study and I'll bring you some.*

It's followed by a wink.

What a fucking loser.

I don't bother clicking on his profile because I know it's going to piss me off.

Setting my phone aside on my toolbox, Daniel sits next to me, an energy drink in his hand. He gives a nod to Red, who's in the parking lot talking to Amber, the chick with the Lexus who thinks Red's her own personal mechanic and will drop everything when she shows up. When he first took over ownership of the shop, he used to cater to customers, but he's been holding back lately and making them actually schedule appointments.

This naturally pisses Amber off because who wouldn't give her everything she wants? Her husband owns half the goddamn town.

"What I wouldn't give to get a hold of her carburetor," Daniel says, pointing to the lady standing next to Amber with the skin-tight jeans on. She looks like she's fucking forty years old.

I shake my head, kinda disgusted with him. "I bet." I don't even know why I'm surprised by his comment either. Daniel pops off with some of the most random shit.

Daniel eyes me seriously. "No really. Her car runs like shit."

I let out a laugh knowing he's lying. "Dude, she's like forty. You're twenty. You don't find that weird at all?"

I know where he's going with his next comment before he makes it. "Raven's six years younger than you."

He leaves his remark at that. Stupid move on his part.

Standing, I toss my burger in the garbage and knock his drink out of his hand. It goes flying right into Rawley who's lying on the ground for God knows what reason.

Whoops.

Rawley grabs the side of his head. "You fuckin' asshole, knock it off."

"Shut up," I grumble, walking away toward the bathrooms. It's then I see Red walking back into the shop, heading for Lenny, who's face is red with either anger or embarrassment.

"You need to fix this, Red," Amber yells after him, following him inside the shop. "My check engine light is on."

Red ignores her, his gaze on Lenny as he whispers in her ear something only she can hear. She seems relieved by it, but still, something is bothering her.

I stop and wait, wondering if she needs anything. She won't look at me and pushes past me inside the bathroom, looking like she's going to burst into tears.

"Find someone else," he barks over his shoulder, slamming his hip into the drawer to close it. "We're not doing it."

Amber places her hands on her hips. She's used to getting what she wants by this move right here, guaranteed. "So you're not going to fix what your little bitch over there broke?"

Whoa. I can't believe she said that to him.

"Nope." Red shakes his head. "You *never* treat my employees like that. She left a fucking vacuum hose loose. It wasn't that big of a deal. Take it up to Portland where you should be taking this car and they'll fix it. I'll refund your money for the valve cover gasket." Red glares, a sweeping glance right past her as he points outside. "Get the fuck out."

Amber doesn't stop there and stands her ground, heaving in a heavy breath. "Okay, so because you're sleeping with her you're going to let this place go to shit? You do *realize* who my husband is, right? I can have this entire shop shutdown. You're actually willing to lose it all for her?"

Lenny's returned from the bathroom, just behind me when Red takes the hammer on the top of his toolbox, he picks it up and tosses it at the wall. Amber jumps, as does Lenny when it crashes to the ground. "I'd burn this motherfucking place to the ground for *her*. So yeah, go tell your fucking husband what a no good piece of shit I am because I refuse to work on your car after you called my girlfriend a bitch to her face and accused her of breaking your car because she's jealous she'd never be able to afford it!"

I'm actually shocked myself Amber said that to Lenny. But then again, I'm not. Turning around, I look at Lenny and I can tell right then it's not what Amber said, it's the fact she fucked up on a car. It doesn't happen often but it happens to even the best mechanics. We've all done it. Only Lenny's way harder on herself then any man would be because she thinks she has to prove herself constantly.

"You okay?" Red asks Lenny when Amber leaves, the tires of her Lexus squealing through the parking lot.

He's pulling her in his arms, trying to wrap his arms around her when she stops him. "I'm fine, Red. You should have let me fix that. All I had to do was tighten the vacuum hose."

He takes a step back and then picks up the hammer he threw, tossing it on top of his toolbox. "She wasn't going to let you fix it. She just came back here to treat you like shit because I won't fuck her." He gives a careless shrug, seeming unbothered by it. "So don't worry about it."

"She's never going to come back here. Why would you do that?"

Red moves toward her again and takes her face in his hands. "I want loyal customers not ones who are looking to break this place apart."

I know what he means and I hope Lenny does too. This place was Lyric's. To understand him, all you had to do was step foot inside those bay doors and know him. His blood, sweat and tears went into running Walker Automotive and it was built on principals and good business. He did things right and never let customers walk all over him. If he didn't want to work on your car because you were a shady piece of shit, he didn't.

Red didn't always see it that way. He looked at it as a business and one he needed to keep afloat. So he took anything people came by with, even if they were only showing up for him. Like in Amber's case.

Since he was shot, his outlook on life and the way he runs Walker Automotive is slowly becoming more of Lyric's way of doing business. Can't say I don't appreciate it because I absolutely loved working for Lyric, and enjoy working for Red too, now that he's not giving me all the shit jobs.

THE ATMOSPHERE IN the shop calms down since everyone's gone home for the night. It's not unusual for me to work late and close up the shop for Red. Mostly because I live upstairs and it's easy for me to do it. I also get more done at night than I do with Daniel working right beside me. I'm sure you can understand why.

I'm still working on a van, a beer in one hand as I ask the engine why it's leaking oil. I have a tendency to talk to vehicles. If only they answered me. It'd make my job a lot easier.

As I'm having a conversation with the van, I hear gravel crunching and dust rising up from the parking lot.

It's Berkley. She's been texting me for a goddamn week and apparently ignoring her texts isn't working. She's another one like Amber, and I'm sure in some way they must be related. Either that or they're taking pointers from one another.

First thing she does when she walks over to me is touch my tools on my tool cart. I do not like anyone touching my tools. It's just one of those things. I have them where I want them and I don't need someone fucking with them.

"Don't touch that." I rip the screwdriver in her hand away and toss it back on the tool cart.

"Geez, you're testy today."

"What are you even doing here? We're closed."

Berkley shrugs. "Saw the doors open and you were here. Thought I could catch you alone."

Downing the rest of my beer, I point to the van. "I'm not alone. There's a van here needing my attention."

UNBEARABLE the TORQUED trilogy

"Can you just fix my brakes, please?" She gives a flip of her hand over her shoulder at her Honda Civic parked in front of my open bay door. "I don't have anyone else to work on my car."

Tossing my empty beer away, I consider it only because maybe she'll stop showing up if I do. Maybe I can finally get her out of my life. Not likely but I can at least try. "I'll do it this one time but stop coming by here. You need to find a new mechanic."

She gives me pouty lips that never work. "You've always worked on my car."

"I can't do it anymore. This is the last time." Letting the van down from the lift, I give a nod. "Move your car so I can pull this one out." I still haven't found the leak but she won't leave so it's better I get this out of the way.

When the van's on the ground, I kick the arms of the lift out of the way so I can back it up. I don't say anything to her for five minutes and she's handing me her keys. "Give me an hour and it'll be done."

Berkley's eyes drop to our hands when she drops the key in my palm. "I don't have anywhere to go. Can I just watch?"

She doesn't want to watch. She wants to try to get me to reconsider.

"Whatever, but no talking." My shoulder bumps hers as I walk by and open the door to her car. It smells like her, lilies and fruit. It's some kind of body spray she wears and I remember loving it when we were together. Now I hate it. I even went to Bath and Body Works after we broke up and asked them to stop selling it.

Imagine their expression. It was one of shock that I would do such a thing but I was also fairly drunk. I proceeded to spend $300 and bought the entire stock they had and then dumped every bottle out.

It made me feel better for about an hour.

When I have the car inside on the lift, Berkley won't stop talking and I'm regretting telling her she could stay. Another thing I hate, besides people touching my tools, is Berkley's endless chatter about nothing. As shitty as it sounds, I get why Rawley jokes that he only gets blow jobs from her. She talks too fucking much. If your dick's in her mouth, at least she can't talk.

I used to think her talking was cute but then it just got on my nerves.

Like now.

Why couldn't she just listen when I told her not to talk?

"Listen." I take the used brake pad in my hand, warning her. "You *have* to stop talking or I'm going to throw this at you."

I wouldn't. I'm not that much of a dick, but she laughs it off as if it meant nothing and continues. For an entire hour. Couldn't tell you anything she said either.

She did need rear brakes and luckily we had some in the back for her car. It takes me another thirty minutes to get both the rear brakes changed and I'm lowering the car down from the lift.

I hand her keys back to her. "You really do need to find someone else to work on your car. It's for the best." We're standing close, about a foot apart and I can smell that body spray. Instantly I'm reminded of our breakup and why she left. I'm also reminded of the fact she cheated on me.

Berkley licks her lips and my gaze follows. I don't know why, but it does. Sensing her opportunity, she places her hand on my chest. "How much do I owe you?"

It's not that I want to do *anything* for free for her, mostly because I still owe so much on that fucking credit card and she should be paying that motherfucker off. But if I do this, maybe she'll leave and stay out of my life. Maybe. So I try it out and tell her, "It's on me."

"I'll pay you," she breathes out, suggestively. I know exactly what kind of paying she has in mind. Before I can step back, she leans in and kisses me.

I react immediately.

"Leave," I tell her, twisting my head away so she can't do it again. My stomach lurches at the thought of her lips on mine. Mostly because I'm immediately reminded of the fact that she's not Raven.

She doesn't lower her hands so I take them from my chest, gathering them in one of mine and letting them fall at her side.

She smiles. She thinks that'll work.

Raising my hand to her hair, I take a fistful of her hair.

"I like that," she breaths, slouching toward me. "You know how rough I like it."

I pull tighter to the point she winces. "I said leave. This isn't happening between us."

"Why?"

"You know why."

Her brow knits as she searches my face for the answer. She's playing dumb but deep down, she has to fucking know *where* she went wrong. She knows.

Swallowing hard, I step away, creating distance, my back hitting the edge of my toolbox. Maybe then she'll see it as my shoulders sag on a sigh and I nod my chin in the direction of the door. "I don't want you here."

I don't care that my words will hurt her. I want her to feel the pain I had when I realized I wasn't the father of the baby we lost. I want that devastating reality crashing on her.

"It's really over between us, isn't it?"

Closing my eyes, I pinch the bridge of my nose as I talk. "It is."

"Seriously?"

I don't understand why she doesn't get it. "Yes. Go home."

She chews on her bottom lip, playing with her keys in her hand as she steps back. "If I leave, that's it. I'm not coming back again."

Our gaze meets. I'm hoping she finally sees it was over for me a long time ago. I made the mistake of sleeping with her a couple weeks after we broke up and I think she thought I'd always be there if she needed some. I'm not *that guy*, which is why it only happened once. Hypercritical of me considering my relationship with Raven? Yeah. Probably.

"That's exactly what I want," I tell her.

There's hurt in her expression, a deep hurt because she knows it's finally over. It's been over for a while but she's finally fucking getting it for once. "I can't believe you're ending us like this."

"No." I shake my head adamantly. "*You* ended us. *You* did that. I'm just sticking to the new plan."

"With everything we've been through, I can't believe you're going to walk away from our history."

I lose all dignity and control I have. "You fucking *cheated* on me, Berkley! You told me you were pregnant with my baby."

That same shocked expression she wore in the bar that night I hinted at this marks her face. "It was your baby."

"See, that's how I know you're lying." I wait for her eyes to meet mine. When they do, I can't help the sarcastic smile. "I *can't* have kids."

"What?"

Resentment punches my chest. "I. Can't. Have. Kids. The medication I'm on made me sterile when I was a kid. Don't blame me for ending us. You did that."

For a moment, she's speechless. It's a goddamn miracle.

"Nothing to say now? I guess being called out on what a lying bitch you are is the only thing that can make you fucking speechless. I'll have to remember that one." Her breath hitches and for a moment, I think I might need to stop, but no, that's not fair to me.

Never once has she considered me in any of this. She's always made the decision and I let her, not anymore. "Maybe I'll pass it along to Rawley?"

I've never seen such agony on her face as I do right then. I hurt her bad with that one. She blinks three times, my words hitting her heart. "Fuck you, Tyler."

She walks away from me, leaving me standing alone in the shop like I wanted.

chapter 14
ROCK BOTTOM

"FUCK," I CURSE, wiping blood off the repair order on my toolbox.

It's Tuesday afternoon and we're swamped, my hands bleeding from the cuts on my knuckles and fingers. You'd be amazed how many sharp parts are under the dashboards of cars and seats. I just fixed a seat where the wiring control went out so it was stuck in the recline position. I had to laugh when I was fixing it because there's only one reason why cars come in with the passenger seat reclined all the way and it's a teenage boy who's brought it in hoping his dad doesn't find out he took his Mustang for a ride with his girlfriend.

Cars are lined up down the street and we're running our asses off trying to catch up. Being the second week in December, it snowed last night leaving the town in about two inches of fresh white powder, which means everyone wants studded tires and their brakes checked.

This morning would have gone easier if Rawley was actually here like he's supposed to be but no, like usual, he shows up at noon.

After Red was shot, he improved for a while but something happened lately and he's fallen off the moral wagon again.

"So man, think Lyric would be proud of the way you're acting these days?" I ask after Rawley throws up in a garbage can next to my toolbox. It fucking stinks and I'm pissed he used *my* garbage can.

Rawley glares, his eyes on the car in front of us and I step away from my garbage can. "Don't fucking act like you're better than me and don't talk about my dad like you'd know if he was proud or not."

We're about ten feet away from one another, a car separating us when I ask, "Why? Does it bother you to know you're a fuckin' disappointment?"

"You know, I've been meaning to ask you, how's my sister?" He looks up at me, smiling. "Break her heart again yet?" Rawley asks. There's laughter behind Rawley's words and it makes me see red. I'm not in the mood for this shit.

"You have no idea what you're talking about." I drop the impact gun in my hand on my tool cart, the thud echoing through the shop causing both Red and Lenny to turn toward us.

"Yeah, sure." Rawley laughs; it's condescending.

"You sure you want to do this right now, Rawley?" I ask, stepping around the car and toward him. "You sure you want to have this conversation, here, right now in front of your brother?"

There's certainly no hesitation in his stare but his words are so far wrong he has no idea anymore. "He doesn't give a shit about me so what does it matter?"

Red does care about him and it pisses me off that he can't see it. I shove him roughly against the wall. "Stop blaming him for your problems."

"Why don't we talk about your problems, *Tyler*." His arms catch him against the toolbox, metal rattling as he eyes me carefully. The smile's finally gone. "You used my sister. Admit it."

194

I admire his bluntness and fight off a smile. There's nothing funny about it but I smile. Maybe that's why he smiled. I'm shaking my head as he watches me—testing and provoking—because he knows I'm going to defend myself. It's only natural. "I love your sister."

Forget the fact that I said I love Raven to him, or everyone else standing around, what I'm focused on is his reaction, *why* he really hates me so much.

"Sure you do. You love her sucking your dick and spreading her legs for you," he taunts.

"That's enough!" Red shouts, his hands on both of our chests. Sure, Red's bigger than I am but I don't even acknowledge him then and lean into his hold, unwilling to let this go.

Rawley's eyes scan my face as if he's studying me. I don't like where this is going and he doesn't either. "I see you've moved back onto Berkley now too. I can't say I blame you, she's a pretty good piece of ass."

"Listen to me, you stupid little shit!" I reach around Red and grab him by his shirt, slamming him up against my toolbox, tools and parts rattling with the motion. "You know *nothing* about what happened between Raven and me. Nothing. Or with Berkley. Just because she's sucking your dick behind the stage after your concerts in a fuckin' bar doesn't meant shit. I *guarantee* you she doesn't remember your dick from any other guy and she'll move on like she did with me, so keep your fucking mouth shut!"

"Her mouth is all I need. It's all she's good for." And he's laughing.

The motherfucker is laughing.

I shouldn't care because Berkley doesn't mean anything to me anymore. It's done between us but the fact that he's standing here provoking me, making me think he's a piece of shit using women, yeah, that bothers me because he seems to have the same mentality as Holden. It's pussy and nothing else matters. Immediately I think of Raven and the fucking shit she's around in college and I see nothing but the anger and resentment for my situation.

Shoving Red aside, I slam my shoulder into Rawley, connecting with his stomach. Our bodies slam against the ground, his head knocking back against the lift when I do so.

Both Lenny and Red are yelling at us to stop but I'm so pissed I can't even think straight. I want to kill him for the things he's saying. He's been like my little brother for years but I want to teach him a goddamn lesson.

Rawley throws his body weight into his punches, a few landing on my jaw, a couple on my cheek with such force blood pools in my mouth. Pain erupts on impact, my own hits landing when I get him off me. There's a blunt crack when I break his nose, crimson leaking from both his nostrils and his nose twisted to the right. He draws his fist back again and nails me in the stomach. It takes my breath for a moment only to have Red yanking at my shoulders.

Neither one of us stop until I can barely put any weight into my punches and everyone is screaming at us.

Red ends up tackling me when blood is pouring from the side of Rawley's head.

"Colt! Help me!" he screams when he's struggling to hold me down.

Colt rolls his eyes, tossing a twenty on the floor where he's standing with Daniel, both smiling. "Nah, twenty says Tyler pulls this one off."

"You useless piece of shit," Red grumbles and then turns his attention to me. "Knock it off!"

I push him back, the adrenaline feeding my strength and I easily knock him aside. I want back at Rawley. He spits blood on the concrete floor. "That's all you got?" he taunts, standing now.

I do the same only to have Red pin me to the wall, his forearm pressing into my throat. "Get the fuck off me!" I shove him back.

He stumbles and comes back at me just as strong. "*No.* What's going on?"

My wild eyes dart around the shop, never landing on anyone. My heart pumps so loud I can hear it in my ears. My body shakes as I say, "Why don't you ask your fucking brother and his big fucking mouth what's wrong."

I can hear Rawley popping off with shit, kicking tools and yelling at me.

"I'm not asking him. I'm asking you what's going on."

There's a crash behind me. Rawley's kicked over my tool cart. Red twists, his attention on the noise when Rawley takes the tool cart, picks it up over his head and throws it. It lands on the windshield of a customer's car.

Dead silence follows and we all look to Red.

"What the fuck?" Red screams, his blistering voice echoing throughout the shop. You could have heard that across the street. I've never seen Red so pissed in my life as he steps toward Rawley. "You stupid son of a bitch! Why would you do that?"

Rawley spits blood at him throwing his hands up in the air to flip his brother, or me, off. "Fuck you! I quit."

"HOLY HELL WHAT was that?" Lenny asks, stepping inside my apartment, her eyes wide and voice a tad frantic.

"Get out, Lenny, just fucking go," I grumble, opening the freezer to look for an ice pack. My left eye is already swelling shut. I'll hand

UNBEARABLE the TORQUED trilogy

it to Rawley, he can most certainly throw a punch. Or twelve. "I don't want to be around anybody right now.

She crosses her arms over her chest. I glance at her standing in my kitchen. She's trying to be nice and give me someone to vent to. "I'm not leaving until you tell me what's going on."

"I'm not asking, I'm telling you." I slam the freezer. "Get the fuck out."

My harsh words do nothing. She plops herself on the couch in the living room. "Nope. Not happening. Talk to me."

"I'm not talking to you."

"I got all night," she warns, putting her feet up on the coffee table.

Grabbing the new bottle of whiskey I bought last night, I sit down at the table with a wet towel.

Lenny stands, walks into my kitchen and opens the freezer and takes out the ice pack I never got out. Sitting down next to me, she pushes it toward me. "Put that on your face. You look horrible."

For ten minutes, I drink about six shots and clean my bloody face off. All the while, Lenny doesn't leave. Instead, I assume she sends a text to Red because I see his picture pop up on her screen several times.

"Did you know you're like the brother I never had?" she asks on minute eleven.

I don't say anything at all. I don't even look at her and do another shot.

"When I called you, crying, on my own, you didn't hesitate to help me."

Another shot.

"I'm not walking away from you because something huge is happening with you and you need someone who's not going to judge you."

Two more shots. Swallowing over the burn, I slouch in the chair, my body and face so sore every expression hurts.

"I can sit here all night," she repeats.

Around the time I can't feel my face any longer, I begin talking, my voice so low I know she has to struggle to hear me. With my stare on my blood-soaked knuckles, I twist the cap to the whiskey in my hand. "I'm gonna tell you a story." She nods so I continue, "There was this guy once… he was out partying with his friends when he meets this girl. Fucking beautiful girl with long legs, flawless tan skin and jet-black hair. She was the bartender and you know women bartenders, they flirt their way to tips. He didn't think much of it, or her flirting until he met her again six months later when she brought her car by to get fixed. Being a bartender in a small town, she couldn't afford a new engine in the car so the guy, the one from the bar, offered to fix it for free if she let him take her out. She agreed and five years later, they moved in together. He thought what they had was real.

"One day, she gets pregnant, and they're happy, or so he thought." I sit forward again, taking one more shot, flinching at the burn it leaves on my open lip. "I mean"—I wipe my mouth once more with the towel when I taste blood, ignoring my ringing phone in my pocket—"he was in love with her, of course he wanted to start a family with her. And then she lost the baby, miscarried. To make her feel better, and knowing he wants to spend the rest of his life with her, he buys a ring. He goes over what he wants to say for days and when he's ready to do it, he comes home from work to find that she's moved out. No reasoning. Just that she wants to find herself. He thinks about it, maybe she's right. Maybe she just needs some time. So he holds onto the ring thinking maybe she might come around after a few days.

"Months go by and nothing, so he puts the ring away. He's at his parents' house one night, his mom trying to talk him into moving on when he tells her that the girl was pregnant, so yeah, it's a little hard for him to move on because he wanted to start a family. He bought a fucking ring. Well, said parent tells him she doesn't know how he got his girlfriend pregnant because she was told when he was younger he couldn't have children. Doesn't add up, right?" I raise my eyebrows at Lenny and I think she knows where this is going, but she never once interrupts me. She just waits for me to finish. "Given, he's mad at his parents because they kept it from him for what, *sixteen years.* So he goes to the doctor. Wants to know for sure, right?" My gaze moves from the bottle in my hand to Lenny, my expression emotionless. "He's sterile. Can't ever have kids. They say he's probably been that way since he was a teenager. So… that longtime girlfriend, the one he bought a ring for, cheated on him. And that's the worst for a guy like him too, because fuck if he doesn't value honesty and commitment. That wasn't even his baby she was pregnant with. Pissed doesn't even do his mood justice and he finds himself at the bar, again.

"This time it's different. There's a friend there. One he's known for years, kind of like a sister to him but she's never been one. She's been more of a tease, something he can never have. Despite their age difference, she's the perfect fucking girl too. Pops off with the funniest shit and always knows how to turn his day around. And she does just that, on a night when all he needed was a friend. Problem is, they get shitfaced and end up back at his place. Though he knows it's wrong, he thinks what the hell? Can't blame a guy for wanting to forget his problems for a little while, right? It starts off simple for them and they find themselves sneaking around because she's his best friend's little sister. The last thing he wants to do is hurt his friend or lie to him because deception is something he knows very well but the truth is, he doesn't want anything interfering with what he and this girl have so they continue to keep things between just the two of them. After six months, she wants more. She wants what every girl wants. A relationship. Commitment. Things this guy *can't* give her. So tell me, what's this guy supposed to do when he's fallen for the girl, but he can't give her forever like she wants when he's not enough of a man to give her everything she deserves?"

Lenny says nothing. For like five minutes. I probably shocked the shit out of her with that story. I think I shocked myself a little because no one besides Red knows I bought a ring for Berkley. That's probably not even the surprising part to her.

Her voice is soft when she asks, "Don't you think what this girl deserves is the chance to decide this for herself? Maybe this guy might be surprised that she still wants him regardless of what he can offer her."

"I can't give her a family, Lenny. She *deserves* a family."

She stares at me like I've lost my mind. And I probably have at this point. The bottle is halfway gone. "What do you mean?"

"I can't... she'll never be pregnant with my child." It hurts to think that let alone say it.

"That's not the only way to make a family," she points out, taking the bottle from me when I reach for it. "You've had enough and you of all people should understand that. I'm living proof and it was your aunt who showed me that."

I do consider what she's saying, I've considered it myself. "She's twenty years old. I don't think I can ever ask her to sacrifice that. What if she changes her mind later?" It all comes back to that guy and the ring and being left with no girl to give it to, sadly. I don't want to ever have that feeling of insecurity again.

"So you're scared she'll be Berkley?"

I stare at her. She saw right through me.

"She's not Berkley, Tyler. You can't make assumptions on her part. You need to give her the benefit of the doubt and let her make up her own mind. She might surprise you."

I'm still twisting the bottle cap in my hand because I want my attention on something else, not Lenny and her seeing the emotion I'm trying like hell to avoid. "So what happens ten years from now when she wants her own baby and wants to feel it kicking inside of her? Then what?"

"I can't tell you what she'd say but you're not even giving her that option. No one can tell you what will happen in ten years, but what I can tell you is that Walkers, Red, Raven... Rawley... all of them... they love and they love hard. You'd be stupid to pass up a chance with her. Absolutely fucking stupid. She's an amazing woman and the best friend I've ever had. Don't let your pride stand in the way just because you feel like less of a man because you can't give her a baby."

Blowing out a breath, I drop the cap on the table and raise my hands to my face, running them over my tender skin.

"How did it happen?"

I peek an eye at her and then drop my hands to my lap. "What?"

"You being sterile."

"It's from my medication."

"And you just found out after Berkley?"

"Yeah." I snort. "My mom didn't think it was important to tell me."

Her eyes soften. "How are you dealing with it?"

Ripping the bottle back out of her hand, I take a shot right from the bottle.

She laughs. "Okay.... So you and Rawley?"

I groan at his name, a reminder of how I got here drinking whiskey in my kitchen in the middle of the day and resembling someone who lost a round in an MMA cage. "He just doesn't know how to keep his fucking mouth shut. He's constantly instigating shit."

I think Lenny knows what Rawley's doing just like I do. He pushes people, makes them see their faults so he doesn't have to look at his own. In many ways, we're a lot alike lately, which is why I usually let his shit slide, but today it didn't.

"Just talk to her. I think you need to give her a chance," Lenny urges me. "There's only one way to find out and that's by telling her how you feel. And tell her you love her."

I raise an eyebrow, my gaze back on the bottle cap as I flip it around in my right hand. "Who says I love her?"

"You did. In the shop like an hour ago. Everyone heard you. And... if you didn't love her, you wouldn't care what she thought about any of this."

I said that? Well shit.

Lenny laughs, standing up and handing me the ice pack again, urging me to put it on my face. "Put this on your face. It's swelling."

When Lenny leaves, I know I have some explaining to do, and I hate having to do that. It's probably why I try not to on all accounts because really, what am I going to say to Raven?

"I'm an asshole with extreme commitment issues, oh, and by the way, I love you so much but please don't want a baby or leave me. 'Cause I can't handle that."

Hell, I didn't really want to tell anyone that.

Letting Raven into my life meant I was taking her choice to have a baby away from her. Would she be okay with that? Could I let her be okay with such a big decision at such a young age?

I don't know about her choices, but I do know I'm in love with her. I have feelings for her that run deeper than friends do. I can't say it started out that way. It didn't for me. I honestly went into this intending to forget about all the shit in my life. But it was bound to happen eventually and I think I knew that risk going into it. Still didn't stop me from doing it.

What I've been denying? Loving her is as automatic as breathing. Every inhale, I fall deeper. Every exhale, it goes deeper, wrapping itself around every part of my being. I couldn't stop it even if I wanted to.

After Lenny leaves, Red comes upstairs. I decide then I'm not telling him about the no-fathering children thing. I already told Lenny and I don't feel like discussing it with Red.

He sits down at the table. "I don't mind that you kicked his ass, because let's face it, he needed it. But what the hell was that?"

I don't have an answer for him. Instead, I slide the bottle of whiskey over to him.

He shakes his head. "I still have work to do. Explain."

"I don't even know what happened down there. It just got heated. I'm not even sure we were even mad at each other, or just everything else." Rawley pissed me off. He did. But at some point while we were throwing punches, I begin to think it had nothing to do with him. It was just a way to get some of that aggression out.

Red eyes the whiskey, and then me. "You and Raven okay?"

"We're…." I draw in a shaking breath. "I don't know what we are. She wants more than friends and I don't know if I can give that right now."

He waits for me to say more and when I don't he asks, "Because of Berkley?"

"I just… I can't do that again." I know it's a blanket response but I leave it at that for a reason.

"So what… did you knock my sister up or something?" He's teasing. I know he is because if he thought I got Raven pregnant, he'd probably hit me again.

"No. That's the least of your worries with me."

Thankfully, he doesn't catch on.

Raven
chapter 15
DANCING ON MY OWN

IT'S MY WINTER break. Fucking winter break before I see Tyler again. Given, it's only been like a week and a half, but still. When you're waiting on someone to call or text, that's like waiting months.

I think he senses when I'm home Friday night, or he just knows because the day I get back to Lebanon for Christmas break he texts me as I'm walking through the door at my mom's house.

Sighing, I sit down on the couch, the lights of the Christmas tree shining in the dimly lit room. In the distance, I can hear Rawley's music blaring upstairs and the shower running which means he's home too.

Tyler: Pizza?

I stare at the message for about three minutes and then reply.
Me: No.

Tyler: Please...

Fuck, why does he have to say please?

Because he knows you and manners with men are your weakness.

Me: Why?

Tyler: Because.

Groaning, I drag myself off the couch. Now I'm curious what he wants. It's the obsessive compulsive side of me that has to find an answer when there may not be one. It's the same part of me that reads the ending of a book because I can't stand not knowing how something's going to end.

Me: Fine. But you're buying.

Tyler: Meet me there at 7.

Damn you, Tyler!
Looking down at my sweat pants and hoodie, I decide to at least put some jeans on. Upstairs, Rawley's coming out of the bathroom with a towel around his waist. He looks at me and then grabs the edge of his towel. "What are you doing here?"

I walk past him to my room. "I live here too." But then I remember what a dick he was at Thanksgiving. "I know you've been upset lately but you better not be mean to Mom on Christmas."

He snorts and leans into the door frame of my room, his arms crossed over his chest and I'm fucking praying that towel stays around his waist. "Whatever, Raven. Don't come home on the weekends and act like you know what goes on here during the week."

He's right. I don't know what goes on during the week but I do know about his fight with Tyler because Lenny told me and I'm curious as to what happened. "Why'd you get in a fight with Tyler?"

Rawley shrugs and steps back. "Ask him." And then he turns around and slams the door to his room.

After changing, I walk downstairs. Mom's standing in the kitchen with a glass of wine in one hand and a cookie in the other, crumbs on her shirt. "Oh, hey, you're home. Yay."

I laugh. She's drunk but I find it cute when she's a bit tipsy. "Are you okay?"

"I'm good. Just enjoying a glass of wine."

I stare at the counter. "Or the bottle."

Her shoulders slump forward. "You're Aunt Carol's in the bathroom. I didn't drink all of that."

Aunt Carol comes around the corner, her own glass of wine in her hand. "Don't let her fool you, Raven. She drank most of that."

I laugh. "I don't doubt that. I get it from her. Anyway"—I nod over my shoulder—"I'm heading out to have pizza with Tyler."

"Okay, be safe!" Mom yells when I'm at the door.

I GET TO the pizza joint fifteen minutes later than I told him. Mostly because it's icy out and also, I wanted him to stress a little, thinking I wasn't coming.

Walking inside, I see him sitting in the back corner in a booth. He looks a bit nervous. I'm sure he's wondering how pissed off I am because I haven't heard from him in the last week. I can't be all that upset with him because I didn't call him either. He was right; my drama is too much for him and as much as I don't want to admit it, Tyler and I aren't meant to be right now. Maybe that's why I agreed to meet with him. Maybe I need to tell him this should be the end of whatever this is between us.

Taking a seat in the booth, I relax against the leather and watch as he inhales a breath, preparing to speak. "You hungry?" he asks, spinning the pie plate to me. I notice he's ordered my favorite, pepperoni and pineapple.

"Yes, I am." I nod, taking a slice of pizza and placing it on the plate in front of me.

It's about five minutes of silence before I catch him staring at me, a grin tugging at the corner of his lips.

"What?" I ask before taking another bite of pizza, wondering why he's smiling at me.

Tyler full-on smiles. "You got sauce on your face."

I notice I have it on my thumb too so I lick it off and moan just because.

His head falls forward on to the table dramatically.

"What?"

He peeks up at me with just his eyes, the rest of his head hidden by his forearm. "You're teasing me."

"You're such a guy. How am I teasing you?"

He chuckles. "You're making it look illicit."

"It's not my fault your mind is always dirty."

Sitting up as we both laugh, he reaches one hand across the table, his long fingers passing over mine.

I pull my hand away, trying to hold my ground. The things he said to me were hurtful and I can't believe he'd think I would just fall right back into this trap.

"I missed you," he says. It's becoming a habit. Piss me off, flirt, tell me he misses me and then fuck me in the bathroom. I'm certainly not fucking him in this bathroom though. No way. I give the dingy pizza joint a glance.

Nope. Not happening in here.

He's comfortably slouched in the booth where we're sitting, his long arm draped over the back of the seat. The neon lights of the pizza sign above his head bathe his dark hair with a glow, and there's a small smile playing on his lips. I literally want to jump across the booth and hump him. But I don't.

"I'm not some girl you can fuck around with and then she's there waiting for you when you're ready," I tell him. "I'm better than this, Tyler. I'm not going to have sex with you this time."

He's taking a drink of his beer when I say that, about the time a waiter walks by too so Tyler naturally chokes on the drink he'd just taken.

"Sorry," I mumble, my cheeks flushing.

"I agree."

I blink, twice. "What?"

"You've never been a girl I can fuck and walk away from, despite my behavior. Don't you see that?" His brow twists. "That's why I'm here. I can't *not* want you."

Is he serious?

"What do you mean you can't not want me? What about my drama? I told you what I wanted and you slammed a door in my face. It's too late for us. I came here because I think we need to stop whatever this is between us."

He's shocked by that. Maybe it's the too late words, but still, he seems a bit shocked. "Don't say that. It's not too late." He shakes his head, his eyes intent on mine. "It can't be. I'm sorry for what I said. I didn't mean it, Raven."

I cross my arms over my chest, only because it makes me appear more intimidating. "You're telling me you didn't mean anything you said that day?"

He considers his words and then says, "At the time I thought I did, but now I realize I was scared of my feelings for you so I didn't say what I wanted to say." I say nothing in reply.

Tyler then stiffens a bit, taking a sharp breath. But he lets it out easily and asks, "Raven, why are you really doing this?" His blue eyes meet mine, waiting on an answer.

I grimace. "Because, I have to protect my heart. You broke it and for once, I'm putting me first. I deserve more than what you and Holden put me through." I don't offer anything else.

"You *can't* compare me to him," he mumbles, his voice like gravel ripping my wounds open.

"You're right, I shouldn't. Because our relationship was completely different. But I practically begged you to love me. In the end you both made me doubt my self-worth."

Tyler leans closer to me in the booth. His voice is almost a whisper it's so soft. "I'm sorry I made you feel that way. I swear I didn't mean to hurt you. I just… I don't know what I'm doing or how to make this right with you." The apology in his voice is enough to make me forgive him, but I don't. I'm not sure I know how to.

My breathing slows. The idea of us falling back into this trap makes my stomach hollow out but what if we're not falling back into anything and he's giving me what I want?

"Raven…." His throat works on a swallow. "*Please.*" His thick lashes lower, hiding his eyes from me. His broad chest lifts and falls as he slows his breathing, getting control. He swallows hard and winces as though he's experiencing actual physical pain. "I want more… with you. You're not the kind of girl someone casually sleeps around with. I know that now. You're the kind of girl you take home to your parents and marry and I'm sorry for making you think otherwise."

My body tenses, and I stare at him with wide eyes. Pain resides there, and a sort of longing to let this be true, but damn, did he just use the words me and marry in the same sentence?

He chuckles. "I don't mean right now. I'm just saying I want you and it's a problem for me because you don't seem to feel that way any longer. I get where you're coming from but if you think this is just me wanting to get back to sleeping with you, it's not. I want to be with you. All in. Love and all that shit."

Is he fucking serious?

Tyler Hemming wants me more than just friends who fuck?

Why would he want that? I mean, he told me in not so many words I wasn't worth the drama. Okay, well, he didn't say that but he sure as shit made me feel that way.

Tyler holds my gaze for another second then clears his throat. "Uh… you shouldn't have to think about it this long." And then he gives me a smile.

Returning his smile, I lean back in my seat. "I just don't know how to answer that." I'm thinking and it's probably not what he was expecting me to say. I mean look at Tyler… most would probably drool over the chance to even have pizza with him, let alone be asked to consider more than pizza and being his fuck buddy. What gives? Why the change of heart?

Seeming annoyed with my lack of response, Tyler's gaze slides away and he takes an extra-big bite of his pizza. "Never mind," he mutters around a mouthful and rolls his eyes.

Okay, that pisses me off.

And I choke on my drink. "Don't say that to me and then say never mind because I don't jump at the chance," I say when I can breathe again.

Tyler just shrugs. I've hurt his feelings but damn it, he's fucking hurt mine too!

"How the hell did you expect me to answer?"

He slouches down further in his seat. "Maybe at least consider it."

"Why?" I squeak. "Why now?"

And he fiddles with his napkin before reaching for his beer. "Why is it so hard for you to believe I want something more than sex?"

Is he for real?

"Uh, because you told me *numerous* times you couldn't and wouldn't fall in love with me. You said you weren't in a place to fall in love and I believed you. For six months I begged you for more and you made it clear I wasn't what you wanted. Excuse me if I'm a little confused here. The last time I looked, I'm still six years younger than you. I'm still your best friend's little sister. I'm still in college with college drama. Still have all the same things in my life that you said you didn't want. So I have to ask, what's really changed? Does this have to do with your fight with Rawley?"

He scowls as if I slapped him with my words and says, "Berkley kissed me."

What? It takes me a moment to process that one, mostly because I want to cunt punch Berkley for kissing him. And then why would he tell me? Is he trying to hurt me? Make me feel bad about myself?

"Good for you then...." It's the only thing I can think to say.

Tyler nods, and I take a breath, my insides suddenly shaky and cold because his eyes have a coldness to them. "She wasn't *you*," he snaps, flopping his hand up and then smacking it against the table, his voice full of remorse.

Stumped by his sudden onset of anger, I stare, the air around me cooling. "Okay."

He clearly thinks I'm judging him—he scowls, his hands curling into fists on the table. He stares stoically at me. "She fucking wasn't you and it made me sick to my stomach that I was fighting my feelings so much. I want you and it's *fucking misery.* I didn't sleep with you because I thought you were *easy* or I wanted to fuck you for a summer. You're better than that and it sucks that it took me so long to get here but you know what also sucks? That you're letting your idea of what you deserve stop you from the reality of you actually having it." He laughs, but it isn't amused. No, not at all. His jaw tenses. "I mean, Jesus Christ, Raven, I'm a fucking man not some college frat boy and I'm asking you for more... *with me.*"

I want to rip out his tongue. We're back to my drama and exactly why I need to end this with him.

More? Of course, it's no secret, I desperately want more but at what cost to my heart? I don't miss that he brings up a college frat boy either. It's a hit to my chest because it just proves my damn point that he doesn't want what's in my life.

Wiping my hands on a napkin, I wipe the condensation from the glass and then take a long drink of ice tea, half tempted to spit it in his face. "I don't think we should see each other anymore. I'm only home for a few weeks and then I need to get back to my college drama."

Absolute silence greets me. Tyler frowns as if he hasn't heard me, but then his chest lifts on a breath and he clears his throat when I stand from the booth. "You're leaving?"

"Yeah."

The neon green light hits the side of his face, highlighting the strong lines of his nose and jaw as he turns to look out the window. The curve of his lower lip plumps before he presses his mouth into a line.

He regards me silently and then nods, not looking at me but at the empty beer in front of him. He gives himself a little shake, then lifts his head. And then he stands and brushes past me.

I'm somewhat stunned by everything that was said, and in a way, relieved. I think it's obvious where we stand and while it hurts to know I caused Tyler pain, at least he knows I'm not going to be his toy any longer.

The cool crisp night takes my breath as I walk out of the restaurant. I can't believe I just ended things with him for good.

chapter 16
I RUN

IF YOU ASK me to name the one holiday I despise more than all the rest I wouldn't hesitate when answering, Valentine's Day. I fucking hate Valentine's Day. This year though, I would have to say there's one higher on that list, Christmas.

It's not that Christmas holds any horrible experiences or memories. Just the opposite actually. This time of year was always a great time in my house. But with my dad being gone and Rawley being a royal fucking shit who refuses to celebrate, it makes it hard to enjoy. It seems this year Christmas serves only one purpose: to remind me my life is like a damn train wreck. I want to close my eyes and wake up after New Year's.

Oh, and Tyler didn't exactly make it any easier. Fucker sent me flowers. On Christmas. Nice gesture, huh? Well it was, but unfortunately, it only sent me into tears because damn it, my heart still wants him, still, despite what my head tells me.

After spending the morning with my mom visiting my dad's grave, and then Nevaeh's with Nova, Red and Lenny, needless to say I'm a bit emotional.

"Is this hard for you?" I ask Lenny when she steps back away from Nevaeh's grave and gives Red and Nova a chance to talk to her alone. We're both crying now.

She considers this for a moment and then shrugs. "No. I mean, she was his first love. And Nova's mom. As much as I love them and want to be a part of their lives, I'd give anything for them to have never gone through losing her."

I'm crying and wrap my arm around Lenny's shoulder. "Jesus, you're too good to be true."

She laughs, kissing my cheek. "So, how's Tyler?"

I side-eye her. "Not awesome. It's complicated. Like *Da Vinci Code* complicated."

Truth is, complicated isn't even the right word. More like shitstorm.

Christmas dinner helps to take my mind off things, at least for a little while. My Uncle Hendrix and his family, along with my mom's sisters, come over and for a few hours, we all try to enjoy the holiday and embrace what is our new norm. I'm thankful when I leave and head to Red's with him, Lenny and Nova because my aunts are staying the week with my mom. I enjoy my aunts in very small doses.

So now here I am, sitting on my brother's couch enjoying Christmas evening with a five-year-old beside me playing with her tooth because Red and Lenny are fucking in the bedroom. It's gross. Not them fucking—there's that too—but I can't stand people touching their teeth. It's repulsive.

"Stop playing with that thing. It's making me sick to my stomach."

Nova drops her hand from her mouth, letting go of her loose front tooth. "Do you think that if the tooth fairy farts, pixie dust comes out her butt?"

"Probably." I'm trying to watch *Christmas Vacation* with Nova but she's more interested in asking questions than actually watching it and to be honest, my minds on other things, or people.

I must have missed one of Nova's million questions because for some reason, she jumps on my lap.

"What are you doing?" she asks, getting in my face and placing both her hands on my cheeks making me look at her.

"I'm thinking."

"Well don't." She grins. "You're not good at it."

"I'm in college. I'm *good* at thinking."

"Is Uncle Ty coming over soon?" Nova pops up off the couch and looks out the window. "I haven't seen him yet today."

God, I hope so. Is it wrong that I want him to?

No, what's wrong is that you want his head between your legs for Christmas.

Groaning, I toss my head back against the couch. "I'm an idiot, aren't I?"

"What's an idiot?" Nova asks, staring at me curiously.

Craning my neck, I hear Red unlock the bedroom door and emerge from the bedroom. "Someone who doesn't make good decisions."

She thinks about that for a minute, her tiny forehead scrunched in confusion. "So like Uncle Rawley?"

"Exactly, kid. *Exactly.*"

Red ruffles my hair. "You staying the night?"

I nod. "Yes. I have no life. Might as well."

He shrugs and nods to the kitchen. "Want some apple pie?"

I stand immediately. "Fuck yes, I want apple pie."

Nova jumps down off the couch. "I want some too!"

We move into the kitchen, and Lenny eventually joins us, flushed cheeks and all. I smile, she glares, and Nova quirks an eyebrow at her. "Are you sick?"

Lenny's a little flustered and shrugs, her anxious eyes darting to me, Nova, and then Red. "No, I'm okay. I was just making the spare bed for Auntie."

What a liar. They don't even have a spare bed but luckily for her, Nova is focused on the pie and not the made-up bed.

Nova shrugs and grabs a spoon. "I want a huge piece, Daddy."

He does as she asks and then gets out three more plates.

Sitting next to me, Lenny looks relieved for the subject change.

"Where's Rawley?" I ask after a mouthful of pie, curious if Red actually knows. I haven't seen him since last night at Uncle Hendrix's annual Christmas Eve party and thought for sure he'd show up for Christmas dinner. But he didn't.

Red makes a face, then corrects it and hands Lenny pie as well. "Haven't seen him since he destroyed a customer's car." Red didn't go to the Christmas Eve party so it explains why Rawley showed up there, and not to Mom's house today.

Lenny had told me about what happened in the shop that day with Tyler and then Rawley quitting, but every time I try to talk to Rawley about it, he tells me to ask Tyler. And the fact that he missed Christmas and Dad's grave today is just a slap in the face. Stupid jerk.

"He better have a good fucking excuse for letting Ma down," Red says, taking a seat next to Nova at the table.

"What did he say when he left that day at work?"

Red takes a slow bite of is pie and then shrugs. "He said some words, made some hands gestures and then quit."

My eyes widen and I stop before taking a bite of my own pie. "Oh, wow." I still can't believe Rawley did that, but then again, I can. It's just like him to throw tantrums. Once when we were kids, I think in the second grade, he was told he couldn't go out for recess because he put gum in some girl's hair. When we came back, the teacher had a surprise when he'd turned over every desk in the class room and ripped down all the posters on the wall.

He didn't like to be told no, or singled out by anyone. Or be made aware of his issues.

It's funny. For being twins, we're complete opposites. One extreme to the other.

A knock at the door brings me out of my thoughts. Nova jumps up to look out the window to see who it is and starts to squeal and runs to the door. "It's Uncle Ty!"

Shit. Tyler. As much as I want to see him, there's a part of me that isn't ready to see him.

"Uncle Ty! Happy Christmas!" Nova yells as she jumps into Tyler's arms.

He catches her and lifts her up to give her a kiss on the cheek, and then picks her up higher to blow a raspberry on her stomach. She giggles uncontrollably to the point he nearly drops her on the floor.

"Merry Christmas, little lady. Have you had a good day?" Tyler walks by the kitchen on his way to the living room and turns to quickly glance in my direction.

There's sadness in his stare and it makes my heart sink to my knees.

Oh, just fuck him in the bathroom so you don't have to see him sad. Make it his Christmas present. Or yours.

The sad part for me is I actually consider it. Mostly because I've never seen him like this.

His eyes are bloodshot and he has bags under them like he hasn't slept. His beard is longer now and his hair looks like he only took enough time to run his hands through it before leaving the house. Actually, that part's sexy, but the rest just screams depressed.

Is it wrong he makes depressed looks sexy?

When he gets to the couch, he plops down with Nova on his lap and hands her a present. Lenny, Red and I move from the kitchen to where they're seated, and I notice the only seat available is next to Tyler on the couch. Fucking figures.

"Auntie, come sit and see what Uncle Ty got me." Nova is so excited I can't tell her no so I walk over and sit down next to Tyler, trying to keep a distance but not be obvious to Nova.

As she opens her present, some kind of My Little Pony set she'd been dying to have, she jumps off and plops down on the floor to play, leaving just Tyler and me sitting on the couch with no Nova to run interference.

We sit in an uncomfortable silence for a few minutes, my skin clammy and armpits prickling before Lenny gets up and asks Tyler if he wants a piece of pie.

"Sure. Thanks. That would be great." As Lenny hands him the pie, I take a minute to glance at him and note again that he looks completely off. It breaks my heart a little more knowing that I'm part of the reason for his appearance. Causing Tyler any kind of unhappiness was never part of the plan as I'm sure now, he never intended to hurt me.

While I'm yet again taking stock of his appearance, Nova moves to stand in front of him, putting her hands on her hips and giving him her serious face.

"You look bad." *My thoughts exactly, kid.* "Why do you look sick?"

Chuckling, Tyler takes a minute to swallow his bite of pie and gives her a soft smile that doesn't quite reach his eyes and then glances my way. "Yeah, well, I haven't been sleeping too well."

She's completely straight-faced when she says, "Oh, well then you should get laid. Works for Daddy when he's tired."

Tyler starts to choke on the piece of pie he just put in his mouth, while I can't help but start laughing. I should point out that a few months' back Nova asked my brother what getting laid meant and he told her it was going to sleep. He'd panicked. I don't think Tyler knows this so it's understandable why he's currently gasping for breath and choking on apple pie.

Once he gets his breathing under control, he turns to me again and looks me dead in the eyes. "Yeah, that's good advice."

After Nova's excitement wears off and she grows bored with playing ponies, we decide to take another stab at watching *Christmas Vacation*.

Thirty minutes into it, I'm still sitting next to Tyler, who has Nova on his lap, her head on his shoulder fast asleep. Suddenly I get the sensation of fingers lightly touching mine and then a hand wraps around, grasping my hand. I don't have to look down to know it's Tyler, but I also can't help my reaction of pulling my hand from under his. His touch is dangerous territory and for my own sanity, I move to get up and find somewhere else to sit, but Tyler again reaches for me. This time he places his hand on my arm.

"Don't get up, please," he whispers. "I'm sorry. Just sit here. For one day can we forget everything else and just sit here?"

I give him a small nod and settle back onto the couch. He doesn't attempt to hold my hand again and I can't help but get mad at myself because a big part of me was hoping he would.

I can't help but wonder what the hell is wrong with me. I know what the right thing to do is, but as I sit here, all I can think is am I making the right decision? Am I making a mistake by refusing to give him more? What I've wanted all along was for him to want more with me and now that he does, I'm pushing him away. Am I an idiot?

No. No, I need to remember why I'm pushing him away. For months, I gave myself to him. Allowed him to have me at his convenience even though he knew I wanted more. Time and time again he refused to allow his feelings to grow and now, now, he decides he misses me and wants more and I'm just supposed to jump into his arms? Not this time.

If there's one thing I've learned through all of this heart ache with Holden and Tyler, it's if I don't start demanding better for myself no one else is going to give it to me.

I'm not going to allow myself to be sucked back into the same game just because he changed his mind. What happens when he gets what he wants and decides he made a mistake?

Once the movie ends, Red offers to take Nova from Tyler but Tyler insists he wants to tuck her into bed.

Watching Tyler walk away cradling Nova to his chest, I can't help the sigh that leaves my chest. Lenny walks over and nudges my shoulder with her own.

"Hey, you okay?" I can tell she recognizes the war going on with me. Truth is, it wasn't too long ago that Lenny was waging her own war against her head and her heart. Luckily for all of us, the heart won out and now I had a best friend and hopefully someday a sister for life.

"Yeah, it's just seeing him with her, knowing how loving and gentle he can be just gets to me sometimes."

"Look, you know I love Tyler." Lenny leans in, her arm around my shoulder. "He's my only family, and I would do anything for him, but you need to remember that I love you too and your happiness is just as important to me. If you truly feel that you're making the right decision, then I'm here to stand by you and help you through it."

With a gasp, I hug her for the reassurance I'm not alone.

As we move away from our emotional hug, both wiping tears from our eyes, Tyler and Red come back into the room with questioning looks. The poor guys can't quite figure out what happened in the five minutes between when they left the room and returned.

Red eyes Lenny cautiously. "Everything okay?"

"Yeah." She gets up and wraps her arm around his waist. "Raven and I were just having a best friend bonding moment on Christmas. We're cool." She moves to take Red's hand and leads him back into the kitchen, leaving Tyler and I alone in the living room.

Crap. Alone again.

There's an awkward silence between us and it breaks my heart a little more because this was never us. I want the days when we flirted and he took every chance he could to make me squirm. We never had a moment of discomfort and it's sad how bad things have become between us when we can't be in the same room with each other without both being uncomfortable.

I look at Tyler and he seems to be struggling. Like he wants to say something but isn't really sure how to say it.

"Everything all right?"

He nods once and points to the door. "Sure. Um, I guess I'm just gonna head out."

"Oh, okay, well, Merry Christmas." There's a huge part of me that wants to grab onto him and beg him not to go because I'm so scared if he leaves now there's no guarantee he will ever come back.

Tyler leans in, almost awkwardly, gently kissing my cheek. He then brings his lips to my ear and gently whispers, "Merry Christmas, Raven. Take care of yourself." Pulling away just as quickly as he leans in, he heads out the door.

Moving from the door to the front window, I watch him walk to his truck only to see him hesitate once he gets to the driver side door. With his hand on the door to his truck, he looks over toward the house, catching my gaze. Again I can see him struggling, wanting to say something but for some reason he's stopping himself as he finally gets into the truck and pulls out to leave.

I'm not sure how long I stand there but I know it's long enough to see his taillights disappear and again I'm left wondering if I'm truly making the right decision. If pushing Tyler away is the right thing to do, surely it shouldn't hurt so much.

BEFORE I GO back to Eugene, I enjoy New Year's Eve with Lenny and Red at Murphy's, the only bar I can get into and not be carded. Rawley's playing and it's the first time Red's seen him since the incident at the shop.

They say absolutely nothing to one another. In fact, Red doesn't even acknowledge him or look in his direction.

We're seated at a booth in the corner not far from the stage, tension in everyone's posture. Lenny's eyes widen when she notices Sophie walk in with a guy. He looks familiar but I can't place his name. I know it's someone we went to high school with though. I can already imagine what my brother's reaction is going to be over this one. In his eyes, despite how he treats Sophie, she's still his and can't associate with other guys.

"Who's that?" Lenny asks, adjusting her black halter top she's wearing. She keeps fidgeting with it no matter how many times I tell her she looks good. Red thinks so too because his hand, the one securely around her shoulders, like the possessive boyfriend he is, hasn't moved since we sat down.

I lean into her so she can hear me over the music. "Not sure. I think I remember him, but I can't think of his name." We watch as they sit at the bar, nowhere near the stage and I know why she does that. She doesn't want Rawley to see.

Well, he has pretty good fucking eyesight on that stage because it's only a matter of time before he notices them.

"Are Rawley and Sophie still messing around?"

Letting my straw fall from my lips, I set my drink down and I roll my eyes. "I'm not sure, probably. They're always messing around. He can't let her go and she just keeps going back for more."

Crap. That sounds vaguely familiar.

My brother is a slut. He's been that way since high school and it all leads back to Sophie Cunning. Sophie was his first girlfriend in high school but they broke up shortly after spring break senior year. It went downhill from there. He started sleeping with her friends and eventually Berkley, Tyler's ex.

"This should be interesting," Red remarks, reaching for his beer on the table. He notices Sophie too.

My gaze darts from Rawley, to Sophie, then back again. You can see it in his motions, the stiffness in his shoulders as he's standing at the mic, his head twisted to the left as Beck talks to him between songs.

He knows she walked in with someone else.

My attention is on them when Tyler sits down at the table. He's drunk already and gives me a wink. See. So familiar. At least he didn't bring a date and he's sitting across from Red so I don't have to technically stare at him. Even though I want to.

He looks good. I love that he's got a beard now. My teeth sink into my lower lip drawing his eyes there. His lips part, a tender sound passing as he lifts his beer to his lips.

Jesus, neither one of us can stop the feelings we have.

Blinking softly, his dark lashes lower, taking a slow drink of his beer. He looks tired, like he hasn't slept in weeks. I know that feeling too.

He and Red talk, words I can't hear over the music. Lenny and I do the same and I focus my attention on those around us as we play detective and attempt to figure out what happened between Rawley and Sophie that would warrant her bringing someone here. Everyone knows Rawley plays at Murphy's on New Year's. It's not a fluke that she accidently stumbled in here with a date. It's a statement to him.

Rawley's good at getting attention on stage so it's no surprise when he kicks an amp over and everyone looks to the stage, Sophie included. He winks at her and grabs the mic forcefully with his right hand, the opening beats of Buckcherry's "Sorry" carrying through the bar. He's not wearing a shirt suddenly either. Probably by design because on his chest is a tattoo that holds meaning to her. It's her name across his heart. My brother is slightly neurotic. Or maybe a lot.

You don't hear him sing slower songs often, and maybe that's why he's doing it now. He's got the perfect voice for this song and always resembles Josh Todd when he sings.

Both Lenny and I stare at Sophie and her reaction as Rawley's rough voice wavers in the dim lit bar. She's bothered by it, especially the song because for once in his fucking life, he's actually saying he's sorry, in a roundabout way.

Sophie blinks slowly, twisting on the stool to face him directly. She loves him, still, and probably always will.

It's then, listening to my brother pour his heart out on stage, I look to Tyler, who's intent on me, finding meaning in the song as well. My heart races, my skin prickling with the force of his stare. A jolt of nausea hits me and I swallow. Fire breaks out over my skin, spreading throughout, igniting the thunderous roar of my pounding heart. Placing my hand over my chest, it's racing, wondering when we will finally get our shit together.

As crazy as it sounds, I'll never be able to move on from him, if I keep seeing him. It'll never happen; that's how much power he has on me.

I stand abruptly and run for the door, needing fresh air. The winter air hits me as soon as the door opens but it offers no relief. None.

The parking lot's crowded, people bringing in the New Year with their laughter while all I have inside me is hurt.

"Stop following me," I tell him when he's standing before me.

Tyler curves an eyebrow at me, waiting on my reaction, running the back of his hand over his jaw before burying his hands in the pockets of his jeans. "You knew when you walked outside a bar, alone, I'd follow." His eyes are cloudy, lost inside.

"No, I didn't know that."

LIAR!

I attempt to move, make it to my car, but he stops me. Moving quickly, he traps me against the side of the building. Every hard line of his body presses me into the side of Murphy's bar and I'm reminded of the night everything began with Tyler Hemming.

He focuses on my lips, knowing what he is doing to me. "I'm sorry if I made you uncomfortable by coming here. Red asked me to come out with them. He didn't realize that we weren't... on good terms." His stare darts from my eyes to my lips and back again. He licks his lips and mine part in response. He always ignites a reaction from me even in anger.

"I can't be around you, Tyler." My breath catches in my throat, and I'm trying to remind myself to focus on breathing. It seems like the moment our eyes actually meet, we're back to being miles away from each other, distanced by what neither of us can say.

"So you can't even be in the same room with me now? Why? We used to be friends." He glares, red-faced, eyes locked on mine, his chest rising and falling faster, clearly struggling to remain in control. Just like Christmas, he wants to say more to me, but there's something stopping him. Pride maybe.

227

"Because it makes it worse for me. Just because I can't be with you doesn't mean it's easy for me to walk away. You hurt me, Tyler. I feel used. I feel like I was just a toy for you to use when you felt it was convenient. And now I'm putting distance between us because I can't resist you. You say you want to be together but how do I know that's not to get in my pants again and then you'll walk away when you want? You're right, we used to be friends but that was before I fell in love and now I can't go back. I can't risk my heart."

His brow pinches together with my words; his scowl set on mine. Cold blue eyes drop to the pavement as he lets go of my hand. Leaning in slowly, he whispers. "Just remember, Raven, I never wanted us to end like this."

Withdrawing, he turns and walks away, the cool night air shocking my face like he's slapped me.

I know exactly how this looks. Here I was a month ago begging him to love me and now I'm pushing him away. I'm in a constant battle with my head and my heart. This girl, the one pushing him away, I'm doing it because I'm tired of compromising my own self-worth.

Raven
chapter 17
VALENTINES DAY SUCKS

AS YOU KNOW, Valentine's Day is the dumbest holiday ever.

Imagine my joy when the hall I live in is having their annual Valentine's Day Kiss Me celebration as I'm trying to make my way back to my dorm room after class. I had seen the signs declaring the annual celebration but I hadn't really put much thought into the fact that it's today. So while I'm unpleasantly surprised to see the crowds gathered, what really shocks me is seeing Holden, drunk off his ass with two girls on either side of him and smiling like the fool I know him to be.

What truly pisses me off though is when he grabs my hand, letting the girls loose and yanks me to his chest, his dusty blond hair falling in his face. "This is the girl I want to kiss."

And he kisses me. Not just any kiss either. He fucking sticks his tongue in my mouth and grabs my ass in the process.

Wide-eyed, the kiss-me twins next to him walk the other way about the time I shove Holden back against the wall he's standing next to.

"You douche dick." I wipe the back of my hand over my mouth. A lot of the times, when I'm super pissed, my cussing doesn't make sense. Like now. "What the hell do you think you're doing?"

It hits me suddenly. The anger and humiliation that he did this in front of twenty or so people and they're all waiting for my reaction. Everyone in the room is staring at me and I'm so embarrassed.

My heart begins to beat rapidly, Holden staring stoically at me, waiting for my final reaction he knows is coming. He stands up straight and takes a step toward me. "Raven, just relax. It's all in fun. You remember how to have fun, right?"

You remember how to have fun, right? I repeat those words in my head several times.

The sting of his cheek and my throbbing hand is my answer to that question. "You have no right to kiss me, ever again."

He humiliated me enough last year, what gives him the right to do it again? I want away from the crowd. Now.

It's around midnight when I'm finally climbing the stairs to my third floor dorm room. After the bullshit with Holden, I may or may not have decided a keg was my date tonight and had a few beers with those kiss-me twins. Turns out they were pretty cool chicks and what really made my night was that we all agreed Holden was a horrible kisser.

STUMBLING DOWN THE hall, I look toward my room and see Tyler sitting in front of my door. Fucking Tyler. It's like he knows when not to show up, and does.

He doesn't move. He's just sitting on the floor, propped up by the door with his head in his hands.

I walk slowly toward him. "What are you doing here?"

He stands immediately, grabbing onto the door frame to steady himself. He then begins to chew nervously on his bottom lip and shoves his hands into the pockets of his loose fitting jeans. He's wearing a dark gray hoodie with the hood pulled up over his head shadowing his eyes. "You didn't answer my texts and I wanted to talk to you."

I want to laugh. But I don't. "What do you want to talk about? I mean seriously, do you honestly believe we have anything more to say to each other?"

There's debate in his eyes. I can tell he's doubting whether he should say anything at all. He pulls the hood off so I can see him more clearly. He's different. Something in his intimidating stare tells me so but I can't place the difference. "After what I saw earlier, I kinda want to talk about you and Holden."

A pain hits my chest. "What are you talking about?" I unlock my door, damn near tempted to slam it in his face, only he follows me inside, obviously wanting answers.

Once inside he tilts his head back and leans up against the wall, looking up at the ceiling. Whatever it is, it's hard for him to say. "You kissed him. I fucking saw you."

"I don't know what you think you saw but that's *not* what happened."

"Don't lie to me. I'm not fucking stupid. I know what I saw. Did you want him to kiss you?" Tyler's body remains rigid and unfamiliar, his eyes on mine waiting for a lie he assumes is coming.

A mixture of shame and regret take over and my stomach dips. "No," I eventually answer without meeting his eyes. How can he think I would want that after being with him?

The very thought of Tyler believing I would kiss Holden willingly hurts, makes my chest burn. I wonder if I would react the same way if I saw him kiss Berkley.

The answer is yes. I would. Hell, I did react that way based on a text message. And even after the last months and the way he's treated me, I'd still have the same jealous reaction. I know I would.

I lick my lips and his gaze follows, his brow furrowing. His anger smolders with an intensity so bright I want to squint. "Bullshit," he snaps, shaking his head.

He's drunk. He has to be. What's with the men in my life? Does Valentine's Day to them just mean Be A Douche Day, treat women the absolute worst?

"What the hell is with guys today? Why is it that you all think Valentine's Day gives you a license to treat women like shit?"

He stands there unsure how to answer my question.

When did Tyler turn into this guy? Something inside of us became clouded when jealousy got the better of us. Our friendship was nothing like it started out as. That closeness is gone and we're left with this, whatever this is.

"*He* kissed *me*." I try to keep my voice down. I didn't want to draw attention to us in here, but I really wanted to scream this next part at him. "I didn't ask for that, Tyler. I'm not, nor will I ever be with Holden again. If you haven't noticed, I don't take back assholes just because they decide they made a mistake."

He seems to soak this in before responding. He nods, tight and tortured, but he doesn't say anything. Lightheaded, I take a seat on the edge of my bed but Tyler doesn't move.

Let me tell you something about Tyler. When pushed, he can and *will* respond like any man. Ask Rawley. I've seen it many times. I've just never been on the receiving end and I'm waiting for the explosion.

I intend to walk outside and get some air. So much had already been said and I'm afraid if he says anything more, I may hate him.

"You know, if you had stuck around for another thirty seconds instead of overreacting, you would have seen me deck him too."

He still says nothing.

I face him, our bodies nearly touching now as we stand near the door. We're so close his breath blows over my face and I know for sure he's been drinking. "*You* don't get to tell me who I can kiss. *You* can't come in here and tell me who I can be with."

He rolls his eyes like he's frustrated that I'm not getting it. "I came because I want you to be with me and instead of talking to me, you're ignoring me."

With my arms crossed over my chest, my fingers are digging into the skin of my arms as I watch him. "Oh yeah? Well, how's it feel?"

He frowns and after about five seconds of thought, he slowly shakes his head. "Is that what this is about? Getting even like I purposely hurt you? Is that what this is?"

I can't believe we're arguing about this. "Tyler, I don't know what this is about. I don't know why you're even here."

He raises his hand to touch my cheek, conflict raging in his eyes. "I'm here because I want to be with you. I miss you."

"No, you're here because you're fucking drunk and lonely."

He shakes his head adamantly. "No, that's bullshit." He tosses his hand lazily in the air and I take a step back against the wall behind my door, the one scattered with pictures of my family and him. He's looking at me now, thick black brows slanting over his eyes in a deep scowl. "Six weeks, Raven. *Six fucking weeks* I've been trying to talk to you. Being drunk only gave me the courage to come here and put an end to it. I'm sure you can relate. You remember don't you? That night in this very room when you were drunk and told me you loved me?"

In my head, I do the math, because I'm weird like that. I'm trying to figure out if it's been six weeks since New Year's and he's wrong, it's been almost eight but I'm not going to correct him on his math. "I can't believe you're bringing that up now."

He stares at me as if I'm missing something obvious. I can see the war waging inside of him because he knows he's not getting anywhere. "Why *wouldn't* I? Have your feelings changed that much that you don't love me anymore?" I can tell by the wavering in his tone those words were some of the hardest he's ever had to say.

Do I still love him?

So fucking much it's sickening.

Tears sting my eyes but the last thing I want to do is cry in front of him. "You don't' get it, Tyler. It's not a matter of not loving you. It's me not wanting to be hurt again."

Disappointed, his head drops and he shakes it back and forth. "I never meant to hurt you."

"I know, but this is me protecting me for once." The words burn in my throat. "My feelings haven't changed but neither has our situation. I'm still in college. You're still you. Twenty-six and *not wanting* drama."

He grimaces with every word. His jaw hardens. *That* hit home.

"Why are you coming in here acting like this is about Holden kissing me and not what it's really about? You're here because of your agenda and getting what you want. Well tough shit because my twenty-year-old drama filled life has no room for you anymore."

Holy hell I've got some balls this morning.

"Jesus!" he says through gritted teeth in a shouted whisper, his tone harsh and louder than before. "Why does it always fucking come back to this? I told you I was sorry for what I said and I fucking meant it."

I'm slow to respond to him. Stunned by the way he's staring at me. "Keep your voice down," I warn him. Pressing my finger to my lips, I point to the door. The last thing I need is people hearing this and calling security.

Tyler lowers his voice and stares at the wall. After a moment, he shakes his head. He sighs. "What the fuck are we doing?" His chest expands, his darkened eyes meeting mine. "Do you wish we would have never started? Is that what this is? Do you regret it?"

His eyes burn into mine, waiting for me to answer him.

Looking away, I say, "No. I would never want that. I don't regret it."

He's silent for a moment, his arms crossed over his chest, his head hanging and eyes on the floor.

"What I regret is that you can't see our problems are so much more than this."

He says nothing. Because he knows.

I shake my head, completely worn out by this and him. "I'm so tired of having this same argument with you."

"Then stop having it," he says, as if it's that easy for me to let go of this.

"You would say that." I can feel the resentment burning behind my words.

"Yeah, I would, because you're forgetting I asked you for more."

"And I *begged* you for more way before you pulled your head out of your ass," I seethe back at him. "Have you ever stopped to think about what *you've* done to me?" I can tell by the look on his face he hasn't. And still hasn't. So I let him know. "*You* made me into the insecure girl who considers herself not good enough for someone like you. How do you think that made me feel? You committed to Berkley but yet me, no, *never*. You never even gave me the option. And now, because you've suddenly decided, I'm supposed to consider forever because you're feeling shitty about it?"

His face hardens, a flood of anger coming with it. His finger points accusingly at me, his breathing so heavy he can barely get out the words. "You don't know a fucking thing about what *I'm* feeling!" He shakes his head again, grabbing the back of his neck, his eyes on the floor, as if I don't deserve their depth.

"So tell me then! You give me nothing, Tyler. Nothing to go on. It's like you're a fucking lock and I'm supposed to know the right combination but I don't."

I repeat my words in my head for a moment because I'm not entirely sure that made sense to him.

When he doesn't answer me, I draw in a heavy breath, ready to explode.

I shift my stance, my hands thrown up in the air. "This is so stupid, Tyler. You tell me you don't want drama but here you are creating it. We're acting like kids."

His mouth twists in a scowl delivered my way. His eyes are hard, lips parting as he speaks. "You don't think I know that?" The bitter laugh returns when he looks up at me.

I find my voice. "Then stop."

Opening the door to my dorm room, intending on getting air, Tyler catches it. His hand, up near the top, slams it closed with little effort, the sound echoing through the room. "You don't say shit like that and walk away."

"Shit like what?" Every time we disagree about anything, we come back to this same argument and these same reactions. "Tyler, we're not even dating yet we fight like insecure high schoolers."

When I turn back to Tyler, his eyes say a lot. "Fuck, Raven!" He starts pacing the place beside my bed. His all-too-cold eyes shift from the floor to me when he stops pacing. Hell, I couldn't even tell if he was breathing at all with how still he'd become. "You think I want this? To be so obsessed with you that I'm fucking hanging around a college dorm hoping you'll give us a chance? You're the one who said you wanted more first, and then I came around to the idea and you tell me no. You've moved on. How could you move on so quickly?"

That's a good question. But then again, it's not all that complicated after what he said to me in the rain. He made me feel like I'd never be good enough for him. Why can't he see what a slap in the face this was to me?

"Because you made me move on. You told me not to love you. What was I supposed to think? You made me feel like I wasn't good enough to be yours. Apparently what we had didn't matter enough to you."

And I'm a fucking idiot. I want to slap my hand over my mouth so I don't say anymore. I know what we had mattered to him. It had to have because he's here now.

He gives me that nod, the one he gives when he was so angry he can't speak. His stomach pulls in, a long deep breath as if to calm himself a little. "It fucking matters, Raven!"

"It matters that you're just being a selfish asshole because I won't put out anymore."

Jesus Christ. I should have stopped at my first stupid comment.

Tyler's anger, when pushed far enough, is a sight I'll never forget. I've heard about it from Red, but never seen him this out of control.

I hear the crash first, my bookshelf on my desk hits the ground and then my laptop smashing against the wall beside me. "You think you've got it all figured out, don't ya?" His words come out in a growl but he keeps his distance from me, pushed back against the wall as if he's needing the separation now more than ever. "You know me, right? I fucked you all summer just for the fun of it and then keep coming back to hurt you more. That was my fucking plan all along. I'm fucking here, right now, trying to get you to see it was more than sex to me!"

We weren't these people. We weren't. I didn't say things like this, and he didn't react this way. Love can make you do some pretty stupid shit sometimes. It's the words you never say that mean the most. The ones on the tip of your tongue, screamed at the top of your lungs to be heard, it's those words that sometimes *need* to be said. Like an "I'm sorry" or an "I love you."

They matter. They really do.

Tyler tips his head to one side, his hands clasped together behind his head. "So is that it? You've decided we aren't going to happen no matter what I say? Do you want me to leave?" he asks, his blue eyes intensely staring at me knowing he crossed the line.

I know what my answer is but I can't manage any words because I have no air supply, but I nod.

While we stand there staring at each other, no words are spoken because none are needed. With one stare, he says all he needs to say. The moments gone, but his eyes are anxious. He's not sure what I'm going to say next, and it scares him. He blinks, and when he opens his eyes again, the depth of his blues are somewhat guarded now.

"Why does it have to be like this?" He moves toward me, coming to stand in front of me.

There's so much I want to say right then, but the moment passes and part of me feels like maybe it's too late. I want to reach up and touch the side of his face. I want his eyes to soften into the blue I know and not the ice that freezes the breath in my lungs and the black consuming his pupils. I want the gentle sensation of his body against mine and the heat it gives me.

I don't have any of that right now. I have this, a situation we both created.

When I don't say anything, his hands find my face, his hair falling into his lashes. I fight my own urge to brush it away from his face and as I watch him, searching his face. I wish I could get inside his mind and understand him better.

His hands are shaking, a slight tremble to them and I can't tell if it's the adrenaline wearing off, whatever he drank before he got here or if he's that nervous of my denial. His eyes seem different too, darker, their depth unreachable.

He brushes his fingertips over my lips, lips that have just been kissed by another. Breathing deeply, he lets his shaking hands drop. He looks completely worn out, with dark circles under his eyes. His face says it all. He's tired of this. We both are.

How does something so simple turn to this, a stream of resentful harsh words spat at one another?

"You shouldn't even be here."

A sadness enters his eyes and when it does, he says, "Believe me, I wish I could leave but I can't." Letting me go, he draws in a deep breath leaning against the wall, it's as if he's been dying to take the breath since he came in here and only able to now. "But that's my problem. I told myself to leave you alone when you told me to, and now here I am, fuckin' angry at your ex and waiting for you to finally put me out of my misery."

I don't even know what to say to that. Am I really causing him misery?

He blows out a shaky breath and then brings the back of his hand to his neck, squeezing. Tyler stands, staring at my ceiling as if he's hoping it holds all the answers. When it doesn't, he drops his stare to the floor and shakes his head.

He turns and heads for the door, stepping over my broken laptop when there's a knock and then a voice.

"Campus police." Of course someone called campus police between the door being slammed and the noise Tyler made when he knocked over my bookcase and threw my laptop.

Knowing he's in trouble, Tyler sighs and takes a step back against the wall letting the officer step inside my room when I open the door.

"We received a noise complaint, Ms. Walker." The officer looks past me and to Tyler, assessing my room with a scan of his eyes. "Do we have a problem here?"

Tyler looks at the ground, and then me out of the corner of his eye. "No problem."

The officer takes a look around my room surveying the mess. "Did you do this?"

"Yeah." He's not hiding anything, but he's also not making eye contact.

"Why?" The officer leans into the door frame, relaxed with his arms crossed over his chest. He doesn't seem too concerned, but he's also not letting Tyler leave and blocking him in the room.

By the way Tyler's hands are shaking, it's obvious he wants to leave. He's had enough and can't even look at me.

"Just a misunderstanding."

I let the words sink in as he speaks them. A misunderstanding? Is that what we were? A misunderstanding? The impact of his words take over and soon tears pool in my eyes.

What was a misunderstanding? Me wanting to kiss Holden?

Yup! That was a big misunderstanding!

My feelings for him?

No, I think I've made myself pretty clear, but he's getting me confused with Berkley.

Or is he referring to his feelings for me?

Every insecurity I have felt since the beginning of whatever Tyler and I had comes rushing back into my mind. I can't believe something so simple as two friends having sex turned into this.

The officer must know there's no immediate threat and backs up. "Is that what happened here or do we need to escort him off campus?"

My stare snaps to Tyler and we're trapped in a moment, one where we see how easily this backfired on us. I breathe in slowly, gathering courage. "No, like he said, it's just a misunderstanding. I'm fine. Just college drama."

Jesus, I'm a bitch! Tyler's jaw tenses at my words. He knows that was a dig at him.

The officer nods. "You know how to reach us if you need anything, right?"

Again, I nod and he leaves a minute later.

I think maybe Tyler might choose now to go, but he doesn't. He lingers by the door like he's struggling to leave just like I'm struggling to let him go.

I watch as he slowly slides down the wall to sit on the floor. "Say it." He runs a frustrated hand and through his hair. "Say there's no chance ever." His voice cracks. "Tell me to walk out the door and never look back."

The pain in his voice ripples through me. I can't do it.

He leans forward and buries his face in his hands. He's shaking his head, as if he can't process what's happening to us. "If you don't want me, end it. I can't take it anymore. I can't end it. You have to do it." His head hangs, his body nearly giving out.

I say nothing.

I can't do it either. The last thing I want is to end it.

His voice evens out but still holds tension. He regards me silently for a moment and I can see there's so much hurt inside his eyes I haven't even seen the half of it. "Raven... just put me out of my fucking misery."

I know exactly what I need to say to him. "We were never together, remember?"

Oh my God, why did I just say that?

He stares up at me for the longest time, like he's trying to diagnose a misfire. Or he can't believe I just said that to him. Sadness rolls through his shoulders, hunching on the onset as he nods, once. Agony floods his eyes.

Sighing heavily, he struggles to stand, leaning heavily against the wall. He runs a hand through his hair and opens his mouth to speak but then clamps it shut again, as if he can't believe my words. It takes him a second to get around his breaking words. He swallows and drops his eyes to the floor. He looks at the door momentarily as if he's trying to decide to leave or speak. I can see the twitch in his jaw right before he locks eyes with me. "You're right." As he passes me, his voice hits my heart with each word. He pauses and leans in so his warmth radiates into me, and I know what I'm going to miss it. With his chest against mine, I can almost feel the beat in his chest and his breath on my face. "Just do me one last favor, Raven. If I text you… *don't* answer it and if you see me walking toward you, turn and walk the other way."

I'm taken aback by his words, and then he's gone.

I stare at the door as it closes, wondering if I should stop him because he's been drinking and I shouldn't let him leave like this. There's something incredibly off about him and his demeanor but I don't have the energy to figure out what it is. I let him go even though every fiber of my being is yelling at me to stop him.

I fucking stare at the door once more because there goes the rest of my heart and I know if he stays, I won't push him away.

Unable to control the sob that leaves my throat, I collapse on the floor next to my broken laptop.

Tyler

Chapter 18
NOT AS PLANNED

"If you don't want me, end it. I can't take it anymore. I can't end it. You have to do it."

MY HEART IS frantic as I walk down the hall, everything we said to one another rushing through me like a tidal wave.

"We were never together, remember?"

How could she have said that?

Easily, it's what you were telling her for so long. You never gave her a reason to think otherwise.

My body shakes from my actions, an all-encompassing tremor from head to toe like I've spent the night in the freezing cold. It rakes through my bones and I shake harder, almost to the point my teeth are chattering. Every step takes an effort I don't have, but make anyway.

Stumbling through the parking lot, I open the door to my truck and sit in silence, the rumble of the big block vibrating my chest. I put my hands on the steering wheel, both of them gripping so hard my knuckles turn white.

Why couldn't she have just put me out of my misery? Why did she have to constantly leave me hanging?

Probably because you did it to her for months.

"You made me move on. You told me not to love you. What was I supposed to think? Apparently what we had didn't matter enough to you."

A pressure in the back of my head swirls like a breeze, but I'm inside my truck. I check the door thinking I left it open but I didn't. There's no breeze, just me and the sound of my truck. With each breath, the intensity increases like a building pressure needing release.

Blinking several times, my eyes shift from the windshield that's scattered with fat drops of bone-chilling cold rain, to my radio. The blue and purple lines dancing across the display light up with the change in the song.

It's a Chris Stapleton song. Taking my right hand off the steering wheel, I punch the display to end the fucking song. I don't want the reminder.

I don't want anything.

My head buzzes, a throbbing sensation in my ears and a rush of blood. I'm in trouble. I know that much, but I put the truck in drive. I stare at my hands again, maybe because they're my only indication of how far out of control this is.

If I saw my face, my eyes might be an indication too. They'd be pitch-black, pupils so wide you'd think I was high. I'd stare at you and you'd know, inside, I was gone.

As I pull onto the freeway, I know what's coming. I usually do. I couldn't tell you afterwards that I know, but when it's happening, in those final seconds leading up to the nothingness that can consume me, I know.

I just wish she believed me enough to know I love her, and that's really all that matters in this world. It's not these arguments and our lack of words. It's love in its purest form. Loving innocently with no consequences. The way *she* taught me, only she was wrong. There are consequences.

It's not until the pressure finally becomes too much, maybe minutes later, maybe longer, that I feel the only relief I've felt in months.

It's not her fault. It really isn't. But it's not like I can tell her that now. Maybe never.

chapter 19
I ALMOST LOVER

"If I text you, don't answer."

I'M AT A loss. How exactly did we end up here? Tyler and I of all people, someone I've known for over half my life. I didn't understand most of what he said when he was here, or why he said it. I'm still in a spin going over and over his words and actions.

Staring at the mess that is my room, I pick up my bookshelf first and then my destroyed laptop, placing it on my desk. Stupid jerk. Why did I let him leave? The look in his eyes, the unsteady darkness in them haunts me. I shouldn't have let him. I know he wasn't drunk but something wasn't right.

It's hours later and I'm drifting to sleep when my phone buzzes on my desk and I jump, my hands scrambling to pick it up, thinking it's Tyler.

It's not. It's Rawley. Fucking Rawley of all people after a month of not hearing from him. The last time he called me was a few days after Christmas, apologizing for not coming and then I saw him on

New Year's at the bar. But not since then. He's starting to remind me of Tyler.

Rawley: Let me in.

I never heard a knock but I open the door and see my brother, looking like hell. His hat's pulled down low, with hair sticking out erratically around the edges and his dark brown eyes are sunken in by nights of sleeplessness.

"You look like shit."

He chuckles, removing his jacket and setting his guitar on the floor. He then flops down on my bed on his back, his shirt pulling up over his stomach to reveal he certainly hasn't been eating either. "Yeah, well, I feel worse than I look if you can believe that."

"I can." Sitting on the floor beside the bed, I lay my head back against the mattress. His hand flops over, rubbing the top of my head.

His breathing is light when he asks, "Why is your room such a mess?"

Rawley knows me and to have a messy room is like the world ending for me. I hate anything out of place. "Tyler. Why are you here? It's like four in the morning."

He sighs, rolling over so he's in a curled position. He smells like a bar: stale beer, cheap perfume and cigarettes. "It's five… or something… but I was playing at a bar just off campus, went home with some chick who lives in this dorm and thought I'd come say hi."

I turn and look at him, my chin on the mattress giving him a disapproving glare only a sister can give. "Or you wanted some place to crash for a little while and didn't want to stay in her room?"

"There's that too."

Patting the pockets of his jeans, he pulls out a joint and raises an eyebrow. I wouldn't say we do this often, but Rawley was the first person I got high with in high school.

I nod. "Sure, why not. I don't have class tomorrow."

Sitting up, he backs up so he's propped against the wall and I sit beside him. His lighter flicks, the joint glowing red and orange for a moment. He hands it to me.

Staring at him, I wonder what the fuck is going on in his head since his outburst at the shop, and then New Year's.

"What the hell is going on with you?"

Shaking his head, Rawley takes a hit off the joint and then reaches for his guitar. "Nothing." He says this as if it's no big deal but I know it is. "Seriously though, what's going on here?" He motions around the room.

"I don't even know. Tyler had a bit of a temper tantrum. I wanted him to love me, and he wouldn't… and then I found out why and then he wanted me and I said no."

My gaze moves to his, the early morning sun starting to peek into my room lighting the side of his face. He hasn't shaved in weeks and has a busted-up lip, and a hickey on his neck. I want to ask, but I don't because it's probably something stupid like a bar fight.

He's nodding, seeming to be listening to me, but then focusing his attention on his guitar. It's then he begins to play the opening notes of "Crazy Bitch" and then turns to me smiling and bobbing his head. He thinks he's being funny but I want to punch him in his face.

"Why would you play that fucking song?"

Rawley smiles and I kind of hate him for it. Raising his hand, he scratches the back of his head and pushes his guitar away. "You're being a crazy bitch."

I don't even crack a smile. "I am not, Rawley."

When he laughs, I don't. I can't. I'm on the verge of tears and I can't believe I'm sitting here smoking a joint with him.

"Hey, I'm just trying to make you laugh." He bumps my shoulder when he passes the joint. "It's what twins are for."

I take the joint next and do the same, only it doesn't offer me the relief I'm hoping it will. "I screwed up with Tyler. I told him I didn't want to be with him when I really do."

"Hey, it could be worse." Rawley laughs, his shoulders shaking. "You could be me." I don't agree with him; though he's probably right.

When I don't say anything, Rawley stares at me. "Did you call him after he left?"

"If I text you, don't answer."

I sigh because it's all I can do. The thought of him breaks my heart and sends a sharp pain through my veins. "No. I let him leave. What would I even say?"

Rawley shrugs and though he's making conversation with me, he doesn't seem like himself tonight. His attention seeming to be on something else. "Tell him you love him and you want to be with him."

I side-eye him. "Oh really? Well, maybe you should take your own advice here and tell Sophie that."

His eyes narrow, the deepest hurt just below the surface. "It wouldn't make a goddamn bit of difference if I did."

In many ways, Tyler and Rawley are very similar, hurt in the same ways, which is why the two of them are at it so often. They're both trying to get the attention off of them by taking out their frustrations on one another.

"Rawley, seriously, what's going on with you?" The only reason I ask is because while he's high, he might actually answer me truthfully. "You're treating Sophie like shit and pushing everyone away from you."

He's quiet for about a minute and staring at his hands. He doesn't look at me when he begins to speak. "Did you know the last conversation I had with Dad, I told him to fuck off and stop trying to make me into Red? Just before he died, I told him to fuck off. My last two words to our dad were *fuck off*." He takes the joint from my hand when I open my window, attempting to push some of the haze out of my room. "My entire life I feel like he tried so fucking hard to make me like him," he says, continuing but staring at his hands. "He didn't do it on purpose, but deep down, he wanted his boys running his shop. I fuckin' get it. I do. It makes sense. I've never wanted it though, but in his eyes, my career choice was the wrong choice. He didn't come out and say it, but I could tell. So I stayed at the shop after he died. You know, make him happy when I couldn't before. But shit, Raven, it's fucking torture. I *hate* working on cars. Nothing gives me the feeling music does. The satisfaction and adrenaline I feel when I'm performing, that's what makes me happy. That shop is Red's. I'm not a part of it and I don't want to be. All I want is music and a stage."

I know there's more. There always is with him. "And what about Sophie? That performance at the bar on New Year's." I whistle in a slow breath. "That was something else."

He rolls his eyes, showing his annoyance. "I *know* I'm fucking up. I don't need a reminder." He's not making any excuses for his behavior; he usually doesn't if you ask him, but then he sighs, his shoulders sagging. Knocking his hat off his head, he brings it down to his lap and groans. "I fucking love her so much but I can't make myself take her back. Out of every girl I'm with, none compare to her. But I can't. Every time I look at her, I think of her deliberately making that choice to break my heart."

"So why keep putting her through it, Rawley. Just end it completely and walk away. Don't keep playing this game of push and pull. It makes you look like an asshole who's purposely trying to hurt her now. Your point was made a long time ago."

"I know.... I don't understand it myself." His forehead creases in deep concentration. "I can't end it with her. I would if I could but I can't do it. I can't get her out of my head. When I take a girl home, I only think about Sophie. It's like every other girl is just trying to fill the aching void in my chest she created and it never works." He shakes his head, running his fingers through his hair and settling his hand on the back of his neck again. It's a motion he does often, but it seems to ease his frustration. "Why'd she have to do it? Why?"

He wants an answer and I can't give it to him, just like I can't give myself one as to why Tyler and I can't work.

"Rawley," I begin, but then think about what I'm saying. "She made a mistake. Put yourself in her position if the tables were turned. You can't constantly make her feel like you're holding it over her head. People make mistakes and sometimes you have to forgive them. Holding a grudge over her makes you the weak one, which you're finding out. It's made you bitter and someone I barely recognize anymore. Forgive her or let her go."

Well fuck, maybe I should be taking my own advice here.

He's quiet, his gaze on the window and the smoke curling around the frame and then out the window with a breeze of crisp winter air. "Dad told me once that you can't love someone until you've had to forgive them. Maybe he's right."

I think he says that to me because we both needed to hear it. My mom always told us the best relationships are the ones that made it through darkness. The ones where people look at one another and see hurt and say, you're worth it.

Tyler's face as he was leaving haunts me. Will we ever be at that point or did I ruin what we could have had?

The thought that I ruined it with him is the worst feeling, one that gnaws at me all morning. He tried and I turned him away. For what?

Well I know why but it still hurts to know he wants more and he can't tell me why.

Raven
chapter 20
WHERE I STAND

A COOL BREEZE moves through my room, chilling me as I curl into my pillow. When I open my eyes, I realize I left my window cracked this morning but the haze remains in my room.

Rawley left at some point and I'm left staring at the window, wondering what to make of earlier this morning.

I think of Tyler immediately and everything he said to me last night. I go over it all, every word and analyze it for its meaning. I'm also reminded, a stirring deep in my chest that I shouldn't have let him leave last night. There was something off. He wasn't drunk but the look in his eyes and the way he was shaking, it just wasn't right. My concern though had been overridden by my need to protect myself and I ignored it. I'd selfishly wanted him gone so I'd pushed aside my own concern and let him go.

I startle when my phone rings. As sad as it sounds, no one calls me anymore. Most communication with my family and friends is through text. Maybe it's Tyler. He said not to answer his texts, but what if he calls?

Sliding one arm out from under my blanket, I stretch across the bed for the phone. Peeking at the screen, I see it's Red.

Groaning dramatically into the receiver, I roll onto my back and stare at the ceiling. "Why are you calling me this early?"

"It's ten in the morning, Raven." He snorts. "Have you talked to Tyler lately?"

My stomach jumps at his name, an indication that his effect on me will never go away. "Why?"

"He didn't show up for work." The sounds of air tools and a lift being raised drown him out and it's everything I can do to hear him. "Have you talked to him or not? I don't have time. We're fuckin' swamped."

My heart pounds erratically, pressing the phone to my ear, struggling to hear him. "Well yeah, I saw him last night. He left about three."

Red's quiet for a second and I hear him drop something. "Fuck. Did he say where he was going when he left? I went upstairs and the place is empty aside from an empty fifth of whiskey. He's never *not* come to work. Do you have any idea where he may have gone?"

Sitting up, I swing my legs over the side of my bed. "Well, no, he left pissed off. We were arguing most of the night and when he left I just assumed he was headed home."

"Okay, I gotta go and call around. See if I can track his ass down."

"Wait, let me know when you find him."

"Yeah, sure."

Scrambling around my room, I throw on a pair of jeans and my Ducks hoodie and head for the door. I don't know where I'm going but I can't just sit in Eugene not knowing where he is or if he's okay.

That feeling I couldn't shake when I woke takes over and roots itself deep in my chest. It hurts, a painful twist thinking he's out there, possibly hurt because I didn't take the time to make sure he was okay before he left.

I know he's an adult and is perfectly capable of taking care of himself but still, this is Tyler we're talking about and I'm always going to care. Always. Regardless of anything that's said or done between us. It's different with him.

I'm ten minutes outside of Eugene on the I-5 heading toward Lebanon when I hear my ringtone. Reaching inside my purse, I dig around for my cell phone, desperate to answer it before it stops ringing.

When I glance at the screen, I see it's Lenny calling and my hands shake as I bring the phone to my ear. "Lenny, tell me he's okay." There's silence on the other end. I think I hear her sniffle but I'm too wound up to really notice.

"I don't know, Raven. His mom literally just called the shop and told Red that Tyler was in an accident. They wouldn't give her much information over the phone other than he was airlifted to Portland."

Airlifted? *Oh God. It must be serious.* Red was airlifted after he was shot and he nearly died.

"Did they say how badly he's hurt? Is he okay?"

She's hesitant to answer. I know she's struggling with the same fears I am because of what happened with Red. "Didn't say. Red's on his way to the hospital. I'm just waiting for Jude and Eldon to come down and help with the shop so I can leave."

"Lenny—" My voice breaks. "Please, if you know something, anything, I need you to tell me. How badly was he hurt? Is he gonna be okay?"

She pauses again and it's excruciating. "I'm telling you the truth, I don't know. She didn't say. Just that he was airlifted."

"I'll meet you at the hospital," I tell her.

"No, pick me up. I'm gonna have Mia pick Nova up from school."

"Yeah, sure. Be there in like forty-five minutes."

I'm doing eighty on the freeway and I know I shouldn't be, but I can just tell the cop it's an emergency, right?

When I arrive at the shop, skidding to a stop in the back parking lot, Lenny's waiting outside for me, leaning against an old Mercury.

Her eyes soften when she eases into the passenger seat. "I know it's easier said than done, but let's try and relax until we know what's happening."

I don't look at her as we're pulling out of the parking lot. I can't because I'll cry. The tears are already there and I don't want to break down. Crying right now would only lead me to thinking the worst and I won't allow myself to go there, not yet.

"This is all my fault," I tell Lenny when we're on the freeway again. "I shouldn't have let him leave when he was so angry. I could tell something was off but I didn't do anything about it."

Lenny reaches over, placing her hand on my shoulder. "Hey, stop thinking like that. There's no way you could've predicted this would happen. Besides we all know how Tyler gets when he's mad. It would have been nearly impossible for you to stop him from leaving if that's what he wanted. He's more stubborn than Red."

A painful lump fills my throat. Did he wreck because of me? Did he forget to take his medication again because of me? I remember seeing him after he had the seizure in the shop. There was blood soaking his face from a cut on his forehead. It was awful and when I asked him what happened he admitted he was so tired from us not getting any sleep the night before he forgot to take it in the morning.

Annoyance claws at my skin, a sick lurch traveling through my stomach.

As much as I feel responsible for this, a realization hits me. With him my life makes sense. The thought of my life without him, it's unbearable.

LENNY AND I RUSH inside the hospital two hours later after hitting traffic. It takes us another ten minutes to find Red upstairs in the waiting room for the ICU.

"They haven't said anything but he's in surgery," Red says, embracing Lenny when she wraps her arms around his waist. "Apparently he drove off the freeway somewhere near Brownsville and took out a barn and some fencing. Rolled the truck. A farmer found him unconscious but at least breathing on his own." He gives a nod to two police officers sitting in the corner.

I process what he's saying for a moment. "He was drinking." My voice trembles over the words.

"Yeah, I gathered that much." Red's face flashes with anger. "Stupid son of a bitch. Why would he be driving after he was drinking?"

Nervously, I chew on my thumb. "Because he was trying to work up the courage to come see me. He wanted to tell me he loved me. He didn't seem drunk when he was there. Maybe a little buzzed and truthfully, something definitely seemed off, but I've been around Tyler enough to know he wasn't drunk. Do you think it's possible he had a seizure? I mean, maybe that's why he wrecked?"

We move to sit down in the waiting area where Red brings his hand up to run over the back of his neck. "As long as he's taking his meds, he shouldn't have, but he hasn't been acting like himself lately so who knows."

He's right. He hasn't been.

For the next four hours, we wait as time passes agonizingly slow with his parents by our side. I wanted to talk to his mom but I had no idea what to say to her, so I remained quiet.

They wouldn't offer any updates other than he was in surgery. Every time we asked, we got the same answer.

I can't think or feel. My mind is numbly unaware of everything going on. Voices seem distant and muddled. Motions seem uncontrolled, my thoughts on Tyler and why I let him leave. I shouldn't have. I just shouldn't have.

Sitting there staring at the nurses' station in the corner, suddenly, I'm worn out. Mostly from being up most of the night, but I hate this feeling rushing through me. The one of being in a hospital, waiting and helpless.

When my dad passed away, they say he died right there on the floor of the shop from a massive heart attack. Red performed CPR on him until the paramedics got there and then they took over, continuing for nearly a half an hour. It was an hour before they finally pronounced him dead, and I was there, waiting with my mom and brothers. Worst night of my life.

When Red was shot, we waited for days for him to come around. I couldn't help but relate all of those instances together into one.

Waiting on the unknown.

IT'S LATE. THE sky dark outside and every time the door opens to the waiting room, I'm chilled to the bone. It's hours after we arrived, but it seems like days. In fact, it's been six hours and thirty-seven minutes since I stepped foot inside this room. On minute thirty-eight, a doctor in navy-colored scrubs and black hair comes around the corner holding his scrub cap in his hands.

He scans the crowd. "Who's the family of Tyler Hemming?"

Red clears his throat, sitting up straighter in the chair giving the doctor a nod and then to Tyler's parents. "We're it."

The doctor looks at the five of us and then sits down in an empty chair across from his mother. Leaning forward his voice is low, maintaining privacy. "Mrs. Hemming, does Tyler have epilepsy or some other condition that would cause him to have seizures?"

His mom has tears in her eyes and nods. "He has epilepsy."

"It explains a lot. As you know, Tyler was in a car accident this morning and brought in unconscious. He had some lacerations to his face, neck and ear. He came out of it for a moment but then went straight into another seizure. A CT scan confirmed he had a brain hemorrhage so we went in and opened a small section of his skull to release the pressure and control the bleeding. We did run into a few complications with his blood pressure and bleeding, but he's stable now. Amazingly enough he didn't break any bones, just the head injury."

His father speaks up right away. "I don't understand. He takes medication to control his epilepsy. What do you think could've caused him to have one?"

That's why he seemed so off. I should have known.

"First of all, it's not completely unheard of for an individual to have a seizure even when on their medication. It's rare but unfortunately, it does happen. Second, we had a toxicology report run and it will be in later because when Tyler was brought in the officers noticed the smell of alcohol on him. It's absolutely possible that a seizure caused him to lose consciousness and run off the road though. It's going to take some time for his head injury to heal, but he should be just fine." He nods to the police officers still sitting in the waiting room. "When his toxicology comes back, we have to report it." Before he leaves, the doctor looks at Nora, Tyler's mom. "He's going to be out of it for a day or two but in the morning, you should be able to see him."

Shaking his head when the doctor leaves, Red stares at the ground, his hands clasped together as he leans forward. "I can't believe he was that stupid."

I don't have the strength to tell Red it's me who was stupid. I let Tyler leave for my own selfish reasons, because I didn't want him to stay, and I should have made him stay. I just hope he wakes up and I can fix this and tell him how much I need him.

Tyler
Chapter 21
REALITY

I'M NOT SURE how long I've been asleep but it feels like days. It's the best sleep I've had in my entire life too. The kind where you dream of nothing. It's just sleep. Which tells me it was probably aided by drugs and not just me being tired.

When I do finally open my eyes, the reality of everything takes a while. It's obvious that I'm in a hospital yet I don't know how I got here. I do have an idea that I had a seizure. The few times I've landed myself in the hospital have been from seizures.

Every inch of me hurts, the dull kind of pain like you're slowly being torn apart from the inside out.

I lie here for a while before a nurse comes in. She smiles at me, tapping her finger to the board. "Nice to see you're awake, Mr. Hemming. I'm Cindy, your nurse. I'm just going to check your vitals and then I'll let the doctor know you're awake."

I don't say anything to her as she goes about her job. I just keep staring out the window and the snow falling wondering how badly I've gotten myself into trouble. I was drinking. But I wasn't drunk. I remember that much. Like a film reel, bits and pieces of the night come back to me and the last thing I remember distinctively is Raven and our argument in her dorm room. The look on her face haunts me.

The door opens again. A tall man in a white coat approaches the chair next to my bed and sits down. "Mr. Hemming, glad to see you're awake. How are you feeling?"

Like shit.

I nod, but it hurts. My body is sore, like I've been hit by a ton of bricks, each one thrown separately. "Sore."

"Any headaches or blurred vision?"

I blink several times. My head's buzzing, a lingering headache around my ears. "A little bit."

"That's expected. You were in a car accident and we had to go in and control a bleed in your brain. A blood test confirmed your blood alcohol content was not above the legal limit."

Oh, thank God.

"Taking that into consideration and factoring in your epilepsy, we are going with the assumption the accident was caused by a seizure. Do you have any memory of the accident or the moments leading up to it?"

I had plenty of memories but I'm not about to share them with this guy I've never met until now. "I didn't take my meds," I admit, remembering my decision to say screw it for just one day. A pang of guilt hits my chest making it hard to swallow. I knew better. I knew better yet I still fucking did it.

The doctor's eyes narrow. "I guess I don't need to tell you how irresponsible that was. You got behind the wheel of a vehicle knowing you were at a higher risk for a seizure. You're lucky you didn't kill yourself or someone else."

Clearing my throat, I ask, "What happened?"

Please tell me I didn't hit anyone.

"You crashed near Brownsville from what the police tell me. Hit a barn and took out some fencing. Didn't do much damage but you rolled the truck. The owner found you and called it in."

There's a knock on the door and Red steps in, giving a nod to the doctor. He then stands at the end of the bed near the window. He doesn't say anything and looks at both of us.

The doctor stands. "Also, your license will be suspended. Any time someone has a seizure, they lose their license for a period of at least three months, sometimes longer."

Fuck. I knew that was coming.

Red clears his throat, taking the doctors attention. "How long will he be here?"

The doctor turns to look back at me. "We're going keep you here for about three more days and then you should be able to go home to your family."

Family? What family? The memories of the argument I had with my parents and the harsh words I said to Raven come crashing back. Though everything's fuzzy, I know I probably destroyed any remaining love she had for me.

Red doesn't miss the look that flashes on my face when he says family. He waits for the doctor to leave before his gaze returns to mine.

I'm the first to speak and say, "Sorry." I know it's probably not enough, but it's the only thing I can think to say.

He shrugs, shaking his head. He's struggling with what to say to me.

It's five minutes at least before he tips his head, a contemplative expression guarding his real feelings. "Look, Tyler, I don't know what's going on with you… but I do know that you're going through some shit and I'm sorry about that. I know I wasn't easy on you with the whole Raven thing, but you fucked up big this time."

I try to draw in a deep breath but it hurts. "I know."

Red walks over and takes the seat the doctor vacated next to my bed. He leans forward resting his elbows on his knees, turning his head so he's looking me in the eyes. "They pulled your license and you're fucking lucky as hell that your blood tests came back below the legal limit or they would be charging you with DWI as well."

Damn. I had it revoked when I was eighteen for a seizure and I knew getting it back was a bitch. You had to go three to six months without a seizure and then go through a shitload of tests just to get it back.

He clears his throat. "I don't think I have to tell you but your job requires you to have a valid driver's license."

I nod, because I know this. You don't think about the consequences when it's happening but the aftermath can be brutal.

His stare remains on mine. "You covered for me when I needed you and I'm gonna do the same for you. You're not losing your job. We'll figure something out."

I nod again, relief washing over me. Drawing in another shaky breath, I say, "I'm sorry, man. I know I've fucked up big time but I'll be damned if I know how I let it get this bad." Tears sting my eyes and it fucking pisses me off that I can't control my emotions.

"We'll get through this." He chuckles, leaning back in the chair beside the bed. "At least you weren't shot, man."

I try to laugh but it hurts my head. "Yeah, there's that."

"Seriously though, Tyler, what's been going on with you? You've been in a downward spiral for months and honestly, you've got us worried."

Ever since Red was shot, he's tried to be more open and accessible. Talking about feelings was never our thing but I guess something changes in you when you've looked death in the face.

"I don't know, man. It's just been one thing after another. After Berkley lost the baby and left me, I went to my parents' house to tell them about everything that was going on." I take a deep breath.

Telling Red is the right thing. He deserves to know why I've been acting the way I have but once I say it, once it's out there, there's no taking it back. "So a month later, I told my mom about Berkley and losing the baby and how upset I was because I was excited about starting a family."

Turning away from him, I gaze at my hands, not wanting to see his expression when I share this next part.

"I expected her to be upset too. I figured being a grandma was something she would be excited about and to lose the chance before she even knew she had it would be hard. But, man, was I wrong. Instead of disappointment in losing the baby, she told me that Berkley couldn't have been pregnant with my baby because my epilepsy medication would more than likely make me sterile. So basically my mom casually informed me that not only would I most likely never be a father, but that my girlfriend of six years cheated on me and got pregnant by some other douchebag then proceeded to tell me it was mine."

Taking a deep breath, I return my stare to Red's and when I do, I'm surprised to see no pity or sadness, but anger.

"Are you fucking kidding me? Why the hell didn't your parents tell you this before?" I know that tone. It's Red's protective growl and even though it may make me sound like a pussy, it makes me happy to know someone is on my side. "Yeah, well I asked that same question and apparently they didn't think it was important enough of a detail to tell me when I was younger and then over time, the right moment for them to tell their son he is most likely sterile never presented itself."

Red sits for a minute, I assume taking in everything I've said, before he leans forward. "Wait, you said that the medication would more than likely make you infertile, but how can you be sure? Maybe you're the exception."

Shaking my head, I return my gaze to my hands. "No. I went and got tested after my mom dropped the bomb and the doctors were right. I'm shooting blanks. Would have been nice to know when I was in high school and spent a shit ton of money on condoms." I try to smile, making light of a difficult conversation, but I don't have it in me.

He sighs, his arms crossed over his chest. "So who the fuck's baby was Berkley carrying?"

"I don't know for sure but I have my suspicions." I clench my hands into fists. I've gone over this in my head at least a hundred times and the only name that keeps coming to mind is Rawley. He's been fucking her for months. Who's to say it didn't start before we broke up? But would he really do something like that? Did he have it in him?

Red knows me and the look on my face. "I know what you're thinking, Tyler, and I just can't believe Rawley would do that. Yeah, he's been acting like a real dick lately, but he's known you most of his life and I can't believe he would cross that line with you."

I shake my head. "Does it really matter? She cheated, got pregnant and then had the fucking nerve to tell me it was mine. I don't know that I would hold it against him if it was him, you know. I'm more upset that she didn't value the six years we were together and threw it away. She probably didn't even know who the damn father was."

Red's quiet for a moment, the two of us looking at the snow falling outside. It's late in the year for it to snow, but apparently the weather was like me and couldn't get it's shit together either.

"Okay, so I get why you've been acting so off lately but what about Raven? Does she know about this?" Red looks over at me, waiting for an answer.

It's the first we've talked about Raven since that conversation in the bar. The one where he hit me for fucking his little sister. Part of me doesn't want to say anything. I'm pretty sure being hit today would suck, but I know he wants to know. "No, I haven't told her," I say, my stare on my IV in my hand "Honestly, it's why I tried to avoid having a real relationship with her for so long. How can I ask her to give up a chance to have a family just to be with me? I mean she's twenty years old. She's in college. She shouldn't be making decisions like this before getting to really find out what she wants."

"Tyler, I think we both know that my sister doesn't do anything she doesn't want to." He chuckles, shaking his head. "Don't you think you owe it to her to make up her own mind? How do you even know she wants kids? You need to tell her about this."

"That's just it. I don't. I haven't told her my reasoning. And I don't think at twenty, she knows what she wants either," I tell him. "How can she? What if I tell her and she doesn't care now, but what happens five or even ten years from now when she sees some couple pushing a stroller down the street and all of a sudden it hits her that she wants that but she's trapped with a man who can't give it to her? What then?"

Red raises his hand to the back of his neck, rubbing it slowly and then lets out a deep breath. "Raven has always been what my grandma used to call an old soul. Ever since she was young, she was always so much more mature and capable of making decisions that were well thought out. Hell, my dad used to joke that she sucked all of the maturity and common sense out of Rawley in the womb. I think you need to give her more credit. She knows what she wants, always has."

I laugh lightly. He's absolutely right. But it doesn't change what I said to her. "Yeah, well that's probably not an option now anyway. Before the crash I went to her dorm room to talk to her and we had a pretty big argument. I left after she told me she didn't want me in her life anymore so I don't think whether I can have kids really matters to her."

He gives a nod to the door, a slow decisive lift of his chin. "Well, judging by the way she acted while waiting to hear from your doctors, I'm gonna call bullshit on that, but that's between you two. Talk to her, man."

There's a pain deep inside my chest when I hear that. "She's here?" After our argument, I didn't think she would have come. Not that I remember everything that was said, but I know shit got ugly.

"She's been here for two days. Hasn't left once."

The pain intensifies to the point where I turn to look back out the window. The snow keeps on falling and all I can think is could it be possible that maybe, just maybe, that even though she said she's not willing to risk being hurt by me again, she still loves me enough to take the leap?

It's then I know Red's right. Enough is enough. I need to tell her why I've pushed her away so much.

IT'S ONLY MINUTES after Red leaves when a red-faced Raven comes through the door. Her eyes are bloodshot, the sleeves of her gray hoodie pulled down over her hands as she wipes her cheeks. While she's been crying and I can't judge whether she's sad or mad so I figure there's a fifty-fifty chance I'm going to get yelled at.

I hold up my hand. "Don't come in here if we're going to fight. I'm highly medicated and there's a no fighting policy."

She laughs and closes the door behind her. "I didn't come here to fight." Taking the few steps from the door to the chair Red was just sitting in, she takes my hand in hers. "You scared the crap out of me!"

"Yeah, well," I chuckle softly, my voice rough from the breathing tube I had, "I scared the crap out of myself and a farmer, apparently." Truth be told, the reality of my decision is what scares me. And the fact that I wasted so much time with Raven because I thought I knew what she wanted. I don't know what she wants.

"What happened?" she finally asks, probably curious if I remember anything.

Though the events are hazy, I remember most of what happened in her dorm. It takes me a minute to reply. I'm staring at her face, remembering everything I love about her, and the real possibility that she can walk out of here and I might not ever see her again. I wouldn't blame her if she did. "I don't remember all of it, but I know I was pissed off that morning because of what my meds had done and decided fuck it, I'm not taking them anymore. I admit, it wasn't the best decision I've ever had." I blew out a breath and stared at her. "And then I went to see you...."

She gasps, shaking her head in disbelief I made such an irresponsible decision but there's confusion written all over her face. Probably wondering why I was upset with my medication. She focuses on the bigger issue at hand when she asks, "What the hell were you thinking, Tyler? You could have died."

"I know. *Believe* me, I know, but at the time I was just so fucking pissed. Pissed at my parents, pissed at Berkley and so damn pissed at my own body for betraying me. I mean, shit, I literally can't control my own brain. I was just tired of feeling so out of control of my own life. So yeah, I knew when I didn't take my meds that morning something could happen." I stare at my hands instead of her face because the disapproving look she's handing me, isn't one I want to see. "But honestly, part of me was okay with that."

Maybe she understands, or thinks she does, or wants to, but she'll never truly get it because I can't explain it.

"I'm just glad you're gonna be okay," she says softly, bringing my hand to her lips.

"Are you?" My voice is rough, my gaze on her, waiting.

"God, Tyler, how can you ask that? Of course I care whether you're okay. You know how I feel." There's a sense of pleading in her tone and I know she's not lying. "Don't you get it, it's not about whether I love you. It's been about you loving me the way I need. You made it clear you didn't want that and then suddenly you did. It's all just going to take some time for me to catch up."

I'm not sure how to tell her this, so I blurt it out. "There's something I'm not telling you, something I should have been honest with you about when I figured out my feelings in the first place."

Her face pales. "What? You're not really dying, are you?"

"No, nothing like that." My hand slides slowly across the white blanket, to the very edge where she takes it. "Do you remember when I walked into Murphy's that night and you asked me what I was drinking away with a bottle of whiskey and I wouldn't answer you?" She nods so I continue, our eyes locked on one another, "That afternoon I had just found out that the medicine I'm on for my epilepsy caused me to become infertile. I had gotten the results back about an hour before I saw you. And not only that, but it meant that Berkley had cheated on me."

For a moment, Raven remains quiet, soaking in what I just told her and her expression is completely unreadable and it drives me fucking insane that I can't hear her thought process. I desperately want to know her reaction to it. Was it anything like mine when I found out? Probably not but I remember the knotting in my stomach, the way my heart raced and the haze of confusion that took over. It was almost as if I didn't know myself anymore.

Raven tilts her head ever so slightly, her only indication she actually heard anything I said to her. My heart races, the monitor beside the bed a clear indication I'm nervous.

Raven blinks, twice, and then reaches for my hand. "God, Tyler. I am so sorry. I can't imagine what that must be like for you."

Relief washes over me but my mind clouds with uneasiness. Mostly because she's not upset, though I still think she has a right to be and maybe that's coming later, but for now, I'll take what she's giving me. "I thought I knew what I didn't want, but I was wrong," I say the words tentatively as if I'm testing them out. "I didn't want to fall in love with you because I didn't want to get hurt. And I didn't want to hurt you in the process, but I did." It's that moment, the one where I have to breathe deeply before continuing to keep from crying and when I do, the words tremble like my heart, knowing this girl, she's the one. Maybe she always has been and it took this to see it. "I thought the best thing for you would be to find someone else because I couldn't give you the life you deserve, but the truth is I can't do it. I'm too selfish. I want you. Hell, I *need* you and even though the thought of you someday changing your mind and realizing you want more than I can give scares the shit out of me, but I can't find it within myself to truly let you go."

Just as I expect, anger rises up in her and her cheeks flush. "I should be totally fucking pissed at you right now for putting me through all this. And if you didn't just have brain surgery I'd totally punch you in the face." My eyes are wide when she leans in and yanks my hand into hers holding it tightly. I'm not sure what she's about to do but she surprises me when she takes a calming breath. "At this point in my life, I'm not ready for kids either and if I am in the future, we'll discuss our options then." Her face is full of strength, shining with a steadfast and serene peace that reminds me of Lyric. "I know it means something to you to father your own, but if it's not a possibility, it's just not. We work around it." Tears spill down her cheeks, and my emotions return, my throat and chest tightening. "I'm not saying no to a relationship with you, because you're the only one I want, but I'm not saying yes just yet. I think we've been through too much to just jump back into things so suddenly. Would you be okay with us taking it slow, just for now?"

I'm such a fucking idiot.

I breathe out the heavy breath I'd been holding. "Yeah, I can take it slow."

She can barely control her crying. It's bordering on hysterical when I give her an emotional chuckle and pull her into my arms. I want to sink to my knees at the thought of losing her.

"I'm sorry, Tyler. For everything I said."

"There's nothing to be sorry for. We both said things we didn't mean. But I have to ask, Raven, what is it that you want?" I ask, my voice uneven as if I'm nearing tears too and I'm not sure if I've ever actually asked her what she wanted.

"I want *you*. I do. If these last two days taught me anything, it's that there's no question about it. I'm in love with you." She holds up her hand. "I still want to take it slow though. We have a lot of things to work out but I know that I want you."

Nodding, I draw back, my hands cupping her cheeks. "What part?"

She sighs, smiling. "All of you."

There's a moment where she watches me, as though she's remembering something, or maybe nothing at all. I'm not sure and I can't tell because I'm more caught up in the fact that she still wants me.

"I'm sorry," she says suddenly crying into her hands, the tears returning. "I'm so sorry. I should have done something to stop you from leaving that night."

Taking her hand in mine, I bring it to my lips. "Hey, don't be. None of this is your fault. You weren't the one who didn't take his seizure medication and then made a complete ass out of himself."

A smile tugs at her lips. "You're right. That wasn't me. *Jesus,* what kind of asshole does something like that?"

"A big one." My laugh shakes through me, causing me to wince while a gnawing pain spreads through my head at the onset.

"What now, then?" she asks finally, clicking the button for the nurse when she notices I'm in pain. Turning to look me directly in the eyes, her expression of heartache and remorse mirror my own. We don't speak, just stare at each other.

"We take it slow like you want and I'll try to be patient."

Tears stream down her reddened cheeks and I quickly wipe her tears away and pull her into my arms, the best I can at least which is a sideways hug.

"Raven," I say, waiting for her eyes to meet mine when I draw back from her embrace. "This may not be the time or the place to tell you this…" my heart thuds louder and then steadies out into a rapid rhythm, "but I love you, and I'm not going anywhere. I'm sorry for the things I said to you. I had no right to accuse you of anything and treat you that way. I'll wait for however long you need me to. I don't know what I can offer you, but I'll give you what I can."

"We—" She starts to say something but stops.

I panic at what her reaction to my words will be and add, "This. Whatever we have is worth waiting for," I say, reaching for her hands. "I love *you*." I blink, nerves taking over.

She nods, slowly, as if she's letting the words sink in. And then she surprises me by saying, "I love you, too, Tyler."

My face spreads into the warm smile. Here I am, lying in a hospital bed in front of the girl I love, and for some reason I might never understand, she actually loves me back.

I still remember the girl who sat in my truck one snowy night, big brown eyes watching me with curiosity as I asked her age, wishing somehow she would have been older. Maybe I knew all along there was something between Raven and me that could only be ignored for so long before it changed.

All my uncertainty of her not wanting a life with me seems silly now. She showed up for me, waited for me, and now I will wait for her.

Looking at her now, why did I ever have fear?

chapter 22
KISS ME

TYLER'S RELEASED FROM the hospital on a Saturday, a week and two days after the accident. For having a hole drilled in his head, I think a week is pretty fucking good. As did his doctor. It just goes to show you when Tyler's determined, he's unstoppable.

I drive home for the weekend to help him get settled in at his apartment. Mostly because he said the idea of having his mother help him use the bathroom wasn't happening but he'd gladly let me assist his wang. Muff kindly agreed.

The doctor advises him to take a few months off work but he can't afford it so he settles with a few weeks and I know even that's pushing it for Tyler. He's never missed a day of work until now.

I move around his apartment, washing sheets, cleaning dishes and putting away his premade and labeled meals my mom made him. I wouldn't say I've convinced myself to be with him in the terms he wants, but I'm here, helping him out and organizing his apartment because it's a goddamn mess and I can't stand it.

Some would wonder why my hesitation, right? He loves me, and I love him. Should be simple. Not exactly.

I'm in the kitchen labeling the pot roast I made when he comes out of the bathroom laughing after taking a shower.

"You didn't tell me I looked like a drunken prank." He stops in front of the counter and smiles at me.

I try not to laugh as I look at his half-shaved head. "Well, I figured you could only handle so much bad news at once."

"True." He runs his hand over the left side of his head that's shaved from the accident and gives a nod to the bathroom. "Can you help me out?"

I'll admit, I miss the longer hair he had. "Yeah, sure." I follow him in the bathroom taking a seat on the counter in front of him. He reaches his hands behind his head, grabbing the neck of his shirt, and pulling it over his head, tossing it to the floor.

My stare is immediately on his chest and then to his stomach. He's lost some weight in the week he was in the hospital but he still looks amazing. Every defined muscle is on torturous display for me. It's really hard not to act on these impulses I have seeing how we're in a bathroom and these rooms are a weakness for us.

His lips twist into a smirk, knowing what's going through my head. I have half a mind to shove my panties in his mouth so he won't smile at me like that. "Stop looking at me like that."

He holds up his hands, turning his smile up a notch. "My bad."

I watch carefully as he pulls out the clippers from under the sink. When his arm lifts, I catch sight of his tattoos. I've seen them hundreds of times but his ink is beautiful, full of red and black designs.

"I've always loved your tattoos." I run my fingers ghosting over the black markings, tracing over them with the lightest touch.

"I'm glad you like them." His voice is rough, as though me touching him is hard for him. Probably about as hard as it is for me being in here with him.

His hands move to my thighs, trailing up them ever so lightly. I shiver, my legs wrapping around his and pulling him to me.

I pick up the clippers. "Ready?"

He nods, giving me a smile. "I guess so."

I'm careful because the last thing I want to do is get the clippers anywhere near the bandage on his head. Relaxing, his eyes drift closed as I pass over his head, thick black beautiful hair I used to thread my fingers through falls onto the floor at his feet.

"I'm going to miss your hair."

The corners of his mouth twitch into a half smile. "It'll grow back."

I know it will but in a strange sense, this, me shaving his head is like a fresh beginning in a bigger sense.

When I'm finished, his eyes open and my heart pounds in my chest, so nervous, but also from the way he's watching me. He's in love with me and I don't think I've ever noticed the look, until now. My heart lurches and it's easy to get lost in the moment when he looks at me like this.

I think he knows what he's doing to me and clears his throat, his hands still on my thighs. "Do you want to watch a movie with me?"

"Sure." At least on the couch I'll probably be less likely to want to have sex with him.

Wrong.

It's clear Tyler's thoughts are not on the movie. Once the opening credits are displayed and his head is in my lap, his left hand is dangerously close to my V and I know D is looking for a little action.

When his hand moves further up, I stop him and Tyler sits up, staring at me. He knows he crossed the line but he doesn't say anything.

I open my mouth to say something but forget what I'm even going to say when I meet his eyes. So instead, I lean in and kiss him because I'm an idiot and I miss kissing him.

Curling his hand to cup my cheek, his lips give me what I need, even harder than what I imagine he will give me. I moan at the sensation, blend of warm and wet soft lips making contact with mine. My hand fists in the fabric of his T-shirt as his tighten around me. Without meaning to, I straddle his lap.

Tyler moans deeply at the change in our position and greedily moves his hands lower over my ass. A spike of nervousness and excitement pricks my skin, settling in my belly. I've missed him so much.

His fingers clench into tight fists around the hem of my shirt. That's when his hard length presses into my center, his hips straining a little closer to capture the friction.

"Raven." He groans, his eyes squeezing shut as a shudder moves through him.

Hearing my name on his lips makes my heart stumble.

I don't have a chance to recover before he growls softly, possessively, against my lips. "You have no idea how much I need you."

By the hardness pressing against me, I have a pretty good idea.

And that's when I stop. He does need me, but not this way. Not yet.

He notices the hesitation and then I move to sit next to him, pulling away completely. Rubbing his hands over his face, he groans before he drops them to his sides. "What's wrong?"

I stand, intending to leave when he grabs my hand.

When he speaks, it's low and deep. With pleading eyes, he presses gentle hands on my cheeks. "Come on, please. Raven... *don't* go. I'm sorry I did that. Please don't leave without giving me hope that we're okay."

"Tyler, we can't keep falling into this trap. If I have sex with you tonight, it's just like all the other times. I don't want to be here for just sex. I want more than that."

It's so hard for me to say because sex with Tyler is so fucking amazing. I want to wash my mouth out with soap for saying I can't have sex with him.

He exhales a huge breath and nods. "I want more than sex too. But I can't have you leave without knowing how you feel. Regardless of not having sex, which sucks, but I need to know." His words send my nerves into a rushed frenzy, my heart hammering as he clasps his hands together between his knees. "I don't know what you want out of a relationship," he admits. "Hell, I don't know if I really know how to be in a relationship but what I do know is I want to figure it out with you. It's up to you, Raven. You're going to have to take the lead because when it comes to this, I'm flying blind."

I understand what he's asking and by the fragile way he's holding onto my eyes. I don't think I can give it to him right now. We need time to figure out what a relationship between the two of us means.

I take his hands in mine, our eyes making contact. "We stumbled into our physical relationship, and I fell hard. We have to take this slow." His face falls with my words and I lose his eyes. "And I'm not saying no, but I feel like if we're truly meant to be, you'll be willing to wait while we build a stronger foundation and in order to do that we have to take it slower this time." Blinking slowly, his stare returns but there's not the same hope there once was. "I thought having a relationship with you would give me the security I needed, but the truth is, the definition I wanted before of boyfriend and girlfriend doesn't mean anything. It's just that. A definition. I think I've learned that when it comes to us, actions speak louder than words and while we can tell each other everything we want to hear, we aren't truly going to be successful in the long term without taking the time to really learn about each other and what the other needs out of this." Sighing, I release a deep breath. "I just can't jump back into what we were. The worst part of this was I wasn't looking out for myself. I went head on into this hoping to snag my childhood crush. If you're asking me if I love you, the answer is yes. But a true relationship needs to be built into more in order to survive. We had sex, Tyler. That's all we had and as great as it is, that's not a relationship that will last."

He nods, knowing there's truth to my words.

Dipping my head forward, I wait for him to look at me. "In order for this to work, you have to come to terms with who you are too. You can't use me as an escape from your life. You need to deal with not being able to have children and what that means for our future. I'm ready to make that sacrifice for *you*, but you have to be ready to make it too. And you need to forgive your parents."

He stares at me, his fingers dancing over my palm as he smiles softly. Raising his hand, he touches my cheek with just his fingertips like he's brushing away an eyelash. "Beauty and brains... how'd I get so lucky?"

I laugh. "Do you understand what I'm saying?"

His hand moves down my neck and then falls away and he nods, once more. "As much as I want to call you mine, I understand we might not be ready for that just yet. I'm willing to do it your way if it means we're getting a chance."

Sitting next to him on the couch again, his lips meet mine and when I don't push him away, his mouth comes back a second and third time, and on the forth, they don't leave mine.

"I love you," he whispers against my mouth. His tongue sweeps gently against mine. "I love you *so much*, Raven, and I'll wait forever for us."

My arms wrap around his neck. "I love you, too."

He closes his eyes. His fingertips press into the curve of my jaw as he holds my head in his hands. "Don't get me wrong, my D will miss your V, but he'll learn to deal with it," he teases, his humor returning.

I throw my head back, laughing. We're so inappropriate. "Muff loves her Wang."

His shoulders shake as a laugh rolls through him. "We need to talk about something else now. All this muff and wang talk isn't good for me."

I snuggle against his side and then stick a pillow between us. "Let's watch this movie."

Just being with him, like this, with everything out in the open is by far the most relaxing night I've experienced in a long time.

I DON'T HEAD straight back to Eugene Sunday night. Instead, I sneak home to grab a few things from mom's house. She's outside watering her newly planted flowers in the backyard so I go back there to check on her. She's been a huge help with Tyler too, and I know she'll be around the shop and upstairs during the day to check on him for me.

Watching Mom in her own world is what I love most. When no one else is looking and she's talking to my dad in the backyard. You know just by seeing her now she's completely at ease. She says she feels him out there, mostly because she loved our backyard and he did too. They spent many nights on the patio together talking, so naturally she'd find strength where they spent time together.

"Oh, hey, honey," she says when she notices me. Setting down the hose, she takes a seat next to me on the patio.

"How's Tyler doing?"

"Seems good. He'll probably need a lot of help tomorrow. I feel bad going back to school."

She waves her hand at me. "Don't, honey. He'll be fine and I'll take good care of him until you get back."

I kind of laugh because I've never really come out and told my mom what's been going on with Tyler and me, but she knows. A mother always secretly knows.

Her eyes move from mine to the table when a lady bug lands on her gardening gloves and stays there. She smiles softly, like it's an inside joke. "Your dad used to hate lady bugs and grasshoppers. Any flying insect with wings made him scream like a little girl."

I laugh too, because I remember that about him. My father was my hero in so many ways but if a bug landed on him, you'd think he was going to die.

"Since he passed, lady bugs always land on me. It's like he's telling me he's always with me."

"How do you manage so well without him here? I mean… I'm… I just can't imagine spending your whole life with someone, raising a family with them and then having them taken from you so suddenly."

She thinks about my question for a moment, tears flooding her eyes and I think maybe I shouldn't have asked.

I fretted over my mom for months after my dad passed away last May. Nervously waiting for the breakdown and the moment I'd have to be there for her to pick up the pieces like she did for Red when Nevaeh died. But Mom has only ever showed strength.

"Things like this." She points to the lady bug who hasn't moved. "He's all around me, in my thoughts, here in this house, the shop. He's all around us and I just"—her hand moves to her chest, over her heart—"he's here. Inside my heart. Your father possessed such a confidence about him you couldn't ignore. Even before I really knew him, he had my attention just off that confidence. He could walk into a room and captivate it just by being there. When he passed, that feeling never went away for me. I can walk outside and it's here, all around me. I can step foot in the shop and know he's there, beside Red, giving him the strength he needs to go on."

I smile, knowing it's true. The lady bug that's on her gardening gloves moves, flies around and then lands on my right hand.

"He's with you too, Raven. He's with all you kids."

"Well then, why can't he knock some sense into Rawley? Maybe turn himself into a spider and bite him," I tease, trying to keep from crying.

Mom laughs, her cheeks warming with the gesture. "Rawley will come around when he's ready. You just have to give him time."

"I can't believe you're saying that after what he did at the shop."

She frowns. "I'm not happy with his behavior, but with Rawley, forcing him to change his ways isn't going to make him do it. He's stubborn and he needs to do this on his own."

She's right, again.

"How are you and Tyler?"

I knew this was coming. Naturally she'd want to know since we hadn't talked about him.

"I gave him a maybe."

"A maybe?"

"Yeah. I didn't want to fall into the trap of just having sex with him." Normally I wouldn't tell my mother this but we were opening up so I just kept going. "For so long I wanted to be with him. I mean,

UNBEARABLE the TORQUED trilogy

you know how much of a crush I had on him. My face would literally turn beat red when he'd come into the room when I was younger."

She laughs, probably remembering me trying to come up with every excuse I could to go to the shop when Tyler first started working there. I wasn't shy about it either. I'd hang out in the shop like I belonged there just to be around him. So yeah, Mom knew I had a huge crush on him.

"So what was the hold up on his part?"

"Well, he kept telling me he wasn't in a position to fall in love. But then every time I came home for the weekend or a holiday, he wanted to get together. Then I wouldn't hear from him. It got to the point where I felt like I was being used. I knew it and he knew it. I was his escape from all the shit in his life he was trying to avoid. So when it finally got to the point where I told him I was done, suddenly he wants to be with me. It wasn't until after the accident that he told me he can't have kids and that's the reason he kept pushing me away."

"Wow, that's a lot. Wait, he can't have kids?"

"It's a long story but the short version is the medication he takes for his seizures caused him to be sterile. You're right. It's a lot and we're a mess, so despite the fact that I want to be with him, I think we have a lot to work through before that happens. His greatest fear is that if we're together and let's say, ten years from now when I'm ready to start a family, then what?"

"And how do you feel about that?"

"There are other ways of making a family. I love him, and I know I can't say how I'll feel ten years from now about having a child of my own, but what I do know is I want to figure it out with him. I think it's more important for us to remember that just because he can't father the child, it doesn't mean we can't a family. There are so many options nowadays and there are plenty of kids in need of a home. Lenny's proof of that."

286

Mom smiles at the mention of Lenny. She absolutely adores her, as we all do. "Yes, she is. Blood doesn't make you family, bonds do."

She's absolutely right on that. Friends are family too.

When you think about it, our presence in the world is tiny compared to the reality of it. It's our presence in the lives of others' that makes the world what it is. Every word we say, every gesture we make, every detail connects you to the presence you make whether you know it or not.

When bad things happen, there's nothing you can do to change them or the circumstances you find yourself in.

I think it's about telling yourself no matter what, you're going to be okay. You can prepare, sure, but there's some things in life you can't prepare for, or how you'll feel when it happens.

Tyler
Chapter 23
WAIT FOR ME

I'M USED TO being alone. I miss Raven and her constant laughter and the way she fills my apartment with her energy. Not having her here with me, my chest feels hollow and I don't like the sensation or the fact that silence greets me so often.

When you're dependent on others because you had your brain operated on, it's surprisingly difficult to do even the simplest of tasks. My memory isn't the best either so while I intend on going to the kitchen, I'll get there and forget why I went in there in the first place.

One certainty at this point, not having a license is definitely for the better, because hell, I'd probably get where I was going and forget why I was headed there in the first place. I felt like my grandpa when he had a stroke and I was constantly driving to Portland or Seaside because he'd forget where he was going and I'd have to go get him and bring him back to Lebanon.

Luckily for me, I live above the shop and people are constantly checking on me. Usually Lenny.

So while I'm lying on the couch Monday morning, there's a knock on my door.

It takes me a couple minutes but when I open the door in just a pair of basketball shorts, I'm expecting it to be her.

"Lenny, I told you I'm fine." I look up; it's not Lenny. It's my mom. "Oh, what are you doing here?"

She frowns, clearly upset with me. "You're my son, Tyler. I gave you space in the hospital, but you're going to talk to me now that you're home."

I knew sooner or later my mom would show up and demand I talk to her. I'm actually surprised she waited this long. I figured when I bailed on Christmas with her and my dad she would have blown up on me. But she didn't. She gave me time. I guess I should give her an opportunity, right?

I scratch my shaved head, but I don't say anything to her. I know I'm being a dick but damn it, I'm still pissed off.

"That's enough," she says, pushing past me with a bag of groceries in her arms. She sets them on the counter and opens the fridge, probably realizing I didn't need any of those because Raven took care of it. "You know, I get why you're mad at me, Tyler." Our eyes meet when I pause, just before sitting back down on the couch. "And I can't tell you how sorry I am but I'm still your mother and I deserve some respect."

I sit down on the couch and push the play button to the movie I was watching, completely ignoring her. I want to punch myself for disrespecting my mother this way.

Grabbing the remote from me, as if I'm a little boy, she turns off the movie. "You're going to hear me out even if you don't want to." She sits across from me, right in the way of my movie. "When you were little, I didn't care about what the side effects were because for the first time, you weren't helpless and having seizures *every* day. Do you know what it's like to not be able to leave your ten-year-old son alone because you're afraid at any moment he can have a seizure and hurt himself?"

I shake my head, because while I've been the one having them, I don't know what it's like for others who witness it, just like they don't understand my side of this. All I know is the lack of control I have, the sense of being helpless. The vulnerability that controls my life.

"When the doctors brought up the side effects of the medication, it wasn't necessary to talk to you about it because you were so young. I don't regret that. There was no need in telling a ten-year-old boy there was a possibility he might be sterile someday. All you needed to know was that for the first time in your life you had a chance to be normal. You had a chance to run and play just like every other ten-year-old. So your father and I, well," she pauses and looks down at her hands, and then back up at me, "We just put it in the back of our minds. I think we both figured the time would present itself and we would tell you then. I know it's no excuse and believe me, I *truly* regret not telling you sooner. But please understand your father and I *never* kept this from you in order to hurt you in any way. It was just the opposite actually. By the time you and Berkley finally got your heads out of your asses and decided to be serious, I was afraid. You were happy and it broke my heart that your father or I would have to be the ones to take a piece of that away from you. I understand it was a completely selfish act, but by not telling you, it protected us from having to be the person who hurt you."

I snort, crossing my arms over my chest like the defiant shit I'm being. "What did you think would happen? Were you going to wait until I got married and then say, well, by the way…?"

"I didn't say I didn't make a mistake, Tyler. We love you. So much. I'm just saying we didn't set out to hurt you and I'm sorry it happened this way. You're the most important person in our lives and I hope eventually you can forgive us."

We stare at one another for a moment, probably longer than she wants and then she stands, knowing I'm probably not ready. And I'm not. I'm a big grudge holder and it's going to take me a while to get over this. I try to put myself in her position if I had a son, but then that just upsets me too because that's not going to happen for me. Regardless, she is my mother and I can't treat her this way.

When she's at the door, I stand up and make the few steps to her. She's crying now and embraces me, her arms around my waist, hugging me.

"I love you, Mom."

She breaks down into sobs. "I love you, so much, Tyler."

"Would you like to have dinner next week? Me, Dad and you?"

She's shocked by my invitation, eyes wide and face flushing. "Yes, definitely. Just let us know when you feel up to it."

"Okay, I will. How about Wednesday night?"

She steps out the door. "Sounds great."

I knew I needed to make an effort with my parents. I couldn't keep holding it against them just because they were trying to protect me. They may have gone about it the wrong way but I know they love me and we need to move past this.

KNOWING I SHOULDN'T, I make my way downstairs to check on the guys and see how work is going this afternoon. As soon as I step foot in the shop, Red gives me that disapproving look. I know it because I used to give it to him when he'd show up after he was shot.

He glances up from the truck he's replacing a head gasket on, reaching for the shop towel on the fender. "You're supposed to be upstairs."

Sitting down on the stool next to his tool cart, I shrug. "I'm bored."

"I know that feeling."

My gaze sweeps over the shop at the cars on lifts, the sounds of air tools filling the metal building. Beside Lenny is a guy I've never seen before. He's younger, probably Daniel's age with blond hair he's got tucked under a Walker Automotive hat. "Who's the kid?" I ask, giving a nod behind him.

"Wesley. He's a friend of Jude's. We hired him as a lube tech last week." He knows by the look on my face what I'm thinking and he's quick to add, "He's not taking your job, man. He's only changing oil." Glancing over his shoulder, he sees him standing by Lenny as she changes brakes on an Explorer, flirting with her. Red looks over at me with an unamused expression. "He's not going to last long if he doesn't keep his eyes off my girl."

I'm only out there five minutes when Mia comes inside the shop, Nova at her feet. The bus just dropped her off and she still has her backpack on. Her brow scrunches when she sees me sitting beside her dad. "What happened to your hair, Uncle Ty?"

I run my hand over my head. "I made a really bad decision and didn't take my vitamins."

Knowing where I'm going with this, Red shakes his head, smiling.

Nova's eyes widen. "So they shaved your head?"

"Yeah."

"Jesus Christ," she mumbles, walking off toward the office.

I burst out laughing, as does Red, knowing she shouldn't say that but it's funny anyway. "Nova, you can't say that."

She says nothing to him and keeps walking. She probably thinks if she doesn't respond, she can pretend she didn't hear him.

Colt makes his way over next with a beer in hand. "So next time you're thinking about taking out a building, why don't you swing by my house," he suggests, smiling. "I got a fence I need to tear down and I'm just too fucking lazy to do it."

I chuckle. "I'll keep it in mind, old man."

"Get back to work," Red tells him.

He raises his hands when Red pushes him away. "I'm just saying, if he's going to run shit over, he'd be doing me a favor."

I'm glad someone finds entertainment in this. Leave it to Colt.

Red points to the door when another car comes in and I'm staring at it. "Go upstairs."

I do as he says, mostly because I don't want to do what he did and come back too soon and then have to take another week off. I have supplemental insurance that will pay for my time off but still, I can't afford to take three weeks off work.

All day I try not to think about Raven, but it's hard. All I do is think about us and where our relationship currently stands. I know she said we're good and basically together, but I finally understand why she wanted a definition with us before. It's maddening not knowing.

It's around six and I'm contemplating fixing myself something to eat when I hear the front door open. The only people who have a key are Red and Raven.

My heart lurches at the thought of seeing her. Gently I turn my head the direction of the door and sit up.

I breathe a sigh of relief when she walks through and turns to close the door. Once she's back facing me, I see she's holding two bags from the Chinese restaurant up the street. "Don't you dare get up, Tyler. Stay on the couch."

I do as she says because I want to watch her walk through the room and when she turns, I get a view of her ass. "You drove all the way back here from Eugene to bring me dinner?"

"Well, yeah." She looks at me quickly, and then away to the bags she sets on the coffee table in front of me, uneasiness masking her features. "Don't make it sound like it's that big of a deal. It's really not."

I study her thoughtfully for a moment, desperately wanting that uneasy look she carries to disappear. "It's kind of a big deal."

She reaches up and tugs at her hair, letting down her ponytail. Her hair spills down around her shoulders as she takes a seat beside me on the couch. "No, a big deal would have been me cooking for you." She gives a dismissive flick of her hand at the boxes on the table. "I brought takeout. There's a difference."

"Oh, well, in that case…." Pausing, I gaze at her speculatively. "It's all good."

It's then I notice she's wearing a T-shirt and sweat pants and while they look good on her, I miss those shorts and tank tops she wore all summer long. I hate winter for this very reason. Less skin visible for me.

"If you're going to play nurse, dress the part." And then I grab a fistful of her shirt and pull her on my lap. I shouldn't be doing it, but as I've said before, I'm not good at following the rules.

She steals a glance at my face when she's on my lap and slides off to sit next to me. "Tyler, I don't have a change of clothes with me. *Don't* rip my shirt."

"Oh, man. That sucks for you. Guess you'll have to play the part of the naughty *naked* nurse."

The corner of her lip curls into a grin. "You have a plan for everything, don't you?"

"If it means getting you naked then yes, I will always have a plan."

"Your plan is pushing boundaries," she tells me, a warning clear in her voice.

Playfully I hold my hands up and scoot away from her picking up a box of noodles and chopsticks. "I'll stop."

We eat mostly in silence, though she asks if I stayed upstairs like I was supposed to today. I lie at first and then grin. "I got really bored and went downstairs. Red yelled at me."

"Well, good. You should rest and get better."

I can't tell her that resting isn't possible with the pent-up frustration I have. If only she could relieve some of it. "Should we watch a movie?" she asks, attempting to distract me from her body.

I know what watching a movie is going to do. She'll lie down and I'll be thinking of all the ways I could cover my body with hers. Groaning, I sit back, running my hands over my face before dropping them on my lap. "Sure."

She scowls at me and the tone of my voice, unknowingly being completely fucking adorable with such a simple gesture. "Don't sound so enthused."

"I don't know how Red did this for so long. I'm fucking bored out of my mind. And horny."

Her cheeks flush. "Well, I can keep you company but we're not having sex."

"When did the naughty nurse have so many rules? In my fantasy of what a naughty nurse would do for me, there were no rules... *or clothes*." My hand moves to her thigh, higher, until she catches it.

Laughing, she stands up, making her way over to the TV and the movies surrounding it. She doesn't even look at the movie she puts in the DVD player and sits down next to me.

I wait a few minutes before I ask, "Will you go somewhere with me?"

There's a heavy sigh, one that I swear comes from her feet. "Tyler, we agreed. No dating. And no, I'm not going to your bedroom with you either."

"*Did* we?" I scratch my jaw. "I don't remember making any rules this time around. And how will this work if we don't date?"

Her eyes never leave my hands and I know what she's thinking. She loves my hands and this is hard for her too. "We haven't *yet*, but we will. And that includes no dinner dates. We'll get to dating soon."

"That's a dumb rule." I point to the now empty containers of Chinese food. "We're literally eating dinner right now."

"This is different. I brought this over and it's takeout."

Her rules make no sense and I think she knows it, but I'm not going to pressure her right now. This is new and we're still trying to figure out what it means. As much as I hated it at the time, I know why Raven pushed me away once I decided I wanted her too.

Now she's afraid if we give it a label, it will hurt worse if it doesn't work. I don't want that either but I'm going with whatever she wants this time.

"Okay, so no going out to dinner?" I'm not liking these rules at all.

She nods, twirling noodles around her chopsticks. "Precisely."

I frown and push the container away from me, leaning back. "I'm going to dinner with my parents Wednesday night."

Her face is expressionless when I say it, but her eyes give her away. "I'll totally go with you for that. Where are we going?"

"Valentino's."

"My last class on Wednesday is at noon. I'll come up after that."

My mind immediately focuses on the word come and she shakes her head when my eyes light up with amusement. Taking the pillow from beside her, she stuffs it between us. I don't care. As long as she's here with me, I'll take it slow, even though I don't want to.

It's something like ten minutes into the movie and I look over at Raven, my sexual frustration amplified as she walks around my apartment making herself at home and making popcorn. "Can I at least touch your boobs?"

She shrugs and sits down with a bowl of popcorn in her lap. Taking my hand, she places it on her boob. "Hell, why not."

I take a handful of popcorn with my other hand. "This is the best movie ever."

She laughs. "Uh huh."

RAVEN DOES AS she says and comes by Wednesday night for dinner. She gets there about an hour before we're supposed to meet my parents. I'm so completely bored that I'm ready when she arrives and sitting by the door like a kid dying to get out of the house on summer vacation.

Downstairs cars are lined up in front of the shop as we come outside, evidence the shop is staying busy. It's cold out tonight, a chill present in the air. Raven pulls the hood of her sweatshirt up over her head and I love that she's not worried about messing up her hair. She's comfortable in jeans and hoodies, much like myself.

"Thanks for driving." I tell her looking over at my truck parked in the corner of the lot that hasn't been touched in nearly a month. It sits with the front end smashed, flat tires and a shattered window covered with a tarp. It's totaled and waiting on the insurance company to settle on the payoff. At least I was smart enough to carry full coverage on it. Naturally, I was at fault and have to pay for not only the property damage I caused but the deductible on my insurance.

Breathing in deeply, I stare at the truck, my 1976 Ford F150 I bought when I was seventeen with my own money.

Raven notices my anxiety for the situation and the consequences I'm facing. She runs her hand over the stubble on my head. "I miss the hair I can pull."

She's trying to distract me and it works. I lean in, my body pressing to hers. With my hand on her hip, I run it up her spine to the base of her neck. Taking a handful of her hair in my fist, I grip it and tug. "I miss pulling yours while you're wrapped around my body," I whisper in her ear. I'm hard instantly and I know she feels it.

"Stop it, Ty." She breathes out unevenly. She can't stop her body from reacting to me. "If you keep this up, I'm leaving and you can go to dinner by yourself."

I drop my hand immediately and take a step back. She stares at me and I want to kiss her so fucking badly, but I know it might push her away. "You started that," I point out.

She nods and takes my hand, walking toward her car. "I know. And I'm sorry."

VALENTINO'S IS THE only Italian restaurant in Lebanon, and quite frankly, the best in the state. It's owned by Nevaeh's father, Tony Valentino, and we're frequent visitors here. I'd say I eat here at least once a week.

I'm not sure what I'm expecting to happen when my parents arrive and we're all sitting together. It's the first time in nearly a year I've sat at a table with them and I hold back a frustrated sigh, but underneath my annoyance, I'm glad Raven's here with me.

"I'm glad you could make it too," Mom says, hugging Raven before she sits down. Her hand finds mine on the table. "You look better, Ty."

Taking the glass of water already on the table, I take a slow drink before saying, "I'm feeling better."

"I hear you're going to University of Oregon. What are you majoring in, Raven?" My dad asks, breaking the ice with her.

"Accounting. Numbers are my thing." Her eyes drop to the glass and the water condensation pooling beneath the glass. Taking her napkin, she wipes it away before taking a drink herself.

I know Raven's a numbers girl. She's very black or white. There's no gray. There can't be. In her mind, there's always an answer. In numbers, you always have an answer, something, a conclusion to a problem.

Maybe that's why she had to have a definition to us for so long. She couldn't handle the gray.

Dad smiles at Raven. He's always liked her. It's then, right then I notice this is a look they never gave Berkley. Maybe they knew from the beginning that the love I felt for her was never going to be the forever kind. The kind I feel for Raven.

We make small talk around the table as we order, the topic of why I ignored my parents for so long never surfaces and I'm glad. I don't want to talk about it.

Raven excuses herself to the bathroom and immediately my mom is asking if we're dating.

"We kinda are," I tell her, not knowing how else to put it. "We're definitely not dating anyone else."

Mom smiles tenderly. "I've always loved her. She's great for you."

I know I didn't need my mom's approval to date Raven, or anyone else's for that matter, but strangely, it's reassuring because they never liked Berkley and certainly never told me they liked her.

I look at my dad. "How's work?"

With a heavy sigh, he runs his hand over his clean shaved jaw. "It's going pretty well. Slow this time of year but it'll pick up." My dad's a custom-home builder and I think in some ways, he was bent by me choosing cars over construction.

Mom leans forward in her chair. "Tyler, we both just wanted to let you know again how sorry we are about everything."

"I know you are and I'll admit, it's going to take me some time," I tell them honestly. It's not something that's going to change for me overnight. But I also want them to know this, me being here is me trying.

They seem relieved by my words and both smile.

When Raven returns, Tony makes his way over to the table. "How's the Hemming family doing tonight?"

Mom smiles. "We're good."

Scooting her chair in, Raven points over her shoulder at a drawing on the wall near the restrooms. I can't make it out clearly, but it looks like three people holding hands and a woman in the clouds. Then beside the little girl is what appears to be a baby. "Is that from Nova?"

Tony smiles at the picture he tells us Nova drew last week. "Lenny and her came in the other day. I just adore Lenny. Such a nice girl for Red, but yeah, Nova apparently asked Nevaeh to send her a baby."

Everywhere you look in the restaurant are reminders that Nevaeh held a special place in everyone's lives and though she's gone and Red's now with Lenny, nothing will ever completely stop the pain inside of Red, Nova, and Tony. It wasn't easy seeing Red lose Nevaeh. I tried so hard to help him through it but there wasn't much I could do to help him.

Lenny, she helps him in ways no one else could, gives him hope at a future, like Raven does with me.

Raven laughs at the drawing and the baby. "I wonder how Red feels about it?"

Tony grins. "Knowing Red, he's probably okay with that." Tony glances at me and shows me a bottle of wine. "You look like you need a drink."

I'd love one… but then my truck flashes in my head and the tarp covering it.

"Nah." I lean back in the chair, shaking Tony's hand. "I'm good." It's rude to pass up the wine, but I'm not giving in. I might not ever drink again after the accident.

Raven stares at the bottle, then me. "You can still have a drink or two."

With my arm around her chair, I shake my head. "I don't need one."

"You're not drinking anymore?" Dad asks, watching Tony pour him a glass of wine.

"No." I didn't tell my parents I had been drinking that night. I actually assumed they knew. It wasn't that I was trying to keep it from them.

I look at Raven, and then my parents. "I had been drinking the night of the accident. I think it's best I don't anymore."

My dad, being a man of very few words most of the time, stirs uneasily in his chair. "Did you get a DWI?"

"No. I was under the legal limit and it didn't cause the accident." Raven's hand finds mine under the table. Awkwardly, I clear my throat. "It was the seizure that caused me to crash."

I'm sure they were aware of what happened since they'd been at the hospital, but I felt the need for them to hear it from me.

"Tyler," Dad begins and I take in another deep breath trying to relax. "We all make mistakes. Don't beat yourself up over it."

The double meaning doesn't go unnoticed by anyone. I remember when I was eight years old, I threw a stick at a girl and it hit her eye. I didn't mean to but for a month she had to wear an eye patch and sleep sitting up because of the damage to her eye. I felt like a complete asshole and my mom sat me down and said: Remember that the greatest lessons in life are usually learned at the worst times from the worst mistakes.

At eight, I had no clue what she was talking about but thinking about it now I finally understand the meaning of what she was trying to tell me.

Yeah, I made a huge mistake driving drunk and not taking my medicine but it didn't mean I had to stop.

WE TAKE OUR time with dinner and talk with Tony for hours. The sky is black, stars out and glimmering above as Raven and I walk up the street to the car. She's staring straight ahead, her focus contained to the pavement. I choose then to finally speak. "Can I hold your hand?"

She watches me warily. "That feels like dating."

"But you let me hold your boobs the other night when we were watching the movie." I'm desperate to hold her close and let her know how much I appreciated her being there for me tonight.

"Oh hell, why not." Her sense of humor surfaces and she smiles. "But don't you dare kiss me on the cheek or open the door for me."

"Got it." I chuckle. "No acting like a gentleman."

It takes me a moment, but I slide my hand out of my pocket and reach for hers. A warm smile tugs at the corner of her lips. I wonder then if she likes the feel of my hand in hers as much as I do.

I can't help it. I want her closer so I pull on her hand, then wrap my arm around her shoulders.

"You're pushing it, Ty."

"I know I am." Drawing in a deep breath, I don't let her go. I can't. "Want me to whisper something dirty?"

"No." She sighs, her eyes on the pavement. "Though you're extremely good at it, I think it'll make it worse, Tyler. I really need us to take it slow. I don't want us to fall back into friends who fuck."

As frustrated as I am that I can't have her now, and the noticeable way the word fuck hits my groin, I understand *why*, partly. There's a big part of me that just wants her to see I want to be with her and there shouldn't be anything stopping us. But she's right. There's a lot about us that we haven't worked out.

Instead of being serious, I pop off with, "We're not fucking so… it's not anything like what we had before."

She elbows me. "You know what I mean."

I stop walking and look over at her, turning her so we're facing one another. Cupping her cheeks, my thumb touches to her bottom lip and I want so badly to part her lips against mine, but I don't. Because of her. "We're different, Raven," I whisper, my voice carrying with the wind. She closes her eyes as if my words hit her suddenly like a heavy weight. "I don't want friends with benefits, so when you decide you want more, I'm all in."

When her eyes open, her smile is patient, tender, and fucking beautiful. "I'm not going anywhere, Tyler. I love you and you don't know how much it means to me that you're willing to wait for the both of us."

She probably doesn't understand how torturous this is for me, but I'll take whatever she's going to give me.

chapter 24
LIKE A WRECKING BALL

FIVE MONTHS LATER
FOURTH OF JULY

IT CERTAINLY WASN'T easy taking things slow with Tyler once his intentions were clear, but I think we both knew for it to work between us, we had to. Even though it was a mutual decision to not define what we have between us, I know we're both on the same page with our commitment. And considering my personality, I'm surprisingly okay with that. I'm relaxed with where Tyler and I are in our lives, and it only assures me he's the right person, because contentment sits in my chest.

We talked endlessly about what the future held for us as a couple and separately. I think both of us wanted everything out in the open so there wasn't anything like, "Well, I don't want the same things as you," conversation later.

We'd both been burned by that already.

We even talked about what happens when I graduate in two years. All my life I've been raised at Walker Automotive and my intention has always been to have a career there. My dreams were my families and not because they had to be, but because I wanted them to be. My plan was to get my degree in accounting and use it by making sure Walker Automotive always ran as a successful business. Red had the shop under control but Mom couldn't do everything in the office. That's where I came in.

Tyler, well, he'd always seen himself working with Red. My dad and Colt started Walker Automotive together and originally wanted Red and Rawley running it when he passed away. We all knew Rawley had no interest in working there so that left Red and Tyler, two people who shared the same vision and level head. Well, for the most part.

Tyler's biggest fear about our relationship, and the reason for us taking it slow, was me eventually wanting a child of my own. He wanted to know without a shred of a doubt, I wanted a future with him regardless of us having a family together or not.

And like I explained to him, carrying his child inside of me wasn't what was most important. Being with him was. And he understood that, in part.

"I get that you want to knock me up, but there's more than one way for us to make a baby," I would tell him.

It was months of discussion that finally led us to today.

I'm finally out of school for the summer and I'm running on Tyler time, which means I'm about an hour late returning from the grocery store. We're not living together, but I'd say I spend more time at his apartment than I do home.

We're heading over to my mom's house this afternoon for our annual Fourth of July party but I had to run to the store to pick up the salad dressing I forgot earlier.

As I pull up to the shop, Tyler's new F250 truck is parked outside but he's yet to drive it. Technically Tyler should have had his driver's license back but when the judge read the toxicology report, they made him attend drug and alcohol classes and be seizure free for three months before he could apply to get his driver's license reinstated.

Unfortunately, he was just about at the three month mark when he had one while we were watching a movie. Scariest fucking thing I've ever seen. Up until then, I hadn't seen one, just the aftermath.

While it was scary, I think in some ways, it brought Tyler and me closer together. To witness him so vulnerable and out of control of his own body was scary as shit, but it still managed to bring us closer together because it allowed me to see that side of him he desperately tried to hide from me.

I'm upstairs cooking the pasta for my salad when Tyler comes out of the bathroom having just gotten dressed. He watches me preparing the salad, his hands on the counter as if he's preparing himself for something.

I stop what I'm doing and stare at him. "What's wrong?"

"As long as you're in my future, having a baby doesn't matter," he tells me right away, as if he's been holding those words in for months. "I just want you to be happy."

His meaning hits me, my heartbeat thumping in my ear. He truly does want me to be happy. All along, it's what he's wanted out of this despite his own hesitations.

I'm not shocked by the conversation because like I said, we've been having these talks a lot. Only I'm not okay with that statement because to me, he's settling and what if we tried in vitro or something where we used someone else's sperm. It all seemed silly to discuss now but in reality, we had to.

He was visibly upset the first time in vitro was mentioned by me, because the idea of another man's baby inside of me was upsetting to him. That's when I realized the severity of this for Tyler. Most women want babies. It's in our DNA to nurture and want children.

Men, they can go either way. Some want them, others don't.

Tyler, coming from a small family of his own, wanted lots of kids. Imagine when he's told he can't. And then on top of that, a man, a possessive man, would need to allow his wife to carry a child that wasn't his. He'd never look into our child's eyes and see himself.

Leaning into the kitchen island, he watches me as I continue with making my salad. "I'm okay with adoption, or that thing where we use a donor"—he waves his hand around—"should you, you know, want that someday."

I want to both laugh and cry at his expression it's that adorable.

Though we haven't declared a relationship, all our talks are based on us being together.

I stop what I'm doing and look up at him. His brow creases. He's waiting for me to say something. "So you're okay with another man's baby in me?"

He groans, shaking his head as he drops it forward. "Don't say it like that, but yeah, if you decide you want to carry the babies, then yeah. But we should use someone we don't know. I might punch the dude if we know him."

Moving around the kitchen island, I stand in front of him. "They have professional services for that, Tyler."

"Well good." Twisting, he moves his hands to my hips. "He can't be a part of our lives."

"You do realize we're like five years from that, right? You have to date me first, marry me, and then we'll get to kids."

He smiles. "I know… and I'd like to mention here I'd like to start having sex with you again. I've got a constant hard-on around you. It's frustrating. It's been five months." In case I didn't hear him right, he holds up his hand, fingers spread apart to indicate the number five, and then repeats it again, silently moving his lips around the word.

I step back away from him. "I have to finish the pasta salad."

He knows this is me pulling back, but only because I need a couple minutes to think of how I want to approach this.

Well those couple minutes turn into like two hours, and Tyler's moving about his bedroom in a pair of gray cargo shorts and a white Hurley T-shirt that clings to his muscles in the most delicious of ways, I'm reminded of how sexy he is and that I know what I want. Not to mention I'm in his room, sitting on his bed. There's that reminder.

And then I scan his face. His hair has grown back about an inch and he just shaved the sides, a reminder of his previous hair cut where I had hair to pull on top. Okay, maybe I'm just missing sex with him. Have I mentioned since the accident we haven't had sex?

It's fucking torture.

"I'd like to start having sex with you again. I've got a constant hard-on around you. It's frustrating."

I should just give in. There's no real reason *why* we shouldn't be.

"You look deep in thought," he says, sitting beside me.

I smile at him. "When did you know you were in love with me, Tyler?"

With his eyes on our hands, he nods. "Thanksgiving. I was watching you eat mashed potatoes." His eyes find mine, humor dancing in them. "Then you mouthed the words 'fuck off' and I fell, right then with gravy drippling down your chin."

Laughing, I shake my head. I knew he wouldn't take it seriously but maybe after the teasing I might get some truth.

Tyler's quiet and I'm nervous as to what he might say next. His head drops forward and he shakes it back and forth like he's gathering courage. "I met a girl when I was fourteen," he says warmly, taking my hand in his and squeezing it. "But she was a little sister, someone I couldn't love because of an age difference. And then life got in the way and shit changed." His lids lower and he sighs, his focus on the ground leaving me nothing but lashes. "Nothing you can say or do would ever make me stop loving you." His eyes find mine again. "I'm forever. Yeah, I didn't fall in love with you like I should have. I staggered my way into it and tried like hell to avoid it, but when it happened, I knew there was no going back from there."

As much as I wanted to pinpoint a day, I couldn't even tell you when I fell completely in love with Tyler. It happened slowly like opening a shaken bottle of soda pop. One tiny movement at a time and then before I knew it, I was so far gone there was also no coming back from it.

I know now what these past five months have taught me. Tyler and I are good at friends, but we're even better at lovers.

"I have to ask you something."

He stares at me, shifting on the bed to face me. "What?

Drawing in a deep breath, my fucking voice shakes when I ask, "Does your D want to go steady with my V?"

Tyler fucking bursts out laughing. He has to hold his stomach even. I didn't think it was that funny, but then he straightens up, eyes me carefully and asks, "Is your muff finally asking my wang to be a family?"

Groaning, I flop myself back on his bed. "Yes or no already?"

Suddenly his body covers mine and waits for me to look at him. When I do, he kisses my lips, once, twice, three times. "It's definitely a *yes*."

Opening my eyes, I watch him though his are closed. He said yes. My heart races at the thought of us finally being together.

"What time do we have to be at your mom's house for the barbeque?" he asks between kisses.

"She said four."

"Plenty of time then."

I laugh. "Tyler, it's like three thirty. We should be leaving."

He shakes his head. "It's been five months. Five seconds would be plenty of time with how badly I need this."

Without hesitation, his mouth crashes to mine and I eagerly oblige. Sucking his bottom lip between my teeth, I bite down slowly and then pull him into me by his broad tattooed shoulders. He moves closer, his mouth firmer and then his tongue eagerly seeks entrance, rushing desire through my entire body.

The kiss could set his apartment on fire. Never has he kissed me like this.

"Please," he whispers. "Please."

Oh, Jesus, it sounds like he's begging me.

The tip of his nose glides up the side of my throat.

"Please what?"

He places his hands beside my head, supporting his weight as he looks down at me. "Let me be with you. All of you."

His fingers trace the curve of my side until they're at the waistband of my jeans. We both stop, just for a second. I'm already aching for this and he knows it. His mouth goes to my ear and his fingers to the skin above my jeans making me shiver.

"Is this okay?" His body tenses, eyebrows squeezing together because he knows I may say no. Just because V was going steady with D didn't mean D could come in yet.

Shut the fuck up, Raven.

"I think you should just take these off," he says, his heart thumping heavily against my chest.

I laugh a little. He's smiling, sure of himself, and I take his bottom lip between mine just to taste before shimmying out of my jeans. Tyler helps, skimming one broad palm down the side of my thigh until I kick them the rest of the way off.

313

"So fucking sexy…." He trails off, his voice thick with need as he separates himself from me.

Standing, Tyler lowers the band of his shorts, freeing his himself for me at the edge of the bed.

Wanting to taste him, I move to my knees taking his hardness between my palms. Running my hands from the base to the tip, I repeat the motions.

Finally, I lower my mouth to him.

"Jesus Christ…." Tyler groans, the intensity in his eyes can only be described as raw hunger. He makes a lot of noises, soft grunts and moans, with one hand tangling in my hair, guiding and encouraging me to continue. All the talk, all the messages and wishing we could be together these last few months have led to this, something neither of us can slow down even if we wanted to.

My body throbs for him, the need so strong I start to shake.

Tyler seems to be on the same page when he stops me, dragging my mouth from him and gently laying me down on the bed.

He hovers at my entrance and then pushes forward an inch. He looks down at me with this intensity, but his smile is playful. "You want my tongue on your pussy, Raven?"

Jesus, I love the way pussy rolls off his tongue. It's fucking erotic and needs to be said daily.

"Yes." I moan, my breath escaping in a whoosh when my lips part.

"Yes what?" His eyes level with mine, tattered breathing making his chest shake, seeming to enjoy my struggle to control my composure. Of course he's enjoying this. The last time we had sex was back in December. "Never be afraid to say what you want."

"I'm not, with you." I breathe out slowly. "I want your tongue on my pussy."

He laughs, once. "Say pussy once more."

I grab onto the little bit of hair that's grown back and tug. "Put your tongue on my V, damn it."

He does as he's told, moving down my body, his eyes closing and inhaling deeply. "Your pussy smells so good."

Tyler and I both sigh when his tongue makes contact with my center. His tongue, wet and warm, is soft and delicate to the touch. Almost tentative in nature, as if he's nervous but still, it's more in the way he holds me in place. As if to say he won't let me go now, even if I wanted him to.

He grabs my hips tighter with one hand, his other working with his tongue to send me over the edge, but what does it is his moan at my reaction.

Writhing in his hands, I scream so loud my voice cracks and I'm left with silent pleas and begging for him to never stop.

When he draws back and stares up at me, I whimper at the thought of him sliding inside me. My thighs immediately clench in anticipation.

"You ready for me, baby?" he asks, crawling possessively up my body. As soon as he shifts forward, I rock against him.

Nodding, I'm unable to hide my excitement. I need him so badly.

It's then he remembers the condom and separates himself from me. The lack of heat from his body is immediate and my nipples harden as I watch him. I want to tell him we don't need one, but I don't want to say anything and remind him of why we wouldn't need one.

Tearing the plastic wrapper of the condom open, Tyler takes the condom between his thumb and forefinger and slides it on. When he's finished, he blinks slowly, eyes so dark, like magical wishing wells you couldn't see the bottom of but knew if you made a wish, it was coming true.

Taking him by the shoulders, I guide him to lie down on the bed, wanting to take control over this.

Breathing in deeply, he watches me straddle him as I make the first move, wanting him to take it easy.

"Look at me." His fingers brush over heated freckled skin. He looks down between our legs, his neck straining as he does so, the muscles in his chest and stomach flexing. "I want to watch your pussy devour every inch of my cock."

Well, I have a new favorite word. Tyler breathing the word cock with his face contorted in pleasure.

As slowly as I can, my legs and arms shaking with anticipation, I slide down on him, down every single thick inch. It takes me a second to adjust, but when I do, relief washes through me immediately, rising up from my center to warm my cheeks.

"Fuck...." A low rumble leaves his chest as he forces me down against him.

In response, a shudder runs through me knowing I'm evoking these reactions from him.

Cursing under his breath, he takes a firm hold on me, fingers digging into my heated flesh

"Don't stop." He slams me down into every movement, refusing to allow an inch of space between us. His hands clutch my hips, rocking me back and forth, a trembling present in his body with every move. "Do you feel how badly I want this?"

I nod, unsure what else to do when he thrusts up into my movements, slow and cautious as I stretch around him. "Probably as bad as I want it."

Any fear I have over this being too soon vanishes, as if it never existed in the first place.

I'm not surprised when we don't say much of anything as he's making love to me, pouring himself into each touch.

For so long a relationship with Tyler was untouchable. Only now, I'm finally seeing and believing that's not the case. I have him. All of him.

Taking a firm hold on my hips, he gives a nod, an indication he wants on top.

He turns me over on my stomach, his chest pressing to my back, his hand moving to my center underneath us. I close my eyes at the sensation of his weight on me.

"Come for me again," he growls in a begging plea at my ear. Shivers dance through me at the roughness of his voice. "I need to feel your wet pussy all over my fingers. And then I'm going to make you lick it off."

Holy. Shit.

His finger makes a pass over my aching center and my body jumps, everything he's doing is too intense, but I want more. He slows his pace and I want to die and scream in his face. He's leaving me hanging, just on the edge.

"No," I plead, my legs straightening out.

"Trust me," he whispers, kissing my neck and ear.

He claims me with measured strokes, knowing how to draw this out. "The longer you deny yourself the release, the better it's going to be."

There's meaning behind those words. For so long Tyler and I denied ourselves one another and that first night together was indescribable, as is this.

Even with my body welded to his, sweat pouring from the two of us, hands slipping and sweet kissing, it's not close enough. I want to crawl inside him and experience everything he does.

My release is intense and stirring needs inside me I didn't know existed. When I've come, my body sedated and rubbery, he flips me over on my back again.

My head snaps back against his headboard when he enters me with one forceful thrust, his hips creating enough power to move my entire body up the mattress. His hot breath fans over me in time with his dominant strokes that slowly kill me with unbridled desire.

Tyler's head falls forward, resting against my forehead, tender involuntary grunts falling from his sweet lips. His sweaty chest slides across my own, and the moan that leaves my lips shakes the both of us.

"God, Raven…." He breathes against my skin, his tongue gliding over my salty sheen. "You're so fucking beautiful. I'm not going to last much longer."

I'm actually impressed he's lasted this long. He moves frantically, moaning and grunting, fisting sheets between fingers and gripping the headboard. We can't slow down. Maybe round two, we'll have more time. But this, this is all about the need.

One of his hands slips behind my head, fisting my hair in his hand. My release is there before I can stop it. He's slamming relentlessly into me, his pubic bone at the right angle, the right touch. The right *everything*.

Riding out my high, bliss pulsing through my veins like a volcano flowing hot lava, I roll my hips into his movements, letting him take me higher and higher until I think there's no coming back from it.

"Oh fuck, I'm gonna come." He yanks on my hair, jerking my neck back. Awkwardly, I twist my head against his grasp to find his eyes.

I wanted so badly to witness the fall, the way he shudders. I need to see it.

His long legs tense, spreading my thighs a little more, his stomach muscles flexing as he pulses into me, steady, panting breaths capturing my own broken ones when our mouths meet. A grunt forces its way from his lips, and then a moan, his mouth moving to my shoulder where he bites down, crying out over his release.

Tyler groans again, his body shaking so badly he can't hold himself up.

When he lets go, I feel every single pulse of him inside of me, the way his dick swells and releases, all of it.

"What's the grin for?" he asks, a smile tugging at his lips when he rolls off me.

My eyes focus on the brightness in his, propping myself up on my forearms. "Your D loves my V."

"Fuck yeah he does." He chuckles softly, head dipping forward to capture my lips.

Raven
chapter 25
RECKLESS

"Is grass gluten-free?"

Red stares at his daughter standing in front of him, his eyes crinkling at the corners. "Maybe, why?"

She hands Red the worm, in two pieces. "He looks hungry and I think his tummy is sensitive so we need to find gluten free grass to feed him."

Red sets his beer down next to him and brushes away a ladybug that's landed on her shoulder. "Well, he's also dead, darlin'. I'm pretty sure gluten-free grass is the least of his worries."

Nova's eyes flood with tears as do mine, for different reasons when I remember my mom telling me about ladybugs and my dad. It's a gentle reminder he's always here with us.

"Do you have some tape?" she asks Red, that same flood of tears spilling over her sun-kissed cheeks. "I'll just tape him together."

I'm actually a little shocked she's nearly crying over a worm. You rarely see that kid cry unless she's throwing a tantrum over something.

I'm not sure how or where, but she manages to find tape.

"Don't worry, wormy," she says, carrying him over to a rock. "Tape is gluten free because it's clear. No additives."

Red looks at me and then Lenny. "What the fuck do they teach at that school?"

Lenny laughs, watching Nova. "No idea."

The Fourth of July party at Mom's house has always been huge. Everyone is invited. Friends, family, neighbors. I'm not surprised when I see Berkley there either, nor am I completely prepared when she approaches Tyler and I as we're eating burgers on the deck.

"I heard about your accident," she says to Tyler, primarily, though she gives me that side-eyed once over. Berkley's never liked me. Mostly because I threw gum in her hair when she first started dating Tyler and she had to cut like four inches off her hair. The gum had Gorilla Glue on it. I never said I was a nice kid. I was in the womb with Rawley. He rubbed off on me a little.

Tyler stares at her, setting his burger down, probably wondering where she's going with this.

And then she smiles at him. "Just wanted to see if you were doing okay. You look good though."

Shut up. Stop talking to him. D and V are going steady and there's no room for your slutty self here!

Tyler nods and leans into my side, a gesture I appreciate so much more than he'll ever know. It's a statement. One that silently tells Berkley he's finally taken for good. "I'm fine."

Bringing her beer to her lips, she takes a drink and then smiles once more. "Take care of yourself."

Never once does she acknowledge me.

"That was awkward," he says, shaking his head and reaching for his burger again.

My heart beat that had suddenly started racing, evens out. "No kidding."

Lenny finds us then and plops down next to us with a bottle of water in hand. "What's this?" she motions to our closeness. "Are you a couple now? Is it out in the open and no hiding?"

Red approaches as she asks, winking at me as if to say he's completely okay with it.

Tyler's arm wraps tight around my shoulder. "Yep."

Lenny glances back at Red. "Told you they'd get their shit together eventually."

Tyler snorts picking up a chip. "It was less than a year ago when I could have said the same thing about you two."

There's certainly no denying that. I think in many ways both Lenny and Red understood our situation, in part, because of what happened between them. Whatever the reason, it's a relief that we're together and we can be out in the open with no hiding this time.

WE'RE SETTLING INTO the night, sitting around eating burgers and ribs, music blaring from a set of speakers to our left when Jude asks Lenny to dance. He's our cousin but he's constantly teasing Red that if he slips up, he's taking Lenny. I wouldn't doubt Jude would try either.

Relaxing back in his chair, Red rakes a hand through his hair. There's a slight smile playing at his lips, the only indication of his annoyance is his tensed jaw. Usually seeing Lenny dance with someone else might set him off but not Jude. He's harmless.

It still doesn't stop him from cutting in though.

He stands and makes his way over to Lenny. "She's *my* girl."

Laughing, she wraps her arms around him only to have him reach around and gather her hands in his.

"I'm not good at this." Red shrugs as the attention in the backyard shifts to him standing in front of Lenny holding something in his hand. I thought it was a beer cap at first but it's clearly no beer cap. "There's a lot of things I could say to you right now. Most of which would be fitting and probably everything you would expect to hear me say. But then I remember we're far from ordinary, and you deserve more than ordinary. You deserve perfection which is everything you are to Nova and me."

Lenny's bewildered stare finds his as I gasp, realizing Red's about to propose to her and his eyes lower to the ring as he places it in the palm of her hand. "Please?"

When she doesn't reply right away, Red looks incredibly nervous, a mannerism I didn't know he possessed, ever.

He laughs, running his hand through his hair. "I fucked that up, didn't I?"

"No!" she gasps, her hand covering her mouth.

Silence envelopes the crowd, as he sighs. "That was a lame proposal, wasn't it?"

"No, it wasn't but are you sure, Red?"

He nods, giving her an almost child-like look. "It's what I want." And when she still doesn't reply, he huffs out a breath. "Lenny... you're supposed to say something." His nervousness was taking over. "I'm sure it's a three-letter word and starts with a 'Y.'"

Her stare drops to Nova at his feet and she winks at Lenny, a gesture she learned from her dad. "Say yes, Lenny. Then you can be my earth mommy."

Red's feet shift. "Still waiting...."

Lenny blinks several times before saying, "It's just that... I'm pregnant."

His gaze lingers on Lenny's stomach and then his brows knit. "You're pregnant?"

Tyler tenses beside me and I squeeze his hand, attempting to offer him something in that moment. I do this because I know it has to affect him in some way that I might never say those words to him. At least not in the context in which he would want to hear them.

"I could have told you that, Daddy," Nova chirps using a nearby chair to jump on his back.

Lenny smiles tenderly at Nova. "I just found out a couple nights ago. Wasn't sure how to tell you yet."

He grabs her shoulders and makes her face him head on and dips his head to catch her eyesight. "Are you serious?"

She starts nodding, holding back tears. "Yes." She then stares at the ground. "Oh shit, I dropped the ring."

Tyler's broad shoulders shake as a laugh rolls out and he whispers to me, "Saw that coming."

"Her dropping the ring, or you knew they'd get married eventually?"

"No," Tyler shakes his head, handing me another beer I didn't know he got for me. "I mean the baby. I walked in on them fucking on his toolbox about a month ago."

"Oh," I giggle and cover my mouth. "Yeah, I've walked in on them in the parts room. They're not very careful at work. It's like they can't wait to get home."

"Nova's there so I imagine they don't have a lot of alone time."

"True."

I can't even describe the moment Red finds the ring in the grass, him on his knees at her feet as he places the ring on her finger and then kisses her stomach.

Squealing, Lenny spins around and faces Tyler and me, flashing the ring. "I'm engaged!"

"And pregnant!" Hugging her tightly, my throat tightens and I whisper, "We're gonna be sisters."

Tyler bumps his fist to Red's. "Congrats, man."

Red's smile is bright, one I haven't seen in years. He's truly happy right now. "Thanks."

"Why did you tell him you were pregnant like it was some kind of deal breaker?" I ask, still so happy for them I can't stop smiling.

Lenny moves her hands to her stomach. "I don't know. I panicked and thought he should know I'm kind of a package deal now."

Red laughs. "Like that would change my mind." In a quick movement, Red has his arms wrapped around her.

"What are you doing?" Lenny yelps at Red when he hauls her up off her feet.

"I'm taking you inside where we can celebrate me making an honest woman out of you. Right now." And then he carries her inside the house.

"Why would he make an honest woman out of her? Did she lie?" Nova asks me, curiously wondering what that meant.

I look to Colt, who's standing beside us now, for an answer.

"She's been naughty. He's going to spank her probably."

My hand flies out to slap Colt on the back of the head. "You dirty old man, don't tell her that."

Nova looks at me, and then Tyler, then back to me. "How'd the baby get in Lenny's belly?"

Tyler and I both stare at her and Colt chuckles. "You're on your own on that one. I'm too dirty." And he walks away.

Nova doesn't even acknowledge Colt, she's waiting on our answer and I'm thinking at any second she might ask if it has anything to do with a V or a D but she doesn't.

Thankfully, Ollie, Nova's little neighbor friend walks up. "I found that baseball we lost."

Nova's eyes light up. "Now we can play again."

Thank fuck.

Tyler laughs and wraps his arm around me. "That was a close one."

"You're not kidding."

Staring at him now, I think back to Lenny being pregnant and his reaction. "Don't worry," I tell him raising my hand up to run over his jaw. He watches me, curious what I'm going to say. "We'll have a family someday."

He gives me a half smile. "I know we will."

I'm not sure he's completely okay with the idea, and I know it might always bother him, but I make a vow right then to always help him through this in whatever way I can. Together.

Leaning in, his lips linger on my ear. "I'm sorry I can't give you that."

I know what he's referring to. A baby. "Don't be," I tell him, meaning the words more than anything I've ever said to him. "You give me what I need."

Though he seems satisfied with my words, the sadness still lingers in his eyes. Pulling me in, his lips brush the top of my head. Not quite a kiss but as if he's drawing in my scent. He sighs and rests his chin on the crown of my head. "I love you."

The lightness of his tone and the gentle way he says it makes me smile. I know I don't need to say it back, but I do.

TINY TWINKLE LIGHTS shine through the yard and Tyler eyes my drink in my hand. "What's that, girl?" His eyes are bright, the side of his face bathed in a warm glow.

I smile. I love it when he calls me girl. Reminds me of when I was younger, tying in my past memories to the future ones we're making right now. "It's half piña colada and half strawberry daiquiri."

He breathes out, uneven and shaky. "Oh man."

I laugh. "Should I go grab a bottle of whiskey and you can pull my hair later?"

"No, I'm off the whiskey these days." He grabs my ass with one hand and squeezes. "But I'd love to still pull your hair."

It's true. Tyler hasn't drank an ounce of liquor since the accident. I'm not sure he ever will again and I'm okay with that. If he thinks it's for the best, then it is.

We laugh, his arms wrapping around me.

Turning the music to country, Hendrix asks my mom to dance about the time Tyler asks me. "So, since V and D are going steady…." He grins, boyish and flirty, his blue eyes shining under the lights of the deck. Turning me, sweeping my brown waves aside, he kisses the back of my neck, swaying to the music and holding me carefully. "Does that mean I can dance with you?"

I turn in his arms, raising my hands, I slide them over his shoulders, our bodies coming together. "Only if you promise to touch my ass in the process." I arch my back, slightly, offering him more.

"Mmmm," he growls, burying his head in my neck, his breath is like a whisper over my skin, one I have a hard time understanding, but know I need it. Drawing back, he tilts his head the direction of the house. "We could go try out your bed upstairs. I bet you thought of me a lot in your bed."

He's certainly not wrong, and I'm about to take him up on the idea when I hear loud voices near the house and a door slamming.

Glancing over my shoulder, I see it's Rawley and his friend Beck. It's been months since I've seen Rawley, but he still texts me randomly. One look at him and I know there's something off about him. He's drunk. Completely shitfaced and hopefully not driving. Beck's at least sober, somewhat. They both look tossed.

I want to run to my brother, beg him to remember who he's hurting by showing up here but the truth is, Rawley's a shell of the person he used to be. If you knew him junior year of high school, and now, you wouldn't think he was the same person. Even his looks have changed, eyes so dark, deep, and unbound.

Mom steps in front of him, her hands on his chest before he makes his way over to Sophie, which I assume is why he's here with the way his glare is intent on her. "What are you doing here?"

He studies Mom's face with eyes we don't recognize, and then licks his lips before asking, "What do you mean what am I doing here?" He's looking past her, and then slowly blinks and eyes our mother with a forced smile. "Isn't this what you wanted, a nice family party? Well, I'm here. It's what you wanted, right?"

Mom shakes her head, disappointment in her eyes and a set frown. "Don't give me your crap. You know damn well I didn't mean like this when I said I wanted you to come."

Rawley throws his arms up, carefree and wild, walking backward away from her. "Well this is what you're getting so take it or leave it."

Hendrix steps toward him, his hand on his shoulder, warning him with cold brown eyes. "That's *enough*, Rawley. Why don't you go get some food and sober up? You're drunk."

"I'm always fuckin' drunk. It's what I'm good at." He shakes off Hendrix's hand. "And you're not my fucking father. You can't just step in and try to act like my father. It's enough I get it from Red what a fucking loser I am. I don't need you doing it too old man."

Rawley walks off, toward the beer.

My heart is in my throat knowing this isn't the end because I know why he's here. He's here to make a scene. I look to Mom, and she brings her hand to her heart. "I just don't know what to do with him and he won't talk to me." She's watching him make his way through the backyard with Beck.

"You know what, Mom, he's almost twenty-one," I tell her, wanting to offer something. I don't want her thinking his fucked-up shit is her problem. "You can't fix him. You have to let him do what he's going to do."

Nodding, she's on the verge of tears, leaning into Hendrix who wraps his arm around her. "I know." She stares at Rawley, and he's staring at Sophie and scowling as he fills a beer.

She puts her hand on her hip. "You said you weren't coming."

"It's *my* family's party." He steps toward her, sipping his beer he doesn't need. "Why are you here? You're not family and the last time I looked, this was a family thing."

Sophie scowls at him. "Don't you dare come over here and try to apologize. I know this is what you expect, fuck up and then you can apologize but not this time. This is the kind of shit I was talking about this morning. You know that, right? You refuse to grow up."

"Oh, I'm not here for forgiveness. We're way past forgiveness, don't you think?" He smirks, condescendingly.

"I can't believe you're acting like this just because I wouldn't *fuck* you," Sophie spits, fed up and giving him what he deserves.

My eyes widen, as do Moms.

Rawley faces Sophie, his face now expressionless. Nodding slowly, he rakes his hand through his hair. "Sweetheart, I'm not looking to fuck you tonight." He gives a dismissive nod to her friend. "Ask Kate."

Sophie's face blanches. She looks to her best friend standing next to her, betrayal written in their locked eyes. "Oh my God, *Kate*.... Is he serious?"

Gasping, I cover my mouth with my hand.

Tyler shakes his head and leans into me. "Jesus Christ, shit's about to get ugly."

It's like an episode of *Jerry Springer*. No lie. There's a moment right then when I look to Sophie and think she's going to murder her friend with her bare hands.

"Tyler, go over there."

Instantly, his body tenses and his hold on me grows more secure. He shakes his head, unsure if he should. "Raven," Tyler says under his breath, "we should stay out of it."

Sophie's friend doesn't say a word, or deny the accusations. Instead, she brings her beer to her lips, as if that's going to distract Sophie. My brother's life is definitely more fucked-up than mine.

Rawley laughs, taking a step toward her, sipping his beer. His voice lowers, but I can still hear him from our place ten feet away. "Hey, I had to get it somewhere. She puts out."

Sophie huffs out a breath and throws what's left of her beer on him and then pushes him as hard as she can. "You're such a fucking asshole, Rawley!"

Rawley absolutely hates to be pushed. Believe me, I'm his twin and if you ever want to set him off, push him off the edge of a bunk bed.

Soaking wet from the full beer down the front of him, he stumbles for a moment and then throws his beer at the fence, the plastic red cup breaking on impact. He straightens himself out and grabs the neck of his shirt and rips it off, throwing it at her feet.

"Pick it up, Sophie," he says slowly, rough with anger, the muscles in his body tensing with each word. His jeans hang low, showing the tattoos across his lower stomach. He points to the ground. "It's where you left my heart, so go ahead, pick the fucking thing up."

Tyler and I exchange a look. He glances around to see where Nova is and she's thankfully not paying any attention to this, nor would she understand what's happening.

Sophie looks down at the shirt, and then to Rawley. "I'm not picking it up. I won't. Fuck. You," is her answer, tears streaming uncontrollably down her face. "You're being a dick tonight. Just leave."

I'm so pissed at my brother for treating her like this I have a mind to run over there and junk punch him.

"Don't' go and try and act like a goddamn victim in this Sophie! You did this. You fucking did." He shakes his head, an annoyance in his glare. "You created this monster. That's on you. I did everything I could to make you…." His jaw tightens, his muscles tensing. "You threw it back in my face. You broke me. *You* fucking broke *me* so this shit's on you. Pick up the fucking shirt," he says again, his voice thick with tears.

"Jesus Christ, no! I'm not picking it up!" she screams with everything she has, causing everyone to stop in shock when she slaps him across the face.

He growls out a forced breath, stepping toward her, anger shaking his body.

I'm suddenly afraid Rawley is about to do something really stupid and I push Tyler forward. "Tyler, *do something*! Don't let him touch her."

I would have never pegged Rawley to lay a hand on a girl but he's not in his right mind and there's no telling what he's about to do.

Tyler moves toward Rawley, his hand on his shoulder. "That's enough, man. Walk away from her."

"This is none of your business, *Tyler*." Scrubbing his hands over his face, Rawley drops them and faces Tyler. He looks at him with pleading eyes and mournful shoulders. You can see the defeat in his whole body. "You know... I know you think I fucked your girl. That's why you hate me so much, isn't it?"

Tyler doesn't say anything at first, he just shrugs his shoulders. But then he mumbles, "I don't hate you, Rawley." His lips barely move over the words, as though he's attempting to keep them between the two of them. "I may not like the way you act, but I *don't* hate you."

"Yeah, well," he spits to the side, unknowingly near my feet, "I didn't fuck your girl. I'm not Sophie. Maybe she fucked Berkley and knocked her up." His glare slices to Sophie. "Or did you take Berkley on vacation with you and show her how to be a cheating whore."

Unable to stop myself, I cry out, "Rawley, stop it!"

He cracks a sarcastic smile my way. "Raven, stay out of this." And then he glances at Tyler. "You don't get to tell me how to handle myself. You led my sister on for months." He then shoves Tyler back. "Fuck you."

I can see where this is going instantly when Rawley shoves Tyler and he immediately stands his ground.

Red rushes out of the house, Lenny following him and that's when I see Nova. I want to run to her, shield her from the destruction that's her uncle but I'm relieved to see Lenny has her.

"What's going on?" Red asks, coming to stand between Rawley and Tyler. "Don't do anything you're going to regret."

"Regret?" Rawley's glare moves to Red. "All I have is regret so what's one more thing?" And then he pushes Red, his hands on the center of his chest. "Stay out of it."

It does nothing to stop Red because he's big as fuck and Rawley doesn't have any size on him, only they're right back in each other's faces. "I'm serious. Back off, Rawley. You don't want to do what you're doing."

"I'm so sick of your shit!" He jabs at his shoulder, another warning to back up.

Red heaves in a heavy breath, scowling at Rawley. "You push me again, you little fucking asshole, and I'm gonna fuckin' deck you."

"Go ahead! Do it! You know you want to!" he screams in his face, hollow eyes lingering to Mom before slowly shifting to Red. "All you've done is look down on me and tell me how to live my life, and I'm fucking sick of it. You're not perfect. Just because Dad left you the business doesn't mean you're Dad. You never gave a shit about me before. Why do you care what I'm doing now?" His voice bellows through the backyard, loud and threatening. I take a step back because his intensity is scaring me. I've never seen him like this. "I get it. You're the good guy. The honorable one everyone looks up to and Raven"—he flicks his wrist my direction—"she's the brains. Going to college like Mom and Dad wanted. You both have it all figured out. Then there's me." He raises his arms up, turning slowly. "The *fuck up!*"

My eyes brim with tears, my heartbeats fast and heavy at the same time. What happened to my brother? Where'd he go? This vulnerable boy screaming at everyone with hollow eyes and the indifferent glares, isn't Rawley. He used to be carefree and loving, cracking jokes and be the life of the party. Now he's fucked-up and broken.

Rawley parts his lips, intent on saying more, but then it passes, and his eyes dart around the yard and to his shirt at Sophie's feet before locking with Red. Throwing his hands up in the air, his shoulders shake, his body trembling and those bloodshot eyes wavering in their control. His hands fall to his head as he turns around and faces everyone, including our mother. I'm really hoping he notices Nova before he says what I think he's going to say.

Red lurks near the fence, a foot away, because I think we all knew this was coming. Everybody watches, waiting to see what Rawley's going to do next.

He throws his arms up again, and screams, "None of you know a goddamn thing! None of you know what my days are like or what I'm going through!" he cries, choking on his words. "Every day I'm judged on everything, but no one takes the time to help me. They just tell me what I'm doing wrong. All I've ever been is the youngest Walker boy, the fuck up. You know what, fuck you for thinking you know a goddamn thing, and ignoring it." Taking the cooler of drinks next to him, he picks it up and throws it across the yard, luckily missing everyone in the way. "Fuck all of you!" he screams at the top of his lungs, his voice breaking and body shaking. He's crying now, it's obvious, but I can't tell if it's from anger or sadness. Maybe both.

Mom nudges Red's shoulder, tears flowing endlessly. "Red, do something."

He looks back at Mom with disbelief. "What the hell am I supposed to do?"

Seeing him come apart like this, I feel like I should know how to reach out to him, but there's no stopping him. The moment comes when he finally notices Nova, crying against Lenny's chest as she ushers her inside the house. She heard what he was saying.

He snorts, his head dropping between his shoulders, shaking remorsefully. "Most of all, *fuck me*." He knows what *he* did. He knows Nova witnessed him at his worst and it's something he can never take back.

As he's walking away, Sophie grabs his hand. "Rawley, please don't do this," she begs. He lets her hold his hand for a second, his chin trembles and he swallows. Their heartache can be seen between them. If they could change this, they would but neither can.

Slowly, he lets go of her hand, shoulders shaking, head bent forward, his breathing uneven and broken. "*Sophie*, this is what I do. I fuck up and I leave." He wipes his eyes with the bend of his elbow. "You should know this by now."

Pushing past her, his shoulder bumps into hers as he storms out the back gate to where I assume he's parked. Beck follows.

I want to go after him, maybe talk some sense into him but Tyler grabs my hand. "Raven… don't." I'm torn when Tyler pulls me in. On one hand, I want to check on Rawley. On the other, I know what Tyler's about to say.

Tyler's eyes fall to mine, to my lips, then back to my eyes. "You need to take your own advice here. All your life you've taken on his mistakes for him. You need to let him handle this one on his own."

As hard as that is to hear, he's absolutely right. I can't fix Rawley. He's going to do, and be, who he wants. He'll call Sophie tomorrow. I know he will. He'll promise and swear and warn, but in the end, it's up to her to stop what's happening and put an end to it. It's up to him to change.

TYLER AND I go back to his place after the barbeque and it's nearing three in the morning but neither of us can sleep. Once in his room, we lie staring at one another, the lingering smells of campfire and fireworks on our skin.

"Do you really think Rawley was the one who slept with Berkley?" I don't know why I ask him, but I want to know if that's what he thinks. The Rawley I know, my sweet vulnerable but brooding brother, would never do that.

"No," he admits. "I doubt it was him. Rawley may be going through some shit, but he's not immoral when it comes to family. I may not like the way he's acting, but six months ago, he could have said the same about me, and he wouldn't have been wrong."

"True."

On his back now, he stares at the ceiling. "I know you said you won't be staying in Eugene this year but…." I smile when he pauses because I know what he's going to ask. I told him that when I came home for the summer in May. It's only an hour drive and not unmanageable so I've decided to live at home this year and save some money on housing. "Will you move in with me?" He turns his head to me when the last word is spoken, waiting on my answer.

At first, I'm stunned by his question, but then again, maybe I'm not. The time we've spent together since his accident has truly given us the strong foundation we so desperately needed and it's also brought us together as one.

"Does D want V living with you permanently? Once you ask her to move in…." I let out a slow whistled breath. Moving my leg, I slide it up over his. "She's here for good."

"It's want I want more than anything." His left hand grasps my thigh as he rolls to face me. "I want to wake up every morning so D can be with V."

"This conversation is getting weird." I sit up in the bed wanting to make sure he's being serious. "Do you really want me to move in with you, Tyler?"

He doesn't move from his place, his hands moving behind his head as if he's completely relaxed. "You practically live here already. It'd make sense."

My stare goes to his tattoos, his chest, and then his eyes. He's right, it would. But I can't just move in because it makes sense. I want to move in because he sees our relationship is heading in the right direction and feels we're ready for the next step.

"Are you sure we're ready for this? It's a big step. Are you scared?"

His face grows serious. "I'm scared of not being enough for someone like you."

I'm not sure where he's going with this. "Like me?"

"You're just… you're you, if that makes sense. You're strong and independent. You don't need a man in your life to be okay. That makes me have to be so much more to keep you." His eyes dance around my face gauging my reaction.

I don't say anything because a year ago I wouldn't have been able to agree with him. But in the time we've been slowly working on building our relationship, I've also been spending time strengthening my self-worth. Never again will I allow Tyler or anyone else to make me feel less than who I am. And never again will I allow myself to accept less than I deserve. So yeah, I know I don't need him, but I want him, and that's all that matters to me. And I know he wants me too, but I can also tell he senses my apprehensions in all this. I want this to be what he wants verses what we should or need to do.

"Raven." He sighs as his fingertips gently touch my cheek to make me look at him. He doesn't say anything at first, blinking slowly, those thick dark lashes that seem like curtains to the beautiful depth his eyes hold. "You and I both know I wouldn't take something like this lightly. You know what I've been through and you know what I'm afraid of. I'm asking you because I see myself spending the rest of my life with you, and I want you here with me."

"I'll move in," I tell him immediately, afraid if I don't, I'll burst into tears before I get the words out.

He pushes me onto my back, hovering above me. His skin's hot against mine. His hands are forceful, taking over, discovering and commanding my attention just as they always do. Just like *he* always does.

Looking over my body, he glances from my face, down, all the way to between my thighs. Holding my wrists captive above my head, he then releases my right wrist, using his free hand to push down on my hip, gripping under my knee and touching my face with the other.

He whispers in my ear, "I love you." And then lifts his face to mine, his breath hitting my lips. His mouth dances across my jaw stopping in their path to kiss my lips and forehead, his nose delicately nudging against mine.

When he finally closes the distance, peppering me with gentle kisses, a sigh of contentment falls from me.

My hands soon find their place on his chest. "I love you," I tell him over and over again.

There are always going to be what ifs in my life. For a person like me, a person who always demanded order and believes every problem has a neat and reasonable solution, the what ifs could be considered unbearable. Lying here, in Tyler's bed, having him touch me and love me in a way only he can, I realize while I might only be twenty, soon to be twenty-one, I know what I want in life and that's Tyler Hemming. The rest will all work out because the strength and honesty in our love, it's undeniable.

Maybe I didn't need to be in control of everything. Maybe walking into Murphy's that night was me being in the right place at the right time as Tyler once said.

author acknowledgments

Writing acknowledgments are always hard for me. Thank you to my family who supports me through it all between the long nights and the sleepless ones where I stay up all night worrying about these stories.

I struggled a lot with Unbearable because I didn't want people to hate Raven, but I also wanted them to understand she's nineteen/twenty when all this is happening and very much naïve to a lot of things. Especially love. So if you were frustrated with her a time or two, so was I! You don't know how many times I thought she was being annoying, but I still didn't change her character. I had to write her the way I did though because it was true to her personality and her.

Tyler, well, I fell for him immediately because what's not to love about him. I write characters the way I see them and trying to persuade me into writing them another way is pretty much impossible. Ask my beta readers. The thing is, these are real instances to me when that's exactly how people act. I want *real* emotions and faults and sometimes people are *unbearably* stubborn and frustrating until they finally see the hold ups.

Thank you to Lauren for making this book what it should be. Couldn't have done it without you. So thankful for the time I was able to spend with you this last month.

Janet, I love you. Thank you for everything you do for me and being there when I need a shoulder to cry on. I honestly believe we were meant to find each other in this life and be family. Can't wait to see you again soon.

Barb, thank you so much for proofreading this book in one day! Love you girl! And thanks for driving me around in a hurricane so I could find a strapless bra for my date, lol. You're the best.

Jill, Marisa, Shanna, Ashely Schow, Ashley Sloan, Rachel... thanks for being there for me when I need someone.

Becky, girl, you make my words shine like the stars. Thanks for being patient while I work on these edits through a hard time in my life and a hurricane.

To my readers, new and old, thank you for taking a chance on me and falling in love with these characters like I have. They've quickly become family to me.

meet THE author

Shey Stahl is a *USA Today* bestselling author, a wife, mother, daughter and friend to many. When she's not writing, she's spending time with her family in the Pacific Northwest where she was born, and raised around a dirt track. Visit her website for additional information and keep up to date on new releases: www.sheystahl.com.
You can also find her on Facebook:
https://www.facebook.com/SheyStahlAuthor

Racing on the Edge
Happy Hour
Black Flag
Trading Paint
The Champion
The Legend
Hot Laps
The Rookie
Fast Time
Open Wheel
Pace Laps
Dirt Driven (Winter 2016)

Behind the Wheel (Release date: TBA)

The Redemption Series
The Trainer
The Fighter

Stand Alones
Waiting for You
Everything Changes
Deal
Awakened
Everlasting Light
Bad Blood
Heavy Soul
Pause (Coming October 2016)
Bad Husband (TBA)

Crossing the Line
Delayed Penalty
Delayed Offsides
Delayed Roughing (Release date: TBA)

Unforgettable Series
All I Have Left
All We Need (Release date: TBA)

The Torqued Trilogy
Unsteady
Unbearable
Unbound (January 2017)